William Hussey is the award-winning author of over a dozen novels, including the Crime Fest award-nominated *Hideous Beauty* and *The Outrage*. Born the son of a travelling showman, he has spent a lifetime absorbing the history, folklore and culture of fairground people, knowledge he has now put to work in his Scott Jericho thrillers. William lives in the seaside town of Skegness with his faithful dog Bucky and a vivid imagination.

WILLIAM HUSSEY

ZAFFRE

First published in the UK in 2023 by
ZAFFRE
An imprint of Bonnier Books UK
4th Floor, Victoria House, Bloomsbury Square, London, WC1B 4DA
Owned by Bonnier Books
Sveavägen 56, Stockholm, Sweden

This is a work of fiction. Names, places, events and
incidents are either the products of the author's
imagination or used fictitiously. Any resemblance to
actual persons, living or dead, or actual
events is purely coincidental.

A CIP catalogue record for this book is
available from the British Library.

Hardback ISBN: 978–1–80418–116–4
Trade paperback ISBN: 978–1–80418–117–1

Also available as an ebook and an audiobook

1 3 5 7 9 10 8 6 4 2

Typeset by IDSUK (Data Connection) Ltd
Printed and bound in Great Britain by Clays Ltd, Elcograf S.p.A.

Zaffre is an imprint of Bonnier Books UK
www.bonnierbooks.co.uk

For Trevor Lewis-Bettison

Chapter One

I FINALLY KICKED THE CHAP OUT of bed around noon. So I suppose I should tell you right off, travelling showpeople have their own secret tongue; a rich and mystifying jargon designed to keep outsiders at bay. You'll pick it up by instinct as we go on, but here's a start:

chap (noun) – general dogsbody, usually male, who travels and works on the fair but is not himself a showman

'*Chr*-ist,' he yawned, spearing an elbow into my ribs and rolling Michelangelo buttocks off the mattress. 'All right, I'm going. God, if only you'd been this energetic last night.'

I shrugged, acknowledging his critique. For two months I'd barely moved from my trailer (a rickety tin box built around the time Neil Armstrong hitched up his wagon and took the human race on tour), yet somehow I'd retained the arms of a stevedore and a physique that could still turn a head.

The chap stepped into his briefs. Early twenties, we'd picked him up somewhere around Hampstead; a student earning a few quid on his summer break by working the London circuit. I was groggy that morning, my brain half-buried in benzos, my body aching from a clearly unappreciated night of going through the motions, but there were patterns even I could read: a smudged ballpoint scrawl on his left hand – *2009 – 1 – AC 302* – a Court of Appeal citation, so a law student; leather wallet with initials embossed in gold, a studiously torn picture of a handsome, middle-aged woman in the sleeve as he flipped it open and checked his cash: a figure cut out, a father disowned?

I grunted at myself. *'Assumptions are your Achilles' heel, Scott,'* my old mentor DI Pete Garris had once told me. *'You should always back up those hunches of yours. Cleverness will only get you so far.'*

'Catch you later, then,' the chap said, pushing a tumble of dirty blond hair out of his eyes. 'Maybe we can have a drink or something? Your treat; your dad doesn't pay enough for me to splash out on booze every night.'

'We'll see,' I muttered. 'Now, get out of it. I need to sleep.'

It was all about sleep, after all. That was why I'd fucked him and then swallowed quadruple my Zopiclone prescription, all washed down with the corpse of a coffee I'd found decomposing on the kitchen counter. Like every night, I longed for that complete exhaustion where sleep comes fast and dreamless.

Zac threw me an indulgent smile and closed the door while I rolled onto my side, blinking at my reflection in the glass of an empty picture frame that sat on the bedside table. A nest of blue-black curls, strong features an unfinished stroke away from pretty, a pair of artless grey eyes that would make Caravaggio swoon. I've tried to be many things in my thirty-one years – reluctant fairground showman, earnest student, hired bone-breaker, CID detective, cleaner of prison toilets – and through it all, my looks haven't betrayed an ounce of hardship. Maybe that's because I haven't stuck at anything.

To be fair, before I found the Malanowski children roasted alive in the back bedroom of their father's shop, I had been a pretty conscientious detective, but as to the rest, the years and the rust just roll off me. Grunting, I tipped the picture frame face down and turned onto my back.

Tucked away in the corral of trailers at the rear of the fairground, the only distinct sound I could hear was an ancient generator gasping itself to pieces. There was the ever-present song of the fair, of course – the somewhat sinister jangle of the carousel's calliope mixed in with jabs of dance music from the Waltzer and the rattle, roar and shake of the rides. If your ear's accustomed, it's almost a lullaby you can drift off to.

The sun beat through the blinds. My eyes hazed, my body uncoiled. And then a blade of light played across the police file sitting on the table at the far end of the trailer, and suddenly my heart was in my throat, a fevered pulse ticking behind my tongue. All at once, I could smell it again: the sting of unburned petrol, the stew of charred children, a stink that eighteen months could not erase.

In my mind, I was back in the street, ducking under the blue-and-white cordon. I saw myself signing my name into the scene log – *DC Scott Jericho* – long, looping letters, full of the swagger of a know-nothing div who thought he could bring sense out of any horror. Forensics whispered by in their Tyvek suits, all their usual gallows humour missing. I knew the reason. I'd been the night duty detective and had taken the call. Even the most sociopathic SOCO knows not to joke when it's a kiddie case.

3

I dotted the 'i' in Jericho and strode into the burned-out shop, past guarded doorways, through to the living quarters at the back, nitrile-gloved hands at my sides, my mind clearing away the clutter of our team and the fire brigade's own forensics unit. I started to sweat. A little rill ran down from my paper hood, the only moisture in this scorched memory of a home. The other officers fell back from the bedroom door as I approached (not badly damaged, I noticed: strange how fires behave) and let me through with a reverence that had nothing to do with me, a lowly detective constable, and everything to do with the clot of misery and despair that waited inside.

The room felt like a holy place long abandoned. There were relics everywhere – twisted, melted things whose purpose only an archaeologist might have been able to reconstruct. Cheery in the gloom, yellow evidence markers surrounded the remains of a big bow-chested wardrobe. The forensics team gave a collective sigh as I reached out and pulled the double doors aside. I frowned then, both in the trailer, where I sat huddled like a tramp in winter, and in the memory. Something had dragged itself into the wardrobe and curled up like a butterfly in its chrysalis.

It took moments to pick the illusion apart; to see that the something had originally been *three* somethings. I think I might then have whispered *No* or *Fuck* or *God*. Three dead kids, arms pulled up like playground boxers, eyes tight shut, drawn together in their love and terror and desperation.

They were with me now in the trailer. A trio of hazy presences standing in the shadows by the door, their eyes full of sorrow and disappointment. Sometimes the Malanowski children spoke to me, mostly they kept their counsel. As the memory fractured so did these phantoms, drifting away like motes of charred skin on the breeze until I was alone again.

I rose slowly to my feet, padded barefoot to the end of the trailer. Garris and his fucking files! Had he come yesterday? Surely I'd have remembered that interfering old bastard picking his way through the garbage of my life and finding a space for himself to perch. I scanned the trailer and saw a cleared nook on the built-in settee. Yes, he'd sat there, between the mounds of my old books and a fortnight's worth of laundry, but when exactly had he visited? No idea.

I'd asked, if he had to bring cases I'd never review, could he at least put them in a non-official folder? Garris hadn't asked why – human details were, as ever, unimportant to him – he just wanted a bit of off-the-record assistance from his former protégé. I stared now at the manila sleeve. A new case, a fresh way to fail. I didn't even open the cover. Tearing the slim contents in two, I was about to shove the lot into the bin when Sal burst through the door.

I've known Sal Myers since for ever. We'd been Traveller chavvies together, our early childhood explorations covering a vast terrain of half-assembled rides, delicate fingers searching where they shouldn't. Now, Sal blew a strand of auburn hair from her face and surveyed the wreckage of my trailer. Something had driven her here in a hurry and she looked royally pissed off. At first, I wondered if it was the recent departure of Zac, and although that turned out not to be the case, she must have seen him leaving and the news that brought her was momentarily forgotten.

Sal looked around with the kind of expression she'd usually reserve for the most dinlo of joskins.

dinlo (adjective) – fuckwitted

joskin (noun) – anyone not a member of the travelling life, especially those that live in houses

I was sweating badly from the flashback, my back honeyed with it, jewels gleaming in my chest hair.

'Had another one up here, then?' She locked freckly arms over the bib of her work dungarees. 'If you're trying to embarrass your dad, you can stop right now. The poor old mush is already walking around like he wants the ground to eat him up.'

'Didn't think you were so intolerant,' I muttered. 'I know some round here are stuck in the nineteenth century, but you?'

'Don't give me that middle-class joskin bollocks,' she spat back. 'No one here cares who you sleep with …'

I didn't believe that. Not entirely. For all their talk of being outsiders, the fairground has its own conservativeness. It holds its people close and likes them to be of a certain type; if divergence exists then such activities are to be carried out in the shadows.

'Screw whoever you like,' Sal continued. In a fairly ineffectual way, she started cleaning up, dishes splashed into the heaving sink, Fairy Liquid added to the toxic jumble. 'That's not what gets your dad down. It's this. Week-old shirts that can stand up on their own, pizza boxes that look like biology experiments, and yes, you poking every slag in sight.'

That wasn't fair on Zac, nor most of the others. I opened my mouth to argue but didn't get past the first syllable.

'I don't know, Scott,' she sighed. 'Maybe you should just go. My Jodie, she idolises you, draws you pictures, bakes you cakes, but I daren't send her round here for fear of what she'll find.'

'Really? I think Jodie's got a broader mind than her mother.' Dragging a pair of blue jeans off the floor, I hitched them over my hips, toed my outsize feet into a pair of sandals, and pulled on a grubby white vest. Dishes crashed under Sal's hands and she turned on me, cheeks flushed.

'So she should just walk in and see you lying spaced out in that pit of a bed? She's seven years old, for Christ's sake. Look, Scott, I've tried, we all have. When you came out of prison, we did everything we could for you – and don't forget, we never begged you to come back here.'

I took a breath. 'Sal, I had nowhere else to go.'

"Course you didn't. If you did, you'd probably never have seen your father again.'

There was no answer to that. She had me nailed with the kind of killer observation that, in my CID days, I'd have reserved for a final interview clincher. My instincts were slow, as I've told you, my gifts – whatever they actually amount to – a shadow of those that had once so impressed Pete Garris that he'd cajoled me into joining the force. Even so, I knew that something was wrong.

'What is it?' I scratched the heel of my hand through the dark bristle of my jaw. 'You didn't come here just to call me a joskin.'

Skirting around her, I flicked open the door, cleared the trailer step and headed for the trestle table I'd set up outside. I poured a bowl of summer-warm water from a canister and was about to soap my face when Sal laid a hand on my shoulder.

'He's here,' she said. 'The skinhead. They found him parnying behind the swing boats like some juk marking its territory. Ted and Johnny are guarding him right now.'

7

'A skinhead?' My laughter was hollow. I knew who she meant. 'Fuck's that gotta do with me?'

Glancing up, I saw a bluebottle at the trailer window. It bobbed and danced there like the resurrected on the Day of Judgement.

'It's the one you put in the hospital,' she said. 'That fascist fuck who set the fire and killed them little Polish kids.' Sal's voice came to me as if she were standing in another room.

'It's Kerrigan.'

Chapter Two

'DON'T.' SAL'S HAND AGAINST MY chest. 'Don't give that murdering bastard an excuse to call the gavvers. You fight him, they'll have you back inside, and pretty soon after Kerrigan'll come for the last pot you pissed in.' I pushed her arm away and she gripped my wrist, her fingers loops of pale steel. 'You won't come back out again. You hear me, Scotty? You'll die in there this time.'

'In there, out here, what's the difference?' I shrugged, realising it was the first honest thing I'd said to her since she'd picked me up from HMP Hazelhurst two months earlier.

Pulling free, I strode out along the backs of the joints, running now, jumping over trailer couplings. A few old aunts and grandmothers called to me from their steps and deckchairs, excitement piping in their cracked voices. They were attuned to the motions of their world and knew when a good punch-up was in the offing.

Out from behind the side ground where the shooting galleries and mirror mazes stood, I jumped the rail of Urnshaw's dodgems. Sparks brawled in the electric cage overhead as I zigzagged between the riders. One of the chaps rodeoing the back of a bumper car shouted a warning to his boss and Big

Sam Urnshaw swarmed out of his booth and caught me by the elbow. This barrel-chested showman hooked something in my eye, the same signal the aunts had noticed, and in an instant, understood.

'You gonna ruck someone?' he hollered over the racket of his ride. I shrugged. 'Does the old man know?'

'I doubt it.'

He whistled and Sam Jr raced over. I'd left the life when I was nineteen, soon after my mother died, and not having grown up with this new generation I was viewed by them with suspicion. They knew my history – that I'd snubbed my heritage and become as near as damn it to a Judas when I joined the force – yet still I was one of them and Little Sam gave me a tight smile.

'Go find Jericho,' his father instructed. 'Tell him his son's on the warpath. On your toes now.'

The kid set off like a whippet.

I didn't want my dad in attendance but it's seldom a showman can have a ruck to himself, so I quickly moved on. Whistles trailed me as other showmen vaulted their counters and stepped in behind. No one asked where we were going or why, they just knew something was about to go down.

We'd come out of a line of side stalls when Sal caught up. She didn't try to argue or pull me away, just marched at my side. Ahead, it seemed that even the punters had begun to catch on and they began to make a path for our procession. Danger's always been part of a fair's allure, right from the days of the knife-throwers and boxing shows, yet those pantomimes were never really what drew the crowds. Joskins know, you see? Deep down they're aware that Travellers live outside the rules by which their own lives are governed and that, if they go to the fair, perhaps they might catch a glimpse of that older, truer danger. Now they lined our route, parents clutching small hands, kids with eyes as round as Ferris wheels.

Kerrigan came into view. He was leaning against a miniature Wild West wagon, part of a set of carousel vehicles. He flashed a grin when he clocked me and jumped down from the ride's runnerboard. Aside from the absence of the plastic mask that had held his shattered cheekbone in place, he hadn't changed much since I'd last seen him in the witness box at my trial.

He sauntered over and held out a sunburned hand. Against that reddened skin, the swastika tattoo shone like a brand. A foolish mistake of youth, he'd told us in his first interview. That lie had been accompanied by his trademark smirk, a sideways tilt of the lips which, within twelve hours, would earn him the most vicious beating he'd ever taken. He'd whimpered then, trembling in the corner of the interview room, pissing his station-issue trousers while half a dozen officers hauled me into the corridor.

Lenny Kerrigan showed no fear now, simply sighed and dropped his unshaken hand into his pocket.

'Ah, but you're a bad loser, Scott. It took me ages to track you down and now I'm here, you can't even play nice. Maybe I oughta get my lads together and give you a lesson in ...'

He stopped. He had made a serious miscalculation. In the world into which he had stepped, family is family, and even the blackest sheep will be protected. It's the Travellers' way, their code almost. There are tales told here, an omertà whisper of paedophiles and women killers who dared to enter this world, of high buildings and hidden foundations that would

11

make a mafioso's hair curl. My people are, by and large, what they seem – generous purveyors of entertainment – just don't presume too much on their smile.

While Lenny had been playing the joker, reinforcements had swarmed in behind me. Thirty or more circled the carousel, men with limbs toughened by labour unknown to the scum that made up the Knights of St George, Lenny's hate group. Leader Lenny shared the same cartoonish physicality as his followers, trapezius muscles hunched up to his ears, biceps ribboned with veins, a head so disproportionate to his inflated body my ancestors might have exhibited him in a pinhead sideshow.

'Brought an army along?' He swallowed. 'Same as always, eh? First, you had the filth to back you up and now you've gone and rolled out the whole carnival.' His bravado was as airy as the drifts of candyfloss that wafted on the breeze.

'What're you doing here?' I asked.

'Free country, innit? Thought I'd scout the place out, might bring me lad along at the weekend. Loves his rides, my boy.'

He had a son roughly the same age as the Malanowski girl, Sonia. We'd tried that angle in the second interview, a gambit of Garris's that hadn't paid off. Usually, the sly old fox was good at reading people, finding chinks in the most psychopathic armour, but he'd misjudged Kerrigan. No appeal to common fatherly feeling had shaken that shit-eating grin.

'I'm not a fan of pikies as a rule,' he continued. 'But I can make an exception for an old mate. You're looking well, DC Jericho.'

I nodded. 'Wish I could say the same.'

He'd had the best reconstructive surgery money could buy: the fact I'd had to sell my house after the civil case he'd brought against me was a testament to that. Still, I'd jumbled his deck pretty nicely and there's only so much a surgeon can do when some of the cards are missing.

'Fair play,' he shrugged. 'Honestly, though, I weren't expecting you to lose it like that over a couple of deep-fried Poles. It's funny, looking back – that old scarecrow Garris just sitting there while you lost your fucking mind. Thought he knew you, I bet. His golden boy. I wonder if he's still proud of you, even though you fucked his case and made him look like a proper cunt. But I got you both, didn't I?' Lost in his victory, he dared to come within striking distance of those twitching fists that had done him so much damage. 'You winding up inside and him brought low.'

'That?' I sketched a smile. 'That had nothing to do with you. I lost it, I failed. Garris is still working, still putting little psychos like you away. All you did was push a lit rag through a letterbox, then scream and cry and piss yourself when I smacked you about.'

Spittle flew. 'Careful what you say. Call me a murderer and I'll see you back in court.'

Sal laughed and pressed her small body between us. 'Get out of here,' she said, looking Kerrigan up and down. 'You're a no-mark coward and that's all you are.'

The smirk reappeared. 'I'm not the one hiding behind two dozen dirty pikies.'

'No,' I nodded, 'you hide behind a balaclava and a greedy lawyer.'

'Do you know what he did when he was inside?' Kerrigan whirled on the spot, arms outstretched. 'This pissy little faggot? Know how he made friends up at Hazelhurst? I've got all the stories if you want to hear 'em. What'll happen when I tell your friends, Jericho? Think they'll still stick up for you after I paint 'em a picture of you on your knees—?'

'Tell them.'

There was a stirring in the ranks, although whether it was anger at Kerrigan or disgust at what they were hearing, I couldn't say. Finally, he dropped his arms.

'They probably won't care, whatever they hear. All half-breeds anyway.'

He moved to step out of the circle, then lunged in as if to nut me. I inclined my head, like a priest keen to hear a penitent's confession.

'You know it was nothing personal, right?' he hushed in my ear. 'Them kids didn't have to go that way. If only their old man had stayed in his Third World shithole. But they won't listen, Jericho. None of 'em.'

'Get out,' I whispered back. 'One minute more on this ground and I will murder you. Do you understand, Kerrigan? I will *murder* you.'

He pushed past me, and just like that, it was over. Hands clasped my shoulder and I listened to the catcalls that accompanied Kerrigan off the ground. A few would probably tail him to his car, but there'd be no violence. They knew my position, and more importantly that of my dad. Old man Jericho was the boss of the firm, the one who negotiated with the authorities for our licences to trade, permissions that can be revoked at the first hint of disorder.

'All right, son?' Sam Urnshaw approached. 'Little Sam says your dad's gone back to the yard to pick up a lorry. I can't get him on his phone.'

I wasn't listening. My blood was up. Kerrigan's arrival at almost the same moment as a flashback of the Malanowski case wasn't a huge coincidence. He might have turned up at virtually any point over the past two months and caught me mid-nightmare, but why come at all? Had he tracked me down just to taunt me? That wasn't his style. Oh sure, he'd lay in an insult or two but they'd almost certainly be doled out in some lonely alley where he and twenty of his goons had gathered in advance. So why wander into the fair alone and unguarded? Once I might have been able to guess but my brain was an idle, lumbering thing. It needed exercise.

I scanned the crowd. Noise everywhere – music, laughter, the clack of barley in the neighbouring field, the tattle of tokens. I took a breath, tasted oil, sweat, axle grease, aerated sugar, the dull smack of a chap's cheap aftershave ...

There. At the corner of the helter-skelter, I saw him, watching as intently as he himself was watched. My heart pounded and, for the first time in a long time, my mind craved a puzzle. A small one, just to get the juices flowing.

'Where are you going?' Sal asked as I made to step away. 'Look, why don't you come back to the trailer? Jodie'd love to see you.'

'Can't,' I shot back. 'Something I need to do.'

I lurched off, away from Big Sam and Sal Myers, in pursuit now of a second monster who had come to the fair.

Chapter Three

THE SKILLS OF A SHOWMAN are born of his trade. First, he must hone the ability to speak the spiel, to chat the chat, to gain the confidence of every kind of punter. Second, his business is observation. A fair might run a week but there'll only be a few golden hours each night in which his living must be earned. In that time, he'll assess tiny gestures: the flutter of a finger over a pocket; the evidence of cash already spent in the form of sugared lips and torn ticket stubs; the firm or carefree steerage of a child. Third, and most importantly, he'll know human nature. The fair is the last great leveller. All human life passes through our turnstiles and, over centuries, we've learned their ways, their quirks and commonalities, the patterns that perhaps only priests and showmen can read.

Some of these gifts I acquired in my first eighteen years living the life, others seem hardwired into me. Strange thing is, it wasn't until Pete Garris pointed it out that I realised these were also the skills of a gifted detective.

I put them to use now.

For obvious reasons, paedophiles are attracted to fairgrounds. Not that showpeople ever give them much of a chance. A strongly worded warning usually sends them on their way, and so I followed this specimen to the northbound exit. He wasn't your typical nonce. He walked with a twitchy gait, his appearance stark among the crowd: a Mohican with flame-dyed side-panels, chin piercing, retro Stones T-shirt hanging off his toothpick torso, pinstriped trousers and neon green trainers. Almost as if he wanted to be noticed.

The fairground fell away and we entered the churned-up field that served as a temporary car park. Families clustered around their saloons, mums and dads distracted by the complexity of infant seats, toddlers galore, ripe for the picking. The human exclamation point I was tailing didn't spare them a glance. He was focused only on escape, and yet ...

Why did he slow when a four-by-four trundled across my path? There were seconds now, ample moments in which to disappear, but the car passed and I located him in exactly the same position. I frowned. I'd seen a lot during my time in uniform, things that ought to have inured me to the sight of the Malanowski kids in their wardrobe coffin, yet nothing of the typical predator profile fitted this guy.

He kept looking back, nervous as hell yet somehow tethered to me. The fair was no more than a throbbing thumbprint in the sky by the time we reached the main road and took our odd little game into the commercial heart of this London commuter-belt town. It was here, amid spruced-up canals and gentrified warehouses, that a possibility occurred.

Was this a trap? A strategy of Kerrigan's to pull me out of the safety of the ground? He comes to the fair and puts on a display, all mock menace, then introduces bait he knows will catch my eye. The nonce is the sacrificial lamb, coerced by

Kerrigan into playing the lure, and if he takes a punch or two before the Knights of St George arrive on the scene? Well, the fascists claim they have no love for kiddie fiddlers.

But all this presupposed a cunning that was alien to Kerrigan, a man who only got away with murder because the lead inter-viewer on his case had beaten the ever-living shit out of him. And anyway, he knew I needed no inducement – if he'd invited me to a meeting, I would have gladly attended.

On now, we passed down a brightly painted quayside at an almost companionable saunter. The guy's shoulders relaxed a little. We were on home turf. Through a narrow alley we came into a Disneyland version of a Dickens' dockyard, its once polluted face scraped back to the bone. From old customs houses, international coffee shops doled out their wares to chattering pricks in business suits.

Out of the dockyard, into another alley. There could be no question about my having followed him now. He even shot me a gutsy little smile, the kind that would've made Jesus climb down from the cross and flip the human race the bird. At the door to a warehouse conversion he stopped, his hand hovering over an entry keypad.

'Please come upstairs. We can talk properly in the flat.' He glanced down at my fists and, for the first time since hearing Kerrigan's name, I flexed my fingers. 'I'll tell you what you need to know, you won't have to hurt me.'

He punched in a code and the door clicked. Stepping inside, he wedged it open, then moved across the vestibule and summoned the lift. I accepted his invitation without question and was soon riding the elevator to the fourth floor and accom-panying him into his studio apartment. We didn't exchange a word until his knees came unhinged and he dropped lightly onto a cream-coloured sofa.

The flat reeked of anonymity. I doubted it belonged to the very individual character who sat before me. A space that might once have housed a single gigantic loom had been compartmentalised with waist-level walls, the kind that could allow you to watch TV in bed while freely conversing with the love of your life as he took a shit next door. There was the usual exposed brickwork and cathedral-sized windows giving a stunning view of the blank wall opposite.

'Can I get you something to drink, Mr Jericho?' He was sweating, his powdered face giving way in minuscule avalanches. 'I think there might be mineral water in the fridge or I could look for some wine, perhaps?'

I crossed the room and took him by the throat. Police are used to playing games. To play them with a reluctant witness used to be my forte – the gentle art of persuasion being one of those showman specialities. It was only when dealing with a particularly hostile suspect I knew to be guilty that my patience would wear thin. In those situations, Garris would usually take charge. Now I was alone, faced with a puzzle that for the first time in two years piqued my interest and a man who, if not yet a criminal, needed a good scare to stop him in his tracks.

Carrying him to one of those big windows, I used my free hand to unsnib the latch and push open the pane. I popped him onto the lead-framed sill and, grasping his shirtfront, tipped him gently backwards.

'I t-told you,' he squealed. 'You don't need to h-hurt me. I'll te-ell ...'

'Speak slowly,' I advised, 'no stammering. I have a headache and Porky Pig was my least favourite *Looney Tune.*'

'I wuh . . .' He closed his eyes, made a supreme effort. 'Will. Just pull me back.'

'Let's see what you have to say first.' I had my sleeve rolled up and he glanced at my straining bicep. He seemed repelled by the sight. I let him drop six inches and his bellow echoed in the canyon below. 'I know what you are,' I told him. 'And believe me, I won't lose any sleep if your brains end up straw-berrying the pavement. So take a breath and try not to shit yourself. Now, why did you come to the fair this afternoon? It wasn't to scope out the kids, was it? Least, that wasn't the main reason. You knew I was on to you, you wanted me to follow, so what the fuck is this all about? D'you think I'm like you, is that it? Thought we could have a nice little sit-down and trade fantasies?'

A curl of disgust rippled his upper lip, as if the very idea of sharing his daydreams was mortally offensive. 'You don't understand, d-do you?'

'There's that stammer again,' I clucked. 'You wanna mess with me? I wouldn't advise it. Did you see the man I was talking with at the fair? The guy with the face that looks like it's had a serious disagreement with several staircases? Who d'you think gave his skull a makeover?'

Tears welled. His chin piercing quivered. 'I kn-know. The professor told me.'

'Professor?' I laughed. 'Are they handing out degrees in kiddie fiddling now?' He gaped at me, as if I'd guessed some impossible truth. I shook him and the window rattled. If I wasn't careful the whole thing could come loose from the mouldered brickwork

20

and I'd make good on my empty threats. 'Why did you wait for me? Who sent you?'

A hundred possibilities. It wasn't only Kerrigan I'd crossed in my years on the force – my arrest record was so formidable some in CID had taken to calling me the 'Fortune Teller', a funfair psychic who mystically foresaw the incriminating details of all his major take-downs. It was a joke laced with resentment. Garris aside, I hadn't made many friends on the job, and even my mentor had kept a certain distance.

Then there were my thug-for-hire years, after I'd left the fair but before Garris had drawn me over that thin blue line. In those best-forgotten days, I'd earned the undying enmity of a host of underworld maniacs. Had one of these finally tracked me down and set up the nonce as a lure? Again, it seemed an overly elaborate scheme.

'Who is this "professor"?' I reeled him out another inch. 'What does he want?'

'I don't know, I swear! His name's Campbell, OK? Professor Ralph Campbell. He contacted me through a friend, someone like me. Campbell rented this flat, told me I could stay here a few days if I gave you a message.'

'What message? And why didn't you just pass it on to me at the fair?'

'It was a test,' he panted. 'If you noticed me, s-saw me for what I was, then he'd be satisfied and matters could proceed. Those were his exact words. I've been hanging around for a week or so, but only saw you today. He'd sent you letters, he said, tried getting your attention that way at f-first, but it didn't work.'

Of course not. Like Garris's case files, every scrap of mail I received was binned unread. Even those dreary letters from the inspector's wife, pestering me about my health and recommending nourishing recipes were discarded.

'So,' I shook him again, 'what's he after? You make him sound like a nonce. If he's in need of a beating, I'll RSVP right away and happily kick his teeth down his throat. Tell me the message and get it over with.'

He shut his eyes, like a character in a movie trying to recall a sequence of digits that'll defuse the bomb and save the city. In the end, it amounted to two simple words. When I heard them I almost dropped him.

'The professor said to tell you that it's happening again. He said ...' The man looked at me, his expression puzzled, as if he too would dearly like to know the meaning behind his words. 'He said that they are dying again. All of them. That only you would be able to see the pattern and put things right. "Tell Jericho," he said, "that they're calling out to him: the dead of Travellers Bridge."'

Chapter Four

EVERY SHOWMAN KNOWS THE LEGEND of Travellers Bridge. There are variations, embellishments, but the version my mother told always had a ring of truth. I remembered her, the chiaroscuro of her pale features thrown into relief by my bedside lamp, her palm pressing on the counterpane that covered my chest.

'*And all at once, they are in the river. Half a dozen, screaming and scratching and clawing for the sky. But not a one ever came out again, and the body of old "Slip-Jointed" Jericho himself was never found . . .*'

Now, hearing the tale referenced by a stranger, I experienced a jolt of mixed emotions. Anger first – rage that a piece of my childhood had been polluted by this pervert's lips. Hot on its heels came curiosity – how had Professor Campbell heard of such an obscure story? Then, that once familiar stirring I hadn't experienced since my final interview with Lenny Kerrigan. A puzzle had forced itself upon me and, unlike the ones with which Garris had tried to intrigue me, this mystery wasn't a collection of abstract facts gathered into one of his files, but a living thing so far unexplored.

'Please,' the nonce whimpered, 'don't let me fall. I'll do wh-whatever you want.'

I hauled him over the ledge and threw him to the floor. There came a prim little *snap*, a finger perhaps, but in the moment he didn't seem to notice. I dropped onto my haunches.

'What's your name? Don't lie, I'll know.'

He nodded, not a trace of guile left in him. 'Jeremy. Worth.'

'Jeremy.' For the first time in a year, I took a Moleskine notebook from the back pocket of my jeans and opened it to a fresh page. It was a habit I couldn't shake, keeping the book on me. In the old days, I'd maintained a scrupulous Major Investigation Book for every case I worked. Disclosable to the defence, these logs were carefully penned with personal reflections unheard of. I decided then that this would be a very different kind of journal. 'Write down your name, address, phone number, email.'

'Listen,' he pleaded, backing across the floor until his shoulders found the leather sofa. 'I don't need to be part of this. All I was asked to do was pass on a message. I don't even know who this professor is or what he wants with you. I'm not important.'

'Oh, but you're wrong, Jeremy. You're *very* important. So important that one day a young "friend" of yours might scribble a note to his loved ones and then take himself to the edge of a tall building. Then I will feel very guilty for dragging you back from the brink and allowing *him* to fall. But that's not ever going to happen, is it?'

He shook his head, bubbles forming at the corners of his mouth as the pain of his broken finger finally pierced through the adrenalin.

'No, because you know I'm clever, don't you? Speak up, no stammering.'

'Yesss,' he fizzed.

'Good. Now, I don't think you've acted on those impulses of yours, not yet anyway, but you're building up to it. What are you? Twenty-four, twenty-five? That means you have some qualms.' I squatted forward, fixed him with my eyes. 'Keep hold of those qualms, Jeremy. Nurture them every day, because from here on out, I'll be watching you. I don't want to hear that you've even glanced sideways at a primary school, are we clear? Now, you might be thinking, how can one man possibly keep constant tabs on me? Well, first, I used to be a copper, and although they don't like me much anymore, I'll be passing on your details and asking them to keep an eye on you too. Second, you've just seen something of how my people work together. There are sections of us all over the country, Jeremy, and wherever you go, we'll be passing your door sooner or later. They have keen eyes too, so you know I'm speaking the truth when I say one slip, just one, and I'll hear about it. Then it won't be a matter for the police. Nod if you understand.'

Although, for the most part, what I told him was bullshit, he lapped it up, like some awestruck disciple who'd just received a testament in stone.

'So write down what I asked. You're right-handed, aren't you?' I glanced at his ballooning finger, already fat as an overcooked sausage. 'Use your left as best you can.'

Moaning, he held the page open with his elbow and made nursery letters with his undamaged hand. When he was done, I scooped up the book and slipped it back into my jeans.

'This professor got hold of you through a friend,' I said. 'Does he know where I can find Campbell?'

'You don't have to go through him.' Jeremy panted against the pain. 'I have an address. Don't you get it? The professor *wants* you to find him.'

A paedophile dispatching a paedophile with a nonsensical message about an old fairground legend. It sounded like something that came into the incident room during the early days of an investigation, the fantastical theory of one of the usual hotline crazies. Did Jeremy Worth know more than he was telling? With a twist of that purpling finger I might have double-checked, but instinct told me the well had run dry. Truth was, I'd already inflicted needless pain when a few questions and well-placed threats would've been enough. So why the brutality?

Rebirth can be a violent process, I suppose.

'Tell me.'

'Ralph Campbell,' he muttered. 'Falls House, Clerihew Lane, Cambridge.'

'You ever seen Campbell?'

'No. I got a letter from him but I lost it. He gave me the keys to the flat, a photo of you from the newspaper, and some money, that's all. He's probably just some fucking lunatic.'

'Probably.' I nodded, and turning away, headed to the door.

'Travellers Bridge,' he called after me. 'I got curious and looked it up online. Took a bit of finding. But all that happened over a century ago, didn't it? So what can Campbell mean by saying they're dying again?'

'We'll see,' I said, my hand on the handle. 'I don't think it'll amount to much.'

But I didn't believe that, not even then.

Sal was waiting when I got back to the trailer. In the interim, she'd had access to the pit and had worked a minor miracle. Plates that looked like they had calcified around the time Vesuvius threw a fit gleamed in a dish rack I didn't know I possessed. Most of my clothes had been taken away, presumably for washing or incineration, and my books were arranged as neatly as possible beside my bed. The bed itself was stripped bare, the carpet hoovered, the windowsills de-bugged. On the kitchen counter, my meds – mostly prescription – had been lined up like denouncers at a Communist show trial.

'You didn't have to do this,' I said, lurching up the step. I was already feeling woozy and wanted her gone. Those little pill boxes were calling to me.

'Had to.' She draped a soiled tea towel over the tap. 'Chernobyl wanted its record back as the world's most toxic shithole. Where have you been, Scott? Don't tell me you went after Kerrigan?'

'No. It was something . . .' I went and sat on the bed, finger-tips trailing the spines of my books: Updike, George Eliot, Scott Fitzgerald, Housman, Fleming, Conan Doyle. Old books, some of them my mother's, others stolen from a variety of libraries long, long ago. 'Sal, you remember Travellers Bridge?'

She frowned, and a glimpse of the redheaded tomboy who'd chased me under clotheslines strung between trailer doorways peeked out. She'd grown into a small, slim woman who carried the disappointment of her years in strands of grey and premature crow's feet.

"Course. We used to scare ourselves silly with that old ghost story.'

'It was just a story, though, wasn't it?'

'Why are you asking about this now? Is it the fête? Don't start getting obsessed with conspiracies cooked up by old showmen, Scott ...' She lifted a hand to my forehead and brushed back a tangle of curls. 'You look better. Better than even a few hours ago. What's happened?'

I took her wrist and kissed the inside of her palm. 'What fête?'

'Uncle Scott! Look what I've brung you.'

Jodie tottered up the step, her arms laden with a fresh pile of shirts. I got to my feet and took the laundry from her. When I placed her gift carefully onto the bed, she jumped up and threw her arms around my neck. I laughed, a sound so rusty I think it frightened her.

Dressed in a corn-coloured blouse and soap-scented dungarees, she was the exact replica of her mother at that age. A cheeky snub of a nose banded with freckles, brown eyes flecked with green, sunset-red hair. I'd never met her father. He was from a circuit up north and, unlike most travelling men who, for good or ill, stick doggedly with the mother of their children, he'd abandoned Sal as soon as she'd shown him the positive test strip.

At around that time I'd been getting out from under a nasty bit of trouble. With mobsters on my back who made Al Capone look like Truman Capote, I hadn't thought it prudent to pay a visit to my pregnant best friend. At least, that's what I told myself.

Unsettled by my laugh, Jodie sized me up with all the unflinching directness of her mother. Then she asked Sal's permission to go and play and, with a flick of her braid, we were left alone.

'She's been imagining you for years,' Sal smiled. 'All those stories I told her about us in the old days. She's built up this picture and—'

'Reality's a fucker, eh?'

'Not always. Make an effort.'

I nodded.

Under the bed, I found a pair of black ankle boots. After changing my red check shirt for a freshly laundered white one, I pulled them on. A light charcoal blazer, crumpled but fairly non-toxic, completed the finest wardrobe I'd worn since being sent down. I ducked my head to the mirror over the sink, grabbed a comb and made the usual pointless effort to bring order to the briar. Then I tapped my pocket for the phone I hadn't charged in over a year.

'Sal, can you lend me your mobile, just for today?'

She handed over the Nokia with all the startled acceptance of a bank teller filling a pillowcase. It was only when I took my car keys from the hook beside the door that she came to her senses.

'Scott, what are you doing?'

I paused on the step, my back turned to her.

'I have a case.'

Chapter Five

I HAD COMPANY ON MY TRIP to Cambridge. By the time the summer storm broke and the rain pummelled the road, the Malanowski children were with me – Sonia, the eldest, in the passenger seat, Pietro and Tomasz leaning over the headrests. The motorway gleamed, eel-slick, the wipers of my ancient Mercedes making feeble work of the deluge.

I tried to ride out the hallucination, but my ghosts were insistent. The boys in the back flickered in the rear-view mirror and made faces at me, tongues poking through fire-nibbled lips, thumbs waggling in the fleshless sockets of their ears. Then Sonia was scolding her brothers and, like the good children they were, they rustled back into their seats.

'Never mind them,' she said. 'They just don't understand, that's all.'

This time it seemed that my ghosts were in a talkative mood. I'd only heard Sonia's voice once before, on a recording of a school poetry recital played during my trial – *Beware the Jabberwock, my son; the jaws that bite, the claws that catch.* Despite her vocal cords being caked with smoke and seared to a crisp, she spoke now in the same warm, slightly accented tones that had echoed around the courtroom and made some of the jurors weep.

Tap-tap-tap went the scalded hand on mine. I dared a sideways glance and saw a Halloween smile.

'The boys are much younger than me, Scott. They don't get that adults just keep making the same mistakes over and over. But it's good that you're going to try. The caravan was becoming very gloomy and we're enjoying the road trip ever so much. Just don't promise things you can't deliver. You promised our dad that you'd put Mr Kerrigan behind bars and that didn't work out too well, did it?'

Behind me in the fast lane, a lorry blared its horn and flashed its beams. I toed the brake and drifted across the carriageway, dropping to a pensionable thirty miles an hour. When I looked again, the children were gone.

I hadn't driven much since leaving jail and the idea of a PTSD hallucination striking at a coasting speed of seventy hadn't occurred to me. I gripped the steering wheel hard. Back at the fair, Zac had given my jalopy a jump-start from his swish little refurbed '67 Beetle (a present from the hated father, perhaps) while Sal assaulted me with a scattergun of questions. I'd kept my answers vague. I didn't want her involved in something I hadn't yet got a handle on. Zac, meanwhile, regarded her with marked jealousy, glances that did nothing for my ego and only made me feel sad for the kid.

My turning flashed out of the semi-darkness and I pulled the Merc into the loop of the exit. The car rumbled over a motorway bridge and plunged straight onto a B-road that was little better than a country lane. In the boot, a dozen or so of my mother's books crashed against each other while those cluttering the passenger footwell jounced like pioneers on a buckboard wagon.

I peered through the rain as the satnav wittered in my ear. Five hundred yards to go. I slowed to a crawl, scanned the narrow road. Fields rolled out on either side, furrows melting under fists of rain.

Suddenly, Falls House appeared to rear up out of the landscape, like one of the mechanised skeletons in old Tommy Radlett's ghost train. Sweeping right, my headlights flooded down a gravel driveway and hit the yellow Ketton stone of the house. The car grumbled to a standstill as I parked up. The front portico had a crenellated roof and a Gothic arch which sheltered the iron-banded oak door. A few green-mouthed gargoyles vomited rainwater from the eaves while a coat of arms, robbed of its heraldic devices by the years, dripped forlornly over the entrance.

The door swung smoothly inwards at my knock. A small, round-shouldered woman of about sixty, dressed almost entirely in black, stood on the threshold. As my eyes adjusted to the light in the hall, I saw that the left side of her face was badly burned. *Like us, like us*, phantom voices chattered in my head.

'Mr Jericho?' she said, the undamaged side of her face lifting into a generous smile. 'Please come in out of the rain.'

'Thank you.'

'Miss Barton.' She nodded as if I'd asked her name. 'We were hoping to see you a little sooner than this, you know.'

'Sorry to disappoint.'

'I'm afraid you have.'

I glanced around the hall. A high-vaulted, dark-panelled room with a long, uncarpeted staircase, it was a paederast's idea of heaven. Almost every scrap of wall was covered with canvases depicting the classical male form, doe-eyed, cupid-lipped, lightly muscled, and sporting tiny, hairless nubs between their legs. On plinths stood a half dozen similar forms, this time in marble, their bodies stuck between the adult and the child. In a few pieces a naked older male was depicted, his solicitous pose innocent enough to the ancient eye. In fact, they would all be relatively inoffensive if they'd been dotted around a gallery, but the sheer number and insistence of them made the room revolting.

'You know what he is, of course? Yes, you've met his messenger boy, so you must.' Miss Barton fingered a small golden cross that lay against her chest. 'I get down on my knees and pray for him nightly.'

'Any luck with that?'

'Mercifully, yes. These days he's practically incapable.'

'You don't sound like you approve of your employer, Miss Barton. Why do you stay?'

'I was his nanny when he was a little boy. Old bonds, I suppose.'

'And do you know what he wants with me?'

She smoothed the crucifix against her stiff white blouse. 'There isn't much that goes on in this house I don't know.'

And with that, she led the way out of the hall and down a wide, wainscoted corridor. Having made his point, the professor didn't seem bothered about continuing his theme in the rest of the house. That, at least, was a mercy. We reached a door inlaid into the wall and Miss Barton knocked and turned the handle.

'Would you like something to drink, Mr Jericho?' she asked.

'No, I don't think so.'

Miss Barton nodded. 'I'll bring you a whisky and soda.' She gave me a final lopsided smile and pushed open the door. 'Just in case.'

'Mis-ter Jer-i-cho! Why have you kept me waiting, sir?'

I followed Miss Barton into the library, where she busied herself at a sideboard, returning seconds later with my drink. Then she inclined her head towards the fireplace and, skirt whispering across the plush purple carpet, left us alone.

Aside from a portrait of a Georgian general that made Genghis Khan look friendly and approachable, this room was hardly decorated at all. By the light of the fire and a solitary standard lamp, I could read a few of the titles of the books which stood in the floor-to-ceiling shelves, the whole collection apparently concentrated on the mid- to late-Victorians. I ran my tongue over my teeth and turned to the man in the wheelchair.

'What can I do for you, Mr Campbell?'

Seated beside the fire, a book face down on his blanketed lap, Campbell's startling blue eyes looked up at me.

'*Professor*, please,' he said. 'Well now, you can take that disapproving look off your face for a start. My crimes were discovered years ago, Mr Jericho. I was drummed out of my profession, incarcerated, and now I have no impure urges at all.' Lifting a thin arm, he smacked the heel of his hand against his groin. 'Chemical castration did wonders to drive out my demons.'

'And yet you still haven't got a single mature cock on your walls,' I said.

A pantomime of distaste played across his gaunt features. 'Forthright. I know that's the showman's way, except when the spiel demands otherwise. All that outside in the hall,' he flicked a birdlike claw, 'why it's art, sir. You're not a philistine, are you?'

34

'I used to be a policeman.' I shrugged. 'I'd call it grounds for interview.'

'What a mercy then that you brought your career to such a stunning conclusion. Please.' He inclined his body to one side, slippered feet swaying a little, and took out a mobile phone. 'Be my guest. I'm sure your former brethren would be delighted to hear from you, especially Inspector Garris.'

I looked at him. 'How do you know about me?'

'Legends, whispers.' He tucked the phone away again. 'Then, of course, there's your family connection to the tragedy of Travellers Bridge, a tale that has always been a particular favourite of mine. It's a wonderful coincidence, really, that you should have such a personal link to the matter in hand, as well as possessing the skills required to investigate the mystery.'

I sighed wearily. 'Tell me why I'm here or we're done.'

He indicated the armchair opposite. 'We have much to discuss and you're such a big fellow, looking up at you gives me quite a crick in the neck.'

At last, curiosity overcame my revulsion and I took a seat.

Putting an age to Campbell was difficult; he might have been anywhere between his late thirties and late forties. His head was practically hairless and his unnaturally smooth chin reminded me of those prepubescent paintings in the hall. Paradoxically, his cadaverousness could have both aged or preserved his features, for although his brilliant blue eyes shone in the shadows of his cheekbones, there didn't appear to be a single line in his waxy skin. Dressed more or less in black, like his housekeeper, the only hint of colour was the faintly violent shade of his lips. I wondered then whether rouging the master's mouth was one of Miss Barton's chores.

35

'You're here,' said the professor, 'because I sent for you. Apologies, by the way, for little Jeremy. I had tried writing but you seemed determined to ignore all communication from the outside world, and I simply had to get your attention.'

'You have it.' I twirled my finger. 'Can we move on?'

'Certainly. But first,' those red lips pouted, 'perhaps a little demonstration, just to sate my curiosity. So many stories told to the private detectives I sent to investigate you. Former colleagues on the force, students from your brief stint at Oxford, your charming friends from that unsavoury period between university and joining the force. All agreed you were quite the detective. And so, anything?'

Indented palms along the line of the thumb, deep but not the ingrained callosity of a lifetime pushing a chair. Although I didn't want to please him, I'm a showman and we like to perform.

'You weren't born disabled,' I told him. 'What happened to you?'

He applauded. 'Prison happened to me. They used my screams to drown out the horror of their own sins. For those with a conscience, I believe it's how one survives such places. But then, you must know all about that. Anything else?'

I looked at him carefully. There was something amiss with his body language, a contradiction that seemed to constantly animate him. His upper torso would suddenly swell and thrust outwards, projecting his inert lower half in a way that clearly caused him discomfort. Then he would fall in on himself again, hunching over his lap as if cowed. He wanted to revel in being a victim and yet at the same time keep a part of it secret.

'It wasn't chemical castration, was it?' I said. 'The people who broke your bones, they did the job properly, didn't they?'

His face went rigid. 'Anything *else*, Mr Jericho?'

'Just one thing. You weren't a professor of history.'

'Why do you say so?'

'The books.' I glanced at the groaning shelves behind me. 'I know what a well-loved book looks like. Creases, dog-ears, shabby spines. All those are brand new, so what's the game?'

'So very close to perfection, but I'll have to award only an upper second, I'm afraid. I am, or *was*, a history professor. As for the books? You know what the police do to one's possessions during a search, especially those of a molester. After I came out of prison, I simply couldn't bear the thought of those big, rough hands on my treasures. And so I bought a fresh set and sent the old books to storage. One day I plan to get some young fellow or other to transcribe my annotations. What a shame, I thought you'd have done your research.'

He was right, I hadn't looked him up. It was a vice of mine which Garris had hated – an overreliance on cleverness and instinct without the proper attention to detail. I could only shrug.

'So I've failed, shall I go?'

'By no means!' Campbell smiled. 'After all, we have yet to discuss yesterday's murder.'

Chapter Six

EVER STOOD ON THE EDGE of a building and been tempted to take that final step into oblivion? Freud called it Thanatos, the death drive. It's that screw-the-risks instinct that makes chancers of us all and probably accounts for the fact that the human race isn't still drawing stick figures on cave walls. I could feel something like it then – the near certainty that I was wading into lethal waters – yet still I leaned forward and asked:

'What murder?'

Campbell smiled, his face more skull-like than ever. 'The third, of course. But we shall get to that.'

From under the open book on his lap, he produced a wireless clicker and thumbed a button. A huge image was suddenly projected onto the blank wall above the fireplace: a paparazzi shot of me and my old mentor exiting the station after our second interview with Lenny Kerrigan.

I knew the shot and the photographer well. After being assigned the Malanowski murders, Maxine Thierrot had hunted me throughout my bail period and, afterwards, lain in wait when Sal picked me up from HMP Hazelhurst a year later. She'd then hung around the fair for a week or two, catching the odd snap, until, despite her fierce objections that my story wasn't over (some of the showmen had overheard her complaining on her mobile), her editor had pulled her from the gig.

I studied the photograph with a detached kind of interest, as if the tightly wound young man towering above me were a stranger. Beside me, Garris looked his usual haggard self, although he retained the cool stare for which he was renowned. Dressed in his usual attire of pinstriped trousers, paisley tie, and cream-coloured shirt with rolled-up sleeves, he looked like the kind of teacher that had died out a decade ago. The only thing that marked him out was the small tattoo on his left wrist; a single red poppy, it was a relic from his army days.

'Detective Constable Scott Jericho and DI Peter Garris,' Campbell said in a scholarly tone. 'This is from almost two years ago, the last time they worked together. Despite a brilliant arrest record and swift promotion to CID, DC Jericho destroyed his career, and almost derailed that of his friend, by violently attacking the prime suspect in the murder of the Malanowski family.

'At his trial, colleagues described Mr Jericho as intelligent, insightful, one of the best case-closers in the business, but also temperamental and abrasive. His only close friend, if we may call him such, was DI Garris, who spoke as a character witness. He considered Jericho the most gifted detective he had ever worked with, possessing an almost unique investigative mind.' The professor clicked again and another Maxine Thierrot shot appeared, this time a grainy picture of me leaving Hazelhurst. 'The private detectives in my employ gathered quite a few juicy titbits about your time inside.' A red laser pointer played around my image's mouth, appearing to turn my lips a similar shade to those of Campbell's. 'Did you enjoy it, I wonder?'

I gave him a shrug. 'Were all your lectures this boring, Professor? I'm surprised the university waited for allegations of kiddie fiddling before firing you.'

His smile fell and he clicked again. 'You're quite right. The recent past is unimportant, but it's my method to move from first principles and I thought you might find my summary enlightening. Never mind. Onwards. Do you know what this is?'

I stared up at the new picture that had appeared on the wall. 'Are you telling me it's real?'

The professor chuckled. 'Yes, indeed. The entire fable.'

A frozen river now bubbled above the fireplace, spanning it, an old bow-backed bridge. It was uncanny. With arches and pediments cobbled together from irregular cuts of Kentish stone, this was the bridge I had always pictured in my mother's bedtime story. Algae had crept up from the river and furred its legs in shades of green. Beyond, I could glimpse the calm meander of the water, caressed on all sides by heavy-headed willows. On the keystone was a plaque with a date that had been eaten away by the elements.

'Travellers Bridge,' I murmured.

'The second,' Campbell corrected. 'The first had been medieval. This nineteenth-century version is an exact replica, built to the order of Mr Gideon Hillstrom, local landowner and mayor of the Oxfordshire town of Bradbury End. It was raised with the aid of public subscription, and much was made at the time of the generosity of the Bradburians, with even the poorest widow donating a penny to the construction. The plaque reads:

ERECTED IN MEMORY OF THOSE SHOWPEOPLE WHO DIED HERE WHEN THE OLD BRIDGE COLLAPSED IN THE GREAT STORM. *'Acclinis Falsis Animus Meliora Recusat.'*

"'The mind intent upon false appearances refuses to admit better things.'"

'Very good,' the professor nodded. 'From Horace, of course. I wonder what Mr Hillstrom and his fellow dignitaries meant by that quotation?'

I tapped my middle finger against my knee, wondering too. 'I still don't understand what all this has to do with a murder you say happened yesterday.'

'You will. Now, apart from my studies in Victoriana, I have a small side interest in what one might call the various subcultures that existed at the time. One of those being the Traveller community. Of course, there had been such peoples for centuries, going right back to the wandering minstrels and jongleur storytellers of the Dark Ages, but it wasn't until the 1800s that the travelling fair as we know it came into being. And one of its highlights was, of course, the freakshow.'

I didn't like him talking about my people. I might have rejected them half a lifetime ago, but they'd taken me back without question in my time of need. The fact this repellent man seemed to know more about them than me was disconcerting. He clicked again and continued.

'Matthew "Slip-Jointed" Jericho.'

The projection of the old daguerreotype glowed against the plaster. My ancestor had been a contortionist, that I knew, but spectacle shows like his had died out years ago and I'd never seen one. Resplendent in a black top hat and tails, Matthew was standing on his left leg, his right wrapped around his back, a naked big toe scratching the inside of his ear. Meanwhile, his arms were cranked upwards behind him, palms inverted towards the floor, fingers twisted at angles that made me want to look away. Matthew Jericho was little more than bone and, apart from the jut of his jaw and a mess of black curls poking from under the brim of his hat, I couldn't see much resemblance to me or my father.

Behind the showman stood a beautifully painted gaff card:

ROLL UP! ROLL UP! JERICHO'S FREAKS – NOVELTIES, CURI-OSITIES, WONDERS OF NATURE (HUMAN OR OTHERWISE), ALIVE, DEAD, OR DYING!

'There were others like him,' Campbell went on. 'Tom Norman, the Silver King, exhibitor of the Elephant Man was probably the best. A much-maligned figure, as most of the freakshow owners were. The truth was that many of these poor souls would've been sent to the workhouse or else starved in the streets, and most were as well paid as the showmen themselves.'

He was right about that at least. The depiction of the Traveller as a sadist who kept his unfortunate employees as beasts in a cage is, as far I know, an old lie. Most were treated as friends and family, and many commanded good salaries or else sold their services to rival companies. It was a way to survive in a time when survival was a day-to-day battle.

'Matthew's show included some of the most spectacular acts of the day,' Campbell went on, and sped through a series of slides. 'Gulliver Rice, the Balloon-Headed Horror.' Another faded daguerreotype, this time of a man with some kind of tumorous malformation of the skull. His smile was kind, his single visible eye twinkling with good humour. 'Maria Landless, the Electric Lady.' A pretty young woman with painted-on sparks rippling from her fingertips. 'Marguerite de Bellefort, the Fat Woman of Wimbledon.' A lady who almost blotted out the bay window in which she sat, her vast chiffon dress barely accommodating the breasts that hung to her ankles. 'And finally, Charlie Buckley, the Dog-Faced Boy.' From his build, I guessed that this last was an adolescent of about fifteen. Apart from a few spare patches around the eyes and nose, coarse hair covered his entire face. I couldn't tell whether Charlie had been a genuine sufferer of hypertrichosis, or 'werewolf syndrome' as it had once been known, or if he was *Duff* (noun: a fairground fake) created by Matthew Jericho.

'It was these five,' Campbell said, 'including your ancestor, who died when the old bridge collapsed in Bradbury's great storm.'

'In the versions I've heard, they were coming into the town for the hop-picking,' I said. 'The fairs were doing badly at the time and showpeople provided cheap labour for farmers in the harvest.'

'That's right,' the professor nodded. 'At that time Jericho was travelling with Moody's Fairground. Most of the showman loads had already made it to the far side of the bridge when Matthew's wagon, carrying him and the rest of the freaks, started to cross. By this point, the rain had been falling hard for five solid days and the swollen river had already burst its banks. Eyewitnesses described hearing a terrible groan that seemed to dwarf the thunder. Through a veil of rain, they watched as the Bradbury-side pier gave way. The horse pulling the wagon shied, tipping its load onto the deck. Matthew was on his feet in an instant, grasping for the reins, when a hoof caught him across the brow and he dropped out of sight behind the parapet. The others rushed to help, but it was too late to save either Jericho or themselves.

'The bridge swayed drunkenly and seemed to turn ninety degrees so that its southern head now faced the flow of the river. The watchers on the bank swear they saw this, although it seems physically impossible. Whatever the truth, the old bridge came apart in an explosion of bricks and dust. When the air cleared, the bodies were gone, some pinned fathoms deep by the debris, others washed downstream where they'd be found a few days later. Only the horse remained, flailing and wild-eyed in the torrent.'

He had told it almost as well as my mother. The only difference was that her version had contained an evolving roster of fictional players whereas his described the real victims of the tragedy.

'Afterwards the bridge was rebuilt as I've described,' he continued, 'and the locals took to calling it Travellers Bridge. So, tell me, Detective, did you find my story interesting?'

'You've painted a vivid picture, I'll give you that,' I said.

'That's only the beginning.' He treated me to a death's-head grin. 'Perhaps you should have that drink now, Mr Jericho.'

Chapter Seven

'**I** DON'T DRINK.'

'Oh, I think you will.' He chuckled, and clicked again. The picture of Charles Buckley, the Dog-Faced Boy, was replaced with a crime scene photograph of a recently murdered monster. Unwittingly, I dropped my hand to the glass tumbler and took a deep gulp of bourbon. It stung my throat, settling me a little. Then I rose and, numb to the reach of the flames, stood in front of the fire. I stretched out my hand and touched the horror above.

'How did you get this?'

'I have my sources,' said Campbell. 'Any information has its price, but what do you make of it?'

That was a question I didn't want to answer, especially to this man who seemed somehow desperate not to be alone with his sin, but I'll tell you, my first reaction was excitement. Here, crucified upon the wall, was a human being who had once held within his now desecrated body all the hopes and terrors of any normal life. Yet, in that instant, he was to me, a corner piece in a puzzle, the dim outline of which I was only just beginning to realise.

The fact he had been decapitated and that his head had been replaced might account for my detachment, I suppose. The victim looked unreal, like a fantastical figure plucked out of some dark fairy tale. Although the strange head that had taken the place of his own screamed for my attention, I forced myself to take in every other detail before the killer's showpiece overwhelmed the rest.

The naked body appeared to have been lashed to the trunk of a tree, coarse rope secured around the legs and upper torso. His hands hung freely at his sides, and unless they had been untied later, my guess was that he'd died elsewhere and then been strung to the trunk. There were several ragged holes and a crusted bloom of blood over his heart, stains running under his armpits, which seemed to confirm that he had been killed while lying on his back.

I stepped closer to the wall, still insensate to the flames. Yes, his fingers were clotted with fresh dirt and I could imagine him gouging the earth in his short-lived agony. From the condition of the body, I guessed he had been in his late fifties, out of shape, with a pendulous beer belly that almost obscured his genitals, but strong with it. Those overdeveloped hand muscles belonged to a working man while his knees were padded over with hardened skin. An idea occurred to me and I turned to Campbell.

'Was this man a showman?'

'No,' he answered. 'But I'd be interested to hear why you think so.'

'The physicality,' I said, returning my gaze to the wall. 'Those callused knee joints, the slight slope and imbalance in his shoulder muscles, the strong calves. Travellers can get that way from continually siting their caravans, pushing against the sides with their preferred shoulder, getting on all fours and guiding the hitch into the coupling. He was left-handed anyway.'

'Very good,' the professor nodded, 'but no. In life, this poor soul was Robert McAllister from Anglesey, North Wales. He had no connection with fairgrounds but he was the owner of the Sweet View Caravan Site that overlooks Benllech Bay, so your conclusions stand.'

Now that I had a name to personalise the victim, shame began to overwhelm my initial excitement. I moved on to the final detail. After death, McAllister's head had been removed with clinical savagery. I pictured it: a shark-toothed saw clenched in a practised fist, the soft yielding of tissue as the edge began to bite and then find purchase in the muscle below. A small whistle of air as it cleaved through the cartilage of the Adam's apple and entered the windpipe. Then, through secret ways, it plunged and, nipping the more or less drained jugular, released an undramatic dribble that barely stained the killer's hand. On then, through the carotid, into vocal chambers where music once played, and finally the scrape and turn of the saw as it found a smoother path between the barrier of the spine. A little jiggling and prising, gripping McAllister's hair and working his waxen head this way and that, and the job is done.

Except it isn't, not quite, for the head must be replaced. Had he come prepared, I wondered? No, the dog's head looked fresh, its muzzle still iced with the foam of its terror. A collie or Welsh sheepdog, ears and chops black, the centre of its face a flash of white that had probably run down to its belly. I couldn't tell how it had been killed but hardly any of its blood seemed have run down McAllister's body. There was no stitching that I could see and the only other option the killer had to complete this modern freakshow was to affix some kind of pole into the human torso and then work the dog's head onto its master's body, for I suddenly felt sure that this was McAllister's own pet.

Campbell confirmed my suspicion. 'Right on both counts. That there is Bestie; apparently the man was a football fan. A sharpened broom handle did the job and poor Bestie's body and McAllister's head were found seated side by side in McAllister's somewhat cluttered caravan. A mercy, I suppose, that the murderer didn't see fit to attach *those* parts.' He tittered. 'Can you imagine?'

I breathed hard and took my seat again. 'OK, so apart from the obvious, what makes you think that this murder is connected to an accident that happened a hundred and fifty years ago?'

'Why the others, of course.' He clicked through two further images. 'Agatha Poole, seventy-eight, found at her villa in the Costa del Luz, electrocuted in an old-fashioned tin bath. Strange, no?' The photograph showed an old, white-haired woman squeezed into a tub barely larger than a wash bucket. Her head had been partially blackened, one arm incinerated to a stub, her naked body scorched and broiled red by the passage of electricity. Driven into the tips of her remaining fingers were what appeared to be thin strands of metal, slender as paperclips, shiny and kinked as if to resemble forks of lightning. 'And here, Adya Mahal, a young girl of Indian heritage who died in the city of Lincoln five days after her nineteenth birthday.' Again, the corpse was naked, this time sitting on a camp bed, sunlight through a red curtain dying her skin. In life, she had probably weighed around twenty-five stone but in death parts of her had been cut away and forced down her throat. That sense of excitement I felt had swiftly curdled, yet still, I leaned forward and asked Campbell to go back to the Electric Lady.

He clicked and the wall turned dark. 'I've prepared a file, you may peruse all the photographs at your leisure.'

'All right.' I swilled the last of the bourbon. 'So we have three murders with ritualistic hallmarks but no common pattern. The methods of killing, of displaying the bodies, there's no consistent MO.'

'Correct,' Campbell agreed. 'But there are one or two connections between the killings. First, the staging of the bodies is suggestive of those who died on Travellers Bridge.' He counted them off on his fingers. 'The Dog-Faced Boy, the Electric Lady, and the Fat Woman of Wimbledon. Only two more to go, Mr Jericho: the Balloon-Headed Horror and your ancestor, the Contortionist, "Slip-Jointed" Jericho. And then there's this.' He reached for a nearby table and handed me three enlargements. 'Found on McAllister's forehead, the sole of Agatha Poole's left foot, and under a flap of Adya Mahal's skin.'

Carved into the dead flesh of each were individual letters: 'A', 'F', 'A'.

'*Acclinis Falsis Animus*: the first three initial letters from the Travellers Bridge memorial quotation. They are dying again, Mr Jericho.' Campbell smiled. 'One by one.'

Chapter Eight

'How did you piece this together?' I asked.

'Inherited wealth and, since my eunuchising, a staggering amount of free time.' Campbell wheeled himself away from the fire and moved to a large desk that stood against a heavily draped window. There, he busied himself with papers. 'I have a little holiday home on Red Wharf Bay, just around the coast from Benllech. I was up there a few days after McAllister's murder and happened to catch sight of it in one of the national papers.' He looked back at me with something like amusement in his gaze. 'You really haven't heard of any of these cases, have you?'

All I could do was shake my head. The truth was, I hadn't picked up a paper since my arrest, hadn't watched the TV news or even glanced at the internet. Now, as Campbell touched the wireless switch again, the wall came alive with a blaze of sensational headlines:

POLICE BAFFLED BY HEAD-SWAP PSYCHO

COULD BIZARRE SPANISH DEATH BE LINKED

TO WELSH MURDER?

SICK SERIAL KILLER LEAVES NO CLUES

'My, how you buried yourself away, Mr Jericho,' Campbell smiled. 'The first two murders were all over the press for a month or two, though the initial furore has died down somewhat. Tentative links were drawn by both the UK and Spanish police and the media. The outlandishness of the crimes was, of course, indicative. But otherwise they have been at a loss to connect the killings and, as is so often the case with the press and the public, bafflement soon turned to frustration and frustration to indifference.'

'But not for you?'

'The police held back a lot of detail, but what I heard struck a chord,' he nodded. 'The whole thing had the flavour of something incomplete. And so, my interest piqued, I hired a couple of private detectives, the same ones who compiled the report on you, and set them to work.'

'So McAllister was the first?' I asked.

'January 18th. Then poor Miss Poole on 3rd March and finally Adya Mahal only yesterday. My little investigative elves are very quick, aren't they?'

'What else have they discovered?'

'Only one other intriguing detail. It went overlooked by the Welsh police, but one of my sleuths discovered it in a paparazzi shot taken of McAllister's caravan the day the murder was discovered. Here, take a look, tell me what you see.'

That thin claw reached out again and passed me yet another enlargement, this time of a dirty trailer window. A small, featureless figure was balanced against the glass, its limbs contorted into strange and unlikely angles. I recognised it as one of those little wooden mannikins with articulated joints that artists use for reference when drawing the human form. The tortured pose of the figure was suggestive enough, but the clincher was the miniature outfit it had been dressed in.

Resplendent in top hat and tails, this was almost certainly meant to represent Matthew 'Slip-Jointed' Jericho himself.

'Were figures left at each crime scene?' I asked, my mouth horribly dry.

'Only at the first,' Campbell told me. 'A calling card, if you will, from our killer. A signal that he had commenced his dreadful task. McAllister's caravan was stuffed with bric-a-brac left behind by visitors to the campsite, and so this wee fellow was easily overlooked by the police. But my detectives have established from friends and neighbours that the mannikin had never been seen before the day of the murder.'

Campbell added a final page and waved the complete file in the air. 'Anyway, it's all here, what little there is.'

I frowned at the slim contents. 'But surely the police must be drowning in information. The British lot and the Spanish force.'

'You'd think so, wouldn't you? But aside from the bizarre nature of the crimes, there was no significant forensic evidence left at the scenes. Indeed, I am the first to have solidly connected the murders. The victims have absolutely no relationship to each other and, as you say, there is no discernible pattern to the ritualism other than that which our special knowledge tells. Without the key of Travellers Bridge, the police are clueless.'

'I think we should inform them,' I said, a trace of reluctance in my voice.

'And you think they'd believe such an incredible theory coming from the likes of me? Or from *you*? Pardon the pun, but haven't you burned those bridges?'

He had a point. Only the flimsiest and most extraordinary thread linked these murders. That I was now convinced of its reality wouldn't do much to sway my former colleagues, but perhaps one of them might listen ...

Campbell coasted over to where I now stood, my back resting against his bookcase. 'Your file.'

I hesitated. Firelight danced across the manila surface and I felt again the spectral touch of a tiny hand in mine.

'I will pay you,' the professor twittered, a hint of panic in his tone. 'Name your fee. Five hundred a day, plus expenses? A bonus, of course, once the case is solved. I don't even ask for proofs that will stand up in court, just a name and a reason.'

I needed money; my resources were dwindling fast and, aside from a place to rest my head, I hadn't asked my father for a handout since I was eighteen. Anyway, the case had already got its hooks into me. Not only the strangeness of the mystery itself but, if I was honest, the air of violence and danger that hung around it. Thanatos again. Taking out my logbook, I tore off a sheet, printed my bank details and handed it to Campbell. He grabbed the scrap of paper like a starving urchin snatching at a heel of bread.

'I leave the course of the investigation to you,' he said. 'I only ask that you make the occasional report whenever you can manage.'

All the urgency of a moment ago had vanished. It seemed odd, but I could've sworn that, having handed over the case, he was now utterly uninterested in it.

'So,' I said, the file clutched to my chest, 'what do you get out of all this?'

His gaze flickered to the well of his lap. 'What remains for a man when he has no passion left? Curiosity, I suppose. A dangerous thing in the wrong hands.'

I shook my head. I didn't buy it, not completely. Superficially, his fixation on the case might be just what it appeared: the gruesome hobby of a man of means whose days were otherwise empty. There was also the somewhat sinister character of Campbell himself that suggested any morbid topic could easily tip over into obsession. Yet for some reason I couldn't quite put my finger on, his explanation rang false. Nevertheless, he had woken me from the constant horror of the Malanowski case and the scent he had started me on was solid enough. Whatever Campbell's true motive for wanting the case investigated, a murderer was at large and at least two more people were in danger.

Without saying goodbye, I closed the door behind me and headed back down the corridor where I found Miss Barton waiting in the hall's paederast gallery. Her burned face hitched into a half-smile so melancholy BB King could've used her as a muse.

'All done?' she asked.

'Not nearly. What do you think of it all?'

She went to the door and opened it onto a landscape that steamed in the aftershock of the storm. The air was thick with the deep, brown odour of the earth and the stagnancy of things unburied. A distant flash of lightning lit up a faraway hillside, and I thought of dog-headed men dripping in the rain, electric ladies murdered by the heavens, a girl choked with the clods of her own flesh.

'I'll pray for you, Mr Jericho,' Miss Barton promised. 'Go well with your God.'

I reached into the passenger seat and touched the case file, reassuring myself that all I had seen and heard was real. It seemed incredible, like something cooked up between Stephen King and the Marquis de Sade. Crawling at fifty along the empty bow of the M11, I wondered, *Who?* I didn't need a name or even a profile at this stage, just the vaguest hint.

The character of the crimes – the deliberate staging of the victims to echo those drowned at Travellers Bridge, the initials from the memorial, the placing of the 'Jericho' mannikin at the first scene – all were prima facie evidence of a link and therefore of someone familiar with the story. A showman? I didn't like the idea, but it was possible.

The story had so many versions, bowdlerised for younger listeners, transformed into almost Jacobean revenge tragedies for older ears, that a few of the old-timers on the circuit must have heard the original. This wasn't the work of some eighty-year-old aunt, however, but might her bedtime tale have inspired a grown-up grandson to murder? We like to think we're different, but just like the rest of society, Travellers have their quota of psychopaths.

There were other possibilities. Someone from Bradbury End maybe? Locals might well be familiar with the legend of the drowned freaks; it could even be taught in their primary school, the distance of years making it no more than a ghoulish titbit of town lore. In that case, the cast of potential suspects could be vast and I had none of my old police resources to fall back on. Where once I might have enjoyed unfettered access to forensic and coroner reports, the HOLMES computer system for cross-checking and managing serial killer cases, and the natural authority that comes with the badge, I now had to rely solely on Campbell's file.

Still, perhaps working a case informally might have its bene-fits. I knew from how the press photographer Maxine Thierrot had tracked me down that the public is often more likely to provide information if they know their name will never appear in any official document. Plus, I no longer needed to justify the loose hunches that had more than once got me into trouble. Now, I could simply follow my nose.

Aside from the good folk of Bradbury End, I was hunting in the dark. It could easily be a lone lunatic who, like the professor, had taken an unhealthy interest in fairground history. A thought occurred and I allowed it space to breathe: I already had the feeling that Campbell was holding something back regarding his interest in the case, but was it possible that he had some direct hand in it? He couldn't have murdered them himself, of course, but what if he had convinced someone else? For a moment, I entertained the absurd image of Miss Barton spearing Bestie's head onto Robert McAllister's corpse.

Two more murders to go, if Campbell's theory held. Why these victims? I'd have to review the file, check that the professor's hired gumshoes hadn't missed anything, but my instinct agreed with their conclusions: these people had no connection. Not business, family, friends, only the fact that they'd been remade into a grisly pantomime of the Jericho freaks.

A service station sparked against the darkness. In response, my stomach growled. I hadn't eaten all day and I was suddenly famished. Under the glare of the forecourt, I topped up my tank and went in search of a sandwich. It didn't occur to me then that, for the first time in months, the smell of petrol hadn't inspired a visitation from my ghosts.

BLT in hand, I waited at the till where an exhausted-looking businessman was swiping his debit card. Bored, I glanced over towards my car only to find a familiar figure leaning against the passenger door.

Lenny Kerrigan grinned and waved.

'Sir?' muttered the attendant. 'I can serve you now.'

'What?' I turned as the businessman shouldered his way past. 'Sorry, I need to – look—' I thrust four twenties onto the counter, 'I have to go. Keep the change.'

'But, sir!'

Anne Boleyn had probably skipped her way to the block with more alacrity than the businessman possessed as he progressed to the exit. Returning the compliment of his shoulder, I elbowed him out of the way, ignoring a cattish shriek as his coffee splashed his hand. Outside, a gust of exhaust fumes hit me. Kerrigan was nowhere to be seen. I ran across the forecourt, jogged a circuit around the station, came back, checked my doors and even under the car. He might possibly have slipped away in his own car or else . . .

'Fucking lunatic!' the businessman called from the window of his Subaru.

Could I have imagined him? I slammed my palm against the bonnet. Of course, I could – nothing more likely. Throwing the unopened sandwich onto the backseat, I pulled into the shadows of the overnight truck stop. There, I took out Sal's phone and dialled the one number I still had memorised.

No one picked up on the first or second attempt. By the glow of the dashboard, I saw that it was a quarter to one, but then, he'd always kept erratic hours, especially when Harriet hadn't been well. I was about to give up when a drowsy voice answered.

'Hell is it? Unless you're being fucking murdered, I'm not—'

'Sir ...' I rested the side of my head against the window. 'Pete, it's me.'

There was a pause during which I wondered if he'd hung up. In the five years I'd known him, I had never been to his house, never met the sickly wife who wrote me letters as if she were a doting aunt. Garris was an intensely private man, sensitive of his wife's needs, but I could imagine him now sitting in a cheery kitchen, Harriet's amateurish watercolours adorning the walls. I'd received a few of these as presents over the years, Garris handing them to me, a mix of pride and embarrassment contorting his usually neutral features. He was often cool, even with his protégé, and yet I never once doubted his love for his wife, nor ever summoned the courage to ask what was wrong with her.

'Just a moment.' A door clicked shut and he was back. 'Is this about the files?' he asked without preamble. 'I brought you a fresh batch the other day. I'm not sure you even knew I was there, but ...' He paused as if remembering some vital fact. 'How are you, Scott?'

'I'm good.' He sniffed at that, sharp as ever. 'I'm better. How's Harriet?'

'Not well.' In all our time together, this was one of the rare moments when I heard weakness in his voice. 'Worse, if anything.'

'Sir, if there's—?'

'What could you possibly do?' he cut in. 'And enough with that "sir" stuff. You're never coming back, Scott, so drop the formalities. Is it about the files? They'll hang me if they find out I've been printing off cases, probably cut my bollocks off too if they discover I've been bringing them to *you*. But, honestly, we could do with some help. There's a case I have running at the moment; the murder of a nurse in Coldharbour Lane—'

'Pete, I need a favour.'

Another pause, another sigh. I could see him, hunched over the kitchen table, phone cradled to his ear. 'This *is* gonna cost me my balls, isn't it? Never mind,' he muttered when I tried a half-hearted reassurance. 'You did me enough favours back in the day. Go on, shoot.'

'Can you look into a guy called Campbell for me? Professor Ralph Campbell. Used to be a lecturer in history, jailed after some kind of kiddie case. I just want a background check.'

I could hear Garris scribbling, then the familiar cluck of his tongue against the roof of his mouth. 'Is this a case, Scott? Something we ought to know about?'

I should tell him. At least two more lives were at stake . . . but Campbell was right; even if Garris bought such a wild story, he was still serving under a cloud for his connection with me. I couldn't risk his career a second time.

'I'm not sure yet. I'll let you know.'

'OK,' he yawned. 'I'll try to have something for you by close of play tomorrow, if not a little earlier. Anything else I can help you with? No? Then please, any more favours you want to call in, can we keep the requests to a more sociable hour? Listen.' I heard a drum of fingers. 'I'm glad you're feeling better. Keep it up.'

The phone went dead and I dropped it onto the passenger seat.

There, something snared my eye: the corner of a cherry-tinted piece of paper poking out from Campbell's file. I knew that shade well, it was the distinctive branding chosen by my father to market Jericho Fairs. Pulling it free, I saw that it was a handbill, the kind the chaps distributed across any new town we rolled into. The text was typically ornate, summoning nostalgia for the old fairs Matthew Jericho might once have known. As this thought flitted into my mind, I read the words and felt a pleasing horror prickle the nape of my neck:

COMING SOON TO BRADBURY END

THE RETURN OF JERICHO FAIR

IN COMMEMORATION OF THE 150TH ANNIVERSARY

OF THE TRAGEDY OF TRAVELLERS BRIDGE

Acclinis Falsis Animus Meliora Recusat!

Chapter Nine

I PARKED UP AND STRODE THROUGH the 3 a.m. stillness. Alert to their duty, the fairground juks strained at their leads and sniffed my heels in a way that would send a stranger's balls squirrelling for cover. Among them, John Webster gave a welcome grunt. I scratched a tattered ear. My mother had bought him in the last year of her life and, because of his love of ripping rats to pieces and leaving them as offerings on the trailer step, had named the boxer dog after her favourite bloodthirsty playwright.

'Hey, boy. Old man still up?'

He looked at me, brow raised, quizzical as a barrister.

At Dad's trailer, I took out the crumpled handbill again. Sal had said something about a fête when I'd mentioned Travellers Bridge – something else too which I couldn't bring to mind. As I was living on the fair, Campbell must have assumed I knew about the anniversary event and so hadn't thought it worth mentioning. But what *did* it mean? That the murders had been inspired by this year's commemoration? Or that the killer had waited, perhaps decades, before setting his plan in motion? Surely even the most cool-headed psychopath would find that kind of restraint almost impossible. Unless, of course, he *had* killed before and had changed his modus operandi after reading about the Travellers Bridge tragedy.

I stuffed the bill into my pocket and tapped my father's door. He had a good-sized chalet at the yard in Kent where he wintered, but for travelling, he kept his simple Colchester, a model pushing forty on whose now-threadbare sofa I had been born. Much less grand than the big Sipsons and Baileys owned by other well-to-do Travellers, Dad kept the Colchester because it was, in his words, 'a showman's trailer, not some joskin's place on wheels.'

'In if you're coming,' he barked.

The 'Chester was in semi-darkness, a single lamp burning on a side table at the end of the locker settee. Unlike most of her generation, my mother had taken the plastic covers off her sofa on the promise Dad would never sit there in his overalls. Now, dressed in immaculate day clothes, he muted the TV and held out his hand. The gesture caught me off guard. Grasping my wrist, he turned my hand palm up.

'Been to Cambridge?'

I shook my head. 'How—?'

'Time you've been gone and the word right there.' I looked at the faded imprint on my hand – *irchang* – and understood. My hands were often closed into fists and the receipt had sweated its impression. 'Birchanger services. Got fuel on the way back. Must have.'

'Why not on the way there?'

'It's still just about readable.'

He nodded at the chair opposite. From my mother, I'd inherited my strong features, from my father, black curls and a broad-shouldered body that dwarfed the armchair. Truth be told, my dad had a face only a mother could love, and I'm not entirely sure my own mother had loved him all that much. It had started, so the aunts told me, with a whirlwind romance, a pull of opposites, swiftly followed by a long, bitter trench of reality. I often wonder what might have become of them if I'd never been born. Divorce, I guess.

'So you've found trouble,' said Dad, leaning forward, spade-like hands between his knees. 'Or trouble found you.'

'You reckon?'

He got up and lumbered to the kitchen area, poured a glass of milk, and returned. For a moment, I wondered if he was going to hand it to me, a bedtime drink for his boy. Sitting again he cradled it to his chest.

'You're talking to me.' He took a long gulp and cuffed the white from his salt-and-pepper moustache. 'That old gavver of your'n has been over quite a lot. Not a bad old joskin, all told. Had him up here for a brew once or twice. He left you a bit of work yesterday, asked after you. So is this his business, or have I got that Nazi fucker to thank for you being up and about?'

'It's nothing to do with Kerrigan,' I assured him. 'It's a case I've taken on. Private client.'

'How's the posh?'

'Not bad. Enough to dent my overdraft, maybe.'

'I told you, I can sort that right now—'

'No.' My father's weathered face corrugated. 'And I don't need any help with Lenny Kerrigan, if you were thinking of going after him.'

'I'm not stupid,' he grunted, 'but sometimes my feelings do get the better of me. Say, I hear of a gorger who comes roaring onto my ground, disturbing the peace.' He spread his hands. 'What am I to do? Now, I know a thing or two about this one, and even if I didn't, that snide little swastika tattoo tells me everything worth knowing. What I have right here is a bit of filth who'd be better off in his box forty years ahead of time. I'm not saying I'd go that far, maybe not even as far as my boy saw fit—' And here the mask fractured for an instant. Was it pride? If it was, I didn't want it. 'But we have ways of calming such a rabid animal right down.'

One of the first books I ever stole from a library was a children's history of the great Romans. I remember sitting on my narrow bed, reading by the light of the fair, the faces of long-dead philosophers and dictators strobing before my eyes. I knew then that my old man had the tongue of Cicero and the guts of Caesar, and I'd loved him for it. That was ten years before I became his Brutus, betraying him in the only way he could never really forgive, by leaving the life.

'Stay away from Kerrigan,' I said. 'I can deal with him.'

He nodded. 'That much is clear.'

I fished in my jeans and took out the handbill. 'I want to know about this.'

'Had those sent out weeks back,' he said. 'Why the sudden interest? You want to run a ride there? I can get you a cushty little set of jets that'd rake it in at a special event like Bradbury End.'

'No, it's not that.'

'Then what?'

'It's the case. It might have something to do with this. The town.' I tapped a finger against the bill. 'I'm not sure how, not yet, but there's a connection.'

He gave me an appraising look, the kind of Cicero glance that could size up a punter at fifty yards and calculate his net worth to the nearest grand.

'Something dangerous? If there's a threat to us in Oxfordshire, I want to know ahead of time.'

'It's nothing like that,' I said and wondered at the lie. Right then, I could feel the tale-spinner inside me, the liar who had tried to win friends at a dozen different schools by inventing humdrum backgrounds. Anything to stop the name-calling before it started: pikey, gypo. Now I let it convince me that I was telling the truth: a random assortment of people had died, there was no threat to the Travellers. 'You don't have to worry.'

A beat. A lone dog barked and Webster answered like a sergeant major demanding order in the ranks.

'Can't ever play it straight, can you? Just like your mother. Leave it out,' he said when I stirred, 'she was my wife and I can speak as I like. So what do you want to know?'

'How was the booking arranged?'

'We were contacted about a year ago by the governors up that way. Blokes called Carmody and Hillstrom. Far as I can tell, Carmody's the errand boy and chief licker of Hillstrom's fat arse. They approached us asking if we'd consider bringing the show back to Bradbury. You're looking pale, what's up?'

'Hillstrom? *Gideon* Hillstrom?'

A superstitious dread washed over me. In that moment, with the trailer painted dusky by lamplight, it seemed almost credible that the same Victorian bridge-builder and mayor of Bradbury End had somehow reached across the centuries and set us all to dance. Wasn't this a ghost story, after all? Serial murderers with a fetish for symbolism are usually a sorry lot, barely more sophisticated than a pimply goth with a hard-on for true crime and death metal. Yet, this case had a care about it that made the whole thing hardly seem real.

Dad reached for his coat, flipped out his wallet, and handed over a gilded business card. 'First name's Marcus, not Gideon.' *Marcus Hillstrom, OBE. Leader of Bradbury End Town Council.* 'First class div, I reckon.' I thumbed the overly embossed honorific and thought my dad was probably right.

'So what's the story?'

'Why the fête, you mean? Probably just a gimmick to give the local economy a boost. Nothing draws 'em like a fair.' He razzle-dazzled his hands, his moustache stretched over the hump of a piss-taking smile. Truth was, the whole business had been living on borrowed time for decades. In a world of on-demand thrills streamed straight into your lap, how could the rickety charm of a travelling fair compete? 'We agreed on a flat fee for the whole thing,' he continued. 'Free round-the-clock rides for the punters. Special events are where the posh is now. You take sweet Fanny Adams with a pay-by-the-ride fair these days.'

'Must've cost them a bit,' I said.

'Local businesses'll pitch in, I suppose. The same respect-able kinds that would've run us out of town once upon a time.'

'Does that mean *we're* respectable?' I half-smiled.

'We're tamed is what we are. They've got new bogeymen to hate now: asylum seekers, starving immigrants trying to earn a crust.' He stretched out his long legs, hip bones cracking. 'Anyhow, Hillstrom said they wanted to mark the anniversary and that his lackey Carmody had found us online. Said the tragedy had become something of a legend up Bradbury way. Not that all of them want us there.'

'What do you mean?'

'Some vote in the council.' Dad sniffed. 'Few of the bigwigs were against it. Thought it was maudlin to look back when the town could be spending money on new projects. Must say, I agree with that. Dwelling on the past never did anyone much good.' He shot me a pointed glance. I returned it as levelly as I could and watched it sway, without defeat, to the framed photograph of my mother that hung above the three-bar fire. 'Anyway,' he looked up, 'can't see how this is any business of yours.'

'Nor can I,' I said, getting to my feet. 'Not yet. Look, I'll be heading off to Bradbury End in the morning. Can I take the trailer?'

His nose wrinkled. 'That old Eccles? I can parny further than that shitbox'll take you. Let me make a few calls and I'll set you up with a brand new—'

'The Eccles'll be fine,' I said, hand on the door. 'And I promise, I'll tell you if things get messy. No trouble will come to the ground if I can help it.'

I was almost out of the trailer when he muttered after me, 'You give that boy Zac a few quid when you're done with him. He's not a bad lad.'

I stiffened. 'And he's not a whore.'

'I didn't say he was.'

His words ghosted with me down the steps. Webster snuffled my palm; whimpered as I left him behind. I padded over mussed-up grass and rain-drenched duckboards, saw a light flicker behind a blind, heard gameshow applause from the TV of an insomniac aunt. Any one of these people would open their home to me right here and now, loan me their life savings if I asked. I glanced down avenues of trailers, laid out with the mathematical precision of master Travellers, and wondered what horrors I might soon bring to their door.

Chapter Ten

MY HAND TREMBLED AND SCALDING coffee splashed across the dead woman stuffed into the makeshift bathtub. The sagging, incinerated sockets of Agatha Poole's eyes stared back at me, almost reproachfully from the photograph. Glancing around the roadside diner, I snatched some paper napkins from a dispenser and blotted away the spill.

I took a breath. Concentrated on my heartbeats. Felt them settle. Then I sorted the crime scene shots back into their manila file. I knew why my hands were so unsteady, why the back of my neck was sticky and damp, why my right leg pistoned under the table like a pneumatic drill. It had nothing to do with the macabre details I'd been poring over for the twentieth time that morning. In fact, there was something emotionally distancing about the gothic imagery of these staged murders – the dog-headed McAllister, the electrically-cremated Agatha, the self-cannibalised Adya Mahal – a sense that they were somehow unreal, like waxworks in a chamber of horrors.

No, it was the withdrawal symptoms that ate my nerves. For the first time in almost two years, I had slept well. No need to seek out meaningless sex to exhaust myself, no need to double down on my Zopiclone prescription. In dreams, I had turned over the puzzle I'd been set by Campbell and found myself waking at dawn, relaxed and eager to begin. It had taken the violent and senseless deaths of three innocent people to give me this respite from my demons – make of that what you will.

But although my mind had hit a kind of reset, my body still craved the daily dose of meds that had held it together for so long. I knew it was dangerous, not to say distracting, to go cold turkey, but I also knew that I couldn't afford a brain fogged by sleeping pills and benzos. Two more lives were at stake and, if I had a hope of saving them, I needed to stay sharp. I'd just have to ride out the next few days as best I could.

That meant ignoring my ghosts too.

Sitting back in the red leather of the booth, I caught sight of plump legs kicking against the backboard. Blackened morsels flaked away from their shoes and fell like dark snow upon the sticky linoleum. I didn't look across the table. I laid my palms flat on the case file and closed my eyes against Sonia's words.

'How funny that you think you can save anyone,' she said, her voice sorrowful rather than unkind. 'Oh Scott, you can't even save yourself.'

I let them whisper and laugh and fade away.

'More coffee, love?'

I blinked up at the waitress, a busty grandmother in a peppermint uniform that clashed horribly with the red, white and blue hokeyness of the American-themed diner. She freshened my cup and sashayed away, a theatrical wink for all and varicose veins that went on for days.

Back to the case file. I took out my notebook and started scribbling. The top hat and tails on the 'Jericho' mannikin looked homemade, probably pieced together from scraps of cardboard and bits of felt – the killer possibly avoiding the use of a branded doll's outfit in case characteristic details or an order history could be traced back to him. Scorch marks on the rim of the tin tub in which Agatha had been transformed into a crude caricature of Maria Landless, the Electric Lady. Burn points at which frayed wires rather than the teeth of electrode clamps had been attached. Other small details in the photos and reports – clean edges to the flesh stuffed into Adya's mouth, indicating a non-serrated blade; no autopsy report yet on Adya, this time remade as Marguerite de Bellefort, the Fat Woman of Wimbledon, but from the amount of blood in her mouth, she must have been alive while her flesh was fed to her. Only lightly bound, so some sedative was probably administered.

All of this – the care, the preparation – tallied with something else suggestive in the police reports: no forensic evidence. Not a hair, not a fingerprint, not a scrap of the killer's DNA to be found at any of the three locations. Did this mean a seasoned predator was at work? I felt it in my bones – despite the savagery of the crimes, a clinical calmness shone through, as if the deaths were not an end in themselves but sketches working towards a larger design. Even with these incomplete flourishes, however, I already believed I had a feeling for the mind working behind them – he had come to his victims with a clear purpose and he had achieved exactly what he intended. No more, no less.

But if this wasn't his first rodeo then what might it suggest about his previous crimes? The recreation of the Jericho freaks was a fixed idea. It had five potential victims and set conditions in which he had to operate: the pattern would always be dictated by the historical tragedy. I know it might sound ludicrous to talk about a psychopath in such terms, but my experience of these monsters told me I was right. Once established, serial killers follow their rituals obsessively, even to the point where it might endanger them.

One of my cases had involved a child murderer who always left a particular brand of baby's blanket clasped in his victim's fist. He must have known we would eventually track him through the purchase of the item but, for him, the compulsion had outweighed any sense of self-preservation.

Could we then say this killer had a thing for restaging historical tragedies? Was that his overriding MO? If so, he had not yet been detected and finding him through a deep dive into unsolved cases would be both time-consuming and difficult, especially as I had no access to police databases.

I sighed and took a swig of coffee. So many alleyways to explore, so many potential cul-de-sacs to get lost down. Once I could have aired my theories with Garris, got his no-nonsense take on my fantastical hunches. I allowed myself a half-smile, thinking back to all those post-shift beers in The Three Crowns where we'd pore over current cases before lapsing into more general chatter. One thing I know my mentor would have come back to was the connection, or lack thereof, between the victims.

They must *be* connected or else why did the killer not simply target random people in Bradbury End? That was the natural locus of the crimes after all. Unless he didn't want the murders to be connected too early. That might suggest he had a link to the victims that could expose him.

But something about this idea didn't sit right. There was a connection between McAllister, Poole and Mahal, something impersonal but significant that I was missing. I sensed it like a word dancing on the tip of my tongue, and strangely enough, I felt that the link had already been made. Not by me or Campbell, but in something someone had said to me recently . . .

I gave it up. I could chase the idea around for hours and get nowhere. Best to wait and let it come to me.

My phone pinged. A text from Zac:

Sal told me you've gone on ahead to Bradbury. Thanks for saying goodbye. You're a fucking arsehole, Scott.

'And you're a good judge of character, Zac,' I murmured.

Truth be told, I had deliberately avoided him this morning. He was a good kid, as my dad had said, and deserved a lot better than some washed-up thirtysomething with anger management issues and delusions of being haunted. If I gave him a couple of days, he'd come to his senses.

And so I'd washed and dressed early, before even the juks had stirred, and crossing the dew-dappled fairground had stopped only to drop Sal's phone back to her. She'd opened the door to her trailer, bedheaded and blurry-eyed.

'Scott? Jesus, what time is it?'

I knew she'd have been up past midnight, minding her candyfloss stall. By way of apology, I handed her a steaming cup of tea.

'Thanks for the loan,' I said, slipping the phone into her dressing gown pocket. 'I've got mine charged up again. I'm heading off to Bradbury End early, so I guess I'll see you there?'

'Wait. What? You're going where?' She shook her head, tumbles of red hair burnished by the dawn. 'Scott, what's going on? Last night you were tearing off somewhere, talking about a case, and now you're heading to the next fair days ahead of schedule?' She beamed. 'Have you worked out something with your dad? Are you running a ride there? Oh God, it'll be just like the old days! We can set up next to each other, make fun of the joskins—'

I laid a hand on her arm. 'It's not that. I do have a case, and somehow it's connected to Bradbury End.'

She frowned. 'Wow. That's quite a coincidence.'

'Isn't it?'

She must have caught something in my tone. 'Just what is this? You're up and about at the crack of dawn, washed and dressed, looking vaguely human.'

I laughed. 'You make it sound like a bad thing.'

'Is it? Look, of course, I'm happy to see you like this. Christ, if you told me yesterday that I'd have some version of the old Scott back, I'd have danced around the fucking maypole. But I know this look.' She brushed back a tangle of curls from my forehead. 'Whatever you've got yourself involved with, it's dangerous. I can see it in your face – the buzz, the thrill.'

I closed my eyes. 'Honestly, Sal, I don't know what you want from me. I lie around all day, taking pills until my eyes rattle in my head, and you bowl up into the trailer and read me the riot act. I find a case, some way to make a living, and that's not good enough either. You can see how I might be a tad confused.'

She set her jaw. 'There are other ways to make a living.'

'I know. I tried them.' I flicked out my hand to past horizons. 'I tried to study, to write, but the world of academia didn't want me. And Harry didn't want me either, if you remember . . .?' I paused, swallowed, closed my eyes for a moment, a face I had loved burning behind my closed lids. I felt Sal's hand on my sleeve. I brushed it off, plunged on. 'Then I tried to earn a crust smacking heads together, and I seem to remember you hating that too. So I tried to step over that thin blue line and that was when everyone here really rejected me. A showman copper? The ultimate betrayal. So yeah, I might have known being a private detective wouldn't be good enough either.'

'Will you listen to yourself?' she snapped. 'The woes of Scott Jericho. Don't you ever wonder why we're all so wary of you? It's because you're like a moth to a flame with this sort of shit. And yes, I'm glad it's dragged you out of all that despair and self-pity, but what worries me is that one day the flame will catch, and it won't just be you who burns.' She then fixed me with a softer look. 'And as for Harry Moorhouse ...'

The waitress reappeared at my elbow, slapping down the bill, jolting me out of memories I'd rather forget. When I took out my wallet, she flapped a dismissive hand.

'Your money's no good here, handsome. The gentleman's already settled it for you.'

I looked up at her. 'What gentleman?'

'Old friend of yours, so he said. Just popped in, paid your tab then headed right back out again. Odd-looking fella, but friendly with it. Very generous tipper. Oh, there he is! See him waving, out by the road?'

She waved, her smile spreading like butter. Following her gaze through the diner's wide windows, I felt my hands close into fists.

Chapter Eleven

'I MEANT TO ASK, THAT CAMERA looking out onto the car park? I was here last week and some bastard backed into my motor and didn't leave a note. I don't suppose I could take a look at your CCTV?'

The waitress gave me a pout that a halibut might have envied. 'I'm sorry, Curly. Kids have been chucking stones at that thing ever since Marco installed it last summer. One was bound to hit the bullseye sooner or later. It's been out of action for months. I could ask around the regulars, though. Maybe someone saw something?'

I treated her to my most winning smile. A lack of car park surveillance suited me just fine. 'Don't worry,' I said. 'But listen, would it be OK if I slipped out the back? I want to play a prank on my generous friend and I don't want him to see me coming. It's just a stupid joke we've had running since we were kids.'

She pressed both hands over her bosom, as if she were a virtuous damsel and I'd suggested a midnight roll in the hayloft. 'Oh, I don't think I could allow that. It's staff only back there and Marco would have my guts for garters.'

My smile was now competing for best in show, dimples working overtime. For good measure, I slipped a tenner into the front pocket of her apron and the dear old thing practically swooned. I took that as the green light. Collecting up my file, I scanned the diner.

'Won't be a minute,' I said, and slid out of the booth.

Much like the establishment itself, the clientele of Marco's American Bar and Grill was an eclectic assortment. Tucked into a siding just off the Oxford road, the converted shipping container was hemmed in on all sides by forest so dense it was a miracle any motorist ever spotted it. A long-extinct neon sign ran across the roof while trellis frames woven with plastic vines made a vain attempt to hide the rusted frontage. A horribly offensive statue of a Native American stood on one side of the entrance, hands raised in surrender to the gun-toting cowboy on the other. Inside was a feeble recreation of a '50s diner, posters for movies I'd never heard of crowding the walls. Still, the coffee wasn't bad.

Among the patrons – a harassed-looking couple trying to wrestle their toddler away from a ketchup bottle; an improbable vicar chowing down a heart attack of a burger; and lined up on stools at the counter, more truckers' butt-crack than you could shake a stick at – I spotted just the man I needed. Tall, broad-shouldered, built like the proverbial shithouse, I thought he could pass, at least viewed from the back.

Casting another glance through the window, I headed down the aisle towards my doppelganger. Drawing level, I dropped to one knee and started fiddling with my laces. The waitress hovered at my shoulder. By knocking-off time, my guess was that she'd have spun this story into something unrecognisable, yet her wildest exaggerations wouldn't come close to the truth.

The guy frowned down at me. And yes, from the front, not exactly my double, but if he played along, that needn't be too much of a problem. He glared, wiped egg yolk from his logger's beard, and in return I tipped him a wink almost as theatrical as the waitress'.

'Hey there, big fella, fancy earning a few quid?'

'Fuck you on about?' he grunted.

Pushing a crumpled twenty across the table, I let him in on the prank. He was to take my place in the booth I'd just vacated, hang out there for ten minutes or so, stay in view of the road but keep his dubious mug turned away from the window. The waitress backed up my narrative, although she didn't look best pleased that he'd received double her original tip. To placate her, I poked another tenner into her apron and she was soon sweetness and light again. Still crouching, I asked if my pal remained at the roadside and she chuckled and waved, confirming he was.

'OK, Grizzly.' I nodded at the trucker. 'You clear on the plan?'

Grizzly rolled his tongue around the inside of his mouth as if seeking guidance from a morsel of unchewed breakfast. 'Run it by me one last time.'

I sighed. 'Take your coffee to the fourth booth and spend ten minutes contemplating the mysteries of existence, the likelihood of alien intelligence, the popularity of ska music, anything you like, only keep your back to the window. Sound good?'

He ran a dirty hand through his matted curls and shrugged. 'Seems weird to me, but it's your dollar.'

'Good boy,' I said, and as he took up position in the booth, I scuttled my way clear of the window. This drew a few curious stares but with food as inedible as Marco's before them, the diners' attention soon refocused on their plates. Meanwhile, the waitress guided me to a swing door behind the till.

'Marco's on a ciggie break, so if you're quick . . .' She reached back and laid an unnecessary hand against my chest. 'Straight through and out the back door. He'll probably be on his phone to that bitch of a wife, so I doubt he'll notice you. Say hello to your friend from me.'

I left her with my most dazzling smile yet and stepped into the kitchen. Tiles greased to a yellowy sheen squeaked under my boots. From the ceiling, a thousand insects hung in wafting graveyards while an unlucky few had escaped only to drop, out of the flypaper and into the fire, onto sizzling hotplates below. Although Marco could never be accused of false advertising – the photos in his laminated menus were honest enough representations – I think that on seeing this breeding ground for botulism, even his least discerning diner might put down their fork.

Making for the back door, I paused for a second at a preparation counter. There, a slimy chicken breast rubbed hazardous shoulders with mould-spotted lettuce. I reached across these delicacies and slid a paring knife from its block. I tested the edge against my thumb – razor-sharp – so either Marco took an unlikely pride in his tools or else this happy little blade had hardly been used. With the flat of the knife pressed against the inside of my wrist, I pushed through the back door.

Birds twittered in the trees that banked up behind the diner. On the other side of the overflowing bins, Marco stood with his back to me, shoulders hunched like a man facing a firing squad. Even from this distance, I could hear the shriek of his wife. OK, so he might well be the world's most successful serial poisoner, but in that moment, I felt for him.

I headed as noiselessly as I could between columns of old oil drums and into the trees. I should have ample time, but my nerves felt raw and I wanted this little sideshow over and done with. I moved quickly through the undergrowth, following the sweep of the forest around the diner to the weed-cracked car park out front. There I paused, hand tightening around the knife.

My friend remained near the roadside, texting now rather than waving. He looked up once or twice and I followed his gaze to my broad-shouldered stand-in, still hunched in the booth. Good old Grizzly.

Time to finish this.

Despite the rumble of the road, I trod carefully, anxious that a snapping branch not give me away. Reaching a row of lorries, I stepped out of the treeline and, moving to the front of one of the cabs, darted another glance at the roadside. Then I broke cover. I stayed low, swept between the cars until I found the one I wanted. He'd upgraded since my arrest, his ancient Fiat Panda traded in for a smart BMW coupé, but the decal in the back window gave him away. A Knights of St George emblem, proudly on show.

My borrowed blade flashed in the light as I went to work. No CCTV, no customers rolling out into the car park just yet. No one to see as I punched holes into four Continental tyres. This done, I dropped the knife and plunged back into the trees, circling around until I was almost level with the road. I had to be fast now, and it had to look right.

Barrelling up behind Lenny Kerrigan, I bellowed *'Booo!'* in his ear.

The fascist thug who had intimidated a hundred girls in burkas on their way to school now leaped out his skin. I practically caught him on the descent and, looping an arm around his neck, held the bastard in a brotherly headlock. Back in the diner, the waitress laughed and waved us away like we were naughty kids while Grizzly shot me a thumbs-up and went back to his coffee. Meanwhile, Kerrigan squealed like a stuck pig as I hauled him into the cover of the trees.

Chapter Twelve

A T THE SERVICE STATION, I'D thought he might be a paranoid delusion conjured out of guilt and pills. But he was here now – the waitress had seen him, he'd paid my bill, and he was currently kicking and struggling against me as I dragged him into the undergrowth. Whatever was going on, I had to end this. Two more lives were on the line and I couldn't afford the distraction of Kerrigan dogging my footsteps.

At a safe distance from the diner, I threw him to the ground. Despite being winded, Kerrigan didn't waste a moment. Scrabbling to his feet, he reached behind to the back of his belt. I didn't need my months in uniform to tell me what was about to happen. Knife attacks are common enough on fairgrounds and by eighteen I'd experienced my fair share. A memory in the dappled gloom of the wood: my father with a wooden pencil in his fist, teaching me what to do if some crazed joskin came at me. I put the old lesson to use.

Kerrigan's was an ornate pig-sticker. I didn't get a clear look, but I thought there was some sort of device on the hilt – probably a Nazi insignia; fascists are so unoriginal. And as sure as night follows day, there was that shit-eating smirk, tugging at the corner of his mouth. The fact that Kerrigan's parents had probably been close relatives might account for some of the stupid, but my guess was that he'd worked hard to nurture an innate fuckwittedness. Why else would he taunt the man who'd already given him the pummelling of his life?

In the end, it was a dull contest. He came at me, jabbing, arms wide, torso unprotected. I waited for the pullback, stepped inside his range of attack, gripped the wrist of his knife hand, and landed a sickening punch against the inside of his elbow. The weapon fell from nerveless fingers and I kicked it across the grass. Meanwhile, Kerrigan's eyes bolted like a pair of skinned eggs and spittle fizzed between his teeth. Holding onto my shoulder for support, he tried to claw my face. I batted his hands away, but he kept at it, so in the end I was forced to nut him square in the nose. His legs came unhinged and he dropped like a scarecrow cut from its pole.

I shook out my fist. Tried not to smile. Sal's words from this morning came back to me: *'You're like a moth to a flame with this sort of shit.'* Much as I might try to deny it, she was right. I was alive again because of violence – the need to avenge it, the need to inflict it, perhaps the need to embrace it before it turned on me. I looked down on this child murderer whimpering at my feet, and forced myself to resist it.

'I'll have you for this,' Kerrigan gasped. 'You think you've lost everything? I'll see you back inside by tonight and then I'll get my lawyers to take that tin can you call a home. I'll have everything your old man owns too – the whole fucking carnival.'

'No,' I sighed. 'You won't.'

Taking him by the shirtfront, I dragged Kerrigan to his feet. He winced as I straightened his collar, a spill of blood issuing from his nose.

'Your fingerprints are on that knife, Lenny. I have witnesses who will testify you came to the fair yesterday and made threats against me—' I hushed him when he started to protest. 'They'll say you did and that's all that matters. You've been following me, stalking me, they'll have you on CCTV, both here and at the garage last night.' Kerrigan didn't need to know Marco's security was out of commission. 'I'll say you came at me with the knife and I was forced to defend myself.' Catching sight of his arm, I frowned and turned his wristwatch to the light. 'And maybe, just maybe, it'll be me who comes for the last pot *you* pissed in.'

He pulled his hand away, cheeks flaming.

'Why are you here, Kerrigan?' I muttered. 'Are you just trying to fuck with me or is it something else?'

Could he be involved in the killings? I wouldn't put anything past this mullering scumbag, let alone the butchery of Adya Mahal, but Kerrigan was your common or garden psychopath. Oh, he'd happily push a lit rag into a building where he knew children slept, but his brutality was circumscribed by the limits of his imagination. I already felt that a subtler and infinitely more dangerous mind than Kerrigan's was at work. Still, his next words troubled me.

'You have no idea what this is all about, do you? The great fucking detective and you can't see what's staring you in the face.'

I gave him a hard shake. 'Are you involved? Three people are already dead and I won't—'

'Yeah, that's right. Three dirty Pole kids and you just can't let it go, can you?' I was satisfied: he had no idea about McAllister, Poole and Mahal, but there was something here I didn't understand, so I let his hateful mouth run on. 'You're in for a big surprise, Jericho. One day soon you'll wake up and realise just how well I've played you, and there won't be a motherfucking thing you can do about—'

Something over my shoulder seemed to catch his eye and his mouth snapped shut. I turned. A spark of silver, like a Tinkerbell in some corny kids' film, darted between the trees. Probably just a trick of the light, but then why had it stopped Kerrigan in his tracks? I shook my head. I had enough mysteries on my plate without chasing fairies through the woods. I pushed Kerrigan aside and, using my sleeve, stooped to collect his knife.

'I'll be seeing you, Jericho,' he muttered, his head thrown back to stop a fresh rush of blood.

I didn't bite back. He'd find out soon enough that he wasn't following me anywhere, at least not today.

Out of the trees, I kicked his flattened tyres and gave the waitress a final wave. She shot me a salacious wink before returning to her customers. Seconds later, I was behind the wheel and hauling my trailer in the direction of Bradbury End.

Theories as to the killer's MO, guesswork about possible connections between the victims were fine as far as they went, but I needed a concrete base for my investigation. As Garris might say, I had to start with first principles. What was the wellspring of these murders? The deaths of the Jericho freaks. That meant heading back to where it all began.

I was about five miles outside of town when my phone rang. I hit the hands-free.

'Mis-ter Jer-i-cho.'

'Mr Campbell.'

His tone was flat, like someone giving a half-hearted impression of the paedophile professor.

'I thought you'd like to know, your first day's payment has been transferred to your account.'

'About that,' I said. 'I've already incurred a few expenses.'

'Text me,' he said airily. 'Miss Barton will see to it.'

A beat. I thought he'd be keen to hear what progress I was making but the silence stretched on.

'You didn't mention the local council had invited my father to set up his fair at Bradbury,' I said. 'A big event to mark the one hundred and fiftieth anniversary of the tragedy, and all of this coinciding with the murders?'

'Indeed,' he yawned. 'Quite the coincidence.'

'Isn't it just.'

A virtual pin appeared on my satnav – a pulsing BRADBURY END moving ever closer. 'Do you believe in such coincidences, Mr Campbell?'

'Why shouldn't I? History is littered with them. Mark Twain's birth and death coincided precisely with the appearance of Halley's Comet; less than a year before John Wilkes Booth assassinated Lincoln, his brother saved the life of Lincoln's son in a near-fatal railway accident. Even for an atheist such as I, the sweep of history can sometimes suggest a designing intelligence.'

'Policemen don't like coincidences,' I said.

'Good job you're not a policeman anymore, then, isn't it?'

I ignored the jibe. 'According to my father, the town council booked the fair a year ago. Six months later, McAllister is turned into Charlie Buckley. Could it be one of the organisers, do you think? The mayor, Hillstrom, is descended from the guy who ordered the rebuilding of the bridge. And then there's his dogsbody, Carmody.'

'A dogsbody making a dog-faced boy?' Campbell tittered. 'Anything is possible, I suppose.'

'Three down, two to go,' I said, more to myself than the professor. 'I think he's going to speed up. The anniversary is in, what, four days? He'll want his masterpiece in place by then.'

'Yes, yes,' Campbell yawned again. 'I'm sure you're right. Godspeed, Mr Jericho.'

The line went dead.

I stared at the phone. The sudden and utter uninterest of a man who had virtually pleaded with me to investigate his pet mystery was another puzzle to add to my growing collection. Perhaps, having handed over the case, Campbell's passion for it would only be reawakened when – and if – I solved it. It was an idea, but not a very satisfactory one. Somehow it both chimed and sat at odds with my earlier thought that his fascination with the case went beyond the explanations he had given . . .

I shook my head. In the end, I decided to file it away with the mystery of those vague promises of Kerrigan's, '*One day soon you'll wake up and realise just how well I've played you.*'

No more distractions. On now, to Bradbury End.

The town itself sat in the bowl of a forested valley. A sign marking the outskirts provoked a wry smile: A PLACE WITH A HISTORY! No fucking kidding. I toed the brake and the car wound down into quaint, meandering streets. The fair and its wide loads wouldn't have an easy time of this – garden walls bulged out into the road while corners jagged at switchback angles. Still, Travellers were used to negotiating tight spots and I was sure the cosy façade of Bradbury End would survive unscathed.

Victorian villas in pastel shades; little old ladies at the bus stop, twittery as fresh-hatched chicks; men with sergeant major moustaches walking droopy-eyed dachshunds; a village post office with an honest-to-God red phone box outside; the local pub, The Old Cock Inn, not a hint of a satirical phallus graffitied onto the flaking sign over the door. Everything achingly, almost artificially, English, like a Hollywood cliché of bygone Britannia.

Except, not quite.

A placard planted proudly in an immaculate lawn screamed:

NO SHARIA! BRITAIN FIRST!
Protest the new Mosque in Bradbury!

Something my dad said last night came back to me, '*They have new bogeymen now.*' He was right. Hate never goes away; it just moves on to fresh targets. Tired of the novelty of the fair on their common, Travellers would once have been blamed for whatever ills were besetting the community and, taking the hint, would pack up their amusements before they could be run out of town. Now we were probably viewed as a harmless eccentricity, as British as that unmolested phone box.

It took a few laps of the town to find what I was looking for. Spotting the homely redbrick building at last, I pulled my trailer up to the kerb and got out. The smell of fresh-cut grass, the sound of a cricket match in a nearby park – all is well in Bradbury End. I looked over at the library.

My heart slammed into my throat.

A man stood in the doorway. A figure from my past, a face I had tried to forget.

When I'd last seen Harry Moorhouse, he had just murdered his father.

Chapter Thirteen

ARRY'S GAZE HAD FOUND MY trailer, a frown crumpling his brow, when an army of middle-aged women crowded in around him, beaming and cooing. I caught snatches of their outrage, 'Never thought I'd see the day'; 'We'll be here first thing with our placards'; 'If Mr Hillstrom and his cronies on the council think they can close our library, they have another think coming'. Harry soothed and encouraged, winning the adoration of all, but then he'd never needed words for that.

I've met many men with kind smiles, some masking horrors you wouldn't believe, but Harry's – open and generous – was a true reflection of his soul.

It was his kindness that had made me love him.

It was his kindness that had made him a killer.

It was the end of my first term at Magdalen and I was huddled up in my old donkey jacket by the fire of The Eagle and Child. The pub was packed to the rafters that night: rugger-buggers hogging the bar and spilling more lager than they drank; tutors clubbed together, tired and demob-happy; townies in the corners, nursing their ales and resentments. I guess it said something about me that, despite the squeeze, no one asked if they could share my table.

I'd arrived in Oxford with such hope, a lamb to the intellectual slaughter. My dad drove me, helped carry my cases through echoing cloisters and up winding staircases to my room that overlooked the river. He barely said a word. Just sniffed and glanced around, as if all this medieval beauty was no more than he'd expected. We shook hands, a thing we'd never done before, and he muttered something about seeing me at Christmas. In my imagining of this moment, I'd had him wipe away a tear and tell me how proud my mum would have been. None of that; just a rough handshake and he was gone.

But still, I was here. I'd fulfilled the expectations of a dozen teachers (the ones who came and taught at the fair during our travelling months and those that welcomed showman chavvies into their schools over the winter) and become the first person in my family to go to university. My mum had given me my love of stories, my teachers had instilled a passion to dig beneath the narrative, now I could be among people who felt the same way I did about books.

That was the dream. It lasted until the end of my first week. Tutors tore my essays to pieces, my observations in class were laughed at. It seemed that loving literature wasn't enough; if you wanted to justify that love, you must dissect it until, staring down at the corpse of the book you'd once worshipped, all you could see were its defects. And if the geniuses I'd revered as a teenager – Austen and Dickens, Hardy and Eliot – were so flawed then what hope was there for my own poor scribblings?

And so I'd stopped volunteering opinions in class and dismissed any idea of joining the college's creative writing club.

In halls, I was treated like an exotic curio. Somehow, word had slipped out about my background and I became the subject of endless interrogation at the college bar. It was mostly good-natured and not particularly class-based. Of course, Magdalen was teeming with public school types who viewed anyone without a private ski lodge in the Pyrenees as an object of pitiable fascination. But even my state school peers were in awe of me. A fairground boy amid these dreaming spires? A Jericho freak indeed.

All I wanted to do was talk to them about *their* world – a place in which books and paintings and art could provoke a tear and you'd never be mocked for it – but they had plenty of friends to discuss such things with. They wanted to hear my story while all I longed for was to escape it. And so I created a persona for myself, brittle and brooding, until, at last, they stayed away.

Some had stopped by my room before leaving for the break. A timid knock, a whispered Merry Christmas, the odd question, '*Are you going back to the fairground for the holidays?*' But aside from a few special events, most fairs are packed up for the winter, the Travellers heading for their yards where, for a few short months, trailers are swapped for static chalets.

My dad would've been at ours, spinning yarns with Sam Urnshaw and Tommy Radlett and the rest. We'd stopped calling each other after the first few weeks, defeated by the challenge of trying to bridge a gulf neither of us could understand. Sal Myers still phoned and updated me on all the news: one of the aunts had broken a hip; there'd been a ruck with some locals at the season-end fair; she'd met a Traveller from up north and they might start seeing each other. How was I doing? Had I made friends with all the other brainiacs?

I stared into the rich amber of my pint. I knew I wasn't suited to Oxford, that it made me miserable, that I didn't like who I was becoming here. But to go back to the life with my tail between my legs? That would be admitting that my dad and his friends were right: that Travellers had no business in a place like this.

Back then, they didn't know that it wasn't just a love of books that made me different, and that going away had been a chance to explore other parts of myself too.

In all that self-pity, I hadn't realised that the pub had fallen silent. I looked up to find the lights dimmed and a group of carollers taking up position on the other side of the fire. Even the rugger-buggers had settled, sipping their pints as quietly as overgrown babies taking the bottle. Firelight danced across the choir, old and young, grey-haired and fresh-faced, so close I might have reached out and touched them. I sat back in my chair, thoughts of Magdalen and ruined dreams forgotten. A boy my age had stepped forward and started to sing.

I wanted to turn away, to hide the tears streaming down my face. It was a Christmas hymn but not one I'd ever heard before. And whether it was his sweet soprano, the simple emotion that animated his features, his beauty, or some combination of all three, he somehow spoke to all my hopes and disappointments.

Afterwards, I lingered until the last drunk had offered his congratulations and the other carollers had left. Then I slipped in beside him at the bar. It didn't occur to me then that he'd been waiting for me to say hello.

'Can I buy you a drink?'

He turned and nodded. 'I wondered when you would. A pint of Batemans, please.'

I signalled the barman. 'You were really good,' I said. 'Amazing, in fact.'

'Is that your considered appraisal?'

'If you can't take a compliment,' I muttered.

'Hey.' He placed his hand on my sleeve. 'I'm sorry. Thank you.'

And he smiled. A warm, open, teasing kind of smile. He was smaller than me, but then most guys are; smooth, delicate features, jade eyes and mouse-brown hair, cheekbones that went on for ever. He nudged his shoulder into my chest.

'Am I forgiven?'

'We'll see,' I smiled back. 'What's it called, by the way? That first one you sang?'

'"*Quem pastores laudavere*"? It's an old German carol. "He whom the shepherds praised." Are you a man of faith . . .?'

'Scott.'

'Scott.'

'Not in anything much.'

He lifted his hand to my face and ran his thumb under my eye, as if brushing away a tear. 'Maybe you believe in more than you think.'

I didn't know what to say to that, so said nothing at all. We took our drinks back to my table and sat there talking until last orders. Then we headed to a late-night bar he knew, found another table and talked some more. When the bouncer kicked us out at 5 a.m. we took our talk to the ancient streets and, eventually, Folly Bridge where we perched until dawn.

I told him who I was, where I came from, what I'd hoped for in Oxford, and he told me about himself in return. A grammar school kid from the Home Counties, as respectably middle class as they came. He was studying musical analysis at Somerville. He was openly gay, out to his friends and family, a cherished only son, and lived for music. It only occurred to me later that, as probing as he'd been about my life, the hard persona I'd used to keep others at bay hadn't made an appearance. The more I spoke to him about the fair and my alienation from it, the easier my words became.

'Take a breath,' he soothed. 'Tell me.'

And I did.

At last, he slipped his small hand into mine. Down by the university boathouses, doors were being pulled wide and practice crafts launched onto the misty river.

'Time to say goodnight, lonely Traveller,' he said.

I pulled him close. 'You mean good morning . . .'

I did go back to the yard that Christmas. It was awkward with my dad, but it had been awkward with him for years and we soon fell into old patterns of meaningless small talk. But I was different. Sal noticed it straight away; I could never hide anything from her. She pressed her forefinger to my nose and beamed, *'You've found someone. Who is he?'* She knew even then, before I'd told anyone on the ground about my sexuality.

The holiday passed with aching slowness and, within hours of being back in Oxford, I was at his door at Somerville.

'Happy New Year, lonely Traveller.' He grinned.

I wrapped my arms tight around him.

By the end of January, we were living together. By February, I knew I loved him. In March, nervous as hell, I told him so, and he gave me a wink and wondered why it had taken me so long. He loved me too, he said. With Harry beside me, I settled

95

down to my studies. I still didn't enjoy them, but if it meant staying in Oxford – staying with him – I'd work my arse off. Those were the happiest months I've ever known – a bright island in a sea of darkness.

At Easter, I met his father and saw immediately what Harry did not – or would not – acknowledge. The man was dying. By summer, the reality of his father's pain couldn't be denied and within weeks Harry had acted upon it. After that, everything changed.

The army of women dispersed and Harry came down the library steps. It was lunchtime and he was probably heading into town for a sandwich.

Heart raging, I stepped into his path. 'Hello, Haz.'

He looked up and, in that moment, didn't seem at all surprised to see me.

'Hello, Scott,' he said, his tone resigned. 'I suppose you're here about the Jericho deaths?'

Chapter Fourteen

'THE MURDERS?' MY MIND REELED. How on earth could Harry Moorhouse know about the random killing of three unconnected people? In all our talk of my life on the fair had I ever told him the story of the Jericho freaks? And if I had …

No. Not this tender man I had loved. He'd killed, yes, but there are degrees of murder, and his was as far away from the psychotic savagery of the monster I hunted as could be imagined. But still, how did he know about the case and what was he doing here?

'Murders?' Harry frowned. 'I thought the drownings were accidental. Nothing I've seen in the research suggests anyone deliberately targeted the showpeople.'

Relief washed over me. 'You're talking about the bridge collapse.'

'Of course. What did you think I meant?'

He smiled, though it was a confused and guarded version of the smile I'd known.

'Nothing. Never mind.' I shook my head. 'But, Harry, what are you doing here?'

'This place?' He glanced over his shoulder at the modest redbrick building. 'I drifted into it, I suppose. After I left Somerville, I tried out a few things before volunteering at our local library. When one of the librarians there retired, I applied for her job and they took me on. Then austerity started to bite and our branch was closed down. Instead of making me redundant, they created this sort of floating position – now I move between about a dozen different branches on a rota system.'

'I see. But listen, what you said just now, it sounded like you've been expecting me.'

'For about a month or two.' He nodded. 'We get quite a few people contacting the library service, asking if we can help with their research. Mostly it's amateur historians, bored retirees looking into their family tree, that sort of thing. Just occasionally something interesting lands in our lap. This ex-Cambridge professor got in touch a while back about the Travellers Bridge tragedy. Said he was fascinated by fairground history and wanted to know more about what had happened to the Jericho freakshow. I didn't . . .' Colour sketched itself across his cheeks. 'At first, I wasn't sure I wanted to get involved. Professor Campbell happened to mention that you might be helping him out at some point and I—'

'Did he know about us?' I asked.

'I don't think so. Why would he?'

'Coincidences,' I murmured. They were becoming practically Dickensian – disparate threads of my life winding together around this case. But, as Campbell had said, coincidences do happen and if I fixated too much on them, I might start seeing patterns in things that weren't there.

'Why did you stay involved?' I asked.

Harry looked away. 'If you were researching for Campbell, I knew we were bound to run into each other sooner or later. After all, here was where you'd always begin, and not just because of the research. I don't think we ever visited a town where you didn't drag me inside the local library.'

He was right. It was a kind of homage, I suppose, maybe an act of contrition too. Being a travelling kid of no fixed abode, it had been difficult to get a library card from the places we pitched up in. And so, with a father who refused to pay for the books I devoured, I had stolen hundreds.

I took a breath. Felt my pulse skip. There was no point trying to avoid it. 'I'm sorry if the idea of seeing me again has upset you. Haz, you know it wasn't my choice to end things the way they did. After what happened, I tried calling and writing; I even turned up at your house. Your family said you didn't want to see me and, in the end, I had to respect that. It was hard, but I came to terms with it. I don't know if you ever got the note I left at your flat when I moved back into halls, but I meant every word. Even if you didn't want to be with me anymore, I needed you to know that I understood what happened with your dad.'

Tears flashed into his eyes and he looked away. 'Don't, Scott. Please. I can't.'

'Hey.' I touched his arm. 'I can leave, OK? Campbell has probably given me all the research material you have anyway. I didn't know he'd already been in touch with the library here. Harry, listen, I have to be in town for a few days, but I can make it so that we never have to see each other. I don't know what happened between us, and I'm not asking you to tell me.

All that was a long time ago. But I don't want my being here to distress you.'

I was turning back towards the road when he snagged my sleeve. 'Scott, wait.' He shook his head. 'Maybe if you come inside we can talk and ... I don't know. Just talk. I've been rehearsing this moment so much in my head, now that it's here everything I thought I'd say has gone out the window. All I know is, I'm glad to see you again.'

It was hard to resist the hope I felt then. For over a decade, Harry Moorhouse had barely left my thoughts. I had tried to replace him, to paper over his memory, but like the ghosts of the Malanowski children, he wouldn't be denied. In fact, it had only been since their deaths that Harry had fallen a little into the background. Perhaps because the comfort of our memories together had felt like an indulgence I no longer deserved.

Now he guided me into the snug little library – an old boy was snoring away in the reading section while toddlers on scatter cushions sat, mouths agape, as Harry's colleague read to them from a pop-up book – and into a cramped back office overflowing with books. I stayed by the door while he flipped the switch on a kettle that nested precariously on the windowsill.

'So are you still writing your music?' I asked as he rummaged in a cupboard for cups. 'Still composing?'

He puffed out his cheeks. 'Come on, Scott, even you have to admit I was never all that good.'

'I admit no such thing! Those pieces you used to play me back in our flat? Haz, they were beautiful.'

He kicked the inside of my boot with the toe of his shoe, an old habit that brought back a flood of memory. 'To a sympathetic ear, maybe. Beneath all that cynical brooding, you were always a sentimentalist. That's why you never took to literary criticism. You get too caught up in the romance of the big picture and can't see the little mistakes staring you in the face. You liked my music because it was heartfelt, but that's all it ever was. Emotional, haphazard, shambolic.'

'You think I'm too emotional?' I almost laughed.

'You were.' He turned to the window where steam from the kettle made a halo around his head. 'Like you said, that was a long time ago. I suppose I don't know who you are now.'

I leaned back against the door. 'Well, I know who you are. A librarian and, therefore, a hero.'

He came over and pressed a warm mug into my hands. 'An unappreciated one, if I am.'

'I heard. Hillstrom and Carmody and the local council are closing you down.'

'They're trying to. Our users have started the fight-back – petitions, marches, the usual stuff. But what about you? I heard you left Oxford soon after I . . .'

Murdered your father? We kept dancing around it.

'You know I never really enjoyed Oxford,' I said. 'I stayed because other things kept me there.'

He looked into his tea. 'And after?'

I didn't want to go into that. A broken heart makes for a dark guiding star and it had led me into many murky places before Pete Garris had found me.

'This and that,' I said.

'Well, it hasn't done you any harm.' He chuckled. 'In fact, you don't look a day older.'

'Really? You do, and better for it.'

It was true. The boy had gone and the man stood in his place. Older, wiser maybe, more himself anyway.

'Please tell me you're still singing at least,' I said.

'Maybe you can guess. Do you still do your old tricks?'

I cast a quick glance around – even amid the office clutter, the clues were pretty obvious. I pointed to a chipped Hello Kitty mug on the desk. 'Honey and lemon, and no cold.' Without thinking, I stepped forward and placed my fingertips close to his throat. He didn't pull away but I let my hand fall. 'You're still singing.'

He moved back to an office chair and took a seat, cradling his cup in his lap. 'And so you're – what? A hired researcher?'

'Something like that.'

'How mysterious. What about your writing?'

I had only ever shared my stories with Harry. After we parted ways, they had remained private scribblings in my notebook, until the Malanowski case and its aftermath had taken away any desire I had left to write.

'I'm back with the fair,' I said.

'What? But you said you'd never—'

'I know. Best laid plans. Anyway, it's not what you th ...'

The office window gave onto the street where my trailer was parked and, as the steam from the kettle cleared the pane, I could make out two figures circling the tin box I called home. One kicked at the wheels and his companion laughed. I put my cup on the desk and turned to the door.

'I'm sorry, Harry. Will you excuse me a moment?'

Chapter Fifteen

I STALKED TOWARDS THE ROAD, AN irrational anger scratching under my skin. During my time in uniform, I had often worked with the kind of officers currently lounging against my trailer. Best practice was usually to send them back to the car to make a report while cooler heads interacted with the suspect. Problem was, there were no cooler heads present that day.

Not mine, not theirs.

'The fuck's going on here?' I asked.

I knew from their shared smirk I'd made a mistake; that the wisest thing to do was wind my neck in. But my nerves were raw. Dealing with Kerrigan at the diner, finding Harry waiting for me in Bradbury End, my hunger to solve these murders and the strange sense that parts of my life were being threaded into the case – all of it coalesced into the frustration that sang behind my eyes.

The officers – both a bit long in the tooth to still be on the beat – kicked their heels against the Eccles and stood upright. They came swaggering to meet me, thumbs hooked into their belts. They had that patronising 'let's be reasonable' air – the kind that, with little provocation, can transform into sanctimonious fury. The first, balding and red-bearded, held up his palm, as if he expected me to rush them.

'Calm down, sir. Now, is this your vehicle?'

'No,' I said, forcing myself to stop. 'I'm just wildly pissed off on behalf of a complete stranger.'

'Goodness me, sir, but you do have a temper, don't you?' The second officer, scrawny and bird-faced, grinned. 'Any reason why you don't like the thought of us in the vicinity of your caravan?'

I shrugged. 'I was hoping to sell it and, to be honest, boys, it's a shitty-enough-looking wreck without two dickheads bringing down the tone.'

'If I could ask you to moderate your language,' Redbeard said, shooting a troubled glance at a host of non-existent passers-by. 'If you've nothing to hide then there's nothing to be worried about, is there? All we'd like to do is take a look inside your charming caravan.'

'On what basis?'

Birdface blinked. 'I'm sorry?'

'You want to search my home, so you either have a warrant or reasonable grounds to consider me a suspect in some crime. What are your grounds?'

For the first time, I wondered if Kerrigan had reported me for assault. It seemed unlikely but nothing about how this day was panning out would have surprised me.

'You're behaving quite aggressively, sir,' Redbeard observed. 'That in itself—'

'Isn't enough. I have video of you kicking my tyres and laying your flabby arses against my paintwork.' I brandished my phone, cursing myself that the idea of actually filming these pricks had only just occurred to me. 'So, do you want to know what I think is really going on here? The fair's coming into town in a few days, you saw what you'd call a "pikey's caravan", and you thought you'd have a bit of fun. I'm not a Romany myself, but mistaken racial profiling is still racial profiling.'

'Now, now,' Birdface placated. 'It's nothing like that.'

I chuckled and stepped around them, giving the fuckwits a wide berth so that they had no excuse to feel threatened and come at me with their batons. At the trailer, I took out my key and opened the door.

'Go on then, fill your boots,' I said, sweeping a welcoming hand over the threshold. 'Just know I'll be taking your badge numbers and putting in an official complaint. Are your records in that department squeaky clean, boys? Is your senior officer going to want to dirty his hands with you again? Or will it be a dressing-down from the chief constable this time? Sir Michael Wishman, isn't it? Yeah, I think he plays golf with my old mate, DCI Pete Garris.'

It was an educated guess, but I could see from their faces that I'd hit the bullseye. Weathered old turds like these don't remain on the beat out of choice. Even if they were happy in uniform, they'd have found cushy admin roles by now. Progression halted by a string of dodgy arrests had been my bet. Now I cashed in the chips.

'Come on,' I sighed. 'I haven't got all day. You up for the tour or what?'

They exchanged narrow glances and Birdface sucked his teeth.

'Just get it shifted,' he said. 'This is a public thoroughfare.'

Redbeard spat on the kerb and they toddled off in search of less challenging prey. I smiled to myself and closed the door. With some of my 'off-prescription' benzos lying around in open drawers, it had been a risk, but I knew that playing nice would have got me precisely nowhere. When bullies bark at you sometimes the only thing you can do is bark back.

'Scott, what was that?'

I turned to find Harry standing behind me, his long nervous fingers twining together.

'That was par for the course when you're a Traveller,' I said.

He looked troubled. I suddenly realised why. In the beginning, before loving him had softened my edges, he had known that old Oxford persona, brooding and tetchy, but this new darkness, this well of rage always stewing under the surface? That was a Scott Jericho he hadn't met. A personality forged in the grief of losing him and refined in the deaths of Sonia Malanowski and her brothers. I decided then that he shouldn't see it again.

'The fair isn't licensed to arrive on the common for a few days,' I said. 'Do you know any local caravan parks where I could set up until then?'

He laid his hand against his cheek, an old anxious habit. 'I've got a driveway at my bungalow. You can park it there, if you like.'

'Haz, I don't think—'

'It'll be fine,' he cut in. 'You'll just need to find somewhere to wait until my shift's over. Meet me back here at six.'

Before I could say another word, he disappeared into the library.

Three hours to kill. I slid behind the wheel of my Merc and headed out of town, finding a siding on one of the rural roads.

I flipped on the radio and listened to news and traffic reports, pop songs and afternoon dramas, taking in nothing. By four, the clouds broke and a drizzle ticked relentlessly against the windscreen. After a while, I went back to Campbell's file but found nothing fresh in those now-familiar atrocities. In all this, I knew I was trying to distract myself from Harry's invitation and what it might mean; just an old acquaintance being kind, my hollow heart told me. Nothing more.

At quarter to six, the sun was blazing again and I drove through steaming streets to find Harry waiting at the kerb. When he waved, I felt a ridiculous lump in my throat.

'Lock's broken,' I said, leaning over and opening the door for him. I snatched the case file off the passenger seat and stuffed it into my side compartment. 'So,' I breathed. 'Are you sure about this?'

He held his leather satchel to his chest, like a shield. ''Course. But if you'd rather not stay?'

I released the parking brake. 'Where's home?'

Home was a suburban cul-de-sac just outside Bradbury End. It took ten minutes or so for me to uncouple the trailer and site it, with Harry's help, in the drive of his bungalow. I asked if I could hook up to his electric and he agreed, waving away any talk of payment. I said I'd get him a bottle of Antinori Tignanello as a thank you. I think we both thought then of his flat back in Oxford, curled up together on the sofa, lips plummy with the aftertaste of his favourite wine.

'So your research for Campbell is a sideline?' he asked as I chocked the trailer wheels. 'You're mainly back working on the fair with your father?'

Despite constant requests, Harry had never met my dad nor been to any of the Jericho fairs. Back then, the idea of those parts of my life colliding had been hideous to me.

'It's a bit of extra cash,' I grunted. 'Campbell found me while researching the Jericho family tree.'

Harry ran his fingers across the mud-splattered side of the trailer. 'You always said you'd never go back.'

'Yeah.' I straightened up. 'Well, a lot's happened since then. By the way, I heard some of the council was opposed to the fair coming here at all.'

He rolled his eyes. 'They're a fun bunch. Last year they put a block on Bradbury's first-ever Pride event. Said it wasn't suitable for a family town. Like we aren't members of families too.'

'Hillstrom and Carmody's work?'

'Mayor and deputy, the gruesome twosome.' He nodded. 'Like the rest of the council, a little to the right of Mussolini. Some people think they're even behind the anger that's being stoked up against the new mosque.'

'I saw the signs on my way in.' I nodded.

'But to be fair, they were all for marking the anniversary of Travellers Bridge. Said it was right to celebrate such a historical landmark in the town's history.'

'You mean the drowning of five people?'

'Tasteful, isn't it?' He winced. 'But hey, what's this?'

I'd been bending down to firm up one of the chocks when he snatched the notebook out of my back pocket.

'I'd recognise these Moleskines anywhere. I thought from what you said that you'd stopped writing. Why would you—?' I spun around, grabbing the book from his hand. He took a step backwards. 'Scott, I'm sorry. I didn't mean to—'

'No,' I said, smoothing the cover with my palm. 'It's OK. I just don't show anyone my stories. Not anymore.'

'Of course. That was rude of me. But look, let's go inside. I'll make us something to eat.'

Following him into the boxy '70s bungalow, I wondered if I should tell him about the case. In a sense, Campbell had already made Harry a part of it, asking him to take on research without revealing the bigger picture. But now that Haz was taking me into his home, was it right to keep him in the dark? The killer I was hunting had his pattern, but without yet knowing the logic behind his victim selection, it was possible he might target the people I was close to, especially if he knew I was on his track.

I raked fingers through my hair. The people I was close to ... The truth was, I didn't want Harry to know about this world in which I felt so stimulated and at home. That moody kid he'd known back in Oxford was as shadowy now as the Malanowski children who waited in the trailer behind me. I closed my eyes. I thought, on balance, I could keep him safe without exposing him to the horrors of the case.

In the end, that turned out to be just another of my mistakes.

Chapter Sixteen

Ella Fitzgerald accompanied me as I wandered around the open-plan living room-kitchen. An old bluesy number, it stirred memories of lazy Sunday mornings in Oxford, slants of dusty daylight, his head resting against my chest.

'Shouldn't be long,' Harry called from the kitchen.

He diced and stirred, intently focused as he always had been when cooking. On the shelves next to his vintage Garrard turntable, I played my fingertips across hundreds of records. Everything here from Renaissance madrigals to gangsta rap. I'd always enjoyed music, but it had never spoken to me the way it spoke to Haz. I was glad he could still get pleasure from it.

My gaze swept other shelves where framed photographs stood among knick-knacks I didn't recognise. Nothing much from our Oxford flat; it seemed that his records were among the few survivors from those days. I saw a couple of familiar photos, though: a cherubic Haz in the arms of the beaming mother who had died when he was too young to remember her and holiday snaps from his teens – Barcelona, Cape

Town, Sydney, a boy shy and sun-flushed. No pictures of the music teacher father from whom he had inherited his passion.

'How long have you been here?' I asked.

He looked up from the stove. 'A year. Just over.'

I peered through the lounge window to the bungalow opposite. A sign similar to the one I'd seen earlier was staked a little drunkenly into the lawn:

SAY NO TO THE NEW MOSQUE! KEEP ENGLAND PURE!

'Lovely neighbours,' I observed.

'Oh yes,' he agreed, following my gaze. 'They're charmers all right. There's going to be some kind of demo against the opening of the mosque this week. There'll be quite a crowd, I reckon.'

'First a library protest and now this,' I said. 'What a vocal lot these Bradburians are.'

'Yup.' He went back to his bubbling pans. 'It pains me to say it, but a small minority will be protesting at both. Pro-library and anti-Muslim. Makes me wonder if they've actually read any of the books they say they want to protect. You know, I think for some of them it isn't the library itself they're interested in saving, it's the simple fact that the building has been there for so many years. Its venerability is the thing that makes it valuable in their eyes, not its purpose.'

I nodded. 'Libraries are revolutionary. When they first started spreading in the 1800s, they were seen as the working man's university. It's no wonder authoritarian governments have never liked them.'

'I remember that speech.' He chuckled. 'I think I got it every time you dragged me around to a new one.'

I smiled. 'Well, I guess you can't have hated me all that much after we finished. I mean, you ended up working in the places I love.'

I'd said it lightly, no edge at all, but my words were met with silence. When I looked over, Harry was standing with his palms planted on the countertop. He kept his head down, as if checking the two steaming plates in front of him.

'Don't you understand what happened back then, Scott? Don't you know why I ...?' When I took a step towards him, he looked up, his eyes bright. 'Doesn't matter. Let's eat.'

'Haz.'

His look became hard – an alien expression for Harry Moorhouse. 'Let's just eat.'

And so we did. Swedish meatballs with mashed potato and lingonberry jam, his Nordic grandmother's recipe and a treat he would rustle up whenever I'd felt down. It tasted just as good as ever and coaxed more memories, harsh as lemon juice in a cut. I ate and tried to divert my mind from the past.

Today had been a wash-out. I'd intended to spend it on local research, laying the historical foundations for the investigation, trying to find any telling detail in the bridge tragedy that Campbell might have missed. I hadn't known then that he had his own researcher on the spot and that everything to be found in the library archive was already in the file. It was time to move on. The crime scene photos Campbell had obtained were all well and good, but I knew from experience that even a cold location can give up its secrets. Tomorrow, I'd head for Anglesey and the scene of the first murder.

'How is it?' Harry asked.

I held up a speared meatball. 'Good as ever. And prepared in lightning speed.'

'I had some ready-made in the freezer.'

'Because it was my favourite and you were expecting me?'

'By the way,' he said, scraping his spoon around the plate, 'there is one other source on Travellers Bridge we could try. Gerald Roebuck. He's a local eccentric and a bit of an old nightmare, really. He runs a kind of unofficial museum out of his front room. Got some interesting stuff amid all the clutter. Anyway, he was my first port of call when Professor Campbell got in touch. There isn't much Roebuck doesn't know about Bradbury End, plus he's a mine of juicy conspiracy theories.'

'Conspiracy theories?'

'You'll find out.' Harry grinned. 'But I'm afraid he's away for a few days. He came in last week and told us his sister up north had been taken ill. Should be back by the time the fair's here, though. I know he's keen to interview the showpeople for his archive on the tragedy.'

'I doubt they'll be able to tell him much,' I said. 'Travellers Bridge was only ever a bedtime story in our circles. I wasn't even sure it was real myself until forty-eight hours ago.'

He stared at me. 'You've only been working on this a couple of days? I don't understand. If the showmen have no information on the Jericho story then why has Campbell employed you?'

It was a good question.

'Local colour, maybe,' I said, returning my attention to my plate. 'We might not be able to give him specifics on the tragedy, but we can bore him to death with stories about the old freakshows themselves. He seems like the obsessive type who'd want that sort of detail.'

Harry looked doubtful. 'I suppose.'

After dinner, I helped him with the dishes. We stood side-by-side, hips almost touching as he swayed to Ella singing 'Summertime'. It almost made me jealous, how he could lose himself like this. I wish I could still do the same with my books.

Twilight was reddening the kitchen when he suggested I take the spare bedroom.

I shook my head. 'I wouldn't want to wake you. I've got an early start, and you remember what I'm like in the morning. Until my third coffee, I tend to crash into things. The bed in my trailer's cosy enough. I could do with a quick shower, though.'

'Of course.' He tapped his temple. 'I should've offered before dinner. Let me get you a towel.'

I let the shower run hot, bullets of scalding water scouring my flesh. My muscles ached from the exercise they'd taken that morning, dragging Kerrigan into the forest. I wondered again about the strange light that had caught his attention – that spark, like a reflection off glass, glittering waist-high between the trees. Something else nagged at me too – the cheap watch strapped around his wrist ...

Dressed again, I rubbed an oval in the steamed mirror. My eyes seemed sharper but I could already feel the need for a Zopiclone nibbling at my nerves. I'd allow myself one sleeping tablet tonight and then see how tomorrow found me. Back in the hall, I called out a thank you to Harry and, receiving no response, guessed he'd already gone to bed. It was full dark as

I left the house, stepping the short distance between the front door and my trailer.

Once inside, I acted on instinct. A single lamp silhouetted the man standing by my bed. He appeared to be going through my medications. I didn't take the time to assess whether it was Kerrigan, one of the disgruntled officers from earlier, or some stranger who might just turn out to be the psychopath I was hunting. Before he had a chance to react, I had my forearm locked around his throat and was lifting him, choking and spluttering, from the ground.

It was his smell that told me I'd made a mistake. His natural warm scent that hadn't changed since those nights we'd spent wrapped in each other's arms. I let him down at once and helped him to the bed where he looked up at me, his eyes huge.

'Haz, I'm so sorry. I didn't know it was you.'

'Christ,' he said, his voice almost a sob. 'Jesus, Scott, what the fuck's wrong with you?'

He got unsteadily to his feet, slapping my hand away when I attempted to help him. I followed him out of the trailer to the bungalow, trying to explain. He didn't look back, just closed the door in my face and turned the key. I stood there on the step, not sure of what to do when the phone buzzed in my pocket.

'Scott, it's Pete Garris,' he said before I could even speak. 'I've got that information you wanted. Professor Ralph Campbell, former Cambridge don, defrocked – or whatever the hell they call it – after the police caught him in a kiddie porn ring. That led to the discovery of actual abuse against a string of minors. He served three years. Came out about eighteen months ago. Got a big compo payout after some other prisoners managed to corner him in his cell and cut off his nuts. Very public-spirited of them, if you ask me. Although they also gave him a pretty brutal kicking afterwards which resulted in some spinal damage. Anyway, I'll text you all the grisly details. Scott ...?'

'Yes. Thank you. Thank you, sir,' I mumbled, my palm flat against the jamb of the door. 'I'm grateful.'

'Look, what exactly have you got yourself mixed up in?' A rare trace of concern tinted my old mentor's voice. 'Why do you need to know about some nutless old nonce living out in the sticks with his nanny? Scott, I think we should talk. Where are you?'

'Bradbury End,' I said hollowly.

'Where? You're breaking up.'

'Yes, Pete, I think we should talk. I might need ...'

I almost cried out. A warm, wet tongue was lapping at the back of my hand. Glancing down, I could hardly believe what I was seeing. Garris was still talking when I cancelled the call and dropped to my haunches in front of the elderly boxer. My dad's old juk whined as I scratched behind his tattered ear.

'Webster? What the hell are you doing here?'

As if in answer, he turned his doleful head and cast sad eyes at the car idling across the street. The driver sat in a band of shadow and I couldn't make out his face. A splash of orange paint ran above the front wheel arch, stark against the Volkswagen's black bodywork. A detail so vivid it had to be deliberate, as if he wanted to be noticed. Beside me, Webster whimpered again, and I suddenly noticed the cardboard container, a little larger than a ring box, attached to his collar. An eye still on the car, I unclipped the box and opened the flaps.

I very nearly dropped the contents.

Wrapped in greaseproof paper was a triangular wedge of human flesh. A piece of Adya Mahal, I had no doubt, for upon the curling skin was a marker pen scrawl – a single letter 'A' for '*Animus*', the third word in the Traveller Bridge dedication. I straightened up and glanced back across the road, locking eyes with the killer who had found me.

Chapter Seventeen

I MOVED SLOWLY AT FIRST, AS if the murderer were an animal I didn't want to startle. Reaching over, I unclipped the trailer door and ushered Webster inside. He went peacefully enough, lumbering up the steps and collapsing almost immediately by the locker settee. Then, the little cardboard coffin still in my hand, I started towards the road.

It was a dry, airless night. Not a breath of wind to stir the pruned bushes and crew-cut lawns of the cul-de-sac. With the moon behind it, Harry's side of the street hugged every scrap of darkness while the windows opposite, and those of the killer's car, dazzled.

My heart hammered. In my mind, I flipped through the images of the file: McAllister strung to the tree, his dog's head lolling from the spike screwed into his torso; Agatha Poole, in her electrified tin bath, lightning twists of silver metal driven into her fingertips; Adya Mahal caught in the apparent act of eating herself alive. Here was the author of those outrages and, at the thought of meeting him, I again felt that dark thrill.

His headlights blazed when I reached the roadside. The engine roared. Of course, he wasn't just going to sit there and let me come for him. The three murders he had committed with such measured brutality were only part of a larger design. Although my understanding remained hazy, I sensed that completeness was vital to his MO, and there were still two Jericho freaks to recreate before this masterpiece was done.

Turning to my Merc, I heard a squeal of tyres as the Volkswagen shot out of the cul-de-sac. Luckily, I had my keys in my pocket and was behind the wheel in seconds. I threw the box of flesh onto the passenger seat, feeling a brief stab of guilt as I did so, as if I'd somehow disrespected the remains of a victim who'd already suffered enough. My own headlights washed over the sleeping bungalows as I hit the throttle and swept out of Harry's drive.

Two red eyes, smoky in the exhaust fumes, flared at the junction. Then the brake lights blinked out and the Volkswagen tore into the streets beyond. In its prime, my Merc might have made up the ground relatively easily. I'd bought it for a song from old Tom Radlett after coming out of prison; a favour to my dad who, in those early days, had imagined I might need a car. Perhaps if I'd looked after it instead of letting it rust while I wallowed in nightmares and self-pity, it wouldn't be groaning and juddering around me now. As it was, all I could do was push the bleating engine to its limit.

We flew on. Careered around darkened streets where austerity had doused the light from every lamppost. My eyes scanned the spaces between cars from which some late-night dog walker might suddenly emerge. I'd taken an advanced driver course during my time in uniform and, as those old lessons came back to me, so did the constraints spelled out by our instructor. The roles of pursuer and pursued are not equal in these situations. When a sociopath is behind the wheel, whoever hunts him will always be at a disadvantage. For a killer who not only saw human life as expendable but delighted in its destruction, the chances of capture were slim.

Still, I aimed to give him a good scare. I owed that much to his victims. And so, cautious as I could be, I sent the Merc shrieking on its way. He led me on a white-knuckle dance around those suburban streets; a chase that made the blood pound in my ears and drove all thoughts of Harry from my head. Jagging out of the estate, we hit a long stretch of road lined with takeaways and convenience stores. Faces made deathly by the fluorescent light of bus shelters stared out at us, and I had no choice but to toe the brake.

The killer did not slow. He slalomed between speed bumps, the Volkswagen's boot bouncing into the air when he caught one. Now illuminated, I saw that his licence plate had been obscured by mud. Not a patch of dirt on the rest of the car. Still, I knew this to be a blind. Like many of his kind, it was clear that this creature indulged in a strange mix of caution and hubris. The total absence of DNA at the crime scenes was telling and yet he had taken the risk of goading me with Webster and the box. He had been working away unappreciated without an audience and now he had one. That would stoke his ego – he wanted to be noticed, hence that flash of orange paint over the wheel arch – but that didn't mean he wanted to be caught. Not yet. And so, although the Volkswagen had almost certainly been stolen, the licence plate was obscured to make me think it was, in fact, his own car.

Leaving town, we plunged into rolling country lanes. As field and meadow flashed by, I wondered again: how had he become aware of me? I'd been on the case just over twenty-four hours and apart from Campbell I hadn't spoken to anyone about it.

Except that wasn't quite true. To varying degrees, six people knew I was either interested in the Travellers Bridge tragedy or actively investigating a case connected to it. Campbell himself and Miss Barton; Sal Myers and my father; Jeremy Worth, who had delivered the professor's message; and now Harry. It might not seem like all that many, but any CID detective will tell you that, as far as an active investigation is concerned, that's a pretty leaky ship. Even if none of them were directly involved – and, for different reasons, it was hard to see how any of them could be – a stray word might have been enough to alert the murderer.

That brought me back to possible suspects. It still seemed that there were only two pools from which to draw: the travelling community or someone in Bradbury End. It was possible, of course, that a random researcher like Campbell had become morbidly fascinated with the story of the drowned freaks, but that seemed like a long shot. Had word spread from Sal or my father, then? Or could Campbell, Miss Barton, or possibly Harry have mentioned something to someone in Bradbury? Someone who had organised the anniversary celebration, perhaps?

These ideas ricocheted through my head as we sped into a tangle of moonlit roads. Branches swatted my window. Trees came together, blocking out the sky. There were passing places every few hundred yards but otherwise, an oncoming vehicle would have no chance. Still, the killer didn't slow. I wondered then how alike we might be and if he too was feeling the exhilaration of the chase. I didn't like the idea and tried my best to bury it.

All at once, we came out of the tree tunnel and onto a double lane that pointed arrow-straight for a mile or more. Cornfields stood on either side, frozen in the breathless night. Only a slight flutter of stalks as they were caught in the killer's slipstream.

My eyes narrowed. Up ahead, two blinking lights had appeared out of the dark.

My head snapped right and I saw the oncoming rush the signal warned of.

'Fuck.'

I kicked down on the throttle.

The Volkswagen also put on an extra burst of speed.

Our engines bellowed at each other as we ate up the road. I thought I might have gained a fraction but another glance across the field turned my blood to ice water. A square of light in the driver's cab and then the impossibly long hulk of the goods train rocketing behind. Sweat tracked down my brow. I swallowed hard. The red crossing lights pulsed ever larger as the flimsy barrier started its trembling descent across the road.

My speedometer shivered at seventy. The opportunity to brake was closing. One way or another, I'd have to commit. Meanwhile, my quarry seemed to have made his decision and started to pull away again. Seconds now, metres in which to decide. So close, I could see the red-and-white stripes on the arm of the barrier; could see the oil-black gleam of the tracks.

The train gave an outraged wail as the Volkswagen flashed across its path, sparks leaping into the night as the barrier met the roof of the car. I'd been too slow. I had no choice. All I could do now was pray that I'd stop in time. My hands cemented themselves around the wheel. In the same instant, my left foot abandoned the throttle and I slammed on the brake.

Wheels locked, rubber burned. The Merc fishtailed across the blacktop. A hundred bits of trash flew in all directions and I heard the smash of my mother's books in the boot. As I spun ninety degrees to face the cornfield, blue-black smoke from the tyres wafted across the windscreen. I'd stopped, but on this side of the barrier or on the tracks? In my panic, I couldn't tell.

I cuffed sweat from my eyes; glanced through the passenger window.

'Jesus fu—!'

The train blared past, barely a foot from the car, its hammer-tread juddering into my bones. Resisting the lunge of my stomach I unclipped my seatbelt, kicked open the door, and pulled myself free. At first, I thought my legs might give way and I clutched at the roof for support. Over a mile long, the engine hauled its tankers and freight across the feathery expanse of the cornfield.

A breath caught in my chest. In the spaces between cargo, I could see a man standing in the road beyond. He appeared like one of those cartoons in a kid's flipbook. A figure that only moved when you riffled the pages. Separated by the trundling mass of the train, I could only watch as he stared back at me through those glancing spaces. In the flashing red light of the crossing, I saw that he was wearing a balaclava and black gloves. He appeared to be of medium height, although since he almost blended into the night, it was difficult to be sure. Before getting back into the stolen car, he held up his hand and waved.

Even then I didn't feel that it was a mocking gesture. More like a sporting salute between opponents. A tip of the hat that said: *Welcome to the game.*

Chapter Eighteen

THE TIDE WAS HIGH WHEN I crossed the Menai Strait, black water frothing as it surged beneath the piers of the great suspension bridge that linked the isle of Anglesey to the Welsh mainland. Summer seemed to have vanished and an autumnal drizzle streaked the windscreen. Beyond the bridge, the island gave over some grudging space for a road that threaded out to its northern shore.

This area was less desolate than some of the last miles of the mainland, where monolithic hills hid their crowns among lowering clouds, but there remained a kind of secretiveness to the country. Nameless lanes appeared out of nowhere, dips in the landscape fooled the eye. I remembered reading once that this had been among the final strongholds of the ancient princes of Wales, and that nationalism still had its natural home among the islanders. Looking about me, I couldn't say I was surprised.

I opened the window a crack and breathed in air salted by the Irish sea. On the passenger seat, Webster growled in his sleep. I reached over and ruffled the scruff around his neck. If only the mutt could tell me who had brought him to Bradbury End.

Returning to the cul-de-sac last night, I'd found the bungalow in darkness. By that time, the thrill of the chase had dissipated and all I could think of was Harry's face staring up at me. The fear in those eyes after I'd mistakenly attacked him. I never wanted him to look at me that way again.

I had stood on the doorstep, raising and lowering my hand, never quite summoning the courage to knock. I knew I ought to pack up and move on. Even without the danger posed by the man I hunted, I was pretty certain that I could bring Haz nothing but misery. But wasn't it already too late? The killer now knew where he lived, might even know of our past connection. At least if I stayed, I could keep an eye on him.

That's the story I told myself. The truth was, after ten lonely years, I had only just found him again. And yes, it wasn't the fairy-tale reunion of my dreams but nor was it the cold rejection I'd dreaded. We had been happy once, and perhaps I was reading too much into things, but he had seemed pleased to see me. Until I'd ruined everything, of course. Now he had glimpsed the violence I trailed in my wake, he probably wanted nothing more to do with me.

It was as I turned back to the trailer, my mind set on leaving, that I saw the note taped to my door. I still had old love letters in that small, cramped hand – keepsakes I cherished. Mouth dry, I unpeeled the note:

Scott, I came to talk things over but you'd gone off somewhere. BTW, where'd the dog come from?! When I opened the door, he very nearly took my head off! Anyway, I realise that you probably thought I was some kind of intruder, so I'm sorry if I reacted badly. Let's talk when you get home tomorrow. Hx

Home.

I'd taken a shaky breath reading that word. He'd had every reason to reject me but instead, he was willing to offer me the benefit of the doubt. It didn't occur to me then that there was no caution in those words, nothing to reflect the fear he'd felt when he looked up at me.

Back inside the trailer, I went to the area where Harry had been standing when I attacked him. My medications with their labels turned to the wall were untouched while a bottle of mineral water stood to one side. That was what he'd been doing, leaving the water and a glass. I rubbed my eyes and rested his note against my pillow. Then I took out my phone and called Dad.

After midnight, and his voice was clear as a bell. I sometimes wondered if he slept at all.

'You rocked up in Bradbury, then? Everything all right?'

'Had a run-in with some gavvers.' I sighed. 'Just the usual sort of dinlos.'

He grunted at that. 'Don't go barnying before we've even built up, son.'

'I'll try my best.' I put the phone on loudspeaker and slipped the cardboard box containing Adya Mahal's flesh from my pocket. Over by the locker settee, Webster continued to dream. 'About the dog—' I began.

'God knows why you wanted to take that poor old juk with you,' Dad muttered.

'You think I took him?'

A pause. 'That's what your note said: *took Webster for a bit of company*. Thought it sounded overly sentimental for you. What are you saying, that you didn't take him? Who left the note under my mat, then?'

'Calm down, Dad. He's here, safe and sound.'

'Then I don't understand what you're saying.'

'It doesn't matter.'

'Scott,' he grunted, 'I want a straight answer: this case or whatever it is you're looking into. You promised me there was no danger to us. Is that still true? Because midnight phone calls do not put me at my ease.'

I stared down at the box in my hands. 'There is someone dangerous in Bradbury End,' I said. 'But I don't have any reason to believe that he'll come after us. He has his rules and I think he'll stick to them.'

'What's that supposed to mean?'

I almost told him then, but some words of my mother came back to me: *'You think the aunts are bad? Showmen are the biggest gossips on any ground, and your dad is just about the worst of them. You want to keep a secret, don't ever speak a word of it in front of George Jericho.'* It was true, middle-aged Travellers like my dad and Sam Urnshaw could while away whole days telling tales. Even if I swore him to secrecy, the truth about my investigation would be all over the fair by mid-morning. Then the killer might really have a reason to target the Travellers.

'You're just going to have to trust me,' I said. 'If there's any direct threat, I'll tell you.'

'Always too close for your own good.' He barked out a bitter laugh. 'Just like your mother.'

I started to remonstrate with him when he launched a curveball. 'That chap, Zac's been asking after you. Fond of you, I reckon. Just be careful you don't drag him into whatever mess you've got yourself involved with. He doesn't deserve to get hurt because of your recklessness.'

The phone went dead and I returned my attention to Webster and the box.

The killer must have come onto the ground in the early hours, taken the juk and left the note. That suggested someone with access to my handwriting. Did that also rule out someone from Bradbury End? Not necessarily. The tabloid paparazzo, Maxine Thierrot, who had continued to stalk me even after my release from prison, had gained access to a report I'd written on our first interview with Kerrigan. Her editor had published it under the banner: DISGRACED COP SABOTAGES MURDER CASE. The story was probably still online, so anyone might study my handwriting at their leisure.

I got up and placed the box in the crisper compartment of my fridge. I knew there was no point handing it over to the police. The smell of bleach on the greaseproof paper was strong. Just like the crime scenes, not a scrap of forensic evidence would be found.

There had been one more surprise before leaving Bradbury. As dawn lit the road leading out of town, I saw the burned-out shell of a car still smoking in a layby. I didn't need to stop. I knew it was the stolen Volkswagen and that it had been left in the hope that I might see it. Another message from the man in the balaclava: *Hurry back, Scott – the fun is just beginning!*

The bay of Benllech sat in the scoop of the village that bore its name. A steep hill on one side plunged down to a stretch of rain-sodden sand and the grey tumble of the sea. On a better day, that water might sparkle, blue as the Adriatic. On the far side, the bay rose again at a gentler gradient to meet the coastal pathways that cut around to Red Wharf Bay where Campbell had his holiday home.

I drove on, past a charming whitewashed café, until I reached the eastern side of Benllech and the gate of the Sweet View Caravan Site. The location lived up to its name with a breathtaking panorama of the beach. I parked up and headed for the reception block. A few families in anoraks were braving the elements, kids with buckets and nets, excited chatter about crabbing pools. Entering the reception, I wiped the rain from my eyes.

'*Bore da.*' I smiled at the young woman behind the desk.

She glanced up from her magazine and slid the lollipop out of her mouth. 'Don't try it on, sweetheart. You haven't got the accent. English?'

'That obvious?' I winced.

She sighed and flipped a page. 'You're tidier'n most, I'll give you that. But English is English. Anyway, if you're wanting a caravan, I'm all out, so a good morning in Welsh and a lush smile won't get you anywhere ...' She glanced at me again. 'I knock off at four, though, if you fancy a pint.' Then, stretching her arms behind her back, she yawned and blinked. 'But maybe not. Gay, is it?'

I laughed. 'You'd make a good detective.'

'Tidy and not Welsh. Had to be gay. So is that what you are, police?'

'Journalist,' I said. Her eyes lit up and she leaned forward.

It was a trick I'd often played during my time in plain clothes. It doesn't matter how much you try to reassure them, witnesses are more likely to talk openly to journos than CID detectives. There's the freedom of being off the record for one thing, plus the fact that media interest in their opinion does wonders for the public's ego. Of course, impersonating a hack was a disciplinary offence, but I'd never been caught and Garris had always appreciated the results.

'Paper or telly?' she wondered.

'Online. Be happy to pay you a little something for your time. Shall we say forty quid?' Her eyes went neon and I kicked myself for going in so high. Still, it was Campbell's money, so I didn't feel too bad. 'I'd just like to ask you a few questions about what happened to your old boss ...'

I made sure I filmed our interview, both to set the scene and so that I could review the footage later. It quickly became apparent that Adele – we'd made introductions – knew next to nothing about her late employer's murder. His body had been discovered by a rambler and the police had found McAllister's head and the torso of his dog, Bestie, inside his caravan. I asked her about the artist's mannikin left propped against his trailer window, the top-hatted figure with its articulated limbs twisted to resemble my contortionist ancestor, and Adele confirmed she had never noticed it amongst McAllister's belongings before the day of the murder. A killer's calling card, just as Campbell had observed. Adele admitted that McAllister had been an OK boss, a bit tight when it came to bonuses, but even that, her tone implied, did not warrant his ritualistic decapitation. And Bestie had been just adorable.

'Bit late in the day for all this, innit?' she said as we finished up. 'Old Bob's been dead six months or more.'

'It's a feature piece I'm doing,' I said, turning off the recording. 'You know the sort of thing. Clickbait for the morbidly inclined? Ten Gruesome Unsolved Mysteries. Spooky Crimes That Will Keep You Guessing.'

She waved her lolly stick at me. 'You want spooky you should go talk to that old witch Debney. Mad as a ferret and stinks twice as bad. I bet your readers would lap up all her ghost story bullshit.'

'Debney?' My mind went back to the file; I didn't recall the name. 'Was she interviewed by the police?'

'I doubt they took much notice of her. But if you can stand the stench, she might be worth a chat.'

'What's her story?'

Adele twirled the lollipop stick against the side of her head. 'Says she saw him that night, is all.'

I tried to keep my voice level. 'The killer?'

'Not just a killer.' Adele grinned. 'The devil himself, so she says.'

Chapter Nineteen

'THOSE LITTLE SLICES OF DEATH, how I long for them.'

'Loathe them, isn't it?'

Miss Debney stared at me. When she smiled, her bloodless upper lip, furred with the trace of a moustache, exposed a cemetery of rotten teeth.

'You know Edgar's work? Oh, but you are most welcome here, then!'

She spread her arms and I tried to concentrate on breathing through my mouth. The name of her hillside cottage, Annabel Lee, ought to have given me the clue as to this former English lecturer's obsession. It had been scrawled on a garden gate glazed with webs and then daubed again, in dripping yellow paint, on the front door. A door that, when opened, I'd almost reeled back from.

It's difficult to describe the smell. I had been the officer first on scene at countless deaths, natural and otherwise; the reek of a putrefying corpse is a rankness that's hard to get used to, but the stench of poor Miss Debney's cottage was something else. A damp, stale, fetid odour, suggestive of the living death of this shunned woman.

'Sleep,' she nodded. 'A curse to both Edgar and myself. Do you know, Mr Jericho, I do not believe that I have actually slept at all in the past fifteen years? Now, you'll tell me that such a thing is physiologically impossible, but I assure you that the human mind can overcome the base needs of the body. In point of fact, I have not eaten since the turn of the millennium.'

Looking at her, I could almost believe it. Dwarfed by the armchair in which she sat, the Witch of Annabel Lee – as she told me the local children called her – appeared like some kind of skeletal puppet. Her clothes, marked with stains I didn't want to guess at, hung loosely from her bones. The sitting room was dark, windows pasted over with old newspapers, but still, Miss Debney's face shone out, waxy in the gloom.

I sat forward on the couch, careful not to touch its crusted cushions. There was no TV that I could see, no radio, no laptop. Just pile upon pile of books. It made me think of my own trailer only a couple of days ago, and I wondered again at the change the deaths of three strangers had brought to my life. Trying to ignore the itching sensation that prickled my skin, I reached over and picked up a collection of short stories: *Tales of Mystery and Imagination*.

'Were you awake the night your neighbour died, Miss Debney?' I held up the book. 'Reading Poe, maybe?'

'*Edgar*,' she corrected. 'He calls me Una and I call him Edgar. We have an understanding. That was why the college sacked me in the end. You see, I could tell my students what Edgar *really* meant in his tales and poetry because he spoke to me.'

'In spirit?'

She drew herself up. 'In *person*. Much as I enjoy the pleasing terror of his masterpieces, I do not believe in ghosts, Mr Jericho.

I am not a child and I am not mad. But in fact, Edgar did not come to me on the night of poor Mr McAllister's passing. I was in my garden—' she wafted a hand towards the window, beyond which weeds had grown waist-high and hidden things chirruped among the stalks, 'counting stars. And the spaces between stars.'

'That must have taken a while,' I said.

'I was distracted,' her brow furrowed, 'by a light. Not a star, but something new and earthly. A will-o'-the-wisp, down near the edge of the cliffs where old McAllister had his caravan. It was winter, you see, January, and that wisp had no business being where he was. Unlike me, the murdered man was no stranger to sleep, you understand?'

'It was winter,' I nodded, 'so the caravan park was closed up. And you're saying McAllister usually went to bed early?'

'Made himself go,' she cackled. 'A skinflint. Used to come up here to pick the blackberries in my garden. Even the children won't do that anymore. Made sure he was all tucked up for the night by seven – lights out, heating off. Plenty of money and yet insisted on freezing himself near to death.'

'Did you know him well?'

'Nobody knows anyone *well*, Mr Jericho. What I knew he chose to show me – McAllister: no family, no loved ones, except maybe that dog of his. Went everywhere together, thick as thieves. People were horrified by what was done to them, but I believe it might even have been an act of mercy. I assure you, McAllister would not have wanted to live a moment longer than that beast.'

'So you saw a light, what next?'

'"*Deep into that darkness peering, long I stood there, wondering, fearing, doubting*—"'

'"*Dreaming dreams no mortal ever dared to dream before*"?' I said.

She gave me a cool look. 'Finally, I decided I must be like Edgar's C. Auguste Dupin and investigate the mystery of the incongruous light.'

'You're not going to tell me McAllister was murdered by an outraged orangutan, are you?'

'It was cold, the night wind screaming off the sea,' she went on. 'I left my cottage and wandered down the hillside into Sweet View. All around me, the white caravans seemed to grow up out of the earth, like rows of silent tombs. Every one locked up, every one dark, except his. When I reached his door, I believe I heard something. McAllister – or perhaps what was left of him – weeping. You'll say I couldn't possibly have heard such a thing, not with the wind braying so, but I assure you I *heard*.'

Although what she said was impossible, I nodded. McAllister had been killed by three puncture wounds to the heart. He would have died almost instantaneously; no time for weeping.

'I knocked. Called out. A shadow there, on the blind!' She pointed at the papered window, and I really believe, in that moment, she was seeing the killer again. 'He was bending over something and when I knocked, he turned his head towards the door. I knew then that it wasn't McAllister. McAllister never moved that way.'

'What way?'

'Patiently,' she said, her flaking brow creased again. 'Considered. McAllister was a lazy man and like all lazy men was easily startled. This man moved through the world as if every surprise had been anticipated and planned for. His shadow paused only

135

for a moment to pull on some kind of mask, and then he came to the door. Came to meet me.'

A mask – the balaclava. I sat forward.

'You didn't see his face?'

She hesitated, one crooked finger tracking down the side of her jaw.

'Yes ... I saw his face.'

Forgetting myself, I took a breath and almost choked. 'He removed the mask?'

Miss Debney laughed. It was an awful sound, like the mad twittering of a caged bird.

'There was no mask. Don't you understand? What I saw on the blind, that was him pulling on his *true* face. There might have been something that looked human underneath, but that wasn't him. He is the darkness and the emptiness and the void. He is anarchy and desolation and the unmaking of things. He is the space between stars. He greeted me on white wings and flew inside the doorway.'

'Did he speak?'

'Entropy does not speak. It unmakes words. It unravels meaning.'

I closed my eyes in frustration. This was my second witness to the murderer and I could get no more sense out of her than I could Webster.

'Why didn't he hurt you, Miss Debney? Why didn't he unmake you too?'

When I opened my eyes again she was gripping her wrist and holding it out to me. 'He saw that *I* saw, and so he did this,' she said, clasping the joint. 'He did this he did this he did this. And his white wings were stained red and his hands

136

were dark and his face was true. Not even the Conqueror Worm may claim him, for he *is* the worm and will feast until he is gorged. Do not think you can stop him. If you dare to try, he will wrap his wings about you and unthread your life until it lifts away like bits of string upon the wind.'

She sank back into her armchair, her hand still clutching that bony wrist. 'Do not bring him back here, Mr Jericho. Do not make me see him again. Even Edgar is afraid of him ...'

Before heading back to Bradbury End, I let Webster out for a run along the beach. I say 'run'. The poor old boy plodded along beside me, snuffling at the sand. When some kids hurtled by dragging a kite, he looked up and gave them a few fierce barks. Still a fairground juk at heart. I reassured them that he was soft as butter and they were all soon making a ridiculous fuss of him.

I watched on, memories of Webster the pup – my mum and I throwing sticks for him on the heath. Those ghosts, almost as real to me as the Malanowski children who now stood watching me from the road. I met Sonia's gaze as she reached down and took her little brothers' hands. Then I turned back to the sea.

Lost as she was, Miss Debney *had* seen the killer. His face – the desolation, the void, the balaclava mask; his dark gloved hands. His wings? What had she actually witnessed in that doorway? Only one thing seemed certain: I had been wrong. Yes, I had guessed that he had his rules, that the five Jericho victims would be his ultimate masterpiece, but I had also imagined that he must take some pleasure in sadism. Yet, here was a witness, one he could easily have disposed of if he'd chosen to, and he had let her live. Did that suggest that the physical deaths of the five, even their desecrations, were unimportant to him? That there was some other purpose these murders might be serving?

All I knew was that Miss Debney's survival had offered me a scrap of comfort: my family and my friends were safe. I did not believe the killer would come for them.

It was a five-hour drive back to Bradbury End. I arrived at Harry's just as a car was pulling up to the kerb. Spotting the Honda Accord, I felt a mixture of trepidation and relief. Face to face, I knew I didn't have a hope of keeping the case from DI Pete Garris, and although part of me yearned for his insight another feared his intrusion. Unlike me, he was still a real detective after all.

I leaned over and opened Webster's door. He jumped out, circled Garris twice, then went to relieve himself behind Harry's hedge. I got out myself, unkinked my neck, and looked over at my old boss.

'What are you doing here, Pete?'

'I'm not sure yet.' He put his hands into his jacket pockets and glanced up at the sky. 'If you've got anything to do with it, probably destroying my career. So come on then, let's hear what sort of mess you've got yourself mixed up in.'

Chapter Twenty

'I LIKE WHAT YOU'VE DONE WITH the place,' Garris said, glancing around the trailer. 'Looking less like a hellhole fit to die in, anyway.'

I handed him a mug of strong black coffee. Thank God he hadn't asked for milk – I wasn't ready to share the contents of my fridge with him just yet. That little cardboard box could wait. I went and sat on the opposite side of the locker settee while Webster collapsed in the space between us.

'All Sal's work,' I said. 'Did you ever meet Sal Myers?'

He smoothed down his tie, his poppy tattoo winking from under his cuff. Honestly, he must have stocks in whatever company produced those paisley horrors. 'Your bosom friend of childhood? Yes, I bumped into her a couple of times when dropping off those case files you never look at. She seemed worried about you. Although . . .' his washed-out blue eyes moved across my face, 'you appear to be doing better. Which begs the question: why have I had your old man on the phone asking me to check in on you?'

'Like Sal, he's a worrier.'

'But it isn't only you that he's concerned about. He senses that this case you've taken on has the potential to spill over and harm the Travellers.'

'I've told him—'

Garris held up his hand. 'Tell *me*. Then, if I'm satisfied, perhaps I can get him to back off.'

I sighed. It was time anyway. I needed a fresh perspective and there was none better than Garris's. I took out my notebook and started flicking back through the pages.

'How did you find me?' I asked.

'How do you find the epicentre of an explosion?' He spread out his hands. 'You trace inwards from the devastation. You told me you were in Bradbury End and so, after a late-night chat with Pa Jericho, I set out first thing. The first natural port of call for a policeman is the local cop shop. I met a couple of officers who had encountered your charming manners only yesterday. They said they'd seen you talking to a librarian. Not difficult to find his address.' He reached into his jacket pocket and took out his well-thumbed notebook. 'Harry Moorhouse. I know that name, don't I?'

There's a lesson here: when discussing cases after work in a confidential nook of The Three Crowns, keep it strictly business. Especially if your confidante is a teetotaller with a photographic memory. God, those boozy chats. I'm not even sure why I used to spill my guts to him; it wasn't as if Garris ever offered me much in the way of sympathy. Perhaps that was the reason. He filled the role of a kind of father confessor, promising neither absolution nor resolution, just allowing me the space to talk.

'The boyfriend from Oxford, right?'

I nodded.

Garris put away his notebook and stretched his arms along the back of the settee. 'I believe you told me once that he—'

'That was in confidence.'

'Off the record. Yes, I remember. Don't look so frightened, Scott, I have enough sadistic pieces of shit on my plate. I'm not interested in pursuing some poor boy who put a loved one out of his misery. I can understand that temptation myself. Good God, I can.'

In all our years together, there had been only a handful of times when I'd glimpsed the man behind the copper. I was probably the closest thing Garris had to a friend on the force, and yet our relationship outside work had been almost exclusively a one-way street. I talked, he listened. But just occasionally that impassive, professional mask slipped.

'How is Harriet?' I said quietly.

'Much the same as when you asked forty-eight hours ago ... Only, no. That's not true. She's worse; yellow with it and pain like you wouldn't believe. I think we both know that it'll only be a matter of time before I have to abandon her to that bloody hospice.'

'You won't be abandoning her, Pete. You've done your best.'

'Oh, I know,' he said. 'I have nothing to reproach myself for. There are just some killers that can't be hunted down and put behind bars, that's all. But let's get back to it. I think you have a story to tell.'

In the end, it didn't take as long as I'd imagined. From Jeremy Worth's introduction to Campbell to my interview that morning with Miss Debney, I placed everything before Garris, including my hazy theories as to the killer's motivations. My former mentor listened as he always had, not a hint of his thoughts crossing his features.

141

'I'd heard about the murders, of course,' he said as I finished up. 'McAllister and Poole's anyway. They were plastered all over the media a few months ago: police baffled, killer remains at large, heads must roll. Basically, a plague on all our houses.' He sighed. 'All right, so let's start with what I think is an assumption on your part: that your ex-boyfriend just happens to be on the scene of a series of murders connected with your family history. When you were together, did you ever discuss the story of the Jericho freaks with him?'

'Maybe.' I crossed my arms. 'I don't know. You're talking over a decade ago.'

'So you're saying his presence here is a coincidence? I thought I'd taught you to be suspicious of coincidences. Let's imagine for a moment that he is your "outside suspect", by which I mean he's not a showman nor a long-time resident of Bradbury End. He became fixated with the story you told him. There are unresolved issues between you. He has killed before—'

'You said yourself that Harry's was a mercy killing,' I cut in. 'His father was in agony and was going to die soon anyway. The humanity behind that act doesn't fit the MO of these murders. And anyway, Harry had only just left me last night when I saw the killer across the street.'

'If he had an accomplice—'

'No. Pete, I know him. Harry could never—'

'You *knew* him,' Garris corrected. 'People can change a great deal in ten years; you know that better than anyone.'

I shook my head, pushing away memories of the man I had been when Garris first met me. 'Harry is the same person he was back in Oxford,' I insisted. 'I'd know if he was capable of this sort of evil.'

'Perhaps. It's true that you can read people better than anyone I've ever worked with.' He stated it not as a compliment but as a plain matter of fact. 'All right, then, let's assume your personal feelings are not clouding your judgement. Another coincidence needs to be considered. Your father tells me that a certain far-right child-killer has been making your life a misery. Do you think Kerrigan could be involved?'

I hesitated. 'I think he *may* have a role. But the whole feel of the case is wrong for Kerrigan. The victim selection, the theme of the recreations, the care taken over the staging of the bodies. Kerrigan's a vicious thug; he doesn't have either the brains or the patience for this sort of thing.'

'Again, what do we think of him as an accomplice?'

'Why would he?' I said. 'And anyway, what advantage could he be to the killer?'

'As a way to distract you?'

'It's possible, I suppose. But, look, Kerrigan started turning up at the fair long before I became involved in the case. The timing just doesn't work. And although it's true that he told me I was in for a surprise – that he'd played me somehow – every mention I've made of the murders he's interpreted as a reference to the Malanowski case. Anyway, forget that piece of trash for a minute. There's something I need you to see.'

I went to the fridge and returned with the cardboard box. I let Garris open it, peeling back the greaseproof paper with the tip of his pen. His eyebrows rose only a little when he saw the contents.

'From your summary, I'm assuming this is a piece of Adya Mahal?' I nodded and, after sniffing the bleached paper, he returned the box. 'I'm sorry, Scott, I have to report this.'

'But what is there to report?' I asked. 'You know as well as I do there won't be any forensics to be gleaned from it. All I have is a useless piece of physical evidence and the ramblings of a convicted paedophile. Apart from the calling card of the artist's mannikin left in the trailer window and the initials of the bridge inscription carved into the bodies, there is nothing to link these victims, either to each other or the historical tragedy. What I've told you is all supposition and theories. But if you can look me in the eye and say that an official investigation, started right now, is more likely to yield results than me working alone, I'll happily hand it over.'

He shifted uncomfortably in his seat, fingers worrying at that paisley atrocity around his neck.

'Come on, Pete. Give me three days. If I've got nowhere by then, you can take it off my hands.'

That inscrutable gaze again. I did my best not to look away. I knew that whatever decision he made, sentiment would play no part in it.

'You've changed,' he said at last. 'Or maybe what I mean is, you've come back. I suppose I'm only sorry that none of the cases I brought you worked that miracle. If you want to know the truth, Scott, the way things were going after you got out of prison, I thought you'd be dead within the year. I'm not usually one for regrets. Wishing you might have acted differently is the ultimate waste of time. But I *do* regret making you lead interviewer on the Malanowski case. Within a couple of years, I might have trained you to control your emotions better, but your temperament was not suited to dealing with scum like Kerrigan.'

'It wasn't your fault, sir,' I murmured.

Something I'd said to Sal came back to me then; words spoken when she'd warned me that, if I went back inside, I'd probably end up dying there. *'In there, out here, what's the difference?'* I had known myself that guilt and anger were killing me by degrees; now things had changed.

'I'll give you your three days.' Garris sighed. 'Make good use of them.'

'I will.'

We went to the small dining table and I spread out the crime scene photographs. 'So, any thoughts?'

Garris traced his finger across the letter *'A'* carved into McAllister's forehead. 'You said these represent the initials of the inscription on Travellers Bridge. Remind me.'

'Acclinis Falsis Animus Meliora Recusat. The mind intent upon false appearances refuses to admit better things.'

'What is he trying to tell us with that?'

'Isn't it just a way of linking the victims to the tragedy?' I asked.

'Perhaps. But a "mind intent upon *false* appearances". Is there something beneath the superficial staging of these murders? Some deeper meaning beyond a psychopathic obsession to recreate the Jericho freaks? Even madmen have their motives, Scott.'

'Do you mean a hatred of people who society perceives as different?' I wondered aloud. 'Maybe he has a deformity himself and projects his self-loathing onto his victims?'

'Or he sympathises with them and it's an act of revenge.' Garris shook his head. 'But I didn't really mean that either. Don't you get the feeling that there's a purpose behind all of this bloodshed? Something separate from the acts of murder and mutilation? I think your idea that he takes no pleasure in any of this could be true. There's a functionality to it all that shines through.'

'I don't know whether that's particularly comforting,' I said.

Garris gave me a long look. 'Oh, it's not comforting at all. It's profoundly disturbing. And unless you catch him, I think much worse horrors are to come.'

Chapter Twenty-One

'**H**AVE YOU CONSIDERED CAMPBELL HIMSELF as a suspect?' Garris asked.

'I have,' I said. 'But, look, that job the other cons did on him, damaging his spine? I don't think he'd even have the strength to overpower a pensioner like Agatha Poole, let alone a working man like McAllister. Plus.' I pointed to a black-and-white shot of Adya Mahal's flat in Lincoln. 'Three storeys up and the lift was out of order the night Adya died. There's just no way.'

'"The mind intent upon false appearances,"' Garris quoted at me.

'You're suggesting that, because I'd think such a punishment was fitting for a man like Campbell, he played up to it somehow? Made his condition appear worse than it actually was?'

'He knew all about the Malanowski case, didn't he? How you served up what you thought was justice to Kerrigan?'

I felt my insides tighten. 'Then he was taking a big fucking risk inviting me to his house. Anyway, we know he can't have been putting it on. You sent me the details of his injuries.'

'Perhaps he's made a miraculous recovery.' Garris gave a wry smile. 'Unless he has an accomplice, of course. Often in cases where two killers act in concert, there will be a dominant personality and one that watches on. A kind of voyeur to the sadism. We've considered whether Kerrigan could be involved, perhaps Campbell paid him to live out his twisted fantasies? Or indeed this Miss Barton. Do you think she'd be physically capable?'

I thought back to the small, scarred woman who had led me through Campbell's paederast gallery. Had her quiet revulsion been an act? I didn't think so, but a mind intent upon false appearances ...?

'She might have the strength,' I admitted. 'I believe Adya was drugged before she was killed, and if Miss Barton took McAllister by surprise? But you're talking about a kind of devotion that goes beyond anything I've ever heard of.'

'It's love,' Garris said bitterly. 'If you'd been in CID a little longer, you might have seen the degradations love can lead to. We don't know what history these two have together, but she's been with him since he was a little boy. Most successful marriages don't last that long. But OK, I admit the MO is completely different from Campbell's past crimes and the physical limitations do seem to rule him out. So we're back to someone in the travelling community or a Bradbury resident. It's such an obscure story it's unlikely someone other than Campbell stumbled upon it and became obsessed.'

'Except he isn't.'

Garris stopped sorting through the photographs and looked up at me. 'I'm sorry?'

'It's odd,' I said. 'But from the moment he handed the case over to me, he seemed to lose all interest in it. Almost as if a burden had been lifted from his shoulders. He hasn't called for updates, isn't interested in my progress. But when I was wavering about accepting his proposal, he ...'

'Yes?'

'He looked frightened. Terrified that I might refuse. And now, total indifference.'

Garris flicked his forefinger against the file. 'But this isn't indifference. This is the compulsive and costly accumulation of evidence. And there was risk involved in amassing it too. If one of the officers he contacted hadn't taken his bribes and had reported him, he'd probably be facing court right now.'

'I know,' I said. 'Right from the beginning, I've had this feeling that Campbell hasn't been telling me the whole truth about his interest in the case. It feels ... artificial, somehow. I can't explain it.'

'There's too much about this business that can't be explained. In fact, one of the only things that seems certain is that this isn't our murderer's first outing. As you've said, the lack of DNA is indicative. I wonder, have you considered a hibernating serial killer?'

I nodded. 'Yes. I think these killings are discrete. They have their set historical pattern that he will attempt to replicate. But it's such a fully formed idea – recreations of past tragedies – and so neatly executed, it feels like a template that's been used before. And if it has, then my guess is that his past murders were either never discovered or, as you say, happened a long time ago. So long ago they've slipped from our memory.'

'Or we didn't appreciate them for what they were at the time,' Garris said. 'Because, like now, the victims appeared to be unconnected and so the murders were never linked.'

'So he repeats this pattern every few years, maybe even every few decades? That must take huge self-control.'

'Well, we know he has that from the arrangement of the crime scenes,' Garris said. 'And there have been many cases of serial killers with big gaps between their activities. If our man fits the typical profile, he's likely to be a loner without a family or normal home life, although he may give the illusion he has one. Then there're all the typical traits: early age trauma, a record of petty offences from his childhood – theft, incidents of arson, maiming and killing animals. You know the sort of thing. He may appear superficially charismatic while having the psychopath's ability to mimic any emotions he doesn't actually feel. I'd say that goes double for this guy.' Garris tapped his pen against the reports. 'This sense of control will be evident in all his actions.'

I scribbled a few lines in my notebook, nodding along as he spoke. There were new insights here but much of what he said accorded with my own feel for the case. Still, it was good to have my theories validated.

'I'll take a look in all the usual databases,' he said. 'See if I can spot him among any old unsolved murders. I'll also take a look at the vics. I think you're right, Scott, they must be connected somehow.'

Finally, he picked up the last photo ever taken of us together, exiting the station after our second interview with Lenny Kerrigan. His lips set into a thin line.

'The Thierrot woman shot this, didn't she?'

'She did.'

'Bloody paparazzi. I know she was bothering you after you left prison. Is she still buzzing around?'

'I haven't seen her for weeks,' I said.

'Well, that's a blessing anyway.'

'Amen. So, any final thoughts?'

Garris stood back from the table where the photos and reports were fanned out like a kaleidoscope of pain and misery.

'Only that ...' He seemed to struggle for the right words. 'It doesn't seem real. Not like an actual case, know what I mean?'

I agreed. Everything about these murders had an air of heightened reality, almost like a detective story. It was as if the players had all been assembled onstage, the set appropriately dressed, the actors' lines rehearsed. Everyone just waiting for the detective to show up and go through the motions. Only he had turned up late, missing the curtain. I said as much to Garris and he agreed.

'Although, what good that idea does us, I don't know. Anyway, I should be heading back home. Harriet sends her best wishes by the way ... Oh, and Scott?'

'Yes?'

'Once you find him, you hand him over to us. You understand?'

'Of course.'

He stood at the door for a while, his gaze never leaving my face. 'I hope to God you do.'

Webster stirred as he pushed the door open. In the next moment, the juk was halfway across the trailer, barking his head off. Harry stood on the step, fist raised as if about to knock. I caught hold of Webster's collar and hauled him back.

'Sorry!' I shouted, hushing the juk as best I could. 'He'll like you once he gets to know you, I promise.'

Harry's frightened gaze flipped between Webster and Garris.

'Hello,' he said holding out his hand. 'Harry. Moorhouse.'

Garris shook his hand. 'Pete Garris. I'm a friend of Scott's. I've heard a lot about you, Harry.' He looked back at me over his shoulder as I settled Webster. 'One more thing before I go, Scott – remember your Sherlock Holmes. Goodbye, Mr Moorhouse.'

Harry moved aside to let Garris pass. A few seconds later, we heard the putter of his Honda turning out of the cul-de-sac. With Webster quieted, we stood looking at each other for a moment, smiling tight smiles.

'I'm sorry about last night,' we said together and burst out laughing.

'You go,' I said.

He ran fingers through that mop of mousy hair. 'I overreacted, running off like that.'

'You had every right,' I said. 'I guess I've just been a bit edgy lately and I didn't expect to find anyone in here. But I appreciated the note. Until I saw it, I was thinking of packing up and leaving—'

'No.' He came forward and Webster stirred at my feet. 'I . . . I'm glad you stayed.'

I knelt beside the old juk and gestured for Haz to join me. Very gingerly, he got to his knees, the look of stark terror on his face making me laugh again. I'd forgotten how scared he was of dogs.

'His bark really is worse than his bite.'

'Like his owner, then?' Harry said, a nervous smile breaking out.

'Just stroke him here, right behind his ear, and I swear he'll love you for ever.'

The low grumble emanating from Webster's belly gradually segued into delighted panting as Harry's fingers got to work. Pretty soon they were both grinning at each other.

'He's a cheap date.' I nodded.

'Hey.' Harry swatted my shoulder. 'Which one of us was that directed at?'

'Take your pick.'

'Where did he come from, anyway?' he asked. Webster was now showing his belly, a geriatric pooch reverting to his puppyhood. 'You didn't bring him with you.'

'A friend dropped him off,' I murmured.

'The one that just left?' He laid his hand against his cheek. 'I'm not sure I liked the look of him. Who is he?'

'He's easy to misread. That was Detective Inspector Peter Garris.' I sighed. 'One of the best coppers you could ever hope to meet . . . and my old boss.'

I suddenly felt tired of secrets. For his own sake, I didn't want to expose Harry to the complete reality of my world, but to keep everything from him – every facet of who I was and what had happened to me in those years since Oxford – that was no basis for starting again. If that was in fact what we were doing here.

'You were a police officer?' he asked. 'Are you still—?'

'No. Not for a while now.'

'Why? What happened?'

As our hands rolled through Webster's fur, our fingertips touched. He didn't pull away.

'I messed up,' I said. 'It didn't end well.'

'I'm sorry,' Harry said quietly. 'I bet you were a good police officer.'

I laughed. 'I was a horrifically bad police officer, but a pretty decent detective.'

'Of course you were! You always beat me at Cluedo. Used all your little tricks as well, I bet. Funny, I never thought of you as a detective, though. So what was he doing here? Was it a social call?'

I almost bust a gut. The idea of Pete Garris paying a social call was like the Ghost of Christmas Yet to Come popping in for a friendly natter.

'Now you're friends, do you fancy taking this old boy for a walk?' I asked. 'There are some things about me you probably need to know.'

Chapter Twenty-Two

I T WAS QUIET IN THE woods. The dank drizzle that had followed me from Anglesey had finally lifted and the last hour of daylight blazed among the treetops. We hadn't spoken much since leaving the bungalow. In fact, Webster had been a welcome distraction, trotting arthritically after the sticks Harry threw for him, allowing me some space to get my thoughts together. Something Garris had said kept nagging at me: '*Remember your Sherlock Holmes.*'

It had been a while since I'd read those old adventures, but one phrase of the great detective resonated: '*When you have eliminated the impossible, whatever remains, however improbable, must be the truth.*'

I glanced at the man walking beside me. I'd assured Garris that there was no way Harry could be involved. I knew him, had loved him, still loved him perhaps. But as my mentor had said, a decade is a long time. Could something have happened to Haz in those years? Some trauma that had twisted him into the faceless monster Miss Debney had seen in McAllister's doorway? Everything I knew about this kind of killer – how their perversions and fixations were moulded in the crucible of abusive childhoods – told me that Harry's involvement was unlikely. As I'd pointed out to Garris, the murder of his father had been an act of compassion, not ritualistic carnage. But still, doubt lingered.

I was stiff after my long drive, joints cracking as I bent down to take my turn with Webster's stick.

'Beautiful place,' I said.

I was being spoiled today – first that wild panorama of the Welsh bay and now the rustic charms of an English woodland. A light breeze crackled the canopy of sycamore and oak; pine needles snapped underfoot. Away to our left, a hidden stream chattered among the reeds.

Harry nodded. 'All part of the smiling face of Bradbury End. Don't be fooled, though. Fly-tippers are always dumping their rubbish into the river. There's a planning application the council are waving through to dig up half the forest for a new super-market. Oh yes, and the police are here every Saturday night, chasing the doggers out of the bushes.'

'Of those three, I sympathise most with the last,' I said.

''Course you do. You always were a champion of the underdog.'

We looked at each other and burst out laughing again.

'Anyway, talking of the police?'

'It was just a chance thing,' I shrugged. 'After leaving Oxford, I tried a few different jobs. None of them really took.' That's right, Scott, start as you mean to go on: all the pretty lies and omissions. I made a fist and remembered some of the blood that had flecked those knuckles in my thug-for-hire years. 'I just didn't want to go back to the fair,' I said. 'I don't know why. Only that it would feel like a kind of defeat.'

Harry crouched to collect the stick from Webster. 'Did you blame me?'

156

'What? No. Why would you even—?'

'Because I was probably the only thing keeping you there. After Dad ...' He stroked Webster's tattered ear, kept his head down. 'After I left, you had nothing much to stay for. You hated your studies, you were never great at making new friends. So you drifted?'

'I did.'

And if only you knew what I drifted into, Haz, I'm not sure you'd be looking at me with such sympathy right now.

'If I'd stayed, we might have figured out the future together, I suppose,' he said.

I hunkered down beside him. Our hands touched as I took the stick and launched it between the trees. 'You didn't owe me anything, Haz. Not an explanation, certainly not any duty of care. I was just grateful for the time we had together.'

His face tightened. We stood, brushed off our knees, and continued down the path.

'So,' he said, 'what happened next? Because as I remember things, you were never all that comfortable around authority. What got Scott Jericho into a police uniform?'

There was a layered question. The steps that led me to become Detective Constable Jericho were simple enough, but the motivations behind them, conscious and unconscious? I guess a psychiatrist might interpret joining the force as the ultimate 'fuck you' to my father. It isn't that Travellers are actively hostile to authority, but almost every minority has a complex history when it comes to the police. It's certainly not a career option taken by any showman I've ever heard of. And by joining up I'd known that returning would not be an easy option.

'Garris interviewed me,' I said. 'I'd been a witness to a case he was investigating. I managed to provide him with a few details that led to an arrest.'

'What kind of case?'

'A child murder. Some poor street kid apparently robbed and cut up and dumped in a canal. The theory was a drug deal gone wrong. The kid was a pusher on the lowest rung of the ladder and the police suspected he'd been dipping into the take. The state of the body seemed to back up the idea. He'd been ...' I glanced at Harry; this was his first glimpse into the shadows of my world, 'made an example of.'

'What do you mean?'

'His face had been mutilated. His nose cut off.'

'Jesus.'

He looked suddenly very pale, which was actually a kind of comfort. I doubted if the killer of Robert McAllister would be so squeamish.

'How did you get involved?'

'I was passing by the canal that night. I happened to hear a splash and then saw a man leaving the scene. By the time I reached the towpath, the body had floated out of sight and I just assumed it was someone dumping their trash. The place was like a graveyard for broken fridges and busted mattresses. Anyway, when I heard about the kid, I contacted the officer in charge, DI Peter Garris. I'd only seen the man from the back, but what I told Garris changed pretty much everything.'

'Well? Don't leave me hanging.'

'The man had a pronounced indentation in his hair,' I said. 'Right around the back of his head at the level of his ears. Grey-haired, around fifty, so probably not a baseball cap. Something he wore habitually, possibly for work. As the streetlight caught him, I also saw this light mud splatter on the back of his left trouser leg. It started at his ankle and reached just below the back of his knee.'

'And?'

'My guess was a hotel porter. The indentation was from his cap. The mud splatter from where he opened taxi doors for hotel guests and then the taxi's back wheel sprayed him a little as it pulled away. Whichever side of the street the hotel was on, he'd always be facing the guest and away from the driver as he opened the door, so it would always be the left leg that got dirty while the right remained clean. He hadn't changed his clothes, so he'd probably come straight from work to meet the kid, which meant the hotel must have been reasonably close by. Garris didn't give anything away while we chatted. He just thanked me for my time and showed me out. It was only later that I heard the kid's stepfather worked as a porter at the Majestic, and that the kid had been threatening to tell his mother about the years of abuse he'd suffered at the bastard's hands.'

Harry blew out his cheeks. 'Wow. So how did things develop from there?'

'My regular back then was a pub called The Three Crowns. It wasn't far from the local cop shop and I'd often see police in there after finishing their shift.' I didn't tell Harry that I'd chosen that particular pub because it was such a favourite of the force. After finishing my own activities for the day, I'd wanted a place where none of my underworld associates would choose to gather. 'Garris spied me in a corner one night and we got chatting. I think I'd impressed him by identifying the porter.'

'I'm not surprised. You always had sharp eyes. I couldn't get away with anything when we were together . . .'

Harry caught himself, and I quickly filled the pause.

'Garris asked me about my background. I told him that Travellers are great observers and are pretty good at weighing people up at a glance. After that night, we met fairly regularly and he eventually started discussing some of his current cases. General things at first, but I always seemed to pick up on a thread or two that he'd missed. It took maybe six months for him to persuade me to fill in the application form.'

'So why did you? Weren't you satisfied in your current work?'

Beating up crooks for other crooks? No, Harry, my job satisfaction wasn't all that high.

'You know I'd always liked puzzles,' I said instead. 'Of course, I had to do my time in uniform before I could join Garris in CID. But even at street level, there were problems to solve. Sometimes what appeared to be a simple mugging could be more surprising than the most brutal serial murder. It's human nature that's fascinating, not the crimes themselves.'

'I can see why that would appeal to you,' he said. 'It was the human drama you loved in stories. I think that's why it broke your heart to pick them apart.'

I'd never really thought of it that way, but Harry was right. I've always been a sucker for a good story.

'Garris used his influence to fast-track me through uniform,' I went on. 'I wasn't much use to him outside CID. That kind of preferential treatment didn't do me any favours with my colleagues, though. They started calling me the "Fortune Teller".'

'Let me guess: because your success solving cases was almost spooky?'

'That was what they said to my face,' I nodded. 'But it was a backhanded compliment. There was jealousy about how I'd progressed so quickly, and then someone found out about my background. Couple that with the rumour I was gay, we get them casting me as the effeminate Fortune Teller. All the usual chauvinism and homophobia, but now with an extra layer of prejudice against Travellers. It was a heady mix.'

'I'm so sorry, Scott. Did Garris try to put a stop to it?'

I shook my head. 'Not his style.'

'But he liked you?'

'Honestly?' I shrugged. 'I'm not sure he likes anyone much. Except for his wife. He was . . .' I took the stick from Webster and swatted the tall grass that fringed the path, 'fascinated by me, I guess. I don't know. I was useful to him, anyway.'

We had emerged into a clearing, the pine-needle path cutting away to a distant band of trees, the bruised sky darkening overhead. The river sounded closer now, though it remained hidden behind a curtain of swaying reed.

As Harry spoke again, I glimpsed three figures waiting up ahead. They sat together on a low stone parapet: Sonia and her brothers, legs dangling, arms folded, charred faces turned towards me. My ghosts waiting for me on Travellers Bridge.

'So what happened?' Harry asked. 'Why did you leave the police?'

The children cocked their heads as if listening.

'I let a killer escape,' I said softly. 'I failed and—'

Away to my right, beyond the hidden river, something sparkled among the trees. A bright pinpoint of moving light, disappearing now between the boughs. The same reflective glimmer, I felt certain, that I'd seen in the woods around Marco's diner.

Chapter Twenty-Three

A LIGHT IN THE TREES THAT seemed to follow me, no matter the forest. Was I actually losing it? I suppose I'd come to view my haunting by the Malanowski kids as a kind of justice. They had seeped between the cracks of my sanity and taken up residence in my broken mind. I could accommodate them, rationalise them, even, because their presence was no more than I deserved. But this pursuing glimmer? That I couldn't make sense of.

Then again, maybe it wasn't a psychological tic at all. I'd taken more than my share of blows over the years – fights with the joskins at school when I'd been a bratty, self-conscious fairground chavvy; endless fists to the skull in darkened alleys during those thug-for-hire years; then the inevitable knock-abouts any young constable experiences. Maybe a bit of wiring had finally come loose, sparking the illusion of reflected light.

Except for that first time near the roadside diner, Kerrigan had seen it too . . .

'Are you OK?' Harry asked, following my gaze.

'Yeah.' I turned back to him, shaking my head. 'Doesn't matter. What were we saying?'

'You were talking about why you left the police.'

I glanced back at the bridge. 'There were three kids,' I said softly. 'Sonia, Pietro and Tomasz. I was the night duty detective and took the call ...'

It took under ten minutes to describe how my life – and, more importantly, the lives of the Malanowski family – had come apart. My voice sounded detached throughout, as if my actions since that night hadn't tortured my every waking moment. It was a deliberate choice. If I'd shown the anguish and grief I was feeling, I knew Harry would have comforted me, and I didn't deserve his comfort. Still, when I reached the part where I beat Kerrigan to a bloody pulp, I pulled back on the detail. It was a cowardly thing to do, but I couldn't risk frightening Harry away.

'You went to prison?' he said in a small voice.

'I got out a couple of months ago.'

'Scott ...'

'It's fine. I deserved jail and more for what I did.'

And you got more inside, didn't you? a mean little voice whispered inside my head.

'You reacted how anyone might have, given the circumstances,' Harry murmured. 'To see those little kids like that.'

'It was no excuse,' I said. 'I was supposed to be a professional. I promised Jan Malanowski that I would put the bastard who murdered his babies behind bars. Instead, I assaulted our prime suspect, making any evidence we had against him next to useless. Any barrister worth their salt could have ripped our case to shreds after that, and the CPS knew it. And so they turned their attention to me. I was the one who ended up inside and all I gave Kerrigan was the keys to my house. I failed Garris and my colleagues, but most of all I failed those kids.'

Finally, my voice cracked and Harry reached for me, as I knew he would. I put up my palm, gesturing him away.

'How was it?' he said. 'Inside?'

'It was justice,' I said simply.

We stood there, letting the burble of the stream fill the stillness. He was searching for the right words, the right questions, and I didn't know how to help him. Maybe this whole ridiculous dream of us getting back together would always flounder at these moments.

'So you went back to the fair?' he said at last.

'It was the only place I could go back to. The only people who would take me back, anyway.'

He flinched at that. 'So what are you doing now? You're not just a researcher for Campbell, are you? There's something else going on here.'

Harry didn't possess the skills of a detective, but he had his own subtle instincts. He had always known when there was something going on with me. At that moment, I felt an almost irresistible urge to tell him everything. To roll the dice and see what came of it. But then I thought back to my debrief with Garris. We had looked dispassionately over the unfolding horror of the case, talking theories and deductions as if these weren't individual lives sadistically cut short. Did I really want Harry to be a part of that darkness? And did I want him to see how drawn I was to it?

'I am looking into something for Campbell,' I said. 'And it isn't just the tragedy of the Jericho freaks. But it is related in some way and I—'

'Something criminal?' He frowned. 'Was that why Garris was here? Scott, I don't understand any of this. How can the accidental deaths of five people over a century ago be something the police are interested in now? Do they think it wasn't an accident? I mean, even if they did, all this happened so long ago.'

'Harry. I just ... I need you to trust me, OK?'

He didn't hesitate. 'Of course. I've always trusted you.'

Then why didn't you stay? The question hovered on my lips.

'I am working a case,' I said. 'And if I could, I'd rather keep you out of it.'

'But why? Is it dangerous?'

'It is to a small number of people. But that doesn't include you.'

'Then why—?'

'Look, there are parts of a police officer's life that he never shares. Not with his partner, not with his friends. Because he knows, if he peels back the surface and shows them what the world is really like, they won't thank him for it. They might even come to hate him. They won't want to, they'll fight against it, but the resentment will always be there. No one can cope with too much reality, you see?'

'How do you cope with it, then?' he asked. 'Alone?'

'I do my best.'

I think he wanted to keep questioning me, but by then we'd reached Travellers Bridge and I had squatted down to read the inscription. It had been eroded by the years, the letters of *Acclinis Falsis Animus Meliora Recusat* worn shallow. I ran my fingers across the motto, scraping away some of the moss that had overgrown it. Then I stood and looked over the parapet into the stream. Where once a raging torrent had claimed old 'Slip-Jointed' Jericho and his caravan, now little more than a narrow brook burbled between the piers.

'They diverted the main river a few years ago,' Harry said as if reading my mind.

'It all looks pretty much forgotten.' I picked a pebble from the bridge deck and dropped it into the dark green waters. 'Makes me wonder why they're making such a fuss of the anniversary.'

He shrugged. 'It has a kind of fairy-tale fascination for the locals, I think. The Contortionist and the Electric Lady and the Balloon-Headed Horror and the rest, all drowning in their river. Every town has its ghost story.'

'Except that these were real people,' I said.

'They were.' He joined me at the parapet. 'Only, we're all characters in each other's stories, aren't we? That's why it's so surprising when the people we know do things we don't expect. It feels as if they've betrayed the role they have in our narrative. I mean, look up there.'

Against the purpling twilight, a breathtaking display was in progress. A billow of birds, bulging and breaking and reforming in the air. As we watched, the swarm suddenly arrowed towards the earth and, in one dark swoop, winnowed the tall grass of the clearing. Then the flock swept on, high above our heads, losing its shape beyond the trees.

'Most young birds return to their nests after their first flight,' Harry said. 'But not swifts. Once they start flying, they don't stop. Not for two years or more. They sleep and eat on the wing, taking insects as they go, swooping down for mouthfuls of water from the rivers. They leave their homes and their parents behind for ever.' He turned to me and touched the side of my face. 'You were supposed to be like that, Scott. You were supposed to fly for ever.'

I cupped my hand over his. 'Harry ...'

I can't say why I didn't see the house when I first stepped onto the bridge. It was certainly large enough – a great, black, ruined presence, the struts of its roof poking through the trees like broken fingers. True, it had been half-swallowed by the forest and the light was failing, but it stood only a few hundred metres from the river. There was a sort of furtiveness to it, as if those boarded-up windows enjoyed watching us from the shadows.

'What is that place?'

Harry followed my gaze. 'The old Matthers-Hillstrom house? Bit creepy, eh?'

'Hillstrom?'

'Ancestor of our current mayor.'

'The same Gideon Hillstrom who built the bridge?'

'That's the guy. I think he built the house a few years later. The Matthers were distant cousins who bought the place from the Hillstroms a couple of decades back. It's been falling to pieces for thirty years or more.'

'But why would Gideon want to build a house overlooking the river where five people died?'

Harry shrugged. 'It's a pretty spot, I suppose.'

I shook my head. 'What happened to it?'

'That's another Bradbury End ghost story. In the late '70s, the last of the Matthers came to live here. The father had died in a car accident the year before and apparently, their family home held too many memories, so his widow decided to move to the ancestral pile. She had one son, a boy of about eight. That local historian I mentioned, Roebuck, he knows all there is to know about what happened, which isn't much. Mother and son kept to themselves and were rarely seen in the town. I think the kid was home-schooled or something. Anyway, one night some local teens got drunk and came up here causing trouble. I guess by then the Matthers' house had got a bit of a reputation. You know what small towns are like.'

'I'm beginning to know what Bradbury End is like,' I muttered. 'Not fond of outsiders?'

Harry gave a grim nod. 'It started with taunts and escalated to stone-throwing and broken windows. The kid got spooked. I suppose after what happened to his dad, he felt protective towards his mother. Anyway, I don't know what he was thinking, but he wrapped some kind of cloth around an old broom handle, doused it in lighter fluid, and set it on fire. Next thing, the whole house is ablaze.'

'Did they get out?'

'I'm not sure. I think the kid survived but maybe the mother didn't make it.'

I stared into the darkening doorway of the ruined house.

All I could think of was the fire-blighted face of Miss Barton looking back at me.

Chapter Twenty-Four

THE ROTTED DOOR YIELDED TO my shoulder and the breath of old house swarmed out to greet us. This wasn't the same kind of stink as Miss Debney's cottage. That had been the cloying odour of a living death; this was the smell of mould and absence and decay. We thumbed torchlight from our phones and swept it through the gloom.

'You'd think they'd lock up the place more securely,' I said.

My voice didn't echo but seemed to sink into the emptiness.

'I reckon they've given up trying.' Harry ran his light across flame-scorched walls covered with graffiti tags. On the floor at the foot of the stairs, a couple of stained mattresses lay side by side, springs twirling through, full of the rusty promise of lockjaw. 'Anyway, the kids seem to have got bored of their local haunted house. Hardly anyone comes here now.'

'Someone's been here,' I said.

Before going inside, I'd secured Webster's leash to one of the porch posts. He now gave us a weary blink and immediately sank his head to his forepaws.

Harry and I stepped over the threshold. Pushing through swags of spider web, we crossed the uncarpeted hall, careful to avoid the broken glass and discarded syringes that littered the floor. At the stairs, I nudged aside one of the mattresses with the toe of my boot and examined the first footprint on the step.

'Trainer, size ten. Fake brand.'

'How can you tell?' Harry asked.

'Pattern of the imprint. The circles are irregular and unevenly spaced. Brands take pride in that kind of nonsense.'

'So what does that tell you?'

'Not much. Other than that, from the sharpness of the print, he was here recently.'

'Do you think it has anything to do with your case?'

It was then that I noticed the top-hatted stick figure carved into the newel post, its limbs set at odd angles, a two-dimensional echo of the artist's mannikin propped in Robert McAllister's trailer window. And below this, a penknife scratch of letters: *AFAMR*. The initials of the bridge motto. The faceless creature who had spared Miss Debney and slaughtered three others had been here all right, and the footprints belonged to him. As he'd turned to carve his calling cards, the outline of his right trainer had been scuffed and blurred in the dust.

'It could rule out an obvious suspect,' I said.

I followed the path of the footprints with my eyes. As I'd said to Garris, unless Campbell was a consummate actor, there was no way he was capable of walking up a flight of stairs unaided. And Miss Barton? Those tiny feet slopping around in a pair of size ten trainers? The image was almost laughable.

I'd taken the first couple of steps when Harry grabbed the back of my jacket.

'What are you doing? This whole building could come down at any moment.'

'I have to check something out,' I said. 'You can wait outside, I won't be a minute.'

His lips set into a thin line, but still, he followed as I edged my way up the staircase. Like the killer, I kept away from the bannister, my shoulder to the wall where the stair was more firmly planted. Nevertheless, the whole structure shuddered as we ascended.

At the landing, I paused for a moment and took in the view of the hall. A large transom window above the door, now masked with bloated boards, must once have flooded light into this airy space. With the rich hue of its rosewood staircase, it would have been an impressive sight. I couldn't help being reminded of Campbell's palatial house in the Cambridgeshire Fens, and suddenly the image of his paederast's gallery super-imposed itself over this hollowed-out hall.

The idea that, despite the footprints, he might have been the boy who grew up here followed me into the first bedroom. Decades of decay couldn't disguise that this had once been a child's room. Stepping inside, I ran my fingers across tongues of curling wallpaper. Beyond a window glazed with webs, the sun had vanished and a shaft of milky moonlight shone against the wall. Here I could make out fire-damaged fawns and satyrs, sea serpents and medusas. Had this been a young Ralph Campbell's inspiration for a lifetime's devotion to history?

Moving to the window, I rubbed a circle in the soot-blackened pane. Directly below: the glint of the stream and the white arch of the bridge, almost spectral in the gloom. For a lonely child shut up here, with only his mother for company, might he have developed a fascination for this view and the local legend that lay behind it? An obsession twisted in some way by the trauma of the fire he had started? Both Garris and I had considered that the murders were not an end in themselves but parts of a design that had some larger purpose. Could it be that the killer was trying to reclaim something of his childhood in these ritualistic acts? Staging his victims like offerings to the past?

The idea had its attractions but again I came back to the fact that it couldn't have been Campbell or Miss Barton who carved the figure and initials on the newel post and then climbed those stairs.

I was still looking down at the bridge when the light caught my eye. There it was again, the shimmer in the trees. Only, was it different this time? Two pinpricks of reflected illumination now? I motioned Harry to join me at the window.

'Do you see that?'

He glanced down to where I was pointing. I held my breath. I had thought Kerrigan had seen it too, but was that just wishful thinking? Maybe I really was losing my mind.

'The light?' he said, and I let go of my breath. 'What is it?'

'I'm going to find out.' I took him by the shoulders and stationed him where I had been standing. 'Wait here.'

'But, Scott—'

I moved as quickly as I dared across the groaning floorboards and into the corridor. The stairs juddered as I took them two at a time. Skirting the used needles and rancid mattresses, I paused at the door. Whatever was waiting out there, I wanted to surprise it, and so took a moment to catch my breath. It was then that an ugly thought ran through my head: just a few days ago, guilt and grief would not have allowed me to stand in this burned-out shell. The flashbacks to the Malanowski home would have overwhelmed me. Was I beginning to leave the ghosts of Sonia and her brothers behind? The idea made me feel sick.

I threw open the door.

There, beyond the bridge, the lights still waited. They seemed duller now, weaker, and unlike earlier today, there were definitely *two* pinpricks shining out.

As I started across the porch, the lights began to flicker between the trees. They were moving, retreating into the depths of the forest. Then suddenly they seemed to swing downwards and, in the next moment, disappeared altogether. I swore under my breath and plunged on, making for the spot where I had first glimpsed them. Behind me, Webster had woken in a fit of barking.

The gravel that carpeted the deck of the old bridge spat out like shrapnel under my boots. On the far side, I was forced to stop and listen. I shouted at Webster to hush and, obedient juk that he was, he immediately quieted. I glanced over my shoulder, back towards the Matthers' house and the boy's bedroom window. Harry stood there, pointing to a place away to my right.

I set off again, heart hammering. Roots caught at my feet, stray branches lashed my face. I stumbled, righted myself, stung my palm against some creeping vine. I could hear him now, breathing heavily, his shadow lunging against the moonlight. A slender figure but out of shape, slowing already. I put on a burst of speed, tore a path through thorn and bracken.

My fingers had just brushed his collar when the ground gave way beneath us. I tried to step back, making a grab for him as he let out a startled squeal. I did my best to pull him away from the dip, grasping the hood of his jacket, but in so doing he tipped us both forward. Though the gully wasn't all that deep, we fell hard, limbs entwined, him kicking out at me as we tumbled. Hitting the summer-hardened earth, his foot connected with my mouth and I tasted a flash of blood.

'You animal!' he shrieked. 'You maniac!'

'*You lunatic! You maniac!*' The words Jan Malanowski had shouted at me from the dock as I was sentenced for the attack on Kerrigan. '*You let him get away.*'

But it wasn't Jan lying on the forest floor, spitting insults at me. I staggered to my feet, took out my phone, thumbed the torch. A stranger blinked in the light – thinning blond hair plastered to his scalp, brown eyes bordering on black, a plump, boyish face scored with the cares of middle age. He was wearing a Gortex raincoat and had a strap twisted around his neck like a noose, something black and heavy hanging from it. I moved my light to the object attached to the lanyard and two pinpricks began to shimmer.

'Who are you?' I demanded. 'Why have you been watching me?'

One of the cracked binocular lenses stared back at me like the elliptical eye of a cat. Even then I knew this wasn't the reflected light I had seen earlier today nor in the wood outside Marco's diner. Maybe it was that knowledge that made me so angry. Just when I thought I'd made some progress with the case, all I had uncovered was a new mystery.

'You animal,' he repeated, unwinding the chokehold of the lanyard as he shuffled away from me. 'You maniac.'

Ignoring the mental echo of Jan Malanowski, I stepped forward and attempted to help the stranger to his feet. He grasped my arm and, as soon as he was upright, thrust his palms into my chest. It was petty, playground stuff, like being shoved by a toddler, but still, it ignited a burst of rage. When he tried it again, I grasped his thin wrist and shook him hard.

'Why were you spying on us? What do you want?'

'Sp-spying?' The blood ran from his face. He had seen something in me, and whatever it was, it scared him half to death. 'I wasn't spying. I was tw-twitching.'

'You're twitching right now,' I said. 'Is that some kind of technical term for a peeping Tom? Hoping to get a glimpse of the doggers in the bushes maybe?'

'Tw-twitching is birdwatching,' he stammered. 'Rare birds. I heard a nigh-nightingale had been spotted here. Then I saw lights in the Matthers' house. It was my public duty to investigate. Next thing I know, I'm being attacked by an an-animal.'

'Careful,' I muttered.

'A maniac.'

I was barely conscious of what I was doing. Hadn't even realised I'd pulled back my fist until Harry called out to me from the ridge above.

'Scott!'

I blinked, lowered my hand, released the stranger. Meanwhile, Harry edged his way down the incline and came to stand between us. He turned to the man, who shrank back.

'Mr Carmody. I'm so sorry. Scott didn't mean to ...'

Carmody, deputy mayor. Errand boy and chief licker of Hillstrom's fat arse, as my dad had described him. Those dark brown eyes flicked from me to Harry.

'You're the librarian, aren't you?' His terror gone, he quickly pulled on the pettiness of his office. 'Yes, I recognise you. Encouraging all this protest nonsense about the branch closures, so we hear. Not your place, of course. A breach of your contract, in fact. And now breaking and entering private property and associating with common thugs.' He gave me the kind of look you'd reserve for an especially pungent piece of dog shit. 'What will we do with you?'

'None of this is Harry's fault,' I said. 'I'm sorry about the misunderstanding. If I can just explain?'

He brandished his phone with a flourish. 'Oh, you can make all the explanations you please. To the police.'

I tried to avoid Harry's gaze. Assaulting the deputy mayor of Bradbury End. That would be my parole conditions breached. By morning, I'd be back inside.

Chapter Twenty-Five

I SAT ON A THIN RUBBER mattress, head in my hands, listening to the drunk in the next cell murdering Bruce Springsteen's greatest hits. 'Born to Run' was being joyfully bludgeoned to death for the twentieth time that morning. Closing my eyes against the glare of the white breezeblocks, I lay down.

A light sweat layered my back and my legs felt shaky. No weaning dose of Zopiclone and benzo for me last night. I thought back to the snap of handcuffs, the sight of Carmody giving his report to one of the officers. Harry's anguished face strobing in the blue lights. He'd seen it again. The rage and darkness that had made their home inside me.

I tried to ignore the ache that memory provoked and focused again on the case. It hadn't been the deputy mayor of Bradbury End who'd been following me. The shimmer I'd seen earlier in the day and near Marco's diner had been a single glint, but perhaps something like Carmody's binoculars had reflected the light. I turned possibilities over in my head: a handheld mirror, a phone screen, even the absurd idea of a monocle. Nothing I could picture seemed likely, so I went back to Carmody himself.

Did his reason for being in the woods at night stack up? When he'd pushed me in the chest, I had noticed a small rectangular bulge in his jacket pocket. A birdwatcher's manual maybe? He had the pettifogging air of a small-town politician, so his sense of civic duty on seeing trespassers in an abandoned property probably rang true. And then there was his sudden change of heart when he heard me give my name to the officers. His boss Hillstrom had been keen for the Jericho Fair to be involved in the town's anniversary celebrations and here he was, making an official complaint against a man of that name. I saw him again in the car park at the edge of the forest, a blue vein throbbing at his temple.

'Perhaps I overreacted,' he'd bleated. 'Can't you just give him a ticking off, Constable?'

Unluckily for Carmody, the officers who'd arrived on the scene were the two I'd humiliated outside the library earlier the previous day. The bird-faced prick and his ginger-bearded colleague.

'Afraid not, sir,' Redbeard had pouted. 'Clear case of assault, you see.' Then, in a whispered aside to me: 'Got ya.'

My mind moved back through the woods to the Matthers' house. Was the story of the mother and son who had lived there really connected to the case? If not, why had the killer visited that burned-out ruin? Perhaps simply as an act of exploration, scoping out the area before he started his grim enterprise. The child's bedroom window did give a spectacular view of the scene of the historical tragedy. But let's say the house was more personally connected to him, who did that suggest? Mayor Hillstrom, whose great-grandfather had built the place? Carmody, who was about the right age to have been the Matthers boy?

Or, despite everything that suggested otherwise, Professor Ralph Campbell? The figure I'd seen in the road beyond the rail crossing had been about the right height and build for both Campbell and Carmody.

I opened my eyes. The drunk next door seemed to have finally completed his massacre of Springsteen's back catalogue. I lifted my hands and examined the cuts and scratches from the forest. All this reflection was pointless. If I was convicted of the assault on Carmody, the remainder of my jail time for Kerrigan would come into play. By the time I got out, the killer would have completed his masterpiece while I . . .

I turned my face to the wall. No. I couldn't go back. Couldn't repeat the things I'd done to survive that place. When Kerrigan had come to the fair, bandying about the rumours, I'd made light of them, but the humiliation of what they'd done to me at Hazelhurst? The degradation? I'd rather die than endure that again.

The cell door screeched open. I turned over just as the custody sergeant entered. He was a wiry man of about fifty with the same patient, no-nonsense expression sported by every CS I'd ever known. Coming forward, he handed me my boots.

'You've been lucky, son,' he said. 'Must have a few friends high up. But then, I guess you knew that from the call you made last night.'

So it seemed Pete Garris had worked a minor miracle on my behalf. Pulling on my boots, I was about to head out when the CS laid a hand on my shoulder.

'Go careful,' he advised. 'Your story's all over the station this morning, and though you acted like a proper twat in that case with the Polish kiddies, a lot of us get it. We've all seen our

179

share of horrors on the job. Times when we'd have liked to have done exactly what you did. I don't need to tell you that's no excuse, but ... Well, there but for the grace of God. Just try and keep out of trouble, all right?'

I promised him I'd try.

In reception, I found two father figures waiting for me. My dad sprang out of a plastic chair, smoothing down his salt-and-pepper moustache, trying his best not to look pissed off. Garris stood also. The dark rings under Pete's eyes suggested he'd probably been up all night nursing Harriet. The thought that he'd had to abandon his sick wife again on my behalf made my stomach curdle.

'You fucking dinlo,' my dad said through clenched teeth. 'What did you think you were playing at? You could've got our licence to trade revoked.'

'That would never have happened,' I replied. 'I'm not associated with the fair.'

'You're *always* associated,' he snapped back. 'You've got my name, ain't ya?'

'Wow.' I nodded. 'Your concern for my welfare is always so touching. You do know I'd have gone back to Hazelhurst if I'd been convicted, right?'

'And whose fault would that have been? You're your own worst enemy, Scott.'

'Gentlemen,' Garris slipped in between us, 'the reception of what I believe you call the "gavvers' gaff" isn't the ideal place for family disputes. Scott, it might interest you to learn that, after you called me last night, I touched base with your father. He immediately got in contact with the mayor and deputy mayor, both of whom agreed to use their influence to get the charges dropped. I then put in a word myself. In that sense, it was a team effort, joskin and Traveller working together. Now, maybe you should shake hands?'

We did, somewhat awkwardly. I still wasn't convinced that saving the fair hadn't been my dad's priority.

'Anyway,' he muttered, 'your boss here has reassured me that this nonsense you're involved with doesn't pose a threat to us. So I suppose I owe you an apology on that score.'

'Yeah,' I said, 'you probably do. I mean, you took a stranger's word over mine.'

'I'd call that the wisdom of experience,' he snorted. 'By the way, we're pulling onto the heath today, so if you could stop assaulting town dignitaries for five minutes, it would be appreciated. And that chap Zac's been asking after you again. Christ knows why.'

With a nod to Garris, he stormed out of the station.

'You know he's right,' Garris said. 'You do have to be more careful. What started you off on this Carmody fellow, anyway?'

Once articulated, the idea of the pursuing light seemed utterly ridiculous, but Garris had known even more obscure hunches of mine to pay off. He didn't dismiss it anyway, though he seemed equally mystified.

'When you were doing that background for me on Campbell, did you find anything about his childhood?' I asked. 'His family, where he was brought up?'

Garris took out his phone and checked through his files. 'Didn't think it'd be relevant so didn't mention it. Ah, yes, here it is. Brought up in Cambridgeshire. Both parents died while he was at university – thank God they didn't live to see what a monster he became, eh? Though, I think parents always know.

181

This Barton woman who had been his nanny stayed on as a kind of housekeeper-guardian figure. Why do you ask?'

I told him the story of the Matthers' house and its occupants.

'Like a Gothic fairy tale, isn't it?' he said as I finished. 'Widowed mother and young son, shunned by the townsfolk, tormented by local children until the inevitable tragedy occurs. But, as you suspected, nothing to do with Campbell and his somewhat sinister nanny. Though, I suppose it fits in with what we were talking about yesterday. That sense of unreality surrounding the case. I don't know, Scott. It feels like a distraction.'

'What about the stick figure and the bridge initials carved into the newel post?'

'You suspect that was the killer,' he said. 'But you don't actually know. It might just be another coincidence. A remote one, I grant you, but this case does seem full of them.'

'OK. But before I let it go, can you check one more background for me?'

He sighed when I gave him Carmody's name.

'He was watching the house last night,' I said. 'And I'm still not sure I completely buy that birdwatching explanation.'

Garris nodded. He looked tired and, for the first time since I'd known him, horribly frail. 'Look,' I said, 'forget about it. Get yourself back to Harriet. She needs you more than I do.'

He shrugged. 'I don't think my wife needs me at all. Harriet went into the hospice this morning. She's so doped up now, I'm not sure she even knows I'm there. I sat by her bed most of last night, holding her hand and ... Nothing. She's as good as gone, poor love.'

'Oh God, Pete. I'm so sorry.'

He blinked at me, dry-eyed as ever. 'She knew I loved her. That's a comfort. As for all this.' He made a vague gesture to the town that spread out beyond the reception window. 'It's actually nice to have something else to think about. I'll check out Carmody with pleasure. What about you?'

I looked again at my hands, scratched and filthy from the forest. 'I have an apology to make,' I said. 'Bridges to mend. If I can.'

'The Moorhouse boy? Just be careful there. You're no fool but sometimes you're too trusting. I'm still not comfortable with the idea of him being here in Bradbury End.' He held up his hand when I tried to argue. 'I'm only saying: be on your guard. For all that hard-man bluster, you're a sentimentalist at heart. It can blind you to what's right before your eyes. Anyway, what's your next move?'

I thought back to Campbell and the crime scenes photographs.

'I think it's time I visited the Electric Lady,' I said.

Chapter Twenty-Six

BACK AT THE TRAILER, I could barely get the key in the lock fast enough. Once inside, I went straight to those pill boxes lined up on the shelf. My head was pounding, my tongue was like a leather strap, and lights danced before my eyes. My hands shook so badly, I almost spilled the bottle of water Harry had left for me. I threw a couple of capsules down my throat and then collapsed onto the bed.

After twenty minutes or so, the trembling stopped. Still, I wound the sheets around my fists and stared up at the ceiling. I'd been stupid to think I could manage this alone. Hadn't I dealt with enough addicts in my time on the force? I should've known trying to wean myself off painkillers and sedatives wouldn't end well. Once the case was over, once I had time to surrender to the withdrawal symptoms, I'd get some help. Until then, I'd have to placate my addiction.

Because that's what it was. Addiction. Just like sex with Zac and the rest. A way to cope and to forget. Except none of it had worked.

Not until Campbell had brought me this case.

I eased myself off the mattress and stood up. The trailer remained steady under my feet. Pulling aside my collar, I took a brief sniff and almost gagged. An overnight stay in a police cell did not make for a pleasing bouquet. If I had any hope of mending bridges with Haz, it would probably be best if I didn't smell like I lived under one. The tremors had been so bad when the taxi dropped me off, I hadn't looked to see whether he was home. Now I squirted some deodorant under my armpits and headed for the door.

An envelope squeezed through a gap in the jamb stopped me in my tracks. My name printed on the front in that familiar hand. I tore it open. This would be his goodbye. He had seen too much of the man I had become and didn't want to see any more.

Dear Scott,

I went to the police station first thing but one of the officers from last night was there and said you were sleeping.

Bullshit. I hadn't slept a wink. Just a bit of extra cruelty on the part of Redbeard or Birdface.

I've had to go into work this morning. Today's the day of the library protest and it's bound to be mayhem. Don't worry about Webster — Val and the girls love dogs and we'll keep him quiet in the back office. I'm enclosing the house key, so if they let you out before I try to see you again at lunchtime, please feel free to use the shower and ransack the fridge.

I hope you're OK, Scott.
Let's talk later, if we can.
Hx

I felt my heart expand in my chest. He hadn't been scared away. We might still have a chance.

If I wanted to carry out my plan for the next stage of the investigation, then I needed to call Campbell. But that could wait an hour. First, I had to see Harry. I took a quick shower, devoured four slices of toast (word to the wise – if you ever happen to overnight at Her Majesty's pleasure, never accept the offer of breakfast), pulled on a fresh T-shirt and trans-ferred my notebook to the back pocket of a clean pair of jeans.

I had no doubt that, confiscating my possessions last night, the police would have tried to read the contents. If they'd been able, I might have had serious questions to answer. From an early age, however, I'd been in the habit of encrypting anything important in a code my father had taught me. Secretiveness runs deep in the travelling community and many old-timers scrawl their account books in this impen-etrable cypher. No tax man has yet broken it. Anyhow, the details of my investigation would have read like badly written poetry.

The traffic was horrendous as I headed into town. I didn't have to look far to see the cause. Up ahead, a dozen brightly painted Travellers' lorries crawled at a snail's pace through the winding streets. I couldn't help but smile. It might be a dying industry, but the arrival of the fair could still work its old magic. On either side of the road, little kids clutched their parents' sleeves and pointed excitedly.

Meanwhile, I drummed my fingertips on the steering wheel. I thought of my dad on the heath, waving rides into their designated spots. I thought of Sal and Jodie setting up their candyfloss stall. I thought of Zac laying out the baseplates of Urnshaw's dodgems. Anything to distract me from the nervous jitter of my stomach. I knew Garris still had his doubts about Harry's presence here, but the idea of him being involved in these murders was preposterous.

Parking in the multi-storey across the road, I made my way to the library. The protest was in full swing, a forest of placards waving in the air. Like the chants, the slogans were all fairly sedate: HANDS OFF OUR BOOKS! SAVE BRADBURY END LIBRARY! RESPECT OUR LIBRARIANS! All they were missing was a polite middle class 'please' at the end. I knew from Harry that, as local government employees, the librarians themselves were forbidden from taking part or even voicing support for the protest. Carmody had said something about it last night, and it was as this crossed my mind that I saw the deputy mayor himself standing at the edge of the crowd.

He and another man – large, red-faced, smiling – were being harangued by a small mob of pensioners. Much as I wanted to head straight in to see Harry, I thought it best to build some bridges here too.

'Mr Carmody, may I have a moment?'

He turned, his look of relief at having been saved from the onslaught of old dears souring when he saw me.

'Mr Jericho. Yes, I wondered if we might—'

'Jericho!' The larger man spun around and, taking my hand, pumped it up and down as if we were both desperately trying to inflate a rubber dinghy. 'Son of the immortal George, I hear. Great-great-something or other of the legendary "Slip-Jointed" Jericho. A pleasure, sir.'

'Mr Hillstrom,' I said, retrieving my hand from his sweaty grip.

'The same. Now look,' he glanced around a little theatrically and dropped me a wink, 'we're all sorry about what happened last night, I'm sure. Unfortunate mistake and all that. But bygones be bygones, eh? Glad to have got it straightened out for you with the Old Bill, weren't we, Alistair?'

Alistair offered a smile so thin his lips practically disappeared. Then the mayor slapped him on the back and I had to grab Carmody before he went sprawling into the road. Physically, Hillstrom was the exact opposite of his deputy. A former rugby prop would have been my guess, that hard-earned muscle turning quickly to fat as middle age bedded in. With a mop of blond hair and a pair of penetrating eyes, he might have been quite a looker in his day, though the clear signs of alcoholism had already robbed him of much of his charm. One thing was certain – this wasn't the lean figure I'd seen beyond the railway crossing.

'I'm grateful for everything you did on my behalf,' I said. 'And I really am very sorry for what happened in the forest.'

'It was a little peculiar,' Carmody said carefully, an eye on his boss's reaction. 'Coming out of nowhere like that and accusing me of spying on you. I mean, do you get a lot of people stalking you, Mr Jericho?'

'You'd be surprised.'

'Well, I wouldn't,' Hillstrom laughed. 'Handsome fellow like yourself. I bet armies of young ladies are forever losing their heads and becoming a nuisance. And you have your father's winning ways, of course. I must say, he charmed the entire town council when he appeared at our organising committee last year. Got the heath for a nominal rent, didn't he, Alistair?'

That invisible smile again. 'He did indeed.'

'I must say, though,' Hillstrom went on, an edge creeping into his voice, 'I would like to know what you were doing at the old family pile. If asked, I'd happily have given you the tour, but the fact is we don't encourage trespassers. Especially with the supermarket deal at such a delicate stage. Have you heard we're redeveloping much of the forest? Very exciting!'

'I was checking out the scene of the tragedy,' I said. 'I noticed the house from the bridge and thought I'd take a look. I'm sorry if I've upset any official town business. I just thought it was curious and wanted to investigate.'

'Investigate what?'

'One or two things that have been puzzling me. For example, why did your great-grandfather build his house so that it overlooked Travellers Bridge? And what did the motto he commissioned really mean? "The mind intent upon false appearances refuses to admit better things"?'

Hillstrom barked out a hollow laugh. 'Who can say? It was all so long ago.'

'And yet worthy of commemoration.' I nodded towards the road where a lorry emblazoned with my father's florid signature was just passing by. 'I must say, I really don't understand your attitude to the past, Mr Mayor. A horrible tragedy is to be the centrepiece of a weekend of celebrations and yet a fine historical building with ties to your own family is to be torn down. And now you're busy closing down your library too.'

'The march of progress, Mr Jericho. The house is practically derelict anyway. And honestly, who uses libraries these days? If a thing cannot justify itself commercially then it is of no benefit to the community. As for the celebrations? Well, we're always looking for something to draw the tourists to Bradbury. Our little horror story is quite charming, don't you think?'

'Five people drowned, Mr Hillstrom.'

'Ah. Yes. I'm sorry, I'd forgotten the personal element. Still, your father didn't seem squeamish about it.'

'Not in the slightest,' Carmody added.

I nodded. 'Must be a great solace to the citizens of Bradbury to have such practical men leading them. By the way, I heard another horror story recently. The last owners of that old house. They were distant cousins of yours, weren't they? The Matthers? Did you know them?'

Hillstrom suddenly looked uncomfortable. 'No. I was very young when they ... Well. It was an unfortunate business.'

'Did both mother and son die in the fire?'

'I don't believe so. That's to say, I'm not entirely sure.'

'Really? That seems— Mr Hillstrom, are you all right?'

A spasm of pain had twisted his features and suddenly he was gripping his wrist.

All at once, I was back in Miss Debney's cottage, that emaciated witch holding out her own withered wrist to me, '*He saw that I saw, and so he did this. He did this he did this he did this . . .*'

Hillstrom smiled through his discomfort. 'A touch of arthritis. Plagues me from time to time. Been a perfect beast these past few days, and such a trying week too.'

190

'Oh,' I said. 'Why's that?'

'The mayor's car was stolen the night before last,' Carmody said.

Hillstrom nodded grimly. 'Police are on it, but I doubt they'll find the culprit. No fingerprints you see. The scoundrel burned it out.'

Chapter Twenty-Seven

I MOVED SLOWLY THROUGH THE PROTESTERS, accepting leaflets and badges, automatically offering words of support. Meanwhile, the sight of the mayor clutching his thick wrist stayed with me. *'He will wrap his wings about you and unthread your life.'* The thin man who had brought Webster to my trailer, attaching a morsel of Adya Mahal's flesh to his collar was not Marcus Hillstrom, and yet there remained the coincidence of that gesture. What did it suggest? Garris and I had considered an accomplice working with Campbell. The same could surely be true of Hillstrom.

A weaker man under the thrall of a dominating personality? It was clear that Carmody stood in awe of his superior, but to indulge in the same perverse obsession? Wasn't that taking deference a little far? Then again, I knew the lengths a submissive character might go to in order to please. A case I'd worked with Garris had concerned a pair of nurses on a maternity wing. One administered lethal drugs to the babies in their care, while the other gave the order. The latter hadn't physically harmed any of the children herself while the former would never have murdered anyone had she not encountered the dominant personality.

Before entering the library, I looked back at the two men. Hillstrom had been evasive about the Matthers incident. Was that just distaste regarding a skeleton in the family closet? Or had he known Mrs Matthers and her son? Could his deputy be that distant cousin? I imagined them as little boys together, playing in the bedroom that overlooked Travellers Bridge, making up stories about the freaks who had drowned there. A shared childhood fascination that had twisted into something darker as they grew.

With most of its regulars outside waving their placards, the library was pretty much deserted. Harry was nowhere to be seen. Over at the issue desk, a young woman with brown ringlets and green fingerless gloves was busy scanning books. Catching sight of me, she beamed and waved me over.

'You're him, aren't you? The old boyfriend?'

'Yes, I—'

She leaned across the desk and swatted me with a bookmark. 'Be good to him. He's an absolute diamond, which I'm sure you know. Even Moira adores him, and it usually takes her months to warm up to anybody. So don't you go breaking his heart or you'll have his fellow librarians to deal with.'

I smiled. 'I promise you, Val, I'll be careful with him.'

'You did the thing!' she squealed. 'He said you can do this trick where you just look at people and know all about them.'

I came around the desk and touched my forefinger to her name badge. 'This gave me a bit of a clue.'

She let loose a gale of laughter and shoved me so hard I almost collided with the shelf behind me. Although she weighed about eight stone, I was pretty certain Val could have taken out Carmody with a single punch. Kerrigan too, come to that.

193

The office door opened and Haz blinked out at us. I spread my arms in a *tah-dah* kind of gesture. Meanwhile, Webster squeezed his head between Harry's legs and gave me a welcoming yap.

'Hush,' Harry said, and the juk looked suitably chastened.

'I see the two of you have become firm friends,' I said. 'Usually that monster has to eat at least three of your fingers before he takes to you.'

'He's been as good as gold,' Harry said, scratching Webster's ear and sending him into raptures.

'OK,' Val said after a pause. 'It's obvious you two have something to discuss. I'll man the shop while the lovebirds have their heart-to-heart.' When I tried to slip by, she treated me to a fairly vicious poke in the ribs. 'Remember what I said, you break our boy, we break you.'

I wasn't entirely sure she was joking.

Webster settled under the desk while Harry flipped the switch on the kettle and I closed the door behind me. Making a fuss about cups and spoons, he kept his back turned.

'So they let you go?'

'They did. Thank you, by the way, for trying to visit. And for the note you left. And for the shower and, well, just thank you.'

He nodded. 'Did they give you a caution? I was lying in bed last night, googling all the possibilities. I guess you're still on parole and so they might send you back to prison if you're convicted. I'm not sure what good it would do, but I could try to have a word with Carmody. Scott, if you had to go back then—'

I crossed the room and wrapped my arms around him. Rested my face against his shoulder. Breathed in the scent of him. He stopped fiddling with the tea things and placed his hand against my face.

'I was lucky,' I said. 'My dad and Garris sorted the whole situation. It's over.'

He let go of a breath. 'Thank God. So your father and the fair are here already?'

'They're pulling onto the heath right now.'

'And that man, Garris. I mean, I've only met him once, but . . .' He shook his head. 'He seemed a bit hard, uncaring, but he clearly thinks the world of you. You're very lucky, Scott, to have people looking out for you.'

I was about to make some comment about my dad's real motives for getting me released when Harry turned to face me.

'What was that last night? The way you were looking at Carmody, it was like you weren't seeing *him* at all. If I hadn't been there, what would have happened, Scott?' I tried to look away but he drew me back. 'You didn't used to be like this when we were together. Yes, I knew you were angry and still grieving for your mum, but there wasn't all this . . .'

He struggled for the word and so I supplied it. 'Darkness.'

'Does it all come from what happened to those little kids? Their blood isn't on your hands, Scott.'

'I let their murderer get away,' I said hollowly. 'He's still out there, walking free, spreading his hate, revelling in what he did. Kerrigan doesn't give a thought to Sonia Malanowski and her brothers, but they haunt me. Every day, every night, I . . .' When Harry tried to reach for me, I very gently pushed him away. 'And it isn't just the kids. Before I joined the force, I did things, Harry. I hurt people. Bad people, but still.'

'Tell me,' he said softly.

'No. I don't want you to know that person. I'm trying to forget him myself.'

He nodded and turned back to the mugs on the windowsill. 'But we can't forget who we are,' he said. 'The things we've done.'

'Haz, what happened with your dad was different.'

'Was it? We're not the same people we were back in that little Oxford pub. That Christmas was a long, long time ago and since then the world hasn't been very kind to either of us. You have your secrets, I have mine, and maybe we won't ever want to share all of them. But accepting that, perhaps we can start again.'

Abandoning the tea, he went and collapsed into the chair beside Webster.

'You can keep your secrets if you like, but I don't ever want you to think you're alone. Even if things don't work out between us, I will always be here. That darkness, that anger, whenever you feel it, you come to me.'

I didn't trust myself to speak. Not at first. He might think that he had changed too, but this was the same sweet, generous soul I'd met all those years ago at The Eagle and Child. The boy who had helped me find my place in the world. Now he was offering to do it again.

'Would you like to come away with me for a night or two?' I asked. It seemed to break the mood and he burst out laughing. 'It'll only be a short trip, but I could do with the company.'

'OK.' He frowned. 'When?'

'Later tonight, if I can manage it. You'll need your passport.'

He considered for a moment. 'Val could cover for me . . . All right, why not? Where are we going?'

'I'd like to keep that to myself, if that's OK?'

'Is it something to do with your case?' When I hesitated, he stretched out and kicked the inside of my boot. 'Fine, you man of mystery, but what about Webster?'

At the mention of his name, the gummy-eyed juk lumbered to his feet and lapped at Harry's knuckles.

'I know you're best buddies now,' I said. 'But my dad can take him back and we can visit any time you like.'

'Does this mean you will *finally* take me to the fair?'

'When it's up and running,' I said. 'And only if you're good. In the meantime, you have work to do and I have a visit to make. I'll text you later with the details of our trip. Come on, boy.'

I took Webster's lead from the desk, clipped it to his collar and started for the door. Harry snagged my sleeve, turning me around.

'When will you be home?'

That word again. I smiled. 'I've got a bit of a drive. Probably around seven, and we may have to head straight to the airport as soon as I get back. Does that sound OK?'

'It sounds very OK.'

A barking Webster made a pretty effective path for us through the protesters and we were back at my car in no time. There, I stowed the old boy on the backseat while I called Campbell. That weary, uninterested voice answered at the tenth ring. He listened with utter indifference to my plan and said Miss Barton would make the necessary arrangements.

'So you've found a Dr Watson, have you?' he muttered.

'I have. It's the librarian you employed to research the bridge tragedy. My ex, as it happens.'

'Really?' he yawned. 'I had no idea you knew each other.'

'Just another coincidence, it seems. Speaking of which, did you ever live in Bradbury End yourself, Professor?'

That sibilant titter greeted my suggestion. 'What an idea! No indeed.'

'And you've never heard of the Matthers family? Mother and son?'

Just the slightest of pauses. 'Never. Are they relevant to the case?'

'I'm not sure.'

Another pause. Then, 'Two days, Mr Jericho. Two days until the anniversary. And two murders to go. Godspeed.'

The line went dead.

Chapter Twenty-Eight

S TOPPING OFF AT A McDONALD's on the way back from Lincoln, my phone pinged almost simultaneously with two messages: confirmation of our travel arrangements from Miss Barton and a report from Garris.

> Looked into Carmody background. Single, no criminal record, solicitor by trade. Born in Aberdeen. Adopted at age 3, grew up in Pembrokeshire. Both parents still alive. No obvious connection with Bradbury until he moved there 5 yrs ago.

My vision of Hillstrom and Carmody as distant cousins growing up together evaporated. It was pretty clear that Alistair was not the Matthers child. That didn't mean, of course, that he wasn't involved in the murders, nor that he wasn't Hillstrom's lean-figured accomplice. The fact the mayor's car had been reported stolen and burned out could simply be a double-bluff on their part. Having said that, could I really see the prim and proper Carmody tearing up the streets of Bradbury End? I read on:

> Also looked into Matthers family. Jonathan and Delia. Mother and son both survived the fire. They left Bradbury

soon after and relocated to the States. As far as official records are concerned, this is where the trail goes cold. There's no mention of them after 1985. Attaching a photo I found in the online archives of the local paper. Rather blurry.

That's all I have. But please, Scott, I don't have to tell you not to rely solely on my research – use that intuition of yours, ask questions, stir things up. I get the feeling something is about to break. Keep me updated. Garris.

'I think you're right, Pete,' I murmured, and echoed those words of Campbell. 'Two days to go.'

Asking questions and stirring things up hadn't got me very far in Lincoln. I'd reached that medieval city on a hill just after noon. Adya Mahal had been a student studying media at the university. Fifty quid from the treasury of Ralph Campbell into the grubby fist of her landlord had gained me access to Adya's flat. There, a sterile, clueless void awaited me. All her belongings had been removed and the police report was accurate in its description of a forensically clean crime scene.

Standing in her bedroom, I had glanced again at the picture from the file. The desecrated body of a young woman with her whole future before her. She had not been a human being to this killer; merely another piece in his great design.

Before leaving, I'd asked questions of Adya's neighbours, posing again as a journalist and pouring Campbell's money into open pockets. No one had seen a thing on the night she died. Adya had kept very much to herself. It was the smell that had finally alerted them. The out-of-order lift and the precipitous stairs up to her apartment had at least confirmed my belief that Campbell would have had no chance of climbing them.

I pushed away my lukewarm Big Mac and took a sip of Coke. Then I clicked the attachment and opened the photograph Garris had found. The black-and-white image looked practically Victorian: a mother in matronly garb clutching the hand of her tiny, pale-faced son. They were standing on that wrap-around porch of the Matthers' house, the shadows of the forest so dense only their faces stood out. Even then the features were little more than scratches in the gloom. Of course, it was possible that these people had nothing whatsoever to do with the case. Still, I was curious. What was their story? I'd have to ask Harry if the local historian Roebuck had returned from visiting his sister.

With no Webster for company, it was a lonely drive back to Bradbury End. Before leaving for Lincoln, I'd dropped him off at his kennel outside my dad's trailer. Amid the organised chaos of building up, I was able to pass through the fair pretty much unnoticed. I hadn't seen my father or Sal and Jodie, though I did glimpse Zac carrying bundles of rider sacks over to the helter-skelter. I'd remembered that he had been asking to speak to me and I almost went across to say hello. The only thing that held me back was the idea that, if I continued to keep my distance, he'd eventually get over this stupid crush. The kid was better off without me.

Then why isn't Harry? said that treacherous voice inside my head.

It asked the question again now.

I turned up the radio, shut out the voice, and drove on.

Back to the case, it was possible of course that the murderer was someone I hadn't considered or even encountered yet. With serial killers that was often the way of it, the eventual discovery of the culprit was more often down to random luck than brilliant deduction. Ted Bundy had been caught because he was pulled over by a traffic cop who then found his murder kit in the boot of his Volkswagen Beetle; the Yorkshire Ripper was nabbed by a probationary constable who ran a random check on his phoney licence plates. Up to that point, neither man had loomed all that large in the police investigations.

Yet something niggled. A sense that, if I hadn't yet met the killer, clues to his identity were already in my hands. And not only that. I felt certain a connection between the victims had also been hinted at. Some words spoken to me at the very beginning of the investigation. The idea dogged me all the way back to Bradbury, though, in the end, I had to admit defeat.

Pulling into Harry's drive, I texted Garris back, thanking him and hoping things were as good as they could be with Harriet. Then I stopped off at the trailer and packed an overnight bag. I swallowed a couple of benzos as I threw the packet into my toiletry bag (just the prescription ones, in case customs decided to take a look). They ought to stave off the shakes until tomorrow morning. I checked my watch: 6.35. Being midsummer, it was light outside and probably still would be when we reached the airport around nine.

Bag in hand, I knocked at Harry's door. There was no answer but the handle turned at my touch and I stepped into the hall. I was about to call out when I heard his voice speaking from the lounge.

'No, he isn't back yet . . . Yes, I understand, we've talked about this and I agreed, didn't I . . .? I'd just like to know what's going on with . . .'

I walked softly towards the open doorway. Harry sat hunched on the sofa, his back to me, the phone pressed to his ear. He nodded twice; tense, sharp movements.

'Yes, I think he bought it in the end . . . Of course. I'll speak to you when we're back. Goodbye.'

He cancelled the call and threw the phone to the far side of the sofa. When I spoke his name, he almost jumped out of his skin.

'Jesus, Scott! How . . .' He stared at me over the sofa back. 'How long have you been standing there?'

I managed a carefree shrug. 'Not long. Who was that?'

His gaze darted to the phone and he laughed. It sounded a little strident, I thought.

'Val. From work. We've been negotiating how many favours I owe her for covering my shifts. I fear the cost in cupcakes alone is going to drive me into the poorhouse.'

His smile seemed natural enough. I smiled back and replayed the snatches I'd overheard in my head. Had that sounded like a conversation with the vivacious young woman I'd met at the library? There had been a stiffness to Harry's tone, a strain, but perhaps Val hadn't appreciated his last-minute request to cover for him. I dumped my bag at the door and went to sit on the sofa.

'Who bought what?' I asked.

Did he stiffen a little?

'I'm sorry?'

'You said to Val, "I think he bought it in the end."'

'Oh. That . . .' He got up and went through to the open-plan kitchen, rooting around in the fridge for ingredients. 'Yes, well, as part of the branch closure we've been encouraged by the council to try to sell off some of the furniture. I was just telling her that one of the local businesses had bought all the desks from the study area.'

'Must be a sad day,' I said. 'How will the closure affect your work?'

'As I told you, I'm on a kind of rotating schedule. I'll still have plenty to do at the other branches I'm assigned to. It'll be librarians like Val who'll be made redundant. But I guess the Hillstroms and Carmodys of this world will come for us all in the end. By the way, I saw a few posters going up on my walk home.'

'For the fair?'

He shook his head. 'Those have been up for ages. These were for the anti-mosque rally. It's all happening in the town centre the day after tomorrow. I hate to say it, but I think they'll get quite a decent turnout.' He laid his hands flat on the countertop. 'When did we become so hateful, Scott?'

I went over, collected up the vegetables and replaced them in the fridge. 'Go and pack your bag. We'll grab some food in town before we head to the airport.'

His smile came a little easier. 'You never told me where we're going.'

'You always liked surprises,' I said.

When he left, I spent a few minutes staring at that phone lying on the sofa cushions. Even if the eternally security-unconscious Harry had used password protection, I knew I could probably hack it by the time he got back. The question was, did I want to? The idea that he could walk in and find me checking his call log was pretty much decisive. Whatever connection we were making was still very much in its infancy. The secrets of our past might in themselves be enough to destroy it before any new relationship even got started. I didn't need to jeopardise things further on the basis of some paranoid hunch. And anyway, his explanation of the call had been reasonable.

That's what I told myself.

It was what I wanted to believe.

In the end, that was just another of my mistakes.

Chapter Twenty-Nine

Located at the edge of town, The Green Man was practically empty. I'd steered Harry away from his suggestion of The Inn on the Heath because I knew that, after a day building up, the nearest pub would be packed to the rafters with Travellers. Don't get me wrong, in their cups you could want for no better company than showpeople. Their stories will keep you on the edge of your seat, their jokes will have you howling; I just wasn't ready for Haz to encounter them en masse. For a joskin, it can be an overwhelming experience.

The conversation since leaving the bungalow had been a little stilted, but by the time our food arrived we were in full flow, reminiscing freely about our time in Oxford. We danced around those final days leading up to his father's death, but the rest of it seemed fair game. The films we'd loved, the books we'd swapped, all our small triumphs and catastrophes and in-jokes were recalled and toasted. That strange phone call – if it had been strange – was forgotten.

He insisted I taste some of his shepherd's pie and, after agreeing it had been microwaved to within an inch of its life, I grinned.

'He who would *not* the shepherd's pie praise.'

Harry smiled. '*Quem pastores laudavere.* You remember?'

'How could I forget? The first words I ever heard out of your mouth. Sweet and soulful and absolutely incomprehensible.' He laughed and I looked around the pub. 'Do you fancy giving me a reprise?'

'What?' He hiccupped. 'Don't be ridiculous.'

'Come on, I haven't heard you sing in years.'

'Nuh-ah.' He took a mouthful of wine. 'I don't do requests. Anyway, it's bad luck to sing Christmas carols in the summer.'

'Who says?'

'An ancient law known only to the sacred order of carollers: *if thou shalt let a festive hymn pass thy lips out of season then thou inviteth great evil into thy presence.*'

'Bullshit.' I laughed.

'Absolutely true!' Harry said. 'And by the way, we don't appreciate outsiders mocking our traditions. Carollers are a proud people.'

I reached across the table and squeezed his hand. 'But could my favourite caroller bend the rules, just for me?'

He looked daggers for a second. Then, composing himself a little theatrically, he began to sing. Just the lightest, faintest sound, hardly above a whisper, and I was immediately transported back to The Eagle and Child, that beautiful face rhapsodic in the firelight. After a couple of lines, he shook his head and started to apologise, saying he was rusty and that he hadn't sung the hymn in years. I was about to tell him that false modesty was very Harry Moorhouse when the pub door swung open and Lenny Kerrigan walked in.

I stood up.

'You have no idea what this is all about, do you? The great fucking detective and you can't see what's staring you in the face.'

His words from the wood rang in my head.

'You're in for a big surprise, Jericho. One day soon you'll wake up and realise just how well I've played you . . .'

Kerrigan hadn't come alone. A dozen or so of his Knights of St George swarmed in behind him. I recognised a couple from our early interviews with the hate group. Beer-gutted, bleary-eyed steroid abusers, they had spent half their lives swilling police station coffee and muttering 'no comment' into our tape recorders. What they were doing here in Bradbury End seemed obvious, but still, Kerrigan's presence reawakened all my old suspicions about his possible connection with the case.

They soon colonised the bar and started bellowing at the landlord.

'We just come through your town,' said a man I recognised as Mickey 'Fatboy' Wallace (Kerrigan's deputy in all but name, we'd once arrested him on suspicion of daubing 'Heil Hitler' in pig's blood on the gates of the local synagogue). 'Do you know you've got fucking pikeys camped out on your village green? Proper stinking up the place and they've only been there two minutes.'

'Now, now, Mickster,' Kerrigan laughed, patting his companion's glistening shaved pate. 'We ain't here for the gypos. Not this time. It's the fucking ragheads we're after, right, boys?' A chorus of approval. 'You heard about this rally on Friday, Innkeep? Hope we can count on your support. Some friends of ours who live round this way invited us over and, I gotta say, it's a beautiful spot. If you wanna keep it that way – good and Christian and pure – I suggest you gather a few mates together and join us on the frontline.'

When I stepped towards them Harry caught my wrist. 'Scott?'

'It's him,' I muttered.

His gaze cut between us. 'You mean the man who . . . What's he doing here?'

'That's what I'm going to find out.'

'Scott, don't—'

But I was already halfway to the bar.

Grabbing one of the Neanderthals by the shoulder and pulling him aside, I stepped into the herd. The knuckle-dragger behind me started to shout something. Kerrigan spun around on his stool and, seeing me, silenced his follower with a look. That shit-eating grin that had earned him his most prominent scar spread like oil across his face.

'Well, look who it isn't. Detective Sergeant Scott Jericho, disgraced. No, no, give him some room to breathe, lads. He likes a few strong boys about him, but we don't want to get old Scotty here too excited, do we? He might start dribbling on the carpet.'

I cut right to the chase. 'How did you find me, Kerrigan?'

'See, this is your problem, Scotty.' He drummed his palms on the bar while the landlord looked on with a nervous smile. 'You think the whole world revolves around you. Now, if I *wanted* to find you, it wouldn't have been all that difficult, would it? I mean, there's ten thousand fucking posters all over this dump with your name on every one of 'em.' This clearly tickled the funny bones of the Knights of St George. I received a few 'friendly' slaps on the back. 'But like I was saying to my mate, the Innkeep here, we're gathered to stop these ragheads opening up their heathen temple. Do you know how many—?'

209

'What I know is how it went down in that forest between us just the other day,' I said. 'If you're back for more of the same, let's cut the chat and step outside right now.'

The laughter stopped like a tap being turned off. I could actually see the landlord's Adam's apple bob as he gulped. Part of me knew that this was mad – only this morning, I'd been lucky to avoid an assault charge that would have seen me back in prison – but that grin. That *fucking* grin. And there, on the other side of the pool table, three little figures with burned faces stood watching me.

'You said that you were playing me somehow,' I grunted. 'So what are you really doing here?'

Kerrigan licked his lips and slid off the stool. Back in the forest, he'd cowered but here he had strength in numbers. He sidled over and prodded me in the chest.

'Guess.'

I looked down at the back of his hand – at the swastika tattoo – and whatever I was going to say died on my lips. I heard again the mad ranting of Miss Debney, '*He did this he did this he did this.*' To ease his arthritis if Hillstrom was the killer, or perhaps to hide an identifying mark? Kerrigan was not the subtle mind behind these murders, I knew that, but as a paid accomplice? Something else that I'd seen in the forest near the diner now made me grasp his forearm.

'That's just about the worst knock-off Rolex I've ever seen,' I said. 'Don't tell me you've run through all my money already? And that Beemer you were driving the other day—'

He pulled his arm away, his face flaming. For a moment I wondered if his Knights might try to defend the commander but they all just stood there, drinking in the drama.

'You owe me for those fucking tyres,' he spat.

'Do I? Or do I owe the company you lease it from? Are you in trouble, Lenny? In need of a bit of ready cash maybe? Is someone paying you to do their dirty work?'

He glanced around the group and did his best to snatch back a little dignity. 'Oh, but have I got a surprise in store for you, Detective Sergeant. Think you're clever, don't you? But you won't see this one coming.'

'Scott, come away.'

We all turned and looked at Harry. He appeared so small, standing there outside the circle. Beyond the pool table, the Malanowski children had vanished, almost as if their watchful vigilance had been transferred to him.

'Please.'

Kerrigan broke into fits of laughter. 'Who's this then, Jericho? Your latest bumboy? Aw, is bumboy scared for his daddy? Poor little shit-stabber.'

I could feel it then, almost like a physical force. The safety Harry offered me and the pull of the darkness. It had never been a factor in our relationship before. Back in Oxford, before my thug-for-hire years, before the rage birthed by the murder of three innocent children, the choice would have been easy. Now it took every morsel of will I had to step away from Kerrigan and take Harry's hand.

'He knows what you did inside, does he?' Kerrigan bellowed after us. 'How you serviced – sorry, I mean *served* – your time up in Hazelhurst?'

'Don't listen,' Harry murmured. 'Just keep walking.'

'Faggots walking on the pink mile!' Kerrigan hooted. 'Backs to the wall, lads!'

When neither of us responded, he hurled one last salvo before we pushed through the door. 'I got a surprise for you, Jericho. The biggest fucking surprise of your life. And I just can't wait to see your stupid face when you find out what it is. Can't. Fucking. Wait!'

Outside, Harry guided me to the car. He was asking if I was OK but I could barely hear him over the blood drumming in my ears. After a couple of minutes just sitting behind the wheel, I turned the ignition and swept us into those narrow winding streets of Bradbury End.

I couldn't know then that Kerrigan was right. A surprise was coming, and soon, only days away now. Looking back, I wonder whether this was the moment that I should have seen and understood everything. But as bitter as it turned out to be, the revelation Kerrigan had in mind wasn't the one that would end up shattering my world.

Chapter Thirty

ALL HARRY KNEW WAS THAT we were heading for Faro and that, once we arrived, I'd be taking us over the Portuguese border into Spain. He must have guessed that the trip was something to do with the case, but didn't ask any questions. I wanted to believe that this was because he'd understood what I'd said about police work: how most of us like to keep our loved ones far away from the misery and violence that pollutes our world. But still, sitting together on the plane, his sleeping head against my shoulder, my thoughts kept wandering back to that phone call.

'*I think he bought it in the end . . .*'

No. I'd reasoned this out already, I didn't want to go over it again. I could trust Harry. I had to trust someone.

But did he trust me? We hadn't spoken much after leaving the pub. He'd seen for himself what I had made of Lenny Kerrigan: the scars that went with that shattered cheekbone. It's one thing to defend someone in the abstract but when you're confronted with the reality of their actions? Sometimes that's a harder thing to reconcile.

We were both exhausted by the time we reached our hotel. I'd hired a car from the Avis rental at the airport and driven us through the Algarve and into a sleepy seaside town near the Andalusian border. Miss Barton had booked a quaint B&B, all trailing bougainvillaea and red terracotta, a stone's throw from the beach. Not that we had much chance to enjoy the view. A glance at the black waves before we said our goodnights and slipped into our adjoining rooms had been about it.

I unpacked my bag, popped a Zopiclone, stripped to my underwear, and collapsed onto the bed. Cicadas chirruped beyond the shuttered window. From next door, the sudden drum of the shower. I reached up and laid my palm against the stuccoed wall. Waited for the pill to work its wonders. Tomorrow we'd visit the scene of Agatha Poole's incineration in her tin bathtub; that sickening recreation of Maria Landless, the Electric Lady. My parole officer hadn't objected when I'd contacted him the morning after my meeting with Campbell to ask permission to travel abroad. Strictly speaking, my movements outside the circuit of the fair were restricted, but I knew from the start that this trip would be a vital part of the investigation. I'd spun the line that I'd got a family funeral to attend and pleaded for twenty-four hours out of the country. I think the poor guy was so stunned that I was up and about and sounding vaguely coherent that he expedited the request to the local director of probation and permission was granted.

My eyelids drooped. In the darkness, I listened to the drifting hush of the sea, imagining a bay far from here where a dog-faced man stood tethered to a tree. Where a raving old woman bowed down before a white-winged demon that clutched at its wrist. Where red poppies grew around the tombstones of decaying caravans. Other figures stepped up to join the sacrificed man – a charred corpse with sparks flying from its fingertips and a girl who gorged herself on her own flesh. A stirring then as yet another pair shuffled in the shadows, waiting to take their place with the Jericho freaks: the Balloon-Headed Horror and the Contortionist. All five looked back at me, silent words on their lips, the secret of their connection taken and scattered by the wind.

Over a quick breakfast on the hotel veranda, the awkwardness of yesterday seemed to have vanished. Harry looked more handsome than ever, the sun lighting his mousy brown hair until it looked like tarnished gold. We chatted about how well we'd slept, the breathtaking view of the whitewashed houses tumbling down to the beach, the stray cats curling their lithe bodies into any scrap of shade. Perhaps he had come to terms with what he'd experienced in The Green Man.

Half an hour later saw us driving through a landscape of plunging valleys carved out by extinct rivers. A few lonely trees clung onto life but for the most part, this was a desolate vista. Away to our right, the Gulf of Cadiz gleamed like spilled ink against the white parchment of the coast.

We crossed over into Spain via the bridge that spans the glistening saltmarshes of the Guadiana River. Once across, I took the first exit, following signs for the little tourist town of Ayamonte. We then climbed a shallow hillside before descending through cobbled streets lined with single-storey houses, then out of town again onto a redeveloped road that eventually led to what had once been an old fishing village.

Here, on Isla Canela – 'the Cinnamon Island' as it was known to the locals – British expat, Agatha Poole had bought her holiday home.

The island itself was a strip of land barely forty metres across, bordered on either side with four-star hotels and apartment blocks. I dropped Harry off at one of the smart *chiringuito* beach bars, telling him I shouldn't be longer than an hour or two. We could then enjoy the rest of the day together before our flight home later that night. He pulled his rucksack from the backseat and, unconsciously I think, leaned over and kissed my cheek.

Then, after a slight pause, he said, 'Whatever you're doing, be careful.'

I watched him pass along the boardwalk, his silhouette wavering in the heat haze, until he vanished into the bar. Then I turned around and followed the satnav the last few metres to Agatha Poole's apartment block.

Money is a universal language and what worked in Lincoln with Adya Mahal's landlord now unlocked the door of Flat 3, Marina IV on the Spanish Cinnamon Island. The custodian of the block, who I'd found downstairs swearing at a malfunctioning pool filter, pocketed his euros and threw me the keys, only asking that I returned them when I was done. What he imagined I was doing here, I had no idea, though I doubted he much cared. The apartment door slammed behind him.

As with Adya's flat, I soon discovered that my long journey had been a bust. All the furniture had been removed and the place was little more than a shell. Still, I now had Campbell's file memorised, so could walk Agatha's home while reconstructing the crime scene in my head. I moved to the master bedroom where the outline of the tin bath had been scorched into the tile floor. Scuff marks showed where the bed had been upended against the wall to make room for the staging of the corpse. At the dismantled electrical socket, safety tape now covered the place where the murderer had pulled out the wires before stripping them down and attaching them to the rim of the tub.

Although technically an elderly woman, Agatha had been relatively fit and yet there had been no signs of a struggle. Would that have been the case if she'd been confronted with someone like Lenny Kerrigan? The autopsy report stated her neck had been broken and that the electrocution had occurred post-mortem. One swift snap and it was all over for Agatha. Again, the idea occurred to me that these deaths were not ends in themselves and that the killer had taken no real pleasure in them.

But his care and experience were in evidence once more. The car he'd arrived in had been bought from a scrapyard over the border for a hundred euro in cash. The dealer was known to the police in both countries and had a reputation for discretion, so it wasn't surprising that he could recall very little about his customer. Male, English, he thought, anywhere between forty and sixty years of age, wearing a baseball cap and sunglasses. Along with the car he had also purchased an old tin bath that he had phoned about in advance and that the dealer had sourced and put aside for him. No, unfortunately, he had mislaid the receipts of sale.

It was out of season when the killer arrived on the Cinnamon Island, most of the bars and restaurants still shut up for the winter. Those in Agatha's block were almost all Spanish-owned holiday apartments and so no one had seen him come and go. The idea of the local Guardia Civil was that an English relative had staged the slaying to make it look like the work of a madman. Agatha's estate had been fairly substantial and, for a time, a nephew living in Seville had been their prime suspect. However, after much questioning, he'd been forced to reveal an alibi involving three prostitutes, a chocolate fountain, and a time-stamped video. It had been the end of his marriage, but he was still a free man.

I dropped to my haunches and played my fingertips around the scorch mark. Like the apartment, the junkyard car left in the basement lot had been wiped clean. I turned to the taped-over socket. Given the state of the corpse, the fuse box must have tripped and been reset a number times before the killer was satisfied with his staging. I thought of that half-fried body lying here, its liquified eyes staring into the dark until neighbour Senora Martinez had discovered it on the third day.

There was nothing else the flat could offer and so I dusted off my knees and headed to the door. It had been a disappointing morning, but at least I got to spend the rest of the day with Haz before our flight home.

I was just locking up when I heard the flap of sandals on the communal staircase. A boy of about ten came into view, a fishing net bouncing against his shoulder. He stopped dead when he saw me, his gaze meeting mine before flicking to Agatha Poole's apartment then to the door across the hall. His eyes were round with fear and, dropping his net to the ground, he turned on his heel and darted back down the stairs.

'Hey, wait!' I called after him. 'I only want to talk.'

But the smack of his sandals didn't slow and his fear told me all I needed to know. This child had seen something, and what he'd seen had terrified him.

I plunged down the stairwell, taking the steps three at a time, my shoulder hitting the wall at each turn as I raced to catch up to the boy. The echo of his breathless gasps reverberated in the concrete funnel of the stairway, the audible catch of terror in his throat. And then a fractional pause, the hush and skid of rubber soles, followed by the softer slap of bare flesh meeting stone. Reaching the bottom of the stairs and the ground-level residents' parking lot, I glimpsed the kid's sandals, one kicked under the chassis of a dune buggy, the other lying against the back tyre of a vintage flame-red Triumph motorcycle.

Silence now. My head flipped right and left. There were around fifty vehicles taking up spaces but otherwise the parking lot appeared to be empty. The only sounds of humanity I could hear was a splash and squeal from some nearby pool and the distant blare of music, perhaps from the beach bar where I'd dropped Harry. Needles of brilliant sunshine pierced the rose-trellised archways that hemmed in the lot and flooded between the bars of the large, automated gate that stood at one end of the complex. A pedestrian gate stood adjacent to this, both exits cumbersome and clanking, as I knew from when the custodian had let me through earlier. In the past couple of moments, I had heard no such sounds and the thorn-riddled archways couldn't be got over or through.

The kid was still here.

'You're safe with me, I promise,' I said in the broken Spanish that, by some miracle, I remembered from school. 'I'm not him.'

An arid breeze meandered through the lot, setting the spiky shadows of thorns dancing across sand-dusted windscreens, rippling the surface of an oily puddle in one vacant space.

'Not the bad man,' I said softly, my gaze lighting on a dark smudge just outside that black pool. A single stain in the shape of a bare toe. 'It's all right, I won't hurt you.'

Bending down, I glanced into the gloom beneath an old flatbed truck. There a pair of fear-bright eyes stared back at me.

'Do you speak English?'

He shuffled further away, small hands clasped together as if in prayer.

'My name's Scott,' I said. 'I was a friend of Agatha.'

'Agata,' he whispered.

'That's right. You knew her, maybe?'

He hesitated. 'She was kind,' he said in English. 'She gave me pocket money sometimes. She stuck up for me with Mama. She was Mama's friend. She didn't deserve what God did to her.'

I shook my head. 'If God exists, he had nothing to do with this.'

'He did!' And suddenly it was as if his anger had made the boy bold. He slid out from under the truck and scrambled to his feet. For a moment, I thought he might run again but his indignation kept him planted to the spot. 'That is what Mama and the Guardia said. That I was making things up or dreaming them, but God killed Agata and I saw Him. I couldn't sleep that night because it was cold and Mama wouldn't put on the heating. So I just lay on my bed thinking warm thoughts. Then the lights from Agata's started flashing on my bedroom ceiling.'

'Your apartment is the one opposite Agatha's?' I asked.

He nodded. 'So I looked out. I thought Agata might be having a disco and the idea made me laugh. But then, a while later, all the lights went out, and even later than that I saw Him open the door.'

I tried my best to keep my voice level. 'What did he look like?'

'He was God,' the boy insisted. 'He was Cristo. He had a white halo and his body was shining. He looked like this.'

He pointed to a miniature painted icon hanging from the rear-view mirror inside the truck. It was a representation of the crucified Christ, hints of gore running from its crown of thorns and the wound cut into its side. With arms spread, this Christ appeared almost to have wings.

'Did you see his face?' I asked.

The boy shook his head. 'But I know it was Him.'

'How?'

He tapped his wrist. 'Because He had a hole right here. Big and red and bleeding. Stigmata, the priest calls it. The hole where the Romans hammered in their nail.'

Chapter Thirty-One

ISS DEBNEY HAD SEEN A dark angel, faceless and terrible, its wings smattered with blood. Senora Martinez's son had seen a Christ-figure, haloed and glowing in its murderous vestments, its wrist bearing stigmata. Separated by age, culture and miles, I had no doubt that these two had witnessed the same killer and had viewed him through the lens of their experiences. For Miss Debney, he had been a phantom conjured from the literature that obsessed her; for this boy, an icon from the walls of his mother's church.

What were the commonalities? A form in white, featureless, but identifiable in some way by its left hand. Hillstrom's spasming arthritis or Kerrigan's swastika. Or wounded perhaps? The boy seemed insistent on a weeping stigmata. But McAllister had died in January and Agatha Poole in early March. What kind of wound could still be open almost three months later?

Another commonality, and this time a reassuring one: he had left both witnesses alive. That seemed to confirm my theory that he took no gratification from the murders but revelled in some deeper purpose they served. Cold comfort for his victims. Colder still, if I didn't stop him, for victims yet to come. But at least I knew my friends and family were safe.

As I questioned the boy some more, a new idea occurred to me. I'd assumed that he had accidentally revealed himself to these witnesses, but did that accord with the experienced murderer Garris and I had profiled? Wasn't there something purposeful about these appearances? He hadn't retreated but had stood for a time and allowed them to drink him in. A madwoman and a little boy whose stories no one would take seriously. Outsiders who only an outsider might listen to. True, no witness had seen him at Adya Mahal's flat but that didn't mean he hadn't wanted to be seen.

It was clear after a minute or two that Alessandro Martinez, as the kid had eventually introduced himself to me, had told all he knew. I handed him a fifty-euro note and his eyes widened again, this time with wonder.

'Don't tell your mama,' I said.

He grinned, and as I started to walk away, called after me, 'Was it Cristo who came for Agata?'

I glanced back. Just a barefoot child, clasping his reward in his little hand. I had felt fear and disgust and, yes, a dark fascination for this killer. Now, looking at the boy he had terrified for no good reason, I hated him.

'It wasn't Cristo,' I said. 'It was only a man. And you don't have to be afraid anymore, Alessandro. He won't be coming back here, I swear.'

Seeking out the custodian, I threw the man his keys. He grunted some kind of acknowledgement and went back to hurling expletives at his malfunctioning pool filter.

My mobile chirruped.

'Can I hear someone swearing in Spanish?' Garris grunted. 'So I'm guessing you're out visiting the scene of the Electric Lady. Find anything?'

I told him what the boy had seen and he made a few positive noises regarding my thoughts. 'Almost peacocking, isn't he? Only, maybe that's not the right way of looking at it. He's not showing off exactly, but ... I don't know, inviting recognition?'

'For his work?' I wondered. 'Or because he wants to be caught?'

'That, I can't say. But I do have some news for you. A name you can tick off your suspect list: Leonard Kerrigan.'

'You're kidding?'

'Is that disappointment I hear? Unfortunately, at the time Robert McAllister was being head-swapped with his dog, our friendly neighbourhood fascist was serving time for assault. Silly boy got himself videoed headbutting a peace activist at a rally. He then put in the boot when she hit the ground.'

'And she sued him, didn't she?' I said, thinking of that fake Rolex on Kerrigan's wrist.

'Believe it or not, he'd already pissed away most of your life savings,' Garris said. 'Half of it going up his nose.'

'And our peace activist came for the rest. Good for her.'

'You don't sound surprised.'

'It confirms a theory,' I said.

'Well, I wish you'd come up with one to link these victims.' Garris sighed. 'I've done another deep dive into files and there's nothing. Other than that they became the target of a certified nutcase with a hard-on for old fairground legends, our vics have zero crossover. I mean, it can't just be a random selection, can it?'

'No.' I stared up at the shuttered windows of Agatha's apartment. 'He wouldn't have come all this way if she didn't mean something. We just have to dig a little deeper . . . Pete, are you still there?' He grunted. 'So I don't know if I should ask, but how is—'

'Hospice tells me she's in her last hours.' He sighed. 'I suppose they know their business. They must develop a nose for it, just like we do. Nurses and doctors and paramedics and police, we get a feel for when death's round the corner, don't we?'

'Pete.'

'Don't say you're sorry. Just go and find that fella of yours. You took him with you, I bet?'

'I know you're suspicious of him, but I—'

'I'm always suspicious of everyone. Which means I'm almost always wrong.'

He hung up, and for a few seconds I stared at the phone in my hand, wishing I could do something for him. It was strange to hear pain in Garris's voice. A man who moved through the agony of others, bringing peace and resolution where he could, while keeping his empathy always in check. Outsiders might see it as coldness but really it was a survival technique essential to all officers who stayed on the force. A technique I had never learned.

I left the car in the street and headed back towards the *chiringuito*. It was a short stroll and the sandy boardwalk was soon under my feet. Up ahead, a perfect beach was dotted with colourful parasols. Kids rocketed past me, skipping bare soles off the baking planks while grandparents trundled behind in electric scooters. It all seemed a world away from the horror of Bradbury End, and at that moment, I was tempted never to return.

Haz and I could find a cheap apartment in a place like this. We could while away our days in the sun, drinking wine, swimming in the sea. Here, without the shadow of the case hanging over us, we could reforge those old links. I shook my head. A nice dream, but I had an obligation, not only to Campbell, whose money I had taken, but to the victims of a killer who wouldn't stop until his design was complete.

A killer who, it seemed, was *not* Lenny Kerrigan. At least, Kerrigan hadn't been involved in the first murder, but did that rule him out entirely? We'd considered the idea of him as a paid accomplice; a distraction arranged by the murderer to keep me off my game. Well, now we knew he needed money, what if he'd been recruited after he left prison? I could certainly see him in the guise of the Englishman who'd bought the dodgy car from the scrap dealer over the border. But that meant the killer had anticipated my involvement in the case and, back when Agatha Poole was murdered, I was still in prison myself. The scenario just didn't work.

At the sound of my name, I looked up. Harry, sitting under an umbrella on the *chiringuito*'s terrace, waving and smiling like I was the best surprise he could have hoped for.

'That didn't take long,' he said as I sat beside him. 'How'd it go?' I wrinkled my nose and he held up his palm. 'Right. Sorry. I know you don't like the idea of me nosing into your shady private-eye world.'

He meant it playfully, but I could hear the disappointment in his voice.

After lunch, we went for a stroll along the beach. Although my mind occasionally strayed, picturing Agatha Poole walking barefoot through these shallows, Harry kept me mostly in the moment.

'I'm sorry this is just a flying visit,' I said. 'Maybe one day we can come back. Spend some proper time here together. Or anywhere. Your choice. It's just ...'

I stopped and turned to him. We had left most of the holidaymakers behind and, wading into the surf, had found a sandbank that stretched far out into the sea. I brushed the fringe from his brow.

'I'm not sure where we are right now.'

He shrugged, his hands finding my hips. 'Let's take things slowly, yeah?'

'Of course. But, Haz, if we really are starting something here, then I need to ask why.' The idea of pushing him away when I'd only just found him again almost made me stop, but if we wanted to move forward then this had to be faced. 'Did you think I wouldn't understand? Harry, he was such a good man and he was in so much pain. That last weekend we went down to see him together, he told us he didn't want to go on. I remember holding you afterwards and ... It was an act of mercy, Haz. Of love. Of course, I understood that. Of course, I did.'

Tears shimmered in his eyes. 'I knew you understood.'

'Then why did you push me away?'

That was when he broke. And that was when I knew. Knew beyond any doubt that, despite Garris's misgivings, Harry had nothing to do with these murders. His heart was too big. It was as simple as that.

'Because you saw,' he said. 'Because you always, *always* saw. You knew as soon as I came back to the flat that night. I told you I'd been at college all day but you did your thing and you saw right through me. My clever boy.' He took my hand and kissed the bowl of my palm. 'I didn't have to say a word, did I? And then half an hour later when we got the call, the pity in your eyes.'

'So if you knew—?'

'It wasn't about that. I didn't ever think you'd judge me for it.'

'Then why?'

'Because you saw what I'd done. The only one who saw. And being with you every day, I'd have to see it too. And I couldn't live like that. This gift you have, Scott, this ability to peel back the layers and get to the truth of people. Don't you know that when you do that, it forces people to see themselves? The lies we tell so that we can cope with the reality of what we are – under that scrutiny it's all stripped away. Can you imagine how frightening that is for people who have things to hide?'

I could imagine it. Harry wasn't the first loved one I'd alienated this way. Once they got to know me, childhood friends had tended to shy away. I'm not sure any of them could have articulated it the way Harry had, but on some level, they'd known this truth about me.

'Then why do you want to be with me now?' I asked.

'Because I've come to accept what I did. In the aftermath, with all the grief and trauma, I couldn't. But now, seeing you again?' His smile was so sad. 'I want you in my life. It's as simple as that.'

But it wasn't that simple. He didn't know all of who I was, and I didn't know all of the secrets he was hiding from me. Secrets kept for my own good, so he thought – to help me, to save me. Secrets kept for the best of intentions. But secrets that would have saved lives, if he'd revealed them then.

Chapter Thirty-Two

SECRETS DIDN'T CONCERN ME THEN. Sitting in the departure lounge of Faro Airport, our hands locked together, not even the case troubled my thoughts. Although I still had confessions of my own to make – about my life before joining the force, about the things that had happened to me up at HMP Hazelhurst – it felt like the final barrier between us had broken down and we could truly start again. In fact, it wasn't until Harry mentioned his name that I remembered I'd meant to ask him about the historian, Gerald Roebuck.

'I heard from him the morning of the library demo,' Harry said. 'Badgering about some research materials he'd loaned to the local archive. He wanted them returned before the branch closed down. I think he was getting back from visiting his sister this afternoon.'

'That's perfect,' I said. 'I could really do with talking to him about the Matthers' house and a couple of other bits and pieces. Could you text him and set up a meeting tomorrow?'

'Why not now?' Harry shrugged. 'He may be obsessed with the past, but he's still got one foot in the twenty-first century. We'll zoom him.'

While Harry set up the video call, I grabbed us a couple of coffees from the ubiquitous Costa. By the time I returned, he was chatting away to a man who looked like a cross between a dishevelled wizard and an old-time bank manager. Gerald Roebuck's ratty grey beard flowed down to the midriff of an immaculate pinstriped suit. Catching sight of me, he flashed out long white fingers, nicotine-stained up to the second knuckle, and beckoned, as if to usher me through the screen.

'You're a Jericho, aren't you?' he wheezed. 'Yes, my friend Harry here has been telling me all about you. Fascinating history from what I can gather. Culturally almost unique. A Traveller detective indeed. I would consider it a great boon if you would deign to share your experiences for my records?'

I took the seat next to Harry and handed him his drink.

'I'd be delighted, Mr Roebuck, but isn't your collection mainly focused on Bradbury End?'

'And the immediate locale.' He nodded. 'But, my boy, don't you know? You are *of* Bradbury End. Your illustrious ancestor old "Slip-Jointed" Jericho perished in *our* river, and so we lay claim to you. Bradburians are like the mafia in that regard – you may try to escape us, but we keep pulling you back in!' He pointed a yellow talon at the screen and hooted like a jackal. 'Anyway, in his short time among us, Harry here has been a perfect godsend for my researches, and so I am more than happy to help out his special friend.'

Haz leaned in and whispered, 'I'll go and look at the planes. Enjoy.'

'Isn't he a peach?' Roebuck winked. 'If only I were thirty years younger and a hundred times prettier. Scandalous, the way he and the girls have been treated.'

'You don't approve of Mr Hillstrom and Mr Carmody's plans for the town?' I said.

The wizard's face darkened. 'Carmody I can understand. He would have been a parasitical leech wherever he decided to suckle. But Hillstrom? His roots go deep in this community. Now he would tear it all up in the name of commerce.'

'But he must have some sense of the town's heritage,' I said provokingly. 'He's supported these commemorative events for the Travellers Bridge tragedy, hasn't he?'

'Pah. Have you yet encountered the oaf?'

I nodded.

'Then you know as well as I that Marcus Hillstrom is about as cultured as your average jackbooted vandal. Indeed, I have my suspicions – and they are only suspicions, mind you – that he's had a hand in all this anti-mosque nonsense taking place tomorrow. Oh, you won't see him among the mob, of course, but I'm pretty sure that, behind the scenes, he's stirred the poisonous pot.'

'Why would he?' I asked. 'If his ideology is just concerned with money?'

'Money comes from power, Mr Jericho. Power comes from the ability to make people believe that you, and only you, can keep them safe. That, in turn, requires a villain or, even better, *villains*. Disorder in the streets might serve the purpose of an ambitious man. Don't believe for a moment that Hillstrom sees his political apotheosis in the mayoralty of Bradbury End.'

'And it seems he's even willing to sacrifice his ancestral home,' I said.

'The Matthers' house?' Roebuck considered. 'Technically that hasn't been in Hillstrom hands since Delia Matthers inherited it from her husband's family in the 1970s. But yes, the principle stands. Marcus would yank out his granny's gold fillings if it would profit him. And ripping up half the forest for this new supermarket will profit him and his cronies a great deal.'

'What do you know of Mrs Matthers?' I asked. 'I heard she emigrated to the States after the fire.'

'You do have a wide-ranging interest in our town history, don't you?' he said curiously. 'Not just the Travellers Bridge tragedy but now the Matthers incident?'

'I saw the house when visiting the bridge,' I told him. 'It intrigued me.'

'Well, I knew *him*.' The historian sniffed. 'The boy, Jonathan, I mean.'

'Really?'

'Oh yes. A peculiar little thing. I was working at the library myself back in those days. I believe it was the only place his mother would allow him to visit unsupervised. I got the sense that, following her husband's death, she developed a morbid certainty that her son would also depart this earthly plane and leave her quite alone. In any event, she kept him close at all times. I sometimes wondered ...'

A troubled look entered his heavy-lidded eyes.

'Yes?' I prompted.

'If the child had set the fire deliberately. Not in anger, not in defence of his mother, not even to frighten away those teenagers throwing stones at their home. But in an attempt to escape the place. To escape *her*.'

'Maybe to escape the view from his bedroom window?' I suggested. 'The story of men and women drowning in that river would give any child nightmares. Or perhaps become an obsession.'

Roebuck bristled. 'We do not use the "o" word in cases of historical fascination. Jonathan Matthers wasn't obsessed, he was ... captivated, shall we say? We would occasionally discuss it together when he came into the library, and yes, he did tend to request the same materials over and over. Lonely boys have their pet projects, Mr Jericho. There is nothing unnatural in that.'

Not unless he grew up to murder three people because of it, I thought.

'The tragedy of the Jericho freaks has always had its students,' Roebuck continued. 'Every few years, I get researchers through the door of my museum buzzing with curiosity. It possesses a grim allure, you must admit. That Grand Guignol sensibility suggestive of gaslight and Victorian intrigue. I mean, the Dog-faced Boy, the Balloon-Headed Horror, the Fat Woman of Wimbledon. It hardly seems real, does it?'

His words chimed oddly with what both Garris and I had said about the case – that sense of unreality, of something artificially engineered.

'This Campbell fellow who contacted our Harry, for instance,' Roebuck went on. 'A new one, I think. I've certainly never heard of him.'

'He was a professor of history at Cambridge,' I said.

Roebuck looked like he'd just swallowed something unpleasant. 'A *professional* historian? How unromantic.'

'I was wondering if I might pay you a visit tomorrow, Mr Roebuck?' I said. 'I've got a few questions concerning the tragedy and perhaps the Matthers family too.'

'Well.' He cocked his head to one side. 'I had wanted to go to the fair tomorrow. See if I could interview one or two of the older generation for my archive.'

'I can provide all the introductions you'd like.' I smiled.

'Perfect!' He clapped those long white hands together. 'Then shall we say after lunch? Harry can give you the address. I do have some work to do in the morning on the flood of '83, but otherwise—'

'Mr Roebuck, what is that?'

As he turned slightly, I'd glimpsed something on the wall behind him. A rectangle of stone with names carved into it. A slab the same size and bearing the same typography as the commemorative plaque on Travellers Bridge. He glanced over his shoulder.

'Oh yes, of course, that might interest you. You're aware of how the new bridge was financed after the tragedy?'

I nodded. 'A subscription was taken up, wasn't it? Local townspeople encouraged to contribute what they could.'

'That's right. However, it was thought only proper that the five families who donated most to the construction ought to receive some special recognition. This was originally intended to appear alongside the commemorative plaque with that rather odd quotation from Horace. "The mind intent upon false appearances—"'

'"Refuses to admit better things,"' I murmured.

'Quite. I mean, there has always been prejudice against travelling people throughout history. I suppose the quote was intended to reference this. A sentimental embrace of the shunned victims of the tragedy by the town in which they'd perished. A commitment that Bradburians would honour their memory by keeping open and tolerant minds.'

'Not working out too well, is it?' I said, thinking of the anti-Islam placards staked into those crew-cut lawns.

'No indeed,' Roebuck acknowledged. 'In any case, our Victorian mayor, Hillstrom reportedly had second thoughts about the additional plaque. Everyone had contributed what they could, you see, and just because some had deeper pockets than others? Well, it smacked of vanity and so the idea was abandoned.'

'But the plaque had already been carved?'

He nodded. 'An interesting curio, it came into my possession a year or two ago.'

I tried to keep the excitement out of my voice. 'Can you focus your camera on it for a moment? I'd like to read the names of those contributors.'

'Certainly.'

He moved out of shot and, lifting the camera from whatever mount it sat in, crossed the room and held it up to the plaque. Unlike the one on the bridge, this had not suffered a century and a half of exposure and so the lettering stood out, sharp and clear. I read:

IN HEARTFELT APPRECIATION TO THE
FOLLOWING BENEFACTORS:
GIDEON HILLSTROM
WILLIAM MCALLISTER
DANIEL POOLE
MARGARET FIELDING
STEPHEN ROEBUCK

I felt my heart in my throat. Here it was at last – that elusive connection between the five victims. Rereading the names, I had no doubt that somewhere in Adya Mahal's family tree the name 'Fielding' would appear. Descendants of all the five major benefactors of Travellers Bridge. And here too the identity of the final victims: Marcus Hillstrom, present-day mayor of Bradbury End and the man who now appeared onscreen before me, speaking words I did not hear.

But there was something else too. A passing comment made to me at the very beginning of the case. Now, with these names ringing in my head, I plucked it from my memory. What had Sal said?

'Don't start getting obsessed with conspiracies cooked up by old showmen . . .'

I focused again on the screen.

'Mr Roebuck, I need to ask you—' I took a deep breath, 'has it ever been suggested that the drowning of the Jericho freaks *wasn't* an accident? That it was deliberately planned somehow? That the townspeople of Bradbury End came together that day and plotted to murder the Travellers?'

Chapter Thirty-Three

*T*HE SINS OF THE FATHERS *shall be visited upon the children unto the third and fourth generations.*

Apart from their vast weddings and funerals, attended sometimes in their thousands, showpeople are not great churchgoers. Still, faith and superstition run in their blood and the old aunts will sometimes pass scraps of half-remembered scripture between each other. This passage had been a favourite of my Aunt Millie and would often be quoted at any joskin punter who stepped out of line.

It rang now inside my head.

'There was talk at the time. Rumours. Hearsay,' Roebuck said, settling back into his chair. 'None of it was proven. Gideon Hillstrom himself is on record as saying they were a wicked calumny. I must admit, it always seemed fanciful to me, but even today some of the older residents of Bradbury will tell you that their grandfathers and great-grandfathers knew it to be true.'

I stared at him. 'That the entire town—?'

'No, no.' He waved a hand. 'Certainly, the townspeople had never welcomed the arrival of the Travellers, but a conspiracy that large would have been unthinkable, if not impractical. No, it was believed that a small inner circle of ... and that they ... the old bridge ... requiring repairs for decades and so weakening a few crucial points ... child's play ... my own ancestor, Stephen Roebuck ... a master builder ... thought to be complicit ...'

The image kept freezing, the historian's words breaking up.

'I'm losing you,' I said. 'Can you hear me?'

'Bad connection ... Come by tomorrow as plan ... We can talk then.'

'Mr Roebuck, listen to me: it's possible that you're in danger. Mr Roebuck?' I got up and started to walk about the terminal, trying to find a stronger signal, but the three bars on Harry's phone indicated the problem wasn't at my end. 'I'm investigating a case and I think someone might have taken this conspiracy theory at face value. I know it sounds far-fetched, but please humour me. This person might blame the descendants of the original— Mr Roebuck?'

The historian cupped his ear, shook his head, and ended the call.

'Fuck,' I muttered. 'Fuck, fuck, fuck.'

I glanced at my reflection, a haunted form in the huge black windows of the terminal building. On the tarmac beyond, planes taxied into allocated spots while shuttles ferried passengers to and fro. Fifteen minutes until our gate closed. I took out my phone and brought up Sal's contact.

'Sc–huh–ott?' she said, battling a yawn. 'What's going on? What time is it?'

'Sorry, I didn't mean to wake you,' I said. 'Is everyone there OK?'

''Course. Are you in Bradbury End? Jodie says she has this big clue waiting for you. I let slip you were working some kind of case and, honestly, she's been running around like a mini Miss Marple ever since you left, asking questions and jotting things down in her notebook. And she's not the only one desperate to see you. Zac won't stop asking me—'

'I'll pop by tomorrow,' I promised. 'But listen, remember when we were speaking about the Travellers Bridge story and you said something about conspiracy theories cooked up by old showmen? What did you mean?'

'Oh God,' she yawned, 'you're not still chasing that old fairy tale, are you?'

'Sal.'

'Urgh. Fine. Just let me get my brain in gear.' I heard a rustle of covers and pictured her sitting up in bed. 'Right, so I remember this time when I was a kid listening to one of the aunts telling the story. We'd all heard it a million times by then, so I wasn't paying too much attention. But suddenly she adds this new bit that I'd never heard before. You know the Travellers were heading to Bradbury to help with the hop picking, right? OK, the story goes that some of the locals didn't much like the idea. Every year the Travellers arrived and undercut their wages. Blah-blah-blah.'

I nodded. This wasn't a new complaint – a few extra pennies earned during the harvest had always supplemented the showpeople's living. Despite the fact there was hardly any evidence they actually depressed local wages, the accusation was always thrown. Again, this was a myth that had now been transferred from Travellers to immigrants – outsiders taking jobs, undermining incomes.

'On top of that,' Sal continued, 'you know how joskins always view us? An invasion, a nuisance, whatever. Unless we're offering them cheap rides and candyfloss, they don't want us around. Well, the story goes that this particular year the uproar got out of hand, even before we arrived. Farmworkers were downing tools, shopkeepers refusing to sell to anyone who sympathised with the showmen. Even the local gavver said he couldn't guarantee the safety of the town. Basically, everyone was in the mood for a good ruck.'

'Panic is catching,' I said, thinking of the anti-mosque demonstration Kerrigan and his crew planned on attending tomorrow.

'Right. Anyway, the Bradbury End bigwigs apparently started to feel the heat. Some of these people were large landowners and they didn't like the idea of us camping in their woods either. Over a couple days, it all reached a boiling point. Citizens pressuring the mayor and the town leaders until they cracked. The old bridge which we always came over had been almost falling down for years anyway. It only needed a little bit of tinkering.'

I shook my head. 'But that's insane. How could they know the bridge would fall only when the Travellers were on it?'

'I didn't say I believed it,' she said. 'But come on, Scott, we've had even worse than that done to us over the centuries. And then there's that saying they put up on the new bridge. Something like: *if you're determined to see people in a certain way then you'll never get past your prejudices.* The aunt who told me the story interpreted that as an admission of guilt. Once they'd seen what they'd done, they realised how wrong they'd been.'

Even if the story of the conspiracy wasn't true (and honestly, it seemed too far-fetched to be credible), some in both communities – Travellers and Bradburians alike – had believed it. I'd once imagined a showman himself becoming fixated on the story, but what if it went deeper than that? What if this was all some twisted revenge fantasy? Payback for the Jericho victims enacted on the descendants of the original conspirators? That might mean the killer was a member of my father's fairground.

Whatever the truth, at least I now had the connection.

'Thanks, Sal,' I said. 'I'll be sure to see you and Jodie tomorrow.'

'Scott, what is this all ab—?'

I cancelled the call and checked the time. Six minutes until our gate.

I went back to Harry's phone and tried Roebuck again. '*The number you are calling is temporarily unavailable. Please try later or send a text.*' I composed a quick message – Call me first thing tomorrow. Urgent. Scott Jericho – and added my number. I then briefly considered calling my dad for Hillstrom's contact details. As he would be the fair's main point of contact on the council, Dad was bound to have it. But how could I explain why I needed it without going into details that would seem fantastical?

I could call the Bradbury End police, of course. Calmly and methodically set out the reasons why I believed two of their prominent citizens were in danger of becoming the fourth and fifth victims of a ritualistic serial killer. I mean, they were bound to take seriously the rantings of a disgraced CID detective, especially one who had just avoided a charge for assault on the deputy mayor. I sighed. The truth was, I still had very little evidence to back up any of my theories.

The only option left to me was one I really didn't want to take.

I thumbed Garris's contact. While the call connected, all I could picture was some overly cheery hospice bedroom, bright floral wallpaper with matching bedspread, as if these imitations of life could somehow balance out all the death. The room softly lit, a plug-in air-freshener spritzing at discreet intervals, a half-open door through which a nurse takes the occasional glimpse. The figure in the bed still breathing and the husband sitting beside her hasn't raised the alarm. Yet. The nurse walks on to the next door. And into this peace, the shriek of my call.

I almost felt relieved when it went to voicemail. At the prompt, I galloped through my message, outlining the victim connection and my concerns for Roebuck and Hillstrom. Then I apologised for calling at all and hoped Harriet was peaceful. *Peaceful?* Jesus Christ. Feeling like the worst piece of shit, I hung up.

A hand on my arm. 'They're calling our flight. Scott, is everything OK?'

For one dark moment, I caught my reflection again in those vast windows. Only it wasn't my face mirrored there and it wasn't the terminal stretching out around me. It was McAllister's trailer, then Agatha's apartment, then Adya's bedroom. And a figure all in white, its wings spread wide, feathers arrayed like a fan of shining blades. A phantom, an anti-Christ, gripping its wrist as blood seeped through its clenched fingers. Maskless now, it looked back at me and grinned. It was my father, it was

Sam Urnshaw, it was Sal and Jodie and a hundred aunts – a carousel of Travellers' faces.

I made my excuses to Harry and lurched to the nearest bathroom. There, I locked myself into the first cubicle and swallowed two benzos dry. By the time our names were being called over the Tannoy, I'd finally stopped shaking.

Chapter Thirty-Four

I LEAPED FROM AN OCEAN OF sleep, immediately alert as my eyes drank in the unfamiliar bedroom. It took a moment to remember where I was and how I'd got here. Arriving home in the early hours, we'd hesitated on the driveway, our bodies squeezed into the narrow space between my trailer and Harry's front door. We'd stumbled over our goodnights until, all at once, his lips were on mine. The next thing I knew, he'd unlocked the door and we were crashing into the hallway, shedding clothes as we went.

Now, I eased my arm from under his head and pulled back the sheets from my naked body. Haz slept on, his brow furrowed, while I hunted out my phone from under the bed. It wasn't until I swiped the screen and saw the time that I realised we'd slept away most of the morning.

'Shit,' I muttered.

Grabbing his dressing gown from the back of the door, I slipped as quietly as I could into the hall. Here, where twists of our clothes still littered the floor, I checked my voicemail.

'*Hello, Scott.*' I knew straight away from his tone what had happened. For once Pete Garris's famous impassivity had abandoned him. *'I'm sorry I didn't get back to you last night. It's Harriet . . . She's gone.'*

'Fuck.' I rested my head against the wall; kicked at my discarded jeans that lay like sloughed snakeskin at my feet. 'Ah, Pete.'

'I wasn't even with her,' he continued. *'I had been, all bloody day and night. I just slipped out for two minutes to grab a cup of tea and . . . Well. One of the nurses here said that's often the way it goes, almost as if they wait for you to step out of the room. I don't know. Sounds like bollocks to me, but you know my views on this kind of thing. She isn't in a better place, Scott. She isn't anywhere at all.'*

He inhaled, and I could tell he was back on the fags. After Harriet had got her diagnosis he'd quit, wracked with guilt that he might have given her the lung cancer that had otherwise seemed such a puzzle to him. She hadn't smoked a single cigarette in her life, not even an experimental puff as a teenager. And so, by the Occam's Razor method of investigation he had always sworn by, the simplest explanation was that he was her murderer.

'I know you'll want to send flowers or some such nonsense. A donation to the hospice would be appreciated. The name's St Hilda's. Anyway, I've been in touch with the CID lads responsible for Bradbury this morning. The problem is, even with your theory about the victim connection – and I agree that you've probably found it, by the way – as far as actual evidence of a serial killer is concerned, we're still on flimsy ground. There's the letter carved into each victim, of course, then the artist's mannikin, and the uniqueness of each staging, but that aside . . .' Another sucking inhalation. *'Well, I've alerted them to a possible threat against Hillstrom and this man,*

Roebuck. I managed to keep the details pretty vague, and they've promised to send a couple of patrol cars to keep a discreet eye out. Still, they'll want something more concrete in due course. Maybe the time's come for you to hand it over as we discussed. I know that's not what you want, but I honestly can't see any other way of progressing things.'

He was right, I didn't want the case taken from me. Not now. In an earlier call, Garris had thought that something was about to break in the investigation. I sensed that too. The moment of crisis was approaching and I needed to be there when the curtain fell.

I kept thinking back to that frightened little boy in Isla Canela and how, whatever reassurances I'd given him, his nightmares would always be haunted by that murderous figure in white. I knew the length of that kind of shadow. It might reach far into his future, stalking him, undermining him, always lurking in the crevices of his life, ready to spring out until finally he would be forced to take action against it – booze, drugs, self-harm, suicide. That was the legacy of this killer, of all killers – not only their intended victims but a hundred other lives, shattered and unmade.

A monster like that deserved to be punished, didn't he?

I deleted Garris's voicemail and opened up Google. The promise of some police surveillance was reassuring but I wanted to check on Roebuck and Hillstrom myself. I still didn't have a direct contact for the mayor but the local government website gave his secretary's number. After ten minutes of teeth-grinding Muzak, she picked up.

'Town hall.'

'Hi, yes, this is Scott Jericho. I'd like a quick word with the mayor, if that's possible?'

'Mr Jericho from the fair?'

Not technically lying, I answered: 'Uh huh.'

'I'm so sorry, Mr Hillstrom has meetings all morning and will then be in the council chamber until after four. Could I get him to call you back then?'

'That would be great. I just need to give you a different number from the one you might have on file.'

I read it out and she laughed. 'You sound a lot younger on the phone, Mr Jericho.'

'Probably all this invigorating Bradbury End air,' I said and ended the call.

In meetings all day. That meant Hillstrom was safe enough for now. I opened my contacts again and dialled Roebuck. It went straight to voicemail.

Behind me, the bedroom door opened and I felt arms loop around my waist.

'You better not be calling your secret boyfriend,' Harry said, his head against my shoulder. 'Or I might just have to have your caravan towed.'

I turned and kissed him. He pulled away, telling me he hadn't brushed his teeth, and I pulled him back saying his bed-mouth tasted just fine. We stayed that way for a few minutes until he shivered and I offered him his dressing gown. I found my bag in the hall and pulled on some joggers and a T-shirt.

Heading to the kitchen, he asked, 'Are you doing anything today?'

'I've got one or two things on,' I said casually.

He went to the sink and started filling the kettle. 'I just wondered, if you weren't busy . . .?'

'Uh-huh?'

'Maybe you could take me to the fair? You promised you would.'

I had promised. Many times. Like almost every non-Traveller I'd ever met, once I'd told him about my background, Harry had become immediately and persistently intrigued. That old allure of the fair, of getting to glimpse behind the curtain, working its magic again.

'If you really want to,' I said, taking a seat at the breakfast bar. 'They should be built up and open by now.'

'Scott, if you'd rather not—'

'No. It's fine. I'd like you to meet them.' *Would you?* whispered that traitor's voice at the back of my mind. Sure, most Travellers are now OK with gay people, but prejudice is like the cancer that had just destroyed Pete Garris's life – it thrives in the dark and is hard to kill. 'You'll just have to take some of them as you find them,' I said. 'They mean well.'

And so it was settled that we'd head down to the heath after breakfast – which was, by the time we'd eaten it, more like an early lunch. I took a quick shower and, while Harry dressed, dropped my bag off at the trailer. There I went straight to those little packets and swallowed a pick 'n' mix variety of pills. My hands had been shaking again and, although I didn't want my thoughts slowed by the drugs, I couldn't afford cold turkey distractions either. By then, it had become a delicate balancing act.

Harry popped his head into the trailer. 'Ready?'

'Yeah,' I said, turning away from the shelf. 'I just need to make a quick diversion on the way.'

The streets were so snarled with traffic there was no point in taking the car. It was opening day and a lot of people seemed to be en route to the fair, but this wasn't the only group heading into town.

Spilling off pavements, lurching into the road, cutting between startled families, dozens of men and women with their inevitable placards: KEEP BRITAIN PURE! NO TO SHARIA! As Harry had predicted, these weren't all the usual far-right suspects like Lenny Kerrigan and the Knights of St George. Among them was a smattering of middle-class Bradburians – friends, neighbours, library-goers. Otherwise decent people who had drunk freely from that poisonous pot Gerald Roebuck suspected Mayor Hillstrom of stirring.

Harry clasped my hand determinedly. This elicited a few jeers and wolf whistles from the skinheads while the other protesters, those without Nazi tattoos, looked at us almost apologetically. I didn't allow them the comfort of an under-standing nod. As far as I was concerned, you're judged by the company you march with.

Partway down the hill, Harry turned us into a street lined with ugly Edwardian houses. More placards were planted here, but at least the chanting had faded to a dull drone. I was pleased to see a police car parked up a little way down the road, two pairs of officious eyes tracking us to Roebuck's gate. My guess was that Garris must have given them a description of me – let the surly giant with the curly hair pass but no one else – because the officers didn't stir from their seats.

Number 29 was pretty much as I might have expected the historian's home to look. A scrap of neglected lawn led up to three muddy steps and a peeling front door. Roebuck's curtains were drawn and a panel of glass in the door nearest the handle had been broken. Seeing this, I asked Haz to wait by the gate.

'Why? Do you think something's wrong?'

I managed a carefree shrug. 'I'm only saying hello.'

But that broken pane worried me. The shards hadn't been cleared, which meant it was recent. Whatever the state of Roebuck's housekeeping, he wouldn't have left it like that. Could someone have slipped past the surveillance team unnoticed? Crossing the lawn and mounting the steps, I had just lifted my hand to the door when it was wrenched open and a strange blade came jabbing out of the darkness.

Chapter Thirty-Five

I SIDESTEPPED THE JAVELIN'S DULL EDGE and, gripping the shaft, pinned the weapon against the door. The figure inside the hall tried to yank it backwards but either I'd surprised him or else he was weak as a kitten. In any event, it stayed where it was. Harry shouted something from the gate and I heard running footsteps behind me. I had to end this and fast. When the door swung as if to close, I kicked it inwards again and a startled yelp sprang out of the gloom. In the same moment, his grip on the javelin vanished.

I was about to push my way inside when Harry grabbed my shoulder.

'Scott, wait!'

'Stay back,' I told him. 'You don't understand what's going on here.'

'Nor do I!' came the voice from the hall.

I rolled my eyes. I should've known. Would that calculating killer who'd left each crime scene as immaculate as a forensic analyst's workbench really have tried to murder me with a spear in broad daylight? It was so ridiculous I almost burst out laughing.

Someone who didn't seem to appreciate the joke was Gerald Roebuck. Sprawled across the carpet, he blinked daggers at me from under tufted eyebrows. Harry squeezed past and started to help the old boy to his feet. Meanwhile, I replaced his make-shift weapon in the vacant mount on the wall beside the door. The smell of cigarettes was almost overpowering, the wallpaper and ceiling coated yellow with nicotine. Even the historian's white hair was dyed with tangerine-coloured streaks.

Hearing footsteps in the road outside, I darted back into the garden and intercepted the officers before they could reach the gate. Luckily for me these weren't my two acquaintances from my first day in Bradbury End and they nodded when I mentioned both mine and Garris's names. I explained there had been a misunderstanding but that a potential danger to Mr Roebuck was ongoing and that their continued presence was appreciated.

By the time I returned to the house, Harry had just about got Roebuck upright and planted him in a chair at the foot of the stairs. Neither seemed to have noticed my brief absence.

'What the hell was that all about?' the historian complained, flashing those long white fingers at me. 'You scared me half to death.'

'Likewise,' I said. 'Do you greet all your visitors with a javelin, Mr Roebuck?'

'Harpoon,' he muttered. 'From an eighteenth-century whaling ship. Nearest thing to hand.'

'I stand corrected.'

He gave me a grudging shrug. 'Bit OTT, no doubt. But it's the third time this week the kids round here have broken that bit of glass. I thought it was one of them coming to leave something unpleasant on the doorstep.'

'So you planned to harpoon them?'

'Just frighten the little bastards, that's all.' He looked to Harry for moral support. 'You're a librarian, you know what they can be like. Anyway.' A pair of beady eyes refocused on me. 'Two o'clock was our arrangement, wasn't it?' Pulling an enormous fob-watch from his waistcoat pocket, he tapped the glass. 'It is now a quarter past twelve.'

I cast Harry a glance. I didn't want to discuss this in front of him. 'You got my message from last night?'

'Urgent, so you said.' I'm sure the smile behind his beard was the height of condescension. 'All researchers believe their pet project is the most important thing in the world. I assure you, it isn't. My time, however, *is*. So if you could return at the appointed hour? Thank you, thank you.'

Fingers with nails thick as orange rind ushered us out. I wanted to put him on his guard but with Haz beside me, it was next to impossible.

'Just don't let anyone in until I come back,' I said.

He didn't appear to be listening. 'By the way,' he called after us. 'I have something for you, Jericho – a little surprise I found on the net after we talked last night. I think you'll find it quite revelatory.'

With a final wave, he closed the door.

'What was that all about?' Harry asked.

'I'd say that was assault with a deadly weapon. He's just lucky I'm not a police officer anymore.'

'And I'd call that evasion. Why did you need to see him so urgently? And why tell him not to open his door to strangers?' When I didn't answer, Haz pulled us to a stop. 'Scott, I'm serious. This case, you said it could be dangerous to a small number of people. Is Roebuck one of them? If you could just tell me, then I—'

I squeezed his hand. 'I've said before, I don't want you involved. If for nothing else then for my own sake. Whatever we have going on between us right now, it's the only good thing in my life. The only pure thing.' It felt like a necessary correction. Because, much as I didn't want to admit it, the case itself had changed my life for the better. 'And it isn't just this investigation,' I went on. 'If we stay together, and if I continue doing this kind of work, I'd always want to keep it separate.'

'For the reasons you told me,' he said softly. 'But I'm not a child, Scott. I've seen a lot of ugliness too. If you trust me, I might turn out to be stronger than you think.'

We went around in that same circle for twenty minutes or more, both of us, as it turned out, keeping our secrets. By the time we reached the heath, we were no further forward.

Banking up behind the woodland that bordered the heath roiled a black billow of cloud, shot through with sickly streaks of yellow that reminded me of Roebuck's tar-stained wallpaper. Though the summer sky remained mostly clear, that dark presence was like a pulsating tumour at the edge of the town, patiently waiting for its moment to spread.

As Harry's hand slipped into mine, I knew I was needed elsewhere. A killer's plan was drawing to its close and yet

254

here I was, about to fritter away precious hours at the fair. But the fact remained, with Roebuck and Hillstrom under protective surveillance, what else could I do? However I turned the current state of the case over in my mind, there were no fresh leads to follow, no further action I could take. All I could do now was wait and hope that some new development, possibly coming out of my interview with Roebuck this afternoon, would provide that final clue that would unmask the murderer.

Still, it felt like a betrayal to the victims as Harry and I joined the crowds streaming through the turnstiles.

Fairgrounds come into their own at night. Unchallenged by the glare and competing distractions of the day, the noise, the lights, the spectacle draw in the punters more easily. Daylight hours are usually when repairs are done, the working innards of rides exposed, spectres from the ghost train laid out upon the grass and revealed as simple malfunctioning mannequins. But that wasn't the case today. It was the opening of the memorial celebrations and, although the lights burned less brightly at noon, the heath was still teeming with punters.

Harry grinned at me like a little kid. And I couldn't help it, despite the anxiety that continued to gnaw at me, I smiled too.

I'd been born a showman. Had spent the first eighteen years of my life among these sights, these people, but suddenly it was as if I was seeing it all afresh through his eyes. The sheer, giddy wonder that makes a travelling fair so special. Watching him zigzag from one stall and ride to another, laughing as he won a plush toy from the hook-a-duck, weaving drunkenly as he jumped down from the Waltzer carriage, I felt both pride and shame. In rejecting some of the things about my people that made me feel like I didn't belong, I had rejected all of it – the joy, the love, the camaraderie. It was Harry who made me see all of that again.

At the dodgems, Big Sam Urnshaw swarmed out of his booth and came over to greet us. I introduced Harry and the old showman's sharp eyes flicked between us. I'd heard Sam joke about 'queers' in the past, but not since I'd come back and I wondered if perhaps he hadn't for a few years now. In any case, he slapped Harry on the back and guided him to 'the fastest car I got'. After bouncing us around the plates for a few minutes, Harry then dragged me away to the Ferris wheel.

Layla Jofford stopped her ride when we reached the top and, glancing down, I saw her snap me a salute. Layla had been a friend of my mum's and we'd always got on well.

'Don't they pause it here so that couples can kiss?' Harry said.

I leaned in. 'They do.'

After honouring this age-old tradition, we took in the view from our swaying gondola: the whole panorama of Bradbury End sitting in its bowl between the hills, the woods away to the north with the thread of the river. Somewhere beneath that green canopy, now overhung with the encroaching darkness of storm clouds, stood Travellers Bridge and the ruined house where a boy and his mother had lived their strange lives. Somewhere inside the compass of this town, a killer waited.

My eyes tracked back to the trailers set out at the edge of the ground. There was something like twenty-five families living and working on my father's fair. That added up to over two hundred individuals. Times that by the number of showpeople currently travelling around the UK and I was faced with a vast suspect pool. True, the story of the Jericho freaks was specific to my family's fair, but such legends are considered common property and I couldn't limit its reach to just our small corner of the community.

Back at ground level, Harry said he had a hankering for sugar so we set off towards the catering trucks. Giddy as ever, he ticked off on his fingers all the rides and attractions he still wanted to take in: helter-skelter, funhouse, and oh yes, he definitely wanted his palm read by one of the ancient aunts. We'd just ordered a couple of hot dogs when I heard my name being called. Webster in tow, Jodie came skipping towards us.

'Uncle Scott!' She threw her arms around my waist while Webster received a rapturous welcome from Haz. 'I've missed you! Did Mum tell you I've been 'vestigating ever since you left? I've really kept my eyes peeled and I've found out loads of clues.' She stopped, breathless. 'Who's this?'

'Jodie, Harry. Harry, Jodie,' I said.

'Oh.' She jabbed an elbow into my hip. 'Is this your boyfriend?'

Harry stood up from where he'd been scratching Webster's belly. He held out his hand and, after a second's hesitation, Jodie shook.

'I am indeed Uncle Scott's boyfriend,' he confirmed. 'And you must be his favourite niece.'

'Goddaughter,' Jodie corrected solemnly. 'I like your floppy hair.'

I laughed. I'd once told Sal that her daughter had an open mind. All kids do, I think.

'Where's your mum?' I asked.

She pointed over to the candyfloss stall where Sal was busy multitasking – one eye on the customers, one on her baby girl.

257

She clocked Harry and twirled a pink-headed stick in our direction.

'The famous Sally Myers,' Haz murmured. 'In the flesh.'

'Mum isn't famous.' Jodie rolled her eyes.

'Why don't you go and say hello,' I suggested. 'Take Webster with you. Me and the munchkin have detective things to discuss.'

This clearly delighted Jodie and she handed over Webster's lead.

'I'll take good care of him,' Harry promised, and together they trotted off towards Sal's stall.

'I like him,' Jodie said after a moment's consideration. 'He's very pretty. Maybe a bit too pretty for you?'

I clutched an invisible dagger to my heart and she giggled. 'So, Little Miss Detective, tell me, what have you found out?'

Grinning, she dragged a notebook from the back pocket of her dungarees. 'I've got, like, a million clues here.'

And so we sat cross-legged together on the grass, smiling punters cutting around us. No one seemed to mind, the good-will of the fair working its magic again. As a cool breeze, full of the promise of rain, suddenly whipped up around us, Jodie talked me through her clues – a discarded cigarette found by the teacup ride (very suspicious); the woman who'd bought six candyfloss bags from her mum but had come to the fair alone (ultra suspicious/possibly just greedy); the stranger who'd taken Webster and hadn't brought him back.

'Did you see this man?' I asked carefully.

She nodded. 'It was a couple of nights ago. Mum thought I was asleep but I wasn't sleepy at all. I saw him through my window and the next morning everyone thought you'd taken

Webster and wouldn't believe me when I said it wasn't you. You're big and tall and this man was sort of skinny-looking. But do you want to know the really funny thing?'

'Tell me.'

Jodie gave me her most serious detective look. 'It'll sound weird, but it's true, I promise.'

'I'll believe you,' I assured her.

'Well, the thing is . . .' she twisted her fingers together, 'that man that took Webster? When I looked at him, his face wasn't right.'

'What do you mean, sweetheart?'

She stared at me. 'It wasn't there, Uncle Scott. His face was all gone.'

Chapter Thirty-Six

H E DIDN'T HAVE A FACE. After Miss Debney and Alessandro Martinez, Jodie was my third witness. She had seen the killer, masked in his balaclava but not wearing his glowing vestments. When I questioned her, she claimed he'd been dressed entirely in black, like a figure cut out of the night. He'd emerged from behind my dad's trailer with Webster on his lead, and dog and man had soon vanished again into the dark. A few hours later, the juk would be dropped outside Harry's bungalow, a piece of Adya Mahal's flesh attached to his collar.

According to Jodie, the murderer moved through the ground with easy familiarity. Hearing this, my heart plummeted. It seemed to confirm what the victim connection had suggested – all this mad butchery was the work of a showman. A showman who most likely belonged to the Jericho travelling fair.

Something Garris had said came back to me then, '*Remember your Sherlock Holmes.*' What was that famous line of Conan Doyle's? When Holmes was asked by an inspector if there was anything to which he wished to draw to the officer's attention, he had replied, '*To the curious incident of the dog in the night-time.*'

Like the dog in that story, Webster had not barked, meaning he must know the killer. Was that what Garris had been implying? That Webster, who had taken a while to warm up to Harry and who barked at practically everyone, had known his abductor?

'Did I do a good detective job?' Jodie asked, drawing me out of my thoughts.

'You're the greatest detective that ever lived,' I told her and rewarded her with tickles.

When she was done giggling, she asked, 'So do you need help standing up now? Because you're old?'

I said I did and she used both hands to haul me upright. Snaking our way through the crowd, we joined a pink-lipped Harry at Jodie's stall. He dabbed my nose with his candyfloss and I tried my best to keep the tension out of my voice.

'I see someone's been having fun.'

'And not just because of the sugar,' he grinned. 'Sal and I have been talking.'

I glanced over at the munchkin's mother. She was leaning against the side of her stall, a Coke in hand, taking a well-earned break.

'I am not liking the sound of this,' I said.

Sal cocked an eyebrow. 'Never let the boyfriend and the best friend swap notes. All kinds of embarrassing secrets might come spilling out. Like that time two slightly high sixteen-year-olds videoed themselves recreating Dolly and Kenny's iconic "Islands in the Stream". Don't look so bashful, Scott, you made a very passable Dolly.'

'And you had the beard for a quite convincing Kenny Rogers,' I quipped back.

She bowed. 'It was always my honour to be your beard.'

Harry burst out laughing and, although she had no idea what we were talking about, Jodie joined in.

'I think I need to walk off some of this sugar,' he said. 'Do you want to give me a tour of the rest of the fair, Jodie?'

Sal nodded and Jodie grabbed Harry's hand, nattering away nineteen to the dozen as she pulled him back into the crowd. Meanwhile, Sal watched me from over the rim of her Coke.

'What?' I said after a solid minute of silent observation.

She shrugged. 'So that's the boy who broke your heart, is it?'

'I don't recall saying anything about a broken heart.' I bristled.

'That was just my brilliant guesswork at the time.' She tossed the empty can into a nearby bin, scattering a swarm of wasps. 'So how did you two bump into each other again after all these years?'

'That's a long story.' She narrowed her eyes. 'For Christ's sake, Sal, stop looking at me like that. Don't you like him or something?'

'That's the thing, I *do* like him. I liked him the first time you told me about him when you came back from Oxford that Christmas. And then, just a few months later, he pretty much destroyed your life, so forgive me if I'm a little suspicious.'

'That wasn't his fault,' I told her. 'He was dealing with some very dark shit back then.'

'But it isn't just that,' she said as if she hadn't heard me. 'I also wonder what he's doing here, right at the moment when you seem to be knee-deep in some very dark shit of your own. Oh, don't look so stressed, I'm not going to restart that old argument. You've promised that this case or whatever it is won't come back on us, and I guess I'll just have to take your word for that.' I cut my gaze away. When I'd made that promise I hadn't known about the connection between the victims. 'It just all seems a bit odd, doesn't it?'

Coincidences, I thought. They were almost the running theme of this case. But coincidences do happen, don't they? Despite what old Travellers might think, not everything is some vast conspiracy. And yet that phone call I'd overheard, apparently between Haz and his colleague at the library, sparked again in my mind: '*I think he bought it in the end . . .*'

'Anyway,' Sal continued, 'what were you going on about last night? I mean, it's pretty obvious that this case of yours is connected to that old story of the Jericho freaks. I just can't for the life of me imagine how.'

'Has anyone around here been asking about it?' I said. 'Maybe one of the younger Travellers bothering the aunts with questions?'

'Scott . . .' she began.

'Please,' I said, 'humour me.'

She glanced over at her stall where one of the chaps was making a mess of negotiating clouds of candyfloss onto their wooden sticks. 'Christ's sake, Martin, it's not brain surgery. Twist and flick, you divvy gorger.' She turned back to me 'It wasn't a Traveller, as it happens. It was one of them. A chap. *Your* chap, in fact. The one you ditched and who's been mooning around like a lovesick teenager ever since you left.'

'Zac?' I frowned.

'That's the cherub. I honestly don't know what they see in you, but he's got it bad. He must have asked me a hundred times to get you to call him. Anyway, he came to me the day the handbills were printed for this here event. Said he was curious, wanted to know what the anniversary was all about. I told him the basic story.'

'Did he pursue it?' I asked.

'What do you mean?'

'Did he want to know specific details? Who died, where exactly it happened, that sort of thing?'

'I don't think so. To be honest, I can't really remember what I told him.'

I mulled it over. We'd picked up Zac in Hampstead a few months ago; a law student working the circuit for his summer job. Although, thinking about it, our chaps didn't usually come from the halls of high academia. There had also been the suggestion of an unsettled home life, I remembered: a snapshot I'd glimpsed in his wallet with a family member torn out. If it wasn't for the fact the dates didn't work, Zac could be an ideal suspect for Jonathan Matthers. A boy who might have come to resent the father who'd died, leaving him alone with that overly protective mother. But Matthers would be at least two decades older than Zac.

Something in mine and Garris's discussion of the killer niggled, however. How had Pete phrased it? '*If our man fits the typical profile, he's likely to be a loner without a family or normal home life, although he may give the illusion he has one.*' Had Zac meant for me to see that snapshot, simply to foster the impression of an existing if dysfunctional family? Was he Garris's loner? A fixated murderer who perhaps wanted to belong to the community he'd decided to avenge?

'Speak of the devil,' Sal said, nudging my arm.

I turned to find Zac jogging towards us.

'I better get back to the stall before Martin burns it down.' She prodded a forefinger into my chest. 'You go easy with him.'

As Zac came bounding up, I tried not to picture those Michelangelo buttocks and focused instead on what I could see. A tight, nervous smile; a day or two of growth on those usually smooth cheeks; shadows under the eyes; fingers raking through a briar of dirty blond hair. He looked jittery as hell, which was reassuring. Unless Zac was putting on an act, our killer was not the jittery type. Only one thing troubled me: another ballpoint scrawl on the back of his hand, this one reaching under his cuff. He was obviously in the habit of making these reminders, and I thought again of a figure in white clutching at his wrist.

'Hey,' he said, a little breathless.

'Hello, Zac.'

I felt like a bastard, but I let the silence stretch out between us. Guilt abhors a vacuum.

'How've you been?' he asked.

'Fine.'

'You look well ... So I'm sorry about that text I sent the morning you left,' he said, his words suddenly rushing together. 'I guess I was upset that you didn't say goodbye and I ...'

I allowed another beat. 'Don't worry about it.' I nodded.

He started twisting his fingers together, almost like Jodie had done minutes before.

'I just thought we'd connected, you know?'

'That was my fault,' I said gently. 'I wasn't in a great place back then and, if I'm honest, I didn't treat you very well. In fact, I suppose I used you. I'm sorry, Zac. You deserve better.'

He stepped forward. 'I don't care about that. But look, I do think that maybe something was beginning to happen between us. I like you, Scott.'

'Zac—'

'Just hear me out. I know you're a bit older than me, but I don't care about things like that.' His fingertips caressed my wrist. 'I suppose I'd like to get to know you properly. Maybe we could start by having that drink we talked about.'

I pulled his hand away. 'I can't.'

'You ... You know, don't you?' He started scratching fiercely at that ballpoint scrawl. 'He told you what I did. That evil fucker, he promised he wouldn't. Scott, I'm sorry. But that morning you left, I was so angry. It felt like you were abandoning me and I suppose I just ... I fucked up, OK?'

I shook my head. 'Zac, what did you do?'

He looked at me with desolate eyes. 'I wanted to hurt you. Wanted to lash out. I don't know. But I cared about you and I—'

'What's going on?' Harry asked, appearing from nowhere and slipping in beside me.

Zac's gaze flicked downwards to where Harry's hand slid into mine. His features twisted, in pain or in anger, I couldn't tell. In the next moment, he was gone, vanishing back into the chaos of the fair.

'What was that all that about?' Harry asked.

'I don't know,' I said.

But already a bleak suspicion was forming in my mind.

Chapter Thirty-Seven

THOSE SILENT AND TUMOROUS THUNDERHEADS were beginning to roll across the heath when Harry insisted we go in search of my father. I was actually surprised we hadn't seen him. Usually, he'd be patrolling up and down the main strip and side grounds, checking the take on his own rides, calculating punter numbers in his head. This went double for any opening day, but no one seemed to know where he'd got to.

Dropping Webster off at his kennel, I mounted the steps to Dad's ancient Colchester and knocked. I can't say I wasn't relieved when he didn't answer. I glanced back at Harry and shrugged.

'Nobody home.'

'That's a shame,' he said. 'I never did get to meet him when we were together in Oxford. Maybe we can take him out to dinner before the fair leaves town? Unless ...'

I came back down the steps. 'Unless what?'

'Well, we haven't really talked about what you're going to do once this case is over.' His gaze roamed around the corral of caravans. 'I mean, when you find whatever it is you're looking for, what will happen to us then?'

Something in the way he said those words ought to have alerted me to what I would discover later. At that moment, however, I took them at face value.

'Then I think you and I should take a little holiday. A proper one this time.'

'Couple up your trailer and hit the road?' He smiled, though his smile looked sad. 'I like the sound of that.'

'Then that's what we'll do.' I checked my watch. 'In the meantime, I better get to my appointment with Roebuck. God only knows what he does to latecomers, but I'm imagining inquisitorial torture devices.'

Harry nodded. 'And I suppose I should look in on the library girls. Smooth things over with Val.'

We said our goodbyes to Webster and headed back towards the main gate.

People were still streaming through, eyes wide, tickets clasped in sweaty hands. They didn't seem to mind the gathering storm clouds, those seething scraps of darkness now racing in the reflection of every windscreen, the sun sparking in the spaces between. Sparking too in Alistair Carmody's binoculars as he trained them on the ponderous revolutions of the Ferris wheel. He stood in the parking area at the western edge of the fair, alone it seemed, his balding head slick as an ice rink, the tip of a pink tongue poking between his teeth. He reminded me of that other watchful loner who had come to the fair – the paedophile, Jeremy Worth, who had originally set me on this strange journey. I wondered then whether Carmody might just be the same kind of predator.

'See you back at the house?' Harry said, kissing the side of my face.

'Sure. In about an hour. And Haz?' He glanced back. 'Be careful.'

'Don't worry,' he said, waving away my concern. 'I'll steer well clear of the protest.'

I watched him go. In truth, it wasn't Lenny Kerrigan and his Knights of St George that worried me. Today, someone far deadlier was lurking behind the pretty façade of Bradbury End.

All the anti-mosque demonstrators appeared to have reached their rally point in the town's east end. At least I didn't encounter any of the placard-waving buffoons as I marched back up the hill. Despite the odd little gust of cool air, the atmosphere felt heavy with the promise of the storm. Soon they'd have to shut down the Ferris wheel in case a stray lightning strike caught one of the gondolas and fried a pair of young lovers mid-kiss.

Thoughts of Zac accompanied me all the way to Roebuck's door. *'I wanted to hurt you. Wanted to lash out.'* I believed I knew what he'd meant. At least it explained one of the minor mysteries that had been dogging me ever since this whole mess began. Once I'd got what I needed from our eccentric historian, I'd go back to the fair and question Zac again. It wasn't a prospect I relished, but it had to be done.

My phone bleeped. A message from Garris:

Just heard from my local CID contact. The idiots have pulled both patrols an hour ago. Apparently uniform has had intel of trouble brewing in town with this mosque protest and it's all hands on deck. I tried to argue our case but being unable to give them full details of the threat, they refused to keep the officers in place. I'm sorry, Scott. Message me back when you can.

'Fuck,' I muttered, glancing up at the empty street.

With everyone seemingly at the rally or the fair, only the breeze moved here, creaking Roebuck's gate on its rusted hinges. Up ahead, I could see the door standing open, almost like an invitation. On a day like this, anyone might want to air their home, yet every window facing the street was closed. Crossing the garden, I paused only to reconsider that broken pane in the door. He'd thought a child had done it. Now I wondered if it had been prepared earlier. So easy then, once the police had left the scene, to reach through and unsnib the latch on the other side.

'Mr Roebuck?'

No answer. I stepped inside.

The daylight seemed to stop dead at the threshold. Beyond, the hall stretched away, almost every inch of wall covered in mounted artefacts and framed historical curios. Not a single personal photograph that I could see. To my right stood the stairs, where even the bannister had been painted yellow by the tarry touch of Roebuck's cigarettes. Further down the corridor, a kitchen with the vague shapes of pots and pans stacked on the drainer.

Before closing the door, I wiped the handle with the hem of my T-shirt and then slipped my hands into my pockets. An old bit of training coming back to me – idle hands might well be the devil's tools but they also had an unconscious habit of touching things and leaving traces. I turned to the sitting-room door. The toe-end of a muddy footprint here. I recognised the same irregular pattern from the impression of the fake trainer I'd seen at the Matthers' house. There was no doubt that it had been made deliberately – there were no other prints on the carpet and the earth outside was summer-hard. He had brought the trainer with him and left this as a trademark for me to find. I stepped around it and used my shoulder to push open the door.

It's a common misconception that a dead body will almost immediately invite hosts of insects. In reality, the blowfly only begins to lay its eggs in a corpse forty-eight hours after the heart has stopped. True, I had once heard a mortician claim that certain species of fly can predict death and start to hover in anticipation. This is in cases of advanced disease, however, where triggering odours play a role. In instances of violent death, the scavengers take a while to gather.

That was why I knew the flies in Roebuck's sitting room were more interested in the spilled milkshake on the carpet than in the corpse. Soon enough their attentions would turn to the figure in the office chair, but for now, that curdling mess at his feet was a more enticing treat. Laced into the odour of sickly-sweet strawberry, I could also detect the iron tang of blood. Strange, because even with his back to me, I could see that Roebuck had been strangled. The ligature mark on the back of his neck stood out, about the width of a thumb, suggesting something thinner than a belt had been used. Perhaps a tie or a dressing gown cord.

The historian's head was tilted forward but he hadn't collapsed to the floor. Though the rope fastened around his upper body and the chair-back was too thin to have been the ligature, it

271

held him in place securely enough. On the cluttered desk in front of him, his laptop screensaver rotated a galaxy of stars. Light, which in the curtained dimness of the room, played eerily across the smooth surface of two floating red balloons.

At first, I thought that the corpse must be holding onto them. That the killer had maybe taped their string to his hands. But then I saw those long white fingers hanging down on either side of the chair and, thinking back to the Jericho freaks, I guessed what had been done to Gerald Roebuck. Those cheery carnival balloons, taken in all likelihood from my father's fair earlier in the day, had been anchored in the most fitting way. For here he was, our fourth victim: a twisted recreation of Gulliver Rice, the Balloon-Headed Horror.

My heart hammered out a thick beat as I rounded the chair. I'd guessed correctly, but still couldn't suppress my disgust.

'Fucking animal.'

But no, no animal savagery here. Just that calm, collected mind at work again. Upon Roebuck's forehead, the carved and dripping letter 'M' for 'Meloria,' the fourth word in the Travellers Bridge inscription. Horrible enough, but this was not the focus of the killer's design. With his latest effort, he had interpreted the recreation in a symbolic sense.

After scooping out the historian's eyes, he'd probably used some kind of long, curved needle to then thread a single string under and between the now vacant sockets. I imagined him standing here, one hand supporting the back of the dead man's head as he pushed the instrument into the left hollow and then, tunnelling it under the gristle of the nasal bridge, had pulled it back out of the right socket. With the thread now moored between the empty eyes, he had drawn it through to equal lengths and, attaching the balloons to either end, had set them bobbing against the ceiling.

I straightened up from my examination. Mixed in with horror and contempt for the crime, I had to admit to a less noble emotion. Relief. This proved, beyond doubt, that Harry was not involved in the case. Except for those few minutes when Jodie had taken him on a tour of the fair, he'd been with me ever since we left Roebuck alive at 12.15. This window of opportunity probably also ruled out Zac. It would be hard for a chap to get away on opening day, and anyway, my suspicions concerning him were not tied to the murders.

Did this also rule out the other Travellers currently in Bradbury End? Not necessarily. Ride and stall owners would have more freedom to come and go. Like my dad, they might slip away for half an hour to chat with their mates or to see how the competition was doing. And where exactly was my father anyway? No one seemed to know. I looked back at Roebuck, that blood-flecked string springing from his eyes like strange optic stalks. No. I didn't always like my father, but I could never imagine him doing something like this.

And yet Roebuck had wanted to go to the fair. That had been part of my deal with him – to provide an introduction to some of the old showpeople so he might interview them for his archives. Had he gone there already? Spoken to someone, let a detail slip that put the killer on edge? Or was he simply selected because he was a descendant of those Bradburians who'd supposedly conspired to weaken the bridge?

I turned from the corpse to the plaque on the wall behind him. The commemorative stone bearing the names of the original benefactors of Travellers Bridge: William McAllister,

Daniel Poole, Margaret Fielding, Stephen Roebuck. These names had all been scored out using, I was certain, blood from the inkwell of Gerald Roebuck's eyes. But one name was missing: Gideon Hillstrom.

I moved across to the plaque, resisting the urge to touch the place where the name had been chiselled away. On the floor below sat a small hammer and a dusting of stone. What did this mean? That Marcus Hillstrom was not to be the fifth victim? That he was, in fact, the killer?

My thoughts were interrupted by the sudden ringing of my phone.

Chapter Thirty-Eight

'You've got that edge in your voice. What's happened?'

I knew what Garris meant, though I didn't like to admit it. The tension, the excitement, the thrill that always came in the closing hours of a case, I could feel it coursing through me.

'Pete, I'm so sorry about Harriet—' I began.

He cut me off. 'You can give me your sympathies later. Tell me.'

I closed my eyes. 'Roebuck's dead. The bastard waited until the surveillance was called off ...'

It felt good to unpack my thinking as methodically as I could. Like the old days, in fact, when we'd pass facts and theories between each other over a pint in The Three Crowns. Garris listened, interjecting only to pose a question or challenge an assumption. When I reached the defacement of the commemorative stone, I heard him take a sharp drag on his cigarette.

'I think it's impossible to say right now what the removal of Hillstrom's name might mean. You said he was in meetings all day?'

'His secretary said he'd call me when he got out at four,' I said. 'But listen, I'm pretty sure the mayor can rearrange his schedule at will. He might easily have slipped away during his lunch hour and paid Roebuck a visit.'

Garris cleared his throat. 'Or it could be this Jonathan Matthers returned? You said Roebuck knew him as a boy?'

'That's right. He said the kid used to come into the library when he worked there. That he was "captivated" by the story of the Jericho freaks.'

'So Matthers might not only have wanted to add Gerald Roebuck to his design but also silence him? I mean, if he was back in Bradbury End and Roebuck recognised him?'

'Possibly,' I said. 'But look, I need to find Marcus Hillstrom. Whether he's the killer or in danger himself, I—'

'No.' There was no mistaking the finality in his tone. 'We discussed this at the beginning, Scott. It's time you handed the case over. Surely you see that? Look, if you wait there, I'll make a call to my contact in the Major Investigation Team. They can be with you inside the hour ...'

But I wasn't listening anymore. Feeling the case slipping away from me, I was picturing all the victims; not just the four unfortunates the killer had remade into such sick caricatures, but Miss Debney and Alessandro and even Jodie. She hadn't known that she'd seen a monster that night, but when the news of the murders broke it would be hard to keep it from her. Then what nightmares might come in the dark?

'Scott, are you there?'

'I'm sorry, Pete, I have to go.'

'Don't be a bloody idiot,' he barked. 'Just listen!'

I cancelled the call. It was a betrayal of my promise to Garris, but I had to see this thing through to the end. I had to be the one to find him.

I was about to take one last look around the sitting room when a knock sounded from the hall.

'Package to sign for, Mr R!'

'Fuck,' I muttered under my breath.

No way I could risk leaving by the front door now. With Roebuck's being one of the first houses, the postman would be in the street for a while. How I'd left things with Garris, I didn't think he'd call the case in until we'd spoken again, and so there was no reason just yet to associate myself with the crime scene. Only one option, then.

The outline of the postie was still lingering behind the glazed portion of the front door when I slipped into the hall. Thank God it was so gloomy, he didn't appear to see me as he knocked and called. Meanwhile, I crept into the tiny kitchen at the rear. One of the milkshake flies had followed me, darting over my shoulder and settling on the handle of the back door. The key was in the lock. I swatted the fly away and used the hem of my T-shirt to turn the key and twist the knob.

I emerged onto a scrubby patch of garden just as the postie dropped his 'Sorry We Missed You' card through the letterbox. I closed the door behind me. Even with most of the street out at the fair or attending the rally, I was glad that the rear of Roebuck's property wasn't overlooked. A high fence ended in a gate that led to a back alley where the bins were kept. Here a tabby cat sunning itself on the paving stones watched me out of one lazy-lidded eye as I passed into the road beyond.

I checked my phone. Garris hadn't tried calling back. I wondered if he'd finally despaired of me or, worse still for my conscience, had left his dead wife and was already on his way to Bradbury End. Striding down the hill, I did my best to ignore the guilt that gnawed at me. My opportunity to reach Hillstrom was already closing and I needed to be focused when I questioned him. It was bound to be a subtle balance, probing his movements without arousing his suspicions.

As I walked, turning the meaning of the vandalised plaque over in my mind, another thought kept niggling at me. Something Roebuck had said that, in the wake of discovering the body, I had forgotten. I tried to coax the memory but it stayed stubbornly out of reach. For the moment, I let it rest and switched back to the plaque. If Hillstrom wasn't the killer but remained a potential fifth victim, then what did the removal of his ancestor's name signify? Perhaps this time it wouldn't be a recreation of the final freak – the Contortionist, Matthew 'Slip-Jointed' Jericho – but something altogether different. Unless of course . . .

'Ah, shit.'

Rounding the bend, I'd almost crashed straight into them. I should have realised that the way to the council chamber would take me via the rally point. Caught up in my thoughts, I hadn't even noticed the chanting. Now the mob pulsated before me, fifty or more faces twisted into hateful laughter, white-supremacist emblems on every T-shirt and bandana. Taking up most of the street in front of the completed mosque, they pushed and tugged at each other like the playground bullies they were.

Only one thing redeemed the scene: shoved to the fringes, I could see from their troubled expressions that the remaining

Bradburians – those who hadn't already left – had realised what a Pandora's box they'd opened. Their placards that earlier in the day had been wafted so proudly now lay heaped at their feet. Meanwhile, a thin line of officers did their best to marshal the thugs.

During my time in uniform, I'd helped police enough demos to read the signals they were telegraphing to each other. The situation was teetering on the brink. All it would take was one wrong word, one stray missile, a misinterpreted glance and the whole thing could go up like a powder keg. I had no doubt that, when it did, Lenny Kerrigan would be at the heart of it.

We locked eyes, the murderer of the Malanowski children and I. He was stationed with his crew on the far side of the street and, at the sight of me, whispered something to his Neanderthal deputy, Mickey 'Fat Boy' Wallace. I watched as this murmur did the rounds of the dozen or so Knights of St George. Then Lenny was taking out his phone and shooting me that shit-eating grin.

I didn't have time for this.

An alleyway, barely wide enough to allow two people to walk down shoulder-to-shoulder, cut away from the road. My footfalls echoed from wall to wall as I took this exit. The sun did not reach here and the chanting behind me soon became muffled again. I'd almost reached the far end when I remembered what Roebuck had said the last time we'd seen him, *'I have something for you – a little surprise I found on the net after we talked last night. I think you'll find it quite revelatory.'*

I glanced back the way I'd come. Could I risk returning to the historian's house? Unless the killer had taken it, there was a chance that whatever he'd discovered might still be among Roebuck's papers. Perhaps on that cluttered desk. And if Garris hadn't called his Major Investigations contact then—

'Where's the other little faggot, eh? Had a lovers' tiff, Scotty?'

Lenny Kerrigan, leading the Knights of St George into the alley. I *really* didn't have time for this. Flipping Lenny the bird, I turned my back on him just in time to meet a colossal fist that slammed the sweet spot between my eyes. For a split second, my vision went dark and I staggered sideways into the wall. Meanwhile, Kerrigan called out to his second-in-command.

'Fuck's sake, Mickster. I said don't start on him until I give the word.'

'Sorry, Len. Got carried away.'

I spun around, flicked the blood from my nose, shook my head until the alley reappeared before me. From the narrow strip of sky above, the first patter of rain began to fall.

'You want to go toe-to-toe with me, Lenny, that's fine,' I grunted. 'But right now I've got more important things on my plate. So move the fuck aside.'

I lunged towards them and at least six jolted back in surprise. Kerrigan held his ground, though the trademark smile faltered.

'Let him come to us,' he muttered. 'Just like we said.'

'I don't know what game you're playing here,' I spat back, 'though I guess it's got something to do with this "big surprise" you've been crowing about. Honestly, Kerrigan, I don't care. You name the time and the place and I'll happily trot along and beat the ever-living shit out of you, just like I did in that interview room.'

Thunder rumbled, finding its voice in the throat of the alley. The rain strengthened and ran like angry tears down Kerrigan's face.

'You got the jump on me!' Some of his followers couldn't hide their looks of contempt as he practically screamed words. 'If you hadn't come at me sudden like that, I'd have fucked you up!'

'You'd have tried. And I'd still have made you piss your pants in terror. You know your problem, Lenny?' Conscious of Wallace lurking behind me, I took another step forward. I noticed that Lenny's Knights had to push at their leader's shoulders to keep him from stepping back. 'You're weak. Hollow right through. All you are is an angry child shrieking at a world it doesn't understand. So step aside, you mewling toddler, and let me—'

I should've seen it. That backwards movement of Kerrigan's hand as he took the crowbar from one of the thugs behind him. But right then something else had caught my eye: the light, the glint, the dazzle that I had first glimpsed in the woods surrounding Marco's diner and then again in the forest by Travellers Bridge. Now it sparked at the shadowy mouth of the alley. Not Carmody's binoculars but a single lens, fixed and focused on me, the glare of daylight reflected in a cyclopean glass eye. Finally understanding what it was, I couldn't help a rueful smile.

The smile was still on my lips when I hit the ground.

Chapter Thirty-Nine

THE PAPARAZZO'S LENS DAZZLED IN the first lightning strike.

I should have known. Of course, it made no sense that she would have just given up. As soon as she'd caught wind of the story – brilliant young CID detective beats suspected child murderer to a pulp – press photographer Maxine Thierrot had stalked my every move. Throughout my trial she'd been there, that ever-watchful camera's eye greeting me as I arrived at court and then lying in wait whenever Garris and I had taken a break. And it hadn't ended there. Eighteen months later, I had found her lurking in the prison car park when Sal came to pick me up. Eventually, her editor had tired of the story and pulled her from the gig, but before that she'd spent weeks hanging around the fair.

Only once had I asked her why she was so fascinated with me. That had been on my last day before sentencing. I remember us on the court steps, Garris trying to pull me away, Thierrot giving me a cool professional shrug.

'It's nothing personal,' she'd said. 'You're just a good story, that's all.'

'Well, now you can put away your little camera,' I'd retorted. 'The story's over.'

'Oh no.' She'd smiled. 'I really don't think it is. Because whatever made you throw your life away, it's still inside you. The violence, the anger? And you know what? I think you'll do it again. Just know, I'll be there when it happens.'

I guess she'd got tired of waiting and had decided to give the story a little push. Only the game she'd been playing with Lenny Kerrigan hadn't worked out the way she'd hoped. I could see that much from her pinched expression as she strode into the alley. That was why, despite the pain in my ribs from the crowbar, I smiled.

'You fucking idiot.' Pushing Mickey aside, she fronted up to Kerrigan. 'Can't you follow a simple instruction? You were supposed to provoke him into attacking *you*. How am I supposed to use this?' She looked down on me as I rolled onto my back, gritting my teeth and laughing against the agony. 'Just look at him. He's the fucking victim here!'

Lenny appeared dumbfounded. I could almost hear the cogs grinding in that primitive excuse for a brain. Predictably, confusion gave way to rage.

'You better give me my fucking money, you stuck-up bitch,' he shrieked at her. 'It wasn't my fault you didn't get the shot when he came at me outside that shitty diner. I got people I owe. Bad fucking hombres who'll cut off my nuts if I don't pay up.'

Thierrot gave one of her indifferent shrugs, the camera swinging from the strap around her neck. 'I was in our agreed position in the scrubland outside the diner, you were supposed to lure him there. By the time I got to you, it was too late to get a decent shot. As for the money, you won a small fortune in damages from our friend here. It isn't my fault that you pissed it all away on coke and hookers. Our arrangement was contingent on you getting me the shot I needed to sell my story. Violent Ex-cop Pursues Vendetta Against Far-right Thug. You didn't deliver that story, so the deal's off.'

The laughter was like blades stabbing at my guts but I couldn't help it.

'So this was how you were playing me, was it? This was your huge surprise? You know, it's funny, Kerrigan. For just a minute, I wondered if you were involved in something much bigger than some slapstick tabloid sting. But no, even this farce was beyond you, wasn't it?'

Thierrot smiled. It might sound strange, but I honestly didn't think there was anything personal in what she'd planned with Kerrigan. It was all just as neat and clinical and businesslike as her well-cut suit and spirit-level fringe. The grey eyes behind her severe spectacles showed no emotion at all as she nodded in agreement.

'You're right, Mr Jericho, I played this very poorly. I certainly should never have involved myself with someone who takes half an hour over his shoelaces each morning. But what I said to you that day outside the court still stands. Whatever this thing is you have inside you, it will show itself again. And I will be there when it does.'

With that, she turned on her kitten heel and swept out of the alley.

It was then that something struck me as odd about the whole arrangement. Thierrot would have been well paid if she had snapped the right picture, but well enough to warrant all this effort and expense? Well enough to involve herself with a poisonous thug like Lenny Kerrigan? The set-up didn't quite ring true, but at that moment a fresh wave of pain rolled over me and made the idea difficult to pursue.

Kerrigan watched his meal ticket depart, a stunned expression on his face. Those rusty gears were working overtime now. I half expected steam to start shooting out of his cauliflower ears. With their leader reduced to a state of apparent catalepsy, Mickey assumed command. It was raining hard now and I knew from my experience policing far-right protests that one thing a fascist can't bear is getting his little bovver boots damp. At Mickey's suggestion, the Knights of St George started to disperse.

Coming to his senses at last, Lenny called after them. 'Where the hell do you think you're going?' He tapped my knee with the crowbar. 'We've got business to settle here.'

The thugs just turned up their collars and continued on their way. They'd seen their glorious leader humiliated, not just by a common 'gypo' but, perhaps worse in their eyes, by a woman. Even the once-loyal Mickey couldn't hide his disgust.

'You do what you want, Len,' he grunted. 'I'm off for a pie and a pint.'

'Get back here, Fat Boy!' Kerrigan screamed. 'That's an order!'

Mickey gave him one last glance, then cast his gaze at the ground where I was struggling to get to my feet. 'That ex-copper might be a pikey, but he's right about you, Len. There ain't nothing to you. No spine anyway.'

Lenny's threats and Mickey's footsteps faded away into the rain. With my face to the dripping wall, my fingers scrabbling for purchase at the bricks as I righted myself, I thought they had left me alone. I ought to have known better. A coward, Fat Boy had called him. Well, cowards don't pass up opportunities like this, not when their enemy is at a disadvantage.

Running steps behind me. The whistle of the crowbar through the air. My spine howling at the impact. A swift follow-up and my right shoulder bellowed. I lost whatever grip I had on the wall and hit the ground again. Rolling onto my back, I saw Kerrigan standing above me, framed against that roiling channel of the sky. His eyes were huge, his mouth drawn into a clown-like rictus, spit foaming between his teeth. He had played his hand and had lost everything. Pretty soon some 'bad hombres' were going to inflict real damage on our Lenny, perhaps make an example of him. I knew the type from my own thug-for-hire years and I didn't fancy Kerrigan's chances. All he now possessed was his rage and the crowbar that he held high above his head.

I tried to raise myself, to kick at him, but the agony in my back kept me rooted to the cobblestones.

'I'm gonna fucking *murder* you!' he screamed.

There was no point reasoning with him, I could see that. I'd dealt with people suffering this kind of extreme psychotic break before and all you could do was pin them down and hope the paramedics arrived before anyone got seriously hurt. In those instances, I'd always had backup, pepper spray, and a baton to resort to. Now I'd just have to hope Kerrigan tired himself out before he killed me.

No point calling for help either. Outside the alley, I could see that the street had been abandoned, discarded placards heaped on the pavement. Sheets of rain rebounded off the road so that even if a passing motorist happened to glance this way, they'd be unable to see anything behind that silver curtain. In any case, the roar of the storm would drown out my cries.

When it came, the blow wasn't a direct hit but a fumbled attack that grazed the top of my head. Even so, the pain was extraordinary. A jagged fork that danced before my eyes, it resembled the lightning carving up the sky. Immediately my stomach clenched and I vomited onto the cobblestones. Kerrigan was saying something – screaming something – but his words didn't matter. In the flashes between the pain, I could see them again: the Malanowski children. My constant companions, they stood at the mouth of the alley. Sonia and the boys, pity in their eyes. Only this time they weren't alone.

He was with them. That dark angel in his balaclava mask, looming up behind my ghosts. That relentless killer who'd visited such cruel deaths upon McAllister, Poole, Mahal and Roebuck. Who would now recreate one more Jericho freak before his design was complete. I wouldn't be able to save Marcus Hillstrom. Wouldn't be able to unpick the puzzle at last. I had failed again.

Just like at the railway crossing, the killer lifted his hand and waved.

In the next instant, the crowbar fell and with it, darkness.

Chapter Forty

OPENING NIGHT AND NOT A soul had come to the fair.

I staggered alone among the stalls and rides, clutching bruised ribs, blood trickling from my torn scalp into my eyes. Amid pulsing lights and the carousel's jangled calliope, I tried to call out for Sal and my dad. Even for Harry, who had so loved his visit to the fair. No one answered. No one moved in the shadows. No one ...

Turning onto the main strip, a carnival tent appeared before me, its red and white stripes running like the blood that dribbled down my face. On a raised dais outside stood a man in pale vestments, his head haloed, his face a dark and howling void. From this emptiness, he bellowed his spiel:

'Roll up, Scott Jericho, roll up! Come and experience the most legendary display of phantasmagoria ever to grace a show-man's stage! Amazing sights to both captivate and horrify the senses! No friend will credit the stories you'll have to tell of the miracles, natural and otherwise, that you will see here tonight! But do not let such considerations deter you! Once in a lifetime – perhaps twice, if Lady Luck is smiling – will you encounter such rare and exotic creatures as these. Roll up, I say, and bear witness to the freaks of Jericho!'

They shuffled out of the tent behind him, four figures who came to kneel in front of the dais. Robert McAllister with his drooling canine jaws; Agatha Poole, shooting sparks from her wire-tipped fingers; Adya Mahal, shoving hunks of flesh into her mouth; Gerald Roebuck staring up at the balloons tethered from his eyes. There was no more preamble. Conjuring a crowbar out of thin air, the killer stepped down from the platform and moved swiftly along the line, smashing skulls as he went.

'Don't you worry, Scott,' he grunted at me. 'Just keep telling yourself, it's only a story. None of it's real. None of it.'

Finally, they lay at his feet and, twirling the crowbar like a cane, he pointed it to an empty space at the end of the row.

'Just the Contortionist left,' he said, a little breathlessly. 'Then the story will be done ... Except you don't want it to be done, do you? No, Scott Jericho always needs a puzzle. To feed him, to connect him to the world, to make him feel alive ...'

My eyes flickered open. In the harsh clinical glare, the phantom figure of the killer vanished, just like it had back in the alleyway. I blinked hard, took a breath, felt it catch around my ribs. Coughing against the pain, I snatched at the plastic cup that was offered to me and managed a few shallow sips.

'Take it easy,' my dad advised. Then, handing me a couple of pills, 'They said to give you these when you woke up.'

I looked into my palm and groaned. 'Paracetamol? Are you kidding me? My head feels like it's been hit by a truck.'

'They've already hooked you up to the good stuff,' he said. 'Even you shouldn't need much more than that.'

I glanced at the back of my hand. A cannula was taped there, the drip stand beside my bed feeding me a bagful of intravenous treats. I guessed I'd just have to wait until the happy vibes kicked in. In the meantime, these weren't my precious benzos but I swallowed the paracetamols anyway.

'How long have I been out?' I asked.

I was lying in a screened-off section of a ward. From behind the curtain came the steady beep of monitors and the indecipherable whisper of doctors and nurses.

'About five hours,' Dad said, collapsing into a chair at the end of the bed. 'Docs think you might have a concussion so they want to keep you in overnight. You looked a proper state when I got here, but they told me there's no bones broken and no internal bleeding.'

I took a peek under the covers and winced. My torso was the colour of a spectacular sunset, all flaming reds and brooding purples. Lifting careful fingertips to my head, I found it swathed in bandages. Just a little pressure at my temple was enough to ignite stars.

'Some old girl out doing her shopping found you in the alleyway,' Dad went on. 'Half-scared her to death, so I heard. Do you remember what happened?'

'Kerrigan,' I muttered.

Dad lifted his eyes to the ceiling. 'Might have known. Had that rally today, didn't they? How did you get yourself mixed up in all that? Playing the hero again or was it something to do with this mysterious case of yours?' When I didn't answer he gave me a knowing nod. 'Keep your secrets, then.'

'I wonder why he stopped?' I said after a moment's silence.

'Maybe he got scared, seeing how bad he'd hurt you. Or else someone disturbed him. Whatever the reason, what he did today won't stand. I told you once that we have ways of calming an animal like that right down. You leave him to us now, son.'

'Dad, I don't think—'

Shaking his head, my father stood. 'I said, leave him to us.'

There was something in his eyes, an anger I'd only seen a couple of times before. I wondered if others had seen the same thing in me in recent years.

'What happened to you today?' I asked. 'We came looking for you at the fair but nobody knew where you were.'

He waved a dismissive hand. 'I had some business to take care of.'

'What business?'

'None of yours, is what.'

I could tell that was the only answer I was likely to get. 'Is my mobile here?' I asked, scanning the over-bed table and bedside cupboard. 'I need to speak to Garris, and there's somebody else I have to call.'

'They're both here,' Dad said. 'The old gavver's just parking his car and the boy's grabbing us some coffees.'

I stared at him. 'You've met Harry?'

'He gave Sal his number today.' Dad nodded. 'So when she heard what had happened, she called him. Seems like a nice joskin. Your boyfriend too, I take it?'

Although I'd come out to my father just before my twentieth birthday, I had never introduced him to anyone I'd dated. In fact, after that awkward, stilted confession in his trailer, the subject had hardly ever been mentioned again. In this day and age, I wasn't the only openly gay Traveller, but for the most part, our existence, while tolerated, wasn't discussed or even acknowledged all that much. This was one of the rare times my dad had referred to it.

'Yes,' I said. 'He's my boyfriend.'

'Sal said you met him back in Oxford. So you what, stayed in touch? Reconnected?'

'Something like that. Look, I—'

A hand tugged at the curtain and a face appeared in the gap.

'Can I come in?' asked Zac. He glanced over at me, his expression a muddle of fear and concern. My dad clapped the chap on the shoulder.

'Don't look so scared, sonny. He's not as bad as he looks.'

'Dad, can you give us a minute?' I asked.

The old man shot me a questioning glance. 'Sure. I'll go and find that boy with my coffee. He must've walked all the way to Colombia to get it.'

I beckoned Zac to pull up the chair to the side of my bed. He did so reluctantly, his gaze landing everywhere except my face. Patches of oil and dirt stained his vintage Spice Girls T-shirt, evidence of a full day's hard labour on the fairground. Fresh sweat plastered the cotton to his torso and my guess was that, hearing the news, he'd run all the way here. He kept raking shaky fingers through those dirty blond locks until I reached over and took his wrist.

'You told Kerrigan I was going to Bradbury End,' I said gently. 'That's how he found me at the diner. Kept his eyes open all the way and just happened to glimpse my Merc in the car park. Zac, why?'

I let go of his wrist and he finally looked me in the eye. 'Because I liked you. I really liked you, Scott. And I know you think I'm just some stupid kid with a crush, but sometimes after we had sex and we'd just lie there for a while and you'd talk to me ...' A tear tracked down the side of his face. He brushed it angrily away. 'I don't have a great home life. My mum's OK but my dad? He takes this weird delight in belittling me. Nothing I do, nothing I achieve is ever good enough for him. I worked so hard to get into law school because that's what he wanted, but then when my acceptance to Warwick came through all he could say was, "Shame it wasn't Oxbridge." So this summer I decided to cut all ties. I couldn't take it anymore – the undermining, the snide comments. It broke my mum's heart, but if I'd stayed in that house, I don't know what would have happened between us. Anyway, I found work on the fair and for the first time in my life, I saw what a real family does for each other. The love, the support. I'm not sure you appreciate this, Scott, maybe because you were born into the life, but that's what Travellers are to each other. Family. And then I met you. This strong, beautiful, damaged man who spoke to me without judging everything I said. I felt at home here. Felt at home with you. And then one day you just up and disappeared on me.'

I remembered the text he'd sent that morning:

Sal told me you've gone on ahead to Bradbury. Thanks for saying goodbye. You're a fucking arsehole, Scott.

'I'm sorry,' I said. 'I honestly thought you were better off without me.'

'So you decided to blank me. Ghost me.'

I nodded. 'And that's why you contacted Kerrigan? To get back at me?'

'He'd been lurking around the fair for a couple weeks, asking a few of the chaps if they'd let him know your movements. I don't know why. He was offering good money, so they said. After you left without a word, I was just so angry. It was easy enough to get his number from one of the guys.'

I thought over what he'd said. The theme of fathers and sons, that search for validation and security obviously chimed with me. And yet, there was something more to it. Something deeper than the surface meaning. Something that strangely seemed to go to the heart of the Jericho murders.

'I didn't mean for any of this to happen,' Zac said. 'I tried to contact you, tried leaving messages for Sal and your dad to pass on. I knew straight away I'd done something terrible. Scott, can you forgive me?'

'It's all right,' I told him. 'You're not responsible for what happened. I'm only sorry I can't be what you need me to be. But listen, you do have a home with us on the fair and we'll always be there for you, Zac. Like it or not, you're one of us now.'

He laughed, fresh tears starting in his eyes. 'Thank you. You don't know what that means.'

I nodded to myself. I'm not sure I ever did. Not until now.

Chapter Forty-One

AFTER ZAC LEFT, I SPENT a few minutes impatiently awaiting the arrival of Garris. My dad hadn't mentioned any news of a mutilated corpse being discovered in Bradbury End – which he surely would have, naturally linking it to the case I was investigating – and so either the police were keeping things quiet or else Garris hadn't yet handed it over to them. I hoped for the latter possibility, though I knew it was unlikely. I'd been out cold for five hours. Even with his loyalty to me, there was no way Garris would put things off that long.

Five hours. More than enough time for the killer to have reached Hillstrom and created his final Jericho freak.

And there was another thought that nagged at me. Something Zac had said about Kerrigan – *He was offering good money, so they said.* That would have been Maxine Thierrot's money, except the same doubt I'd had back in the alleyway now returned to me. Would a paparazzi of Thierrot's experience and judgement really expend all this effort and resource on a story that, in the end, might not pay off? It seemed unlikely. Although if Thierrot was only acting as a kind of middleman, giving instructions and passing on cash, then who had bankrolled Kerrigan's persecution of me and to what end? And was all of this linked to the killings? If so then was it possible that Thierrot, perhaps unwittingly, knew the identity of the murderer?

An elbow nudged the curtain aside and Harry stepped into the cubicle. He didn't look as worried as Zac and so I guessed he'd been here a while and had got used to the sight of me. Taking the seat Zac had just vacated, he rested his hand against my thigh.

'Do you want to see?'

I nodded, and pulling out his phone, he snapped a photo. Then he perched gingerly on the side the bed, his shoulder nudging mine, and showed me the damage. All in all, I'd expected worse. Clearly, Kerrigan had laid in a few more sly blows after I'd passed out but despite a black eye and a whole heap of swelling, I considered myself lucky.

'Well, I'm not going to win any beauty pageants for the next few weeks,' I said. 'But you should've seen the other guy.'

'Why?' Harry asked. 'What did you do to him?'

I smiled. Smiling hurt. A lot. 'Nothing much. He's just an ugly fucker is all.'

'I suppose it was the man we saw in the pub that night? Kerrigan?' Harry sighed. 'Scott. He could've killed you. How is this ever going to end?'

I wasn't sure how to answer that. My dad's vague promise that he would 'calm Kerrigan down' worried me. I didn't want him or any of the showpeople putting themselves at risk pursuing a vendetta on my behalf.

'There might be CCTV evidence,' I said. 'Enough to nail him for the assault. Don't worry, it'll all work out.'

This was some premium bullshit. I knew there were no cameras in that alleyway. Still, it seemed to help ease Harry's mind.

'We should get away from here,' he said, slipping off the bed. 'Couple up your trailer and hit the road, just like you said. I know you've got this case going on, but can't you just . . . I don't know, leave it be? Everything you've said about being an investigator, all the darkness you don't want to show me, doesn't that tell you something?'

'Haz?'

He didn't respond and so, groaning, I sat up on the edge of the bed. My ribs seemed to swim inside me, floating in a sea of pain. Nothing like the pain that I'd suffered behind the walls of HMP Hazelhurst, however. I looked down at the hands in my lap, tried to stop them from shaking. It was time.

'They hurt me, Harry,' I said in a tiny voice. 'In prison, they hurt me very badly. The other prisoners. When they found out I was ex-police, they . . .' It rose before me, the shower block with those filthy, blood-streaked tiles, pink rivulets diluting as they gurgled towards the drain. The corner in which I laid huddled afterwards, a fire like nothing I'd felt before burning inside my guts. 'I can't . . .' I took a breath, felt it catch. 'I can't tell you what they did to me. I just . . .'

He came to me, this man I had found again in the howling emptiness of my life. He asked no questions, just wrapped his arms very gently around me.

'Scott,' he whispered. 'Oh, Jesus.'

'That's the world I don't want you to see,' I told him. 'Part of it anyway. And you're right, it isn't a healthy place for me, but if I turn my back on it then innocent people will suffer. People I can help. Maybe even save.'

'You're a good man, Scott Jericho,' he said, his voice hoarse. 'And I think I need to tell you something—'

'Oh. I'm so sorry. I'll come back.'

I glanced over Harry's shoulder to where Garris stood just inside the curtain. The strip lights bleached his already pale skin until it shone like crumpled paper. The poor sod looked done in, his eyes etched red, grief chiselled into every line of his already worn face. When Harriet had been well, he'd turned up to work immaculately attired, trousers pressed, shirt starched. Now, his creased suit seemed to hang from him.

'No. No, it's fine,' Harry said, pulling away. 'I said I'd drop by the fair on my way home anyway. Let Sal know how you're getting on. She said to tell you she's sorry she can't get to the hospital tonight but that she'll pop in first thing tomorrow.' He leaned in again and, finding an unswollen corner of my face, planted a kiss. 'I'll call later. I can come back and we can talk if you like.'

With that, he gave Garris a shy nod and disappeared through the curtain. Meanwhile, I clenched my teeth against the grind of my ribs and shuffled back onto the bed.

'Sorry I've dragged you back into this,' I gasped. 'You don't need all this crap on your plate. Not right now.'

Garris remained standing. 'It's a welcome distraction,' he said. 'We've had weeks to make the funeral arrangements, so there isn't much I can do other than sit at my kitchen table and stare into space.' When I started to offer my condolences again, he waved them away. 'Let's get to it, shall we?'

'Hillstrom.' I nodded. 'Have you—?'

'One thing at a time.' He gripped the back of the chair but didn't sit. 'Your father tells me this was Kerrigan's doing?'

I filled him in on all the details, including Maxine Thierrot's apparent plan to catch me in her tabloid sting, adding that I suspected there was something more to the whole business. Garris nodded.

'We ought to have guessed a dumb fuck like Lenny Kerrigan wasn't plotting something on his own. As for Thierrot, I agree. She might well receive a big one-off payday for a shot of you attacking Kerrigan, but there must be juicier stories for her out there. But if you're thinking the killer set up this whole sideshow, perhaps paying Thierrot to dog you and also involve Kerrigan, what would be his motive? It hardly fits with his MO for these murders.'

I shook my head. 'Perhaps to just muddy the waters? I don't know. But come on, Pete, you're dancing around something. Is it Hillstrom? Is he dead?'

Garris sighed and finally collapsed into the chair. 'Marcus Hillstrom is alive and well. At least he was at eight-fifteen tonight when I dropped by his house on the way here. He was a little annoyed at you for having missed his call at four o'clock, but when I explained what had happened he was all sweetness and light. Sends his best wishes. Not the sort of thing that ever happens in "our dear little town". He does want to know why the police are suddenly so concerned for his welfare, but I said we'd explain it to him in the morning. Which we *will*, Scott.' He shot me a sharp glance. 'This has already gone far enough.'

'So you've been in touch with the local CID?' I asked.

'No,' he said. 'Not yet.'

'Why not?'

'Because after I got off the phone to you, I jumped in my car and headed straight to Bradbury End. I suppose I wanted to talk some sense into you before you started tearing off on some mad crusade. If you want to know the truth, Scott, I'm frightened for you.'

I cut my eyes away. 'You don't have to worry about me.'

'But I do. I worry what you're going to do when you find this killer. Not for his sake, but for yours. What you told me about Maxine Thierrot, how she said there was something inside you – that rage you unleashed on Kerrigan? She might be a parasite, but she's right, isn't she? If you give way to it again, it will destroy you.'

I shook my head. 'So you came to Bradbury.'

He sighed. 'To Gerald Roebuck's. You weren't there.'

'No, I'd already—'

'Scott. Neither was he.'

'What?' I stared at him. 'What do you mean?'

'I found the door unlocked. The house was empty. No corpse waiting in the sitting room with balloons for eyes. Just a scribbled note on his desk for his cleaner: "*Gone back to Hull to visit sick sister. Please water plants.*" Other than that, no spilled milkshake, no feasting flies, no defaced plaque on the wall.'

Pain throbbed at my temples as I tried to make sense of what Garris was telling me. 'So he came back after I'd gone? Cleaned up, disposed of the body somehow, removed the memorial stone? Why?'

'It's just another chapter in the story, isn't it?' Garris said. 'I mean, things like this don't happen in real murder cases. Abducted dogs, vanishing corpses. The truth is, the guy who started all this has been fucking with you, right from the very beginning.'

Ignoring the shriek of my torso, I sat forward. 'Pete, what do you mean?'

He reached into his jacket and pulled out two thin envelopes, one white, one brown. 'I think I know who's behind all this. And I think we've made a big mistake, Scott. He covered his tracks well, set up his new identity so perfectly that even when he was arrested the false documents must have fooled the authorities. My guess would be that he'd committed similar crimes in the States under his birth name and that he or the mother wanted to return home for a fresh start. But old habits die hard. Not long after he settled in Cambridge, he was arrested again.'

'You're talking Campbell and Miss Barton.'

He handed over the envelopes. 'Or Jonathan and Delia Matthers. I got one of our tech boys to clean up that old photograph from the online archive. Take a look.'

I pulled out the print: there was the little, pale-faced boy standing on the wrap-around porch of the Matthers' house. It was still impossible to match him exactly with the repulsive 'professor' who had first set me on this strange journey. There was no doubt about the other figure, however. Taken before the fire, in the photograph her face was undamaged, but this was clearly a younger version of the woman who'd introduced herself as Campbell's devoted nanny.

I looked at Garris and shook my head. 'No. It's too easy.'

'Most of the time finding murderers *is* easy; you know that.' Garris tapped the second envelope. 'And I think this proves it beyond much doubt. I found it on Roebuck's desk with a note inside addressed to you. It's Campbell, Scott. He's been playing you all along.'

Chapter Forty-Two

THE HANDWRITING, SPRAWLING AND SPIDERY, was a match for the other scribbled notes and memoranda I'd seen on Roebuck's desk:

As promised, Mr Jericho — that little surprise I found on the net. Even as a boy, Jonathan always did have a taste for the dramatic.

I slid the paperclipped note from the corner of the printout. It was a downloadable theatre programme from a touring production of *The Importance of Being Earnest*, then playing at a small community venue in upstate New York. The production had taken place just over five years ago, and although the face of the actor playing the Reverend Canon Chasuble was less cadaverous than that of the man I'd first met in Cambridge, there was no mistaking those blazing blue eyes. Beneath the headshot that Roebuck had circled ran a brief bio:

Jonathan Matthers is an accomplished thespian of both Broadway and the London stage. His credits include . . .

I handed the printout back to Garris.

'Broadway and the London stage is probably a bit of a stretch,' he said. 'If he'd been that famous, I would have found him easily enough online. Roebuck really had to go digging for that hidden treasure. But a career as an actor is suggestive, don't you think? Anyway, I'd guess that, when the father died back in the '70s, he must have left his wife and child pretty well off. False documents good enough to fool the police don't come cheap.'

I shook my head. 'He was the one who started me on the case. Pete, listen, we've said before how obsessive these murders seem. How the killer's main motivation isn't necessarily the individual deaths but the accomplishment of the complete design. The full recreation of the Jericho freaks. Why would he imperil that by hiring a detective to investigate his own crimes?'

Garris took a moment to consider his answer. 'We assumed that some overall design was his motivation, but we don't know that for sure. What does ring true is the idea that this whole thing is like a story. It has the feel of something fabricated. And if it is a story, well then, every good yarn needs both its hero and its villain. Who better to play the part of crusading detective than a descendant of old "Slip-Jointed" Jericho himself? Can't you see the irresistibility of that idea to a man who had been obsessed by the tragedy since boyhood?'

I shook my head again. The painkillers were starting to fog my thoughts. Everything Garris was saying tallied with my initial suspicions about the child whose bedroom window had overlooked the bridge, and then there was Roebuck's confirmation of Jonathan Matthers' morbid interest in the tragedy, as well as my own conviction that, right from the start, Campbell

303

hadn't been telling me the whole truth about his interest in the case. But still, there was something wrong with this picture. And it wasn't just the obvious objection that I now put to Garris.

'His disability. There's no way he could have killed McAllister and the others. He couldn't have even climbed the stairs to Adya Mahal's flat.'

Garris looked at me almost pityingly. 'He'd researched you, remember? You told me about that strange presentation he gave before getting down to the murders. He knew all about your background and what had happened with the Malanowski kids and Kerrigan. He created a persona for you to deduce, one that might appeal to your strong sense of justice: a man who hurt children but who, unlike Kerrigan, had been punished for it. A punishment that would satisfy the rage inside you. And being satisfied, you bought the lie. He acted the part of a man who had suffered a vicious attack and because you saw what you wanted to see, you fell for it. I think Jonathan Matthers is perfectly capable of these murders.'

'His books,' I murmured. 'He told me he'd bought new ones when he came out of prison because he couldn't bear the thought of how the police had handled them during his arrest. He hadn't read a single one, had he? "Professor Campbell" doesn't exist.'

Garris folded his arms over his stomach. 'These killings always had a touch of the theatre, didn't they? The way they were staged?'

'We said he might have killed before,' I reminded Garris. 'That there was that sense of experience and calculation at the crime scenes.'

'It's possible. We'll have to notify the police in any location Matthers resided. See if there are any unsolved murders that coincide with his time living there.'

But again something didn't chime with me. 'A paedophile murdering adults?' I said.

'It's an unusual MO, I grant you,' Garris conceded. 'But thinking about it, your theory that the murderer might also be behind the whole Thierrot-Kerrigan sideshow fits Matthers very neatly. He is probably our only suspect who has the resources to pay for such a thing. As to why he bothered setting up that particular aspect of the business, we'll know more once we interview him. In the meantime ...' he creaked to his feet, a hand in the small of his back, 'you concentrate on getting better. I'll notify my contact in the local CID tonight. If the hospital releases you in the morning, it might be useful for us to meet with him tomorrow and get a forensics team down to Roebuck's. But only if you feel up to it. And Scott?' That hooded look again. 'I meant what I said before. You leave him to us now. Your part in this case is over.'

As soon as Garris vanished behind the curtain, I ripped the securing tape from the back of my hand. Then, pinching the end of the cannula between thumb and forefinger, tore the needle out of my vein. The pain was so minuscule next to the shriek of my ribs I barely noticed it. Luckily someone had left a pack of cotton wool on the cupboard by the bed and, pulling it open with my teeth, I pressed a wad to the puncture point. The bleeding stopped within a couple of seconds.

In the cupboard, I found my boots and a travel bag containing toiletries and a change of clothes. I guessed Harry must have brought them from my trailer. I pulled on a pair of jeans, a fresh T-shirt and jumper, every movement sparking some new agony. My phone I discovered in the bag's side pocket along with my wallet. By the time I'd laced my boots, I was a little breathless.

Sitting on the bed, I thumbed the killer's contact.

'Mis-ter Jer-i-cho,' came that piping voice. 'And what can I do for you?'

My hand tightened around the phone until the casing squeaked. 'Are you at home, Professor?'

'Where else would I be on a night such as this?'

'I'm going to pop over in about an hour,' I said. 'I think you deserve an update on the case.'

'No need, sir. You can perhaps email me your report at a later date.'

'One hour,' I said, and cancelled the call.

No one tried to stop me from leaving the hospital. The nurses on the ward seemed busy enough with the patients demanding their attention to pay much heed to one avoiding it. In fact, it was only when I reached the taxi stand outside that anyone challenged me.

'Sure you're all right to be going home, mate?' asked the cabbie as I groaned my way onto his backseat. When I asked if he could take me all the way to Cambridge and back for double his usual fare, his concern seemed to vanish. Giving him the address, I added two further requests:

'Get me there as fast as you can and please don't talk on the way.'

The storm had quieted during my unconscious hours, though dark clouds remained, dragging their swollen bellies across the moon. As we swept out of town, the drowned fields on either side of the road glinted like spilled oil. It made me think again of the killer from my dream, his face a blank and howling void.

Did Jonathan Matthers' face fit that emptiness? Were his the eyes that had watched me from beyond the railway crossing? Physically, he fitted that lean, gangly form quite well. And so was Garris right? Had I let myself be deceived because the terrible fate he claimed to have suffered in prison satisfied my brutal instinct for justice? I had been abused and degraded inside a prison myself and so wasn't it fitting that someone whose crimes dwarfed my own should endure a much worse fate? One that I might also project onto Lenny Kerrigan.

And yet.

As a final puzzle piece, Matthers would not slip neatly into position but had to be hammered home. I closed my eyes. Bit my lip against the pain blooming through the failing opioids in my bloodstream. As the miles and minutes flew by, I tried to turn Matthers this way and that, to force him to yield to the role Garris and I had imagined for him. But he would not yield. Instead, I kept catching whispers in the darkness of my mind, like dissenting voices shouting from another room.

'This the place, mate?' the cabbie called over his shoulder.

I glanced down the long drive to the looming hulk of the house. At that moment my phone chirruped – a missed call from my dad. I guessed the hospital must finally have realised they were a patient short and contacted my next of kin. I put the phone on silent.

'Wait for me here,' I said. 'I shouldn't be too long.'

'Be as long as you like. But why don't you let me drive you up there? Honestly, mate, you look like you're about to drop.'

But I didn't want the taxi's headlights announcing my arrival. First, I wanted to get a peek at Jonny boy and his dear old mother.

I was almost at the house, one hand cradling my ribs, the wind wrenching at me, when a volley of barking cut across the fields. I stopped dead. Some lonely dog, perhaps alerted by a stranger's scent. I suddenly thought of Webster and the curious incident of how he had remained silent when the killer came for him in the night. Could I imagine that loyal fairground juk going off willingly with Jonathan Matthers?

Matthers, who I now saw through his study window, standing freely in front of the fire, his hands stretched out to the flames. Matthers who walked to the decanter on the sideboard and poured himself a drink. Matthers who nevertheless could *not* walk because DCI Pete Garris, my mentor, my friend, had told me he couldn't. Garris's words came back to me:

'Got a big compo pay-out after some other prisoners managed to corner him in his cell and cut off his nuts ... Gave him a pretty brutal kicking afterwards which resulted in some spinal damage.'

Those details hadn't been part of Matthers' fake identity. What Garris had told me concerning the attack upon him in prison had come from Pete's research into the incident. Details he claimed to have gathered from official sources. But if they had been fabricated then only one person could have invented them.

308

I felt the ground shift beneath me. Felt the world tilt. Felt the final puzzle piece slip smoothly into place. I should have seen it back at the hospital but my pain and the opioids had dulled my thinking. Now the truth about Peter Garris came crashing down and, with that truth, a way to verify it.

Taking out my phone I quickly looked up the number and called.

'St Hilda's Hospice, how may I help?'

My throat was so dry I could barely get the words out. 'I want to make a donation,' I said. 'In memory of a patient who's just passed away. Is that possible?'

'Of course. I'm so sorry for your loss. May I have the patient's name?'

'Harriet,' I almost sighed the word, 'Garris.'

I heard the clack of a keyboard. A short, murmured conversation. Then:

'I'm sorry, we don't appear to have had a patient of that name. Are you sure—?'

'No,' I said softly. 'You wouldn't have.'

Because Harriet Garris didn't exist.

Chapter Forty-Three

I DIDN'T SEE IT ALL AT that moment, but I saw enough. And what I saw planted a new pain deep inside me. A pain keener than any physical hurt inflicted in that alley back in Bradbury End. During all those boozy after-work chats in The Three Crowns, I'd felt that I had found not just a colleague but a friend. More than that: a father to stand in for the one who had never understood me. True, there had always been a certain reticence on his part, a professional distance bordering on the emotionless, but this? This, I had never imagined.

What Peter Garris really was had struck me at almost the same moment as my realisation that he'd invented Jonathan Matthers' prison injuries. It was then that I remembered the conversation in my trailer. The one during which we'd picked over the file and speculated on the nature of the killer. In his analysis, Garris had been describing himself:

'If our man fits the typical profile, he's likely to be a loner without a family or normal home life, although he may give the illusion he has one.'

And what an illusion Harriet Garris had been. A painfully shy woman, kind but reclusive, living in the shadow of her forthright and accomplished husband. A husband who, in his undemonstrative way, had loved her so much he'd even taken pride in those amateurish watercolours of hers. A caring, nurturing soul who had written homely letters to Garris's disgraced protégé. Letters I had answered, scrawling my thanks onto prison notepaper.

Had he enjoyed reading them? I wondered. Had he laughed at their expressions of pathetic gratitude?

I stepped towards the house, ran my knuckles across the brickwork, grating them until they bled. That anger Maxine Thierrot had seen inside me was kindled again. All that time Garris and I had worked together, all the praise he'd heaped on my intuition and insights, all the monsters we'd hunted down and put behind bars, I had never guessed that the most heinous of them all walked beside me. Oh, but he must have taken such sweet delight in that.

I drew my hands away, flicked my blood against the stone. I could feel the hunger for those little packets back in my trailer. Part of me wanted to blot out this hateful truth; part of me wanted to rage against it. I tried to calm both instincts. Tried to focus. Questions remained: why would he kill these people? Why would he attempt to frame Jonathan Matthers? What's the purpose of it all?

Again, that conversation in the trailer came back to me. Perhaps there was no purpose other than a deranged killer's sick game. What I had always interpreted as professional reticence was in all probability the heartless void of a true psychopath. A cold-blooded predator who, in order to disguise himself, had learned to mimic human emotions while feeling nothing himself. I'd met more than my fair share of such men; to creatures like these, the infliction of pain is purpose enough.

311

Pain – the Jericho victims' and my own. He had killed them in mockery of me, of the life I'd been born into, of its legends and traditions. In that sense he was like Zac's father; the parent who sneered at their child's achievements. Only unlike Zac's father, he had pretended to be proud of mine. Wondering what I had done to make him despise me was a pointless exercise, I knew. The rat's maze of a psychopath's mind defied any empathic logic. But still, I wondered . . .

Enough. I'd ask him myself before the night was over. First, I needed to speak with Mrs Matthers and her son.

I didn't have to knock. The iron-banded oak door swung open at my approach. That guilt-ridden, round-shouldered nanny I had first seen fussing with her crucifix and giving dark hints about her employer greeted me again.

'My dear Mr Jericho,' she said. 'What on earth has happened to you?'

I closed the door behind me.

'The question is, what has happened to you, Miss Barton? Or do you prefer Mrs Matthers?'

'Who?' She clutched at the golden cross lying against her breast. 'I'm sorry, I don't under—'

Mocking applause echoed out from the corridor beyond the paederast's gallery.

'Bravo, Detective! Bravo! So you have penetrated our secret. How ever did you guess?'

Jonathan Matthers came striding into the hall. He still appeared painfully thin but gone was the strangely ageless professor tucked up in his chair. This figure was immediately more vibrant, animated by a sort of manic energy. His speech was different too. No more of that lisping haughtiness but a lazy American drawl. Only his lips appeared the same, sporting that faintly violent rouge.

He circled the hall as I spoke, occasionally pausing to admire one of those prepubescent statues, occasionally skipping, once or twice stopping to lay a hand against his mother's burned cheek. She meanwhile remained impassive.

'There was always something that didn't ring true about your performance,' I said.

That brought him to a halt. He pouted. 'All the world's a critic. So tell me, darling, what fault did you find in our dear Professor Campbell?'

'His uninterest,' I shrugged. 'All that hyper-excitement while you were briefing me about the murders, all that desperation to attract my interest and get me to take the case. Then, as soon as I did, complete indifference. Not even a scrap of curiosity about my progress, despite the fact you were paying me a frankly ludicrous fee. Someone tonight presented you to me in the role of a dark storyteller, manipulating me like a character in a murder mystery, yet surely if that were true you would be hanging on every development. But no, you had no interest because you already knew the solution to the mystery.'

Jonathan squealed and clapped his hands as if I were a magician who had just pulled a rabbit out of his hat. 'Very good, Detective! But not just because I knew the solution to your petty mystery, but because I *wasn't* interested. I assume you know all about my childhood in Bradbury End? Well then, I will admit to a passing fascination with that tawdry tale of the drowned freaks. How could I not? Incarceration forces one to find hobbies in one's immediate environment.' He cast his mother a sour glance. 'She'd never let me out of her sight, you know? And so yes, I became interested in the tragedy. Even plagued some pitiful old bore at the library with questions about it. But honestly, until Inspector Garris darkened our door, I hadn't thought about it in years. Other interests came my way as I grew.'

He winked at me and I felt my bloodied fists twitch.

'How did Garris find you?' I asked.

'He said we were perfect, didn't he, Mother? Perfect! He'd been researching the Travellers Bridge tragedy, you see, and came across our story. Said we were ideal for a small drama he was contemplating. He gave me my character of Professor Campbell and mother the role of Miss Barton. Not a born actress,' he said out of the corner of his mouth, 'but she did quite well, I think. He briefed me all about you, too. I must say, he's a most unnerving fellow, but undoubtedly the best director I've ever had. Told me how to push your buttons without going too far. Warned me that if I did, I might end up like that Nazi chap you put in the hospital.'

'When did he first contact you?'

'Oh, I forget.' He waved an airy hand. 'Six months ago, was it, Mother?'

Delia Matthers gave a silent nod.

'And he blackmailed you into all this?'

Another wink, this time accompanied by a titter. 'He discovered I'd been naughty again. We left the States a couple of years ago, just after I got out of prison. I won't go into all the details, doubtless you'd find them sordid. Suffice to say, I'd been on tour with a production of *Joseph* – my Pharaoh was the talk of Seattle – when some of the children in the cast started bleating about my conduct. Anyway, we decided on a fresh start back in the home country. Truly, Mr Jericho, I'd intended to mend my ways, but the flesh is weak. During his research into us, Mr Garris discovered certain slips in my online behaviour and threatened to expose me if I refused to play along with his game. Bearing in mind my previous conviction, that would have meant a lengthy prison sentence.'

'Did you know what he was planning from the outset?' I asked.

'Oh, the murders?' That old uninterested tone entered his voice again. 'Yes, I believe he went into all that. I mean, he had to so that I could brief you about them during our little tete-a-tete.'

'So you knew that he intended to slaughter five innocent people?'

'I didn't relish the idea of it, if that's what you're thinking,' Jonathan snapped. 'But what alternative did I have? Five strangers set against my own liberty. You might think it selfish, but for me, that wasn't a difficult decision.'

'And for you, Mrs Matthers?'

At last she spoke. 'It wasn't just about Jonathan being sent back to prison, Mr Jericho. You think you know this man, I assure you, you do not. I have spent two-thirds of my life disguising the true face of a monster.' She cut her eyes to the grinning figure of her son. 'Next to Peter Garris, I'm an amateur.'

'What did he say to you?' I asked.

She didn't flinch. 'He said he would murder us both. After detailing every mutilation he was going to perform upon these poor people, he said that all of that would be nothing compared to what he would inflict upon us if we didn't go along with his plan. And he would kill Jonathan first, slowly, agonisingly, while I watched.'

I closed my eyes. Saw the rage dancing in the dark. 'You could've gone to the police.'

'With what evidence? Just the word of a convicted child molester and his mother against that of a distinguished detective. And anyway, would you take such a risk with your own child?'

Would I with Jodie? She wasn't even my daughter, but if a sadistic killer threatened her life, what wouldn't I do to protect her? I turned back to Jonathan.

'You paid Maxine Thierrot to follow me, to try to catch me out attacking Lenny Kerrigan. Why?'

'Another of his little ideas,' he replied. 'I would hire her as a freelancer and, on top of the fees she earned from me, she could sell any resulting photos to the tabloids. She would employ Kerrigan on my behalf to stir the pot, to dog your footsteps and nettle that famous temper, but he was to remain unaware of my part in the arrangement.'

'Did she ask what your interest was in me?'

'She was naturally curious, but Garris instructed me to say that my motives were my own. And of course the fee was exorbitant, so that kept her curiosity in check.'

'But why?' I asked again. 'What was the point of that part of his plan? What was the point of any of it?'

'Oh, you must ask him that yourself.' Finally, Jonathan Matthers' idiot smile fell away. 'Bad men don't always have motives that people like you would understand, Mr Jericho. It's just in them: the compulsion to inflict harm. I did get the feeling that it was personal, though. Do you think he hates you? Wants to torment you? It's all about power, after all. These bad things we do.'

Chapter Forty-Four

'WHY DID YOU REALLY SET the fire back in Bradbury?' I asked Jonathan Matthers.

I'd grown sick of his paederast's gallery and was now standing just outside the front door. Down at the end of the long driveway, the taxi waited, a light rain stippling the glare of its headlights. Inside the doorway, Jonathan and his mother looked back at me.

He shrugged. 'Because I hated her. I think she always knew what I was and didn't like the idea of me being around children my own age. My father knew too. You discussed it before he died, didn't you, Mother? What to do with me. Father had found me, you see? Playing games with one of the neighbour boys. Then word got around and my parents decided the best thing to do was to move us lock, stock and barrel to some old family home Dad had inherited. But before we could all sail off, poor old Pops departed on his own journey, right through the windscreen of his vintage Jaguar.

'I suppose she thought she was honouring his final wishes, keeping me locked away. Anyway, the night those teenagers came to throw stones at our house, I decided I'd had enough. If I couldn't escape my prison, I'd burn it down around us. After that, Mother changed.' Smiling, he caressed the burned side of her face. 'She realised she couldn't stop me playing the games I wanted to play. Not for ever. And so she gave in.'

I looked at the tiny, diminished form standing beside him. All she could do was shake her head.

'He's my son.'

It was the only explanation she had.

'And because of him, because of you, four innocent people are dead.' My rage kicked against me and I answered it. 'That young man who first made contact with me at the fair – Jeremy Worth. I suppose Garris must have blackmailed him too.'

Jonathan nodded. 'I never met him, but yes. As far as I know, he came to Garris's attention via some online misdemeanour that a police colleague was investigating. He hadn't actually done anything in the real world, if you catch my drift, but Garris had enough to frighten him.'

'Online *is* the real world,' I spat back. 'Real kids suffer. So let me tell you what I told Jeremy: I have my eye on you now, Jonathan Matthers. From this moment on, you so much as look sideways at a child and I will end you. Do you understand? I will *fucking* end you.'

A strange expression crossed Delia Matthers' face when I spoke. Though she had protected him all his life, I wondered whether such an outcome would be wholly unwelcome to her.

'You're no different from him,' Jonathan shrieked as I turned my back and hobbled away into the night. 'You're killers both!'

Killers both.

The phrase ghosted me all the way to the road. Perhaps he was right.

Tonight would tell.

'Back to Bradbury?' the cabbie grunted as I collapsed into the backseat.

'Give me a second.'

Gasping against the pain, I leaned forward and slid the partition between us closed. I then looked at my phone. More missed calls from my dad. I suddenly felt a stab of guilt followed swiftly by a fresh tide of anger against Garris. His crimes, his depravity, had made me doubt my own people.

It was time.

I made the call.

'Hello, Scott,' he said. 'What mischief have you been getting yourself into?'

There was a lightness to his tone, a humour I'd never heard before.

'Lost for words? Well, well. Your father has been on the phone. It appears you've vanished from the hospital. However much you might respect me, I knew you wouldn't be capable of just handing over the case. In fact, I counted on it. So I assume you've been to see Mrs Matthers and her charming son?'

'I have,' I said. 'And I know what you are.'

He laughed at that. 'To paraphrase the old Travellers Bridge inscription: a mind intent upon false appearances will always fail to recognise the truth. That was your mistake, Scott. You saw in me what you wished to see.'

'Well, I see you now,' I said. 'And I'm coming for you.'

'Of course you are, my boy. I'd expect nothing less. Bradbury End library, then. I'll be waiting.'

The line went dead.

The library. Harry.

Christ, why hadn't I seen it before? After all, Harry was another of those improbable coincidences that had made the entire atmosphere of the case seem so unreal. He had been placed in my way, a character from my past reintroduced into the narrative to play his role as companion, as lover, as suspect, and now, perhaps as victim. Manoeuvred into position by a blood-soaked storyteller, probably using the same technique he'd employed with Jonathan Matthers. Blackmailed, but how? The answer was obvious, and it honed my fury into cold, hard hatred.

I don't remember ever telling Garris the story of the Jericho freaks. Lost in a haze of booze in our corner of The Three Crowns, unburdening my past to this man I had trusted, I suppose I must have. I'd told him many other fairground stories and legends; all, I now realised, at his prompting. What I do remember, is spilling the secret of the only man I had ever loved. How, in an act of mercy, Harry had taken his father's life and then afterwards rejected me. Garris must have recalled that conversation and hunted Harry down. Another piece of scene-setting, ready for my arrival in Bradbury End.

Haz had claimed that he'd been in town for over a year, but the inconsistencies of his story now occurred to me. Roebuck mentioning Harry's 'short time among us' and his fellow librarian Val saying something about a colleague Moira warming up to him after just a few months. Whatever corroborating evidence Garris could possibly have unearthed concerning his guilt, it had worked its magic. Harry Moorhouse had come to Bradbury and played his part to perfection.

The question was, like Jonathan Matthers, had he known about Garris's larger plan? I shook my head. He might have deceived me, but I could never believe that of him.

I brought up his contact and hit call. It went straight to voicemail.

'Harry, it's Scott. I know everything, OK? Listen, I need you to go to the fair right now. Stay with my dad until I come and get you. We can talk then. If Garris calls, don't pick up. I still ...' I rested the back of the phone against my forehead for a second. 'Doesn't matter. Just do as I say.'

I hung up and tapped the partition.

'Bradbury End library. Fast as you can.'

While the cabbie performed a three-point-turn in the narrow lane, I took a last glance at the Matthers' residence. But it wasn't the occupants of that soulless house I was thinking about. I was remembering Harry in the sitting room of his bungalow, on the phone to Val, so he'd said. '*Yes, I think he bought it in the end ...*' Bought what? The possibility of an old lover returned? Of romance rekindled? Had all of it been an act directed by Garris? That moment we'd shared on the beach of Cinnamon Island, had he scripted each word?

Even if he had, I didn't care. I still needed to make sure that Harry was safe.

At close to midnight, it was a clear run back to Bradbury. Still, every minute passed like an hour. Both Garris and Harry's phones kept going to voicemail. I left messages – threats for the former, repeated pleas to seek sanctuary for the latter. I called Dad too, told him I was OK, asked him to look out for Harry. When he said he could tell by my voice something was wrong, I hung up. I wouldn't put him or any of the Travellers at risk by telling them about Garris.

Finally, the cab pulled up outside the darkened shell of the library. Except, not quite dark. A single light burned in the windows. I heaved myself onto the kerb and the cabbie wound down his window. I handed over my card.

'Pleasure doing business,' he yawned. Then, giving back the card, he glanced up at the still-troubled sky. 'Weird night, eh?'

'You don't know the half of it,' I said.

The wind groaned. In the distance, I could hear the whipcrack of tarpaulin and the clanking of steel guy ropes. The night-time chimes of the fairground. I wondered then if I'd ever see it again. Ever walk among those stalls and rides, listen to the stories of old showmen, find the safe embrace of that community I had once rejected. I hoped so, but first I had to face this creature who stood now in the doorway of the library.

I lumbered up the path, agony coiling around my ribs like hot wires. By the time I reached the entrance, I'd had to dig my nails into my palms to stop myself from screaming.

'Is he here?' I gasped. 'If you've hurt him—'

This man I had trusted, this father who had given my life some purpose, smiled in a way I had never seen before. He no longer looked the exhausted, grief-stricken wreck that had shuffled into my hospital cubicle. Those emotions were like the makeup of a clown, now rubbed away to reveal a face untroubled by such human weakness.

'Harry is fine,' he said. 'I just popped by the bungalow to borrow his key to this place. I left him safe and sound, I assure you. But, please, Scott, continue your thought.'

He led the way inside. The door sighed shut behind me.

Decommissioned, the library had been stripped bare. This in itself struck me like an act of violence, like a murder even, the heart of the place torn out.

'If you've hurt him,' I said, 'I *will* kill you.'

At the issue desk, he turned and, folding his arms across his chest, nodded.

'I really think you might. You've always had that potential. I saw it many times before you finally unleashed it on Lenny Kerrigan. It was one of the things that fascinated me about you. That and those keen insights and intuitions, of course.'

I barked out a bitter laugh. 'Not keen enough, though, eh?'

He shrugged. 'I don't judge you for not seeing me as I am. My disguise was years in the making and honed to perfection long before I met you, Scott Jericho. Even so, in giving in to my curiosity about your talents and recruiting you to the force, I knew almost immediately that I'd made a dreadful error. But we'll come to that. Why don't you ask the question you're burning to ask?'

'Why?' I said simply. 'Why all this horror and bloodshed? Were you mocking me? My family, my background, was it all some sort of twisted, spiteful parody? Did these people die because you hate me, Peter?'

He looked genuinely surprised. 'You think I did this to mock you?'

'I don't know,' I said.

He shook his head. 'My boy, I did it to save you.'

Chapter Forty-Five

'SAVE ME?' I ECHOED. 'WHAT do you mean?'

He waved my question away. 'Indulge me first. You know how I've always enjoyed seeing how your mind works. Tell me how you unravelled my clues.'

I could see that we were playing this game on his terms. Unless I wanted to beat the answers out of him, of course. I wasn't discounting that idea, wasn't even sure right then that either of us would leave that place alive, but for now I was willing to play along.

'Your clues.' I nodded. 'That's right. Because it was your mystery story, wasn't it? Even before you gave your little hint about how unreal the case seemed, how manufactured, I'd sensed it too. The most extraordinary serial killer investigation doesn't have this many oddities and coincidences.'

'Always told you to mistrust coincidences.' He smiled.

'What put me onto you tonight began with Webster,' I said. 'Your hint about Sherlock Holmes finally landed. If Jonathan Matthers had tried to take him then Webster would have alerted the whole fair. He was bred to be a guard dog after all. So it had to be someone the juk had become familiar with. Someone who had been visiting the fair on a regular basis, checking in with my dad, delivering those case files I never reviewed. I remember Webster seeing you outside Harry's bungalow when I got back from Wales. He'd barked his head off when he first met Haz, but with you, he just wound around your legs like you were old friends. You'd been the one to mention the curious incident of Webster in the night-time and so would have known it couldn't possibly have been Matthers who came for him. And then I realised you had also provided that information about the injuries Matthers sustained in prison. They couldn't be wrong, unless you had invented them.'

'If you remember, I told you not to rely solely on my research,' he said, his smile wider than ever. 'But to follow your own instincts. It was always an Achilles' heel of yours, Scott. Not to double check information from what you assumed were trusted sources. Cleverness will only get you so far, you know.'

I offered a smile of my own, a bleak acknowledgement of his critique.

'Anything else?' he asked.

'I'll tell you if you can give me a guarantee that Harry is OK,' I said.

He nodded. 'That seems fair. Just a moment.'

Garris took out his phone from his rumpled jacket pocket and dialled. When the call connected he put it on speakerphone. Haz's voice, fearful and tremulous, echoed around the empty library.

'What's happening? You have to tell me. I did everything you wanted me to, just as you said. But please, *please* tell me . . .' I could hear the emotion catch in his throat, 'is he OK?'

Into all this darkness, cutting even through the hatred and rage that roiled inside me, I felt the reassurance of Harry's love.

There was no pretence in his words. This was the same bright, compassionate, generous man I had first met all those years ago in Oxford. Whatever he'd done, he had done it for me.

'Scott is with me right now,' Garris said. 'He was likewise concerned about your welfare and wanted the reassurance of hearing your voice.'

'I'm so sorry, Scott,' Harry cried. 'You have to believe me, I never—'

'Remember our arrangement, Mr Moorhouse,' Garris cut in. 'Be where we agreed in, what shall we say, half an hour? If things conclude satisfactorily between Scott and me, you may still see him there. Although that very much depends on how he reacts to my final proposal.' Garris ended the call and replaced the phone in his pocket. 'I instructed him not to answer any of your calls tonight, by the way. Oh, and one other small detail that's probably been troubling you – he knew nothing of the murders.'

I closed my eyes. 'What did you tell him?'

'That my plans were my own.' He shrugged. 'He obviously knew that something was going on. Kept demanding reassurances that, if he played along, no one would get hurt. I soothed his anxieties as best I could, though I wonder in his darkest moments what he imagined I was up to. And then there was always the risk that, once you became involved, you might reveal the details of the case to him, but on balance I thought not. It's almost the police officer's code, isn't it? To keep all the horrors away from the people they love. And why would you frighten him off when you'd only just found him again?'

'Why did you involve him?' I asked.

He spread his hands. 'Man cannot live by puzzles alone. Not even you. Harry's role was to intrigue, to distract, to wrongfoot you. To add another layer to the drama. And as a clue, of course, to the entire artifice of these murders. Another almost unbelievable coincidence that might suggest that the true motive at work wasn't anything to do with some absurd fixation on the historical tragedy of Travellers Bridge, but solely upon you. Your background, your history. I suppose you've guessed how I coerced Harry into coming to Bradbury End?'

'You exploited what I told you about his father.'

Garris tapped his jacket pocket. 'A small confession: all those conversations in The Three Crowns? I happened to record everything you ever told me.'

I stared at him. 'Why?'

'That's the crux of the whole matter,' he said. 'For now, let's just say I was fascinated by you. I had been ever since we first met over the case of that boy drowned by his stepfather. I'd never met anyone like you before, Scott. Your showman background, the unique talents your upbringing had given you, so perfect for a detective. And then that darkness, that potential for extreme violence which almost felt like a mirror of my own. Except yours, while equally destructive, had not only a quality of empathy and justice but was still a living, breathing thing.'

'What do you mean by that?'

'One thing at a time,' he sighed. 'Being fascinated, I wanted to keep a record of our conversations. I've been living such an empty life these past few decades, I enjoyed filling my spare hours listening again to your insights into our cases and the unburdening of your personal history. By the way, Scott, you mustn't think this was a cynical exercise. I really did appreciate the trust you placed in me and I hope that, by providing a friendly ear, I was able to help you come to terms with all those demons.'

'Don't fucking dress it up,' I said. 'I trusted you and you betrayed me.'

'I'm genuinely sorry you feel that way,' he said softly. 'I hope that by the end of tonight you might feel differently. But to get back to Harry. I tracked him down easily enough. You'll be pleased to hear that he still had very deep feelings for you. So deep that, when I played him the recording of your drunken admission of his crime, his first thought was for you. I told him that I wanted him to relocate to a place called Bradbury End and that at some point you would make an appearance there. He was to act surprised and, without being obvious, offer you a path back into his life. Again, it might reassure you to know that he had always regretted how things ended between you and that this was the least objectionable part of my plan. I told him that if he refused to follow my instructions, I'd have to make the recording known to the police.'

'You threatened to get him charged with murder.'

'You really do underestimate him, Scott. Harry wasn't concerned with his fate. I made it clear to him that, as a convicted criminal and an ex-police officer, you would inevitably be charged as an accessory to murder after the fact. That was more than enough to get him on board. But now, I've talked enough. Over to you.'

Outside the wind seemed to be picking up again, finding gaps in the old library and moaning like a man in torment.

'Once I realised it was you, lots of other details fell into place,' I said. 'All those forensically immaculate crime scenes? Either the hallmark of an experienced killer or a seasoned CID detective who knew how to clean up after himself. That idea then led me onto a vision of the murderer that two witnesses had interpreted according to their particular background and culture. Miss Debney saw you as a Gothic phantom, a dark angel with glowing wings. To Alessandro Martinez, you were a Christ-figure in haloed vestments. They were both describing the same thing: a killer in a forensic officer's Tyvek suit, its white cotton material translucent with a light source behind it ...'

My eyes snapped to Garris's left hand and the final detail of Miss Debney and Alessandro's visions became clear. When you become used to seeing something you no longer see it at all. A new feature on a friend will stand out – a fresh scar, a sudden physical weakness, a radically different haircut – but even the most identifying mark will pass unnoticed if it has always been there. The poppy tattoo on Garris's wrist, for instance. The souvenir of his army days.

'When the old woman in Anglesey saw you coming out of Robert McAllister's caravan, you covered your wrist,' I said. 'But in Spain, I think that identifying mark slipped your mind. When the boy saw you, he believed he was witnessing a vision of Christ, the red of the poppy like a bleeding stigmata.'

'Stupid of me,' Garris conceded.

'Perhaps. Or perhaps you wanted him to see. With McAllister, you were just starting out, with Agatha Poole you might have thought it was time to start leaving me a few breadcrumbs. Incidentally,' I pointed at the paisley atrocity around his neck, 'I'm guessing you used that to strangle Gerald Roebuck? It fits the ligature mark.'

'You always hated my ties,' he smiled, smoothing it against his shirt. 'And honestly, I hate them too. But they were dear Harriet's favourites, and so ...'

'She was a very effective bit of camouflage for you.' I nodded. 'A sociopathic police officer never moved by the inhumanity he witnessed might have started raising suspicions. But a devoted husband who poured all his emotional energies into a neurotic and reclusive wife? How could anyone imagine him as a monster?'

Unknotting the tie, he tossed it onto the desk behind him. Again the wind shrieked, throwing grit against the windows, groaning like a soul in agony.

'I *was* a monster, a long, long time ago.' His smile became nostalgic, sentimental even. 'I look back now and cringe. How I ever got away with it, I'll never know. Perhaps one day I'll trust my stories to you, Scott, as you trusted yours to me. But now I think it's time I answered your question. Why did I become a monster again? Why did these poor people have to die? The answer is simple. They were sacrifices made on the altar of Scott Jericho.'

Chapter Forty-Six

'I CAME OUT OF HIBERNATION FOR you, Scott. You'd have been dead within the year if I hadn't.'

I felt the world tilt again, felt the ground shift under my feet.

'What do you mean?' I asked.

Garris gave me a long look. 'You know what I mean.'

'No.' I felt sick. All the physical pain of my injuries suddenly seemed insignificant. Background noise to the shrieking horror of what I was hearing. 'Please don't tell me you ... Jesus, why would you think I'd want such a thing?'

He shrugged. 'You wouldn't want it. That wasn't a consideration. It was for your own good, Scott, surely you must see that? And I didn't relish the barbarity of it. Not for a second. This might be difficult for you to believe, but those crimes I committed when I was a young man – the thrill of watching the light go out of their eyes, the little tokens I'd take away with me afterwards – I haven't felt the urge to revisit any of it. Not for years. Men like me can lose the taste for the kill, you know. Don't you remember that we agreed there was a larger purpose behind all this staged savagery? That it felt as if the murderer was going through the paces, taking no pleasure from the deaths themselves? I didn't torture them. I killed them quick and clean.'

'You desecrated them afterwards.'

'And their desecration enticed you, didn't it?' he said quietly. 'You must believe me, all of this was a last resort. You were spiralling, sinking, losing yourself. Haunted by the ghosts of those children and by the guilt that you had failed them. Friends and family offered you every comfort and solace they could. You rejected them. It was as if you'd decided that the only atonement you could make was your own slow and inevitable destruction.'

My thoughts flew back to the trailer. To those days and months before the case had reawakened me to the world. I had been sinking, as he said, drowning, pushing away every hand that reached out to save me. And now I realised that only Garris had found a way.

'I tried first with the files,' he went on. 'Any unusual case I could get my hands on, I brought to you. First in prison and then after you were released. Nothing worked.'

'But wait.' My voice sounded distant, hardly my own. 'By the time I got out, you must have already killed McAllister and Poole.'

'The Jericho murders were always my backup plan,' he said. 'If I'd ever been successful with one of the other cases, I would have happily abandoned the whole idea. But it became increasingly apparent that only something very special would connect with you.'

I felt the gorge rise in my throat. 'You treat their lives so lightly. Like an insurance policy.'

334

'I'd be lying if I said I felt anything for them,' he admitted. 'But as I say, I took no joy in what I had to do. Those two witnesses you mentioned? The boy and the old woman? Easy kills if I'd chosen to dispose of them. I let them live because it was simpler to do so.'

'So you killed to provide me with a puzzle?'

'A very special puzzle, designed specifically to draw you in, to fascinate and captivate you. A murder mystery full of all the Gothic trappings of a Victorian freakshow. A conundrum personal to your family history, to awaken not just the brilliant mind of Scott Jericho but all those complex and troubling aspects of his life. A riddle that, if it worked, might just save you.'

'But why do you care? You have no empathy, no real emotions. All of that is just an act you put on to hide what you really are.'

'I don't care.' He frowned. 'At least, I think I don't. It's difficult to explain.'

I laughed, turned away, stalked to the door and back, my hand pressed to my ribs.

'Try,' I said. 'Four people are dead because of what you did for me.'

He closed his eyes, spoke in the gentlest voice. 'It was an act of contrition, I suppose. When you've never experienced guilt before, it can be a troubling emotion. I brought you into the force because I was fascinated by how your mind worked. How you could apply those skills of the showman – observation, deduction, knowledge of human nature – to the world of criminal investigation. But once I'd made you part of that world, I began to understand that the risk to my security was too great. Meeting up now and then in The Three Crowns, I could maintain the illusion of Detective Inspector Peter Garris. Having you at my side every day as a colleague in CID, however? You'd eventually see through the mask I'd so carefully cultivated. One day you'd expose me.'

'So what did you do?' I asked.

'I waited.' He sighed. 'Waited for that other aspect of your personality that I found so intriguing to assert itself. I knew your rage would undo you in the end, it just needed the right case. And then Lenny Kerrigan came along and set that fire. As soon as I heard you were the night duty detective, I decided to put you in charge of the interview. After that, I hardly had to do anything at all, just sit and wait for the darkness to come roaring out of you.'

Some of Kerrigan's words came back to me then, '*It's funny, though, looking back. That old scarecrow Garris just sitting there while you lost your fucking mind . . .*'

'It was a matter of personal survival, but I had regrets. Kerrigan was the path that led you to prison and disgrace. In killing those children, he was effectively killing you too. And I couldn't have that.'

My hands curled into fists. 'And so you decided to add four more deaths to my conscience?'

He frowned. 'Why would you see it like that? These are my murders.'

'Committed to save *me*,' I roared at him. 'Surely even a psycho like you can understand that I'd rather have died than have any of this happen?'

'I gave you a chance to live again.' He shrugged. 'It's up to you what you do with it.'

336

'I'll tell you what I'm going to do with it,' I said. 'I'm going to make sure you're convicted for every one of these murders. I'm going to see you rot in jail for the rest of your life.'

He shook his head, almost sadly. 'No, Scott. You're not. As you know, there isn't a scrap of evidence to link me with any of the crime scenes. Jonathan Matthers and his mother know that if ever they speak a word of what passed between us, I will release full proofs of his most recent offences. In your own interests, Harry won't corroborate your story and so it will be your word against mine. I have an immaculate professional record; you are a violent convicted offender. But let me offer you another solution to our impasse.'

He circled the librarian's desk and went to that little back office where Harry and I had once drunk tea and danced around our past. I think I might have already guessed what waited inside. It's difficult to remember now, my memories are so muddled up with the pain and guilt and despair of that night. But I think I knew that it wasn't the wind that groaned behind the door.

'As I told you, I was never interested in the murders themselves,' Garris said, his fingers closing around the handle. 'The recreation of the Jericho freaks served their purpose and so I stopped with Gerald Roebuck. But I had always intended one last victim, for the sake of neatness, and perhaps as a final offering to my old friend Scott.'

'Hillstrom,' I murmured.

Garris shook his head. 'Don't you remember I removed his name from the plaque? No, not a descendant of that conspiracy imagined by old showmen. A conspiracy cheerily relayed to me by your father, by the way, when I once asked him about the story. Marcus Hillstrom might have his faults, but I think you'll find my final Jericho freak a much more deserving candidate.'

And with that, he opened the door.

It took me a moment to understand what I was seeing.

On the floor of the office:

The killer of the Malanowski children, reimagined.

The man who had taken everything from me, recreated.

Lenny Kerrigan, born again as Matthew 'Slip-Jointed' Jericho.

Broken and reset, his limbs now followed curious new angles my eye did not want to follow. I thought again of that daguerreotype I'd seen projected onto the wall above Jonathan Matthers' fireplace. My ancestor, the Contortionist, his left leg squirrelled around his back, his arms cranked behind him, his palms so inverted it appeared that the wrists must have snapped at the joint. But while these twists and dislocations had been natural for Matthew the same couldn't be said for the strangely crablike figure now hunched before me.

At first, I didn't understand how he could be alive. But then Garris went to him, and producing a syringe, stabbed the needle into his chest. Kerrigan's eyes flew open and he gasped as the adrenalin hit his bloodstream.

It was then that I noticed the letter carved into his forehead: 'R' for *Recusat*, the final word from the bridge inscription.

I staggered back from the horror of it. This wasn't a corpse I could calmly analyse and assess, but a still-living human being. The agony and dark wonder of his position shone dully in Kerrigan's eyes. I think his mind must have broken then, because instead of screaming, he chuckled. It was the most chilling sound I'd ever heard.

Meanwhile, Garris went to the windowsill where the kettle stood and picked up a small, bright blade.

'You understand now? Why I had Jonathan Matthers employ Maxine Thierrot and our friend here to dog your footsteps? It wasn't a sideshow at all. It was to ensure Mr Kerrigan's presence in Bradbury End at the crucial moment. *This* moment. Our fifth Jericho freak.' He lifted the scalpel to the light. 'If I hadn't have intervened, he would have killed you back in that alley, Scott.'

I nodded dumbly, remembering the figure in the balaclava standing behind the children.

'And he will kill others too, if we let him.'

I almost laughed at that. 'How can he now? With what you've done to him.'

'All I've done is saved you from yourself,' Garris said softly. 'Again. How did you think it would have ended between the two of you? With his hatred and your rage? There would always have been blood.'

'Bluh – bluh – bluh,' Kerrigan garbled. Then giggled. Then shrieked.

'Isn't this the justice of Scott Jericho?' Garris said, kneeling beside this thing he had created and stroking its bald head. 'Isn't this what your ghosts have been crying out for?'

I turned away from the room and looked back into the dim recesses of the library. There, between a pair of empty shelves, three dead children waited for my answer. Sonia, Pietro and Tomasz Malanowski, hands held tight, made one in their love and terror and desperation. No pity had been shown to them.

No mercy. Not even a passing thought for all their dreams and hopes and potential. Nothing offered to these innocents but agony and hatred.

I didn't look back.

'If you kill again ...'

'You'll be waiting for me, Scott, I know.'

I nodded. 'Where is he?'

'I think you know where,' Garris said.

Then another voice, barely human now:

'Juh-i-co. Huh-elp. Muh-ee.'

I shook my head, and stumbling out of the library into the night, left the killers to their dark work.

Epilogue

OCTOBER

A SCATTER OF DYING LEAVES SHIVER their way down a respectable suburban street, chattering under family saloons parked in the driveways of identikit houses, scurrying across well-groomed lawns where the grass is sugared with the first frost of autumn. It is early; only the odd lambent-eyed cat stalking the pre-dawn shadows and throwing sly glances at the freshly carved pumpkins that sit in darkened windowsills and upon icy doorsteps.

From the vantage of my ancient Mercedes, I watch one sleek black creature sidle its way right up to the killer's front door and then, perhaps thinking better of it, turn and chase the leaves to the end of the street, and beyond. I pinch the bridge of my nose, rub my eyes, flip down the sun visor and look at myself in the narrow mirror.

As always, my reflection is misleading. A handsome mask showing none of the terror that haunts my dreams. Looking at me, a stranger might never guess what I'd endured only a few months ago in the charming Oxfordshire town of Bradbury End. Physically at least, I have healed, and with Harry at my side, I now rarely feel the pull of those little pills and packets.

I had found him that final night right where Garris promised I would, waiting for me at the midpoint of Travellers Bridge, his back turned to the old Matthers' house. We didn't speak at first, only stood there as the wind soughed through the trees and the river ran black beneath us. It was only when I clutched at the parapet that he rushed forward and, holding me as gently as he could, told me that everything would be all right. That whatever Garris had done, we'd survive it, together.

That he loved me.

Weeks have rolled by since then, and I have never revealed to him the full horror of the plot in which he played such a crucial role. He hasn't asked, although I know he wonders. He must, especially when he wakes me from my nightmares, holding me like he held me on the bridge, promising it will be all right.

For now, we continue to live together on the fair. We work, we contribute, we find peace in the heart of the community. My dad has taken very strongly to Haz and he's a great favourite of Webster, of course. Sal tells me he's too good for me. She's right, as always. Meanwhile, Jodie delights in a new uncle, who isn't as grumpy as Uncle Scott. As for us, we tell each other we're happy.

Some days I even believe it's true.

I flip the mirror shut and pull the key from the ignition. It's time. Stepping onto the empty pavement, I start towards the house, the only one in the street where a figure stands at a downstairs window, as if waiting to greet an old friend. Silhouetted against the light from his living room, Pete Garris raises a hand to me and, mad as it sounds, I am tempted to wave back. He had been my mentor, my friend, almost a father.

342

And then the image of him in the library comes back to me, the shining scalpel in his hand, the ruined creature at his feet. And so my own hand closes into a fist and I walk on, crossing the garden, falling under the dawn-dark shadow of his house.

The bizarre murders committed for the sake of Scott Jericho have never been linked. Gerald Roebuck was listed as a missing person by his sister, who died a month later. With no fresh leads and no living relatives to put pressure on the police, the case was quietly dropped. That other missing person, Leonard Kerrigan, received a little more attention. Due to our past associations, I was interviewed by the Bradbury police but when no less a person than DI Peter Garris provided me with a watertight alibi for the night of Kerrigan's disappearance, I was quickly exonerated. When Kerrigan's widow was made aware of the debts he'd left behind and of the 'bad hombres' to whom he owed such sums, she soon agreed with the official theory that he had either met with a sticky end or else fled the country.

Only one person didn't seem convinced by this explanation. One afternoon about a week after his murder, I received a text message from Maxine Thierrot:

Shame about Kerrigan, isn't it? But don't worry, Scott.
Next time I'll be there with my trusty camera.

Of course she made no mention of her deal with 'Professor Ralph Campbell'.

I've dropped in on the Matthers a couple of times, just to remind them that I'm watching. Jonathan told me, following instructions received from Garris, that he had terminated all

343

contact with Maxine Thierrot, settling his debt with her and informing her that his personal interest in my case was over. Whatever she made of that, I have no idea.

Mrs Matthers, meanwhile, seems thankful for my visits, her son less so. I've told him I want his paederast's gallery dismantled in time for my next call or I will take it apart myself. With a sledgehammer.

Now I mount the step and press the bell. Through frosted glass in the front door, I watch the killer step out into the hall and come forward to meet me.

DI Peter Garris has taken early retirement from a glittering career in CID. Crushed beneath the grief of losing his beloved Harriet, he hadn't felt able to go on facing the petty ugliness of the world. Old colleagues reached out and invited me to his retirement do at The Three Crowns. I'd never been all that popular among them but 'you were always his favourite,' they said. Suffice to say, I didn't RSVP. But just like with the Matthers, I continue to check in on him.

To make sure he's keeping his promise.

Suddenly the wind picks up, spinning a weathervane, rattling the plastic bones of a Halloween skeleton hanging from a neighbour's porch. It's a smart little street this, modest and nondescript, the ideal place for a monster to hide in plain sight. Quiet old Mr Garris now spends his days tending his back garden. Behind this perfectly ordinary house, a large new flowerbed has been dug out in the eastern corner. It catches the last of the afternoon sun and he has planted marigolds there in memory of his darling Harriet. They grow fast and thick and were her favourite flower, so he tells the neighbours, who can't seem to recall ever having met the poor woman. Very reclusive, an invalid, they think. Anyway, it's a charming spot and the secret it holds will remain hidden.

For now at least.

The door swings open.

The monster smiles.

'Hello, Scott,' he says. 'Won't you come in?'

Glossary of Traveller Slang

chap: a worker on the fairground who is not himself a showperson.

chavvy: a traveller child

dinlo: an idiot; a moron

div: (see dinlo)

gavvers: the police

ground: abbreviation for 'fairground'

joskin: a non-traveller (see also gorger)

juk: a fairground dog; usually a watchdog

muller: to die or murder

posh: earnings, wages, profit

ruck: a fight

Acknowledgements

This book could not have been possible without the early encouragement of authors JD Kirk, Alex Scarrow, JE Mayhew, Alex Smith, and David J Gatward. Thanks for setting me on the criminal path, boys! I also owe huge thanks to early readers of Killing Jericho for their insights and advice: Hanna Elizabeth, Dawn Andrew, Debbie Scarrow, Jacqueline Beard, and Stephanie King. Advice pertaining to the 'gavvers' and their ways was provided by my dear friend, CID officer DS David Bettison. All mistakes are, naturally, my own.

Donna Morfett, crime fiction fan supreme and wonderful interviewer and blogger, has been a great support to me throughout. As have the members of the UK Crime Book Club on Facebook; special mention to Caroline Maston, Samantha Brownley and the whole admin team.

As ever, I owe undying gratitude to my brilliant agent Veronique Baxter at David Higham Associates for believing in Scott's journey. Thanks also go to Clare Israel who handles my TV/film rights.

This book only exists because of the passion and belief of my wonderful editor Ben Willis. I'll never forget our first conversation about Killing Jericho – I knew straight away that Scott and his adventures would be in the safest of hands. It really has been a delight working with you, Ben. Onwards to book 2, 3 and beyond! Thanks also to Isabella Boyne, Ciara Corrigan, and Jon Appleton.

Thanks, as ever, to my family – almost all showpeople themselves – for long talks and reminiscences about fairground life and legends. Scott Jericho may be fictional but the world he inhabits is as real and vibrant as anyone could wish. I hope readers will be intrigued, not only by this story and future instalments, but by a glimpse behind the curtain of this still largely hidden way of life.

Keep reading for an exclusive extract from the next
Detective Scott Jericho thriller ...

JERICHO'S DEAD

Coming soon

Chapter One

THE ONLY CORPSE I FOUND in the killer's attic was a skeletal mouse, its papery bones encased in webs and buried under piles of old clothes. Looking down at the tiny body, I allowed myself a wry smile. I was pretty sure this rodent had died of natural causes.

I turned off my phone light and started back through the open hatchway. The foldaway steps creaked under my weight as I descended to the landing. Having grown up in a Traveller's trailer, I'd never developed that traditional childhood dread of attics. Instead, my nightmares had concentrated on the shadowy space beneath our home—a cramped, oily gap into which hideous monsters might crawl and lie, breathlessly listening to my heartbeat above.

I hadn't known then that all monsters possess a human face.

One of the blandest and most inconspicuous of faces now stared up at me from the back garden. I remained at the landing window for a moment, returning his gaze. Impassive as ever, Peter Garris, retired detective chief inspector and dormant serial killer, raised his hand and waved. He was dressed in gardening gear, cut-off Wellington boots, mud-stained corduroys, a checked shirt, and a ridiculous straw hat to keep the hard October sun out of his eyes. No sign of the paisley tie his late wife had insisted he wear every day to work.

That fashion atrocity, as well as the fiction of Harriet Garris herself, had all been part of his act. A carefully calibrated performance to divert attention from the hollow shell that, like those monsters under our trailer, lay patiently concealed. The house in which I stood was yet another layer of that perform-ance. From the outside, it appeared to be the residence of any other middle-class, middle-aged widower. A neat two-up, two-down in an unremarkable suburban street, its patch of front lawn dutifully mowed, its curtains drawn at 8:30 every morning, just the hanging baskets outside the door in need of a little watering. But such oversights were to be expected. Poor Mr Garris was, after all, still in the first stages of grief.

Except he wasn't. Like love and regret and compassion, grief was unknown to him. And anyway, Harriet had never existed. I wondered if Garris' neighbours, delivering their sympathy cards and hearty casseroles, might have recoiled a little had they ever stepped over this threshold. Not because there was anything obviously disturbing here. Garris didn't display trophies from his victims on the mantelpiece nor make lamp-shades out of their hides. No, it was the emptiness that would have unnerved them. Not a single family photograph adorned these walls, not one cherished keepsake to relieve the clinical tidiness. It was a home as vacant as the killer who occupied it.

I turned away from the window.

Heading downstairs, I wondered not the first time, could there be a storage unit somewhere? A garage lockup perhaps, anonymous and paid for by the year? And does he visit this place, like an old man recalling the glory days of his youth, running hands nostalgically over humming freezers and specimen jars cloudy with formaldehyde? That last night in Bradbury End, he'd confessed to taking tokens from the victims of his early kills, all the while promising that those savage appetites had left him for good.

If such a place existed, and I could find it, then all this futile watching and searching might be over. I could lay proof before the police that even DCI Garris' reputation could not withstand. Because without corroborative evidence it was impossible to move against him. The twisted murders he'd committed four months ago, all in an effort to save me from my own self-destruction, could not be traced back to him. He'd slaughtered five people without leaving behind a scrap of DNA. But those early kills, before he'd joined the force and had no knowledge of forensic procedure, if there were traces of those and I could get at them?

I stepped off the last stair. There was, of course, a more immediate solution to all this. I could make an anonymous call, suggesting the police take a look in the eastern corner of Garris' back garden. Moving through his immaculate kitchen, with its sparkling pans and glinting knives hanging from their hooks, I stopped at the patio door. He was standing there, right beside the burial plot. If the police dug beneath those fast-growing marigolds, they would find the shattered corpse of a child-killer. But in discovering Lenny Kerrigan they would also unearth other secrets. Ones that could endanger the person I loved most in this world.

Before stepping outside, I caught my reflection in the glass of the door. Harry had been going on at me for weeks about needing a haircut. He was right. A mess of blue-black curls were currently spilling over my ears. Otherwise, I looked better than I had in years. A combination of Haz's homecooked meals and the hard labour of working on my dad's fair had recut muscle I'd lost during my time in prison. Still, there was something I didn't like about the winter-grey eyes of this figure. A hunger, a restlessness, a kind of yearning.

I gripped the handle and slid back the door.

Garris straightened up from where he'd been pruning the marigolds. His gaze, lifeless as it seemed to me now, flicked across my face.

"So, are you satisfied that I've been behaving myself, Detective?" When I didn't answer he bent again, and plucking a faded petal, popped it into his mouth. "*Calendula officinalis. Give 'em a patch of blue sky and a drop of sunlight, these beauties will flower whatever the month. Perfectly edible too.*" He nudged his boot against a clump of dirt. "*Of course, the right kind of nourishment in the soil helps tremendously.*"

I looked down at the marmalade hue of the flowers. The fascist murderer Lenny Kerrigan had died horribly, limbs snapped and twisted into strange new formations, yet some remorseless part of me still resented the beauty of his grave.

"Come now, Scott," Garris said. "Petulance doesn't suit you. If I'm going to continue to permit these unannounced spot-checks, the least you can do is to be civil."

Clasped in the pockets of my trench coat, my fists twitched. "You'll permit them," I said. "Whether I'm civil or not."

He chuckled. In the old days, before I'd discovered his true nature, Garris had rarely laughed. "I've seen you watching the house, you know? Hunkered down in a different car each time, keeping your weary vigil. Random days of the week, all in an effort to catch me out. I assume you borrow the cars from your fellow Travellers? I must admit, I miss my visits to the fair, nattering away to your father and all the old showpeople. Perhaps one day—"

"You ever set foot on any of our grounds, I'll bury you neck-deep in that flowerbed," I said. "And let the fiercest of our juks have at your face."

"But not my pal Webster, eh?" he replied evenly. "How is that good boy?"

He smiled a self-satisfied smile. But there were limits to even my old mentor's cleverness. He thought I'd been clumsy in my efforts to surveil him. He ought to have known better. If I'd used my own car to keep watch on his movements, he'd have known straight away something was amiss. By taking the apparent precaution of different vehicles on different nights, I'd allowed him the satisfaction that he'd seen through my plan. A smugness that had, in turn, lulled him into a false sense of security. It was stretching my income to breaking point, but the private detectives who monitored Garris in my absence provided the reassurance I needed. He rarely went out and received no visitors. I was as certain as I could be that his urge to kill had not been reawakened by his recent activities. But it was a temporary solution. I couldn't go on paying the detectives forever.

"You're very uncommunicative these days, my boy." He sighed. "Remember those chats of ours in the Three Crowns when you'd dazzle me with your insights? And it wasn't all business, was it? After the third or fourth pint, you would confide in me as a friend. I really did value your confidences, you know."

I almost laughed. "So much so you used them against me."

He blinked. "Not against you. To help you. I can't understand why you still refuse to see that."

"Of course you can't. Because you're a monster. You killed five people because you thought it would save me. And do you want to know the worst part? It *did* save me." I turned my face to the cold blue sky. "And now I have to live with those deaths on my conscience. I know you'll never wrap your head around what that means, but you should know that barely a night goes by when I don't wake up screaming. That's the life you've given me."

He nodded, wiping his palms down the front of his shirt. "That sounds unpleasant. But even the worst nightmares fade in time. And really, what was the alternative? I remember one of those boozy midnight chats, after all of our cases had been put to bed and we'd moved on to more philosophical subjects. We agreed, did we not, that this is it?" Creaking to his haunches he picked up a morsel of dirt and crumbled it between his fingers. "Earth to earth, and not a hope of heaven. You have a dual soul, Scott. The romantic who loves his books and stories and the realist who sees life as it truly is. Like me, you've witnessed people die. Watched as the light goes out of their eyes. Have you ever detected even a hint of something beyond?" He chuckled again and dusted off his palms. "If I hadn't set you the puzzle of the Jericho freaks then all you'd be right now is a name on a gravestone."

He was right. This was my philosophy. Even the ghosts of the Malanowski children had been nothing more than echoes of my guilt. Spectres now supplanted in my mind by new figures. But in the real world, there were no lost souls crying out for vengeance and no justice except that which we make for ourselves.

"How are you, Scott?" he asked, straightening up again. "Seriously, I remain concerned for your welfare. There's a certain look in your eye that worries me. Because you're bored, aren't you? And in your case, boredom leads to uneasy thoughts."

He tipped the brim of that absurd straw hat, and with his eyes, followed a smoky contrail across the sky.

"I really think it's time you found another puzzle."

Chapter Two

I'D FELT LIKE KILLING HIM then. Because he was right. For a few months, I'd thought that Garris' terrible sacrifice on my behalf had truly reawakened me to the world, and that in finding Harry again, I had also discovered an anchor that would keep me tethered to it. From now on I could do without puzzles. Could do without the lure of injustice and violence that demanded the wicked be punished and the innocent saved. Because Haz's love for me was a brighter, saner star to guide my life by.

But slowly, surely, it had begun to gnaw inside me—the hunger for a problem and the desire to make bad men pay for their brutality. Perhaps I'd never be rid of that need. Perhaps it was hardwired into me.

So why not start with *this* bad man? It would be simple to end him—my forearm around his throat, hard as granite as I dragged him into the house. Garris' was a sheltered back garden, the neighbours' windows discreetly angled so that no one could possibly have seen him burying Kerrigan's broken body. No one to see now if I hauled the killer back through the patio door. No one to hear his muffled cry before I cut off his airway.

I had never killed before, but during my thug-for-hire years, between leaving uni and joining the force, I had come close. More than once, if truth be told. I knew I had it in me. Garris knew it too.

"But you won't," he said as if reading my mind. "Because that really would be the end of you. And anyway, I still have the recording I took in The Three Crowns, as well as a few other bits and pieces that would inevitably lead to Harry Moorhouse's arrest on the charge of murdering his father. I know, I know," he said, waving aside an objection I hadn't raised. "The poor man was desperately ill, in agony, it was a mercy killing. But you know as well as I, that if it went to trial, there'd be no guarantee of clemency. Well then, if anything untoward should happen to me, I've arranged for the proof of his guilt to be released."

Rage scratched behind my eyes. I did my best to tamp it down.

"Honestly though, Scott, all this conflict is unnecessary," Garris went on. "If you won't take my word that I have no desire to kill again, then I'm perfectly happy for you to continue monitoring my activities. In fact, I welcome these catch-ups. I was never much of a people person, as you know, but that mind of yours? It still fascinates me."

Leaning in, he tapped his forefinger against my temple. In that instant, as I cut my gaze towards him, I saw something in the dead marble of his eyes. Just a flicker of emotion, the stunned realisation that he'd gone too far.

"Don't," I said.

And he recoiled as if I'd struck him.

I left Garris standing beside Lenny Kerrigan's grave, the stamp of some newfound fear on his haggard features.

Back behind the wheel of my ancient Mercedes, I clenched my fists until my knuckles cracked. Then I let go of a long breath, turned the key in the ignition, and headed out of the estate, finding a dual carriageway, the motorway, and finally a string of country lanes that led towards home. As ever for a Traveller, 'home' was a constantly shifting location. Currently, it meant a muddy field on the outskirts of the tiny Fen city of Aumbry. More specifically, a forest clearing where we'd been booked for a special event due to take place in four days' time.

I barely noticed the passing miles. Instead, I ran through the possibilities, as I had a thousand times since discovering Garris' true nature. And just like all those other times, I came to the same conclusion: there was no way out of this nightmare. Even if I found evidence of his past murders, I couldn't expose him without also exposing Harry's secret. I might kill him and happily accept the consequences for myself, but that again put Haz at risk. No matter how much I worried at it, a solution refused to present itself.

All I knew as Aumbry's cathedral spire appeared on the horizon was that my former mentor was right. I needed the diversion of a new puzzle. The sooner the better.

Patches of the vast medieval woodland that once blanketed much of this landscape flashed past my window. Reaching the signpost for "Purley Rectory"—now adorned with half a dozen flashier signs announcing both the fair and the special event—I turned right onto the forest road. It had recently been re-tarmacked, the bracken bordering it cut back to the treeline. I toed the brake. Traveller chavvies had taken to playing in these woods and their chase games were apt to spill into the road without warning. Predictably, there had already been noise complaints from the few neighbouring farms.

Away to my left, I spotted a child-sized skeleton as it raced between the trees, and all at once, I was thrown back to a long-forgotten October afternoon. Like little Joey Urnshaw, I too had insisted on wearing my costume every day leading up to Halloween. I think we must have been open in Hampstead back then because I remember my mother guiding me across the heath towards the posh houses that sat in the vale. As we walked hand-in-hand, she'd told me all the spine-tingling tales she could remember from her favourite ghost story writers— classics by the likes Algernon Blackwood and MR James. I'd hung on her every word until we reached the attractive Victorian villas that abutted the heath. There I'd dashed from house to house, ringing doorbells and shouting 'trick or treat!'

Hardly a door was opened to us and traipsing homeward, my plastic cauldron had rattled with only a scatter of sweets. My mother said nothing, though I can still picture the look on her face. A pinched fury that made her lips pale. Traveller chavvies never did well at Halloween, not compared to the local kids, but this was a new low. We'd stopped at a shop just outside the fairground where she purchased enough pick-and-mix to fill a dozen novelty cauldrons. Then, brushing back my curls, she'd said, "Don't mention this to your dad. It'll only make him wild."

Even then I'd wondered if it wasn't her own anger that worried her. I have very few memories of my mother losing her temper, but when she did it was always a sight to behold. Everyone avoided her during those times, even my father. Now, caught up in this memory I hadn't thought of in years, I wondered if perhaps the rage that so often coiled under my own skin might have deeper roots than I'd realised.

Emerging into the huge clearing, I parked in one of the hundreds of bays that had been spray-painted onto the ground just outside the fair. It was late afternoon and dusk was already stealing in. Soon, every generator would be switched on and those vague columns and spirals that loomed against the sky would define themselves into thrill rides and Ferris wheels. In the meantime, only the glow of trailer windows and my own headlights relieved the gloom. That, and a border of multicoloured bulbs flashing around the billboard that overlooked the carpark:

IN PARTNERSHIP WITH JERICHO FAIRS,
EVERTHORN MEDIA
WELCOMES YOU TO
PURLEY RECTORY
THE MOST HAUNTED HOUSE IN BRITAIN
JOIN US THIS HALLOWEEN NIGHT
FOR A LIVE EDITION OF TV PHENOMENON
GHOST SEEKERS
WITH RENOWNED MEDIUM DARREL EVERWOOD
SPOOKY FUN FOR ALL THE FAMILY!

I got out and stood beneath the pulsing glare. I liked this no more than my father, but in recent years special events around which a fair could open for a few days were a necessary evil. For some time, the travelling fair had been a dying industry, its overheads enormous, its appeal to the public little more than a fading sense of nostalgia. To survive we had to piggyback on more modern spectacles. This haunted house bullshit was just the latest in a long line of stunts that, to my mind, cheapened the purity of our heritage.

The aspect of the whole thing that grated most was to see our family name associated with a two-bit chancer like Darrel Everwood. In principle, I had no problem with harmless con artists. In fact, it could be argued that showpeople themselves had their roots in thrills and spills trumpeted with dubious claims. But Everwood was no benign sideshow huckster. His claim to communicate with the dead was not only absurd but deeply damaging. For one thing, there was the case of Debbie Chambers, the little girl who had gone missing from her front garden just before Easter.

In an interview with a leading tabloid newspaper, Everwood had claimed that the child had died only hours after being taken and had been buried somewhere close to the Chambers' residence. For Debbie's parents, clinging to any scrap of hope that their daughter might still be alive, the subsequent media shit-storm had proved devastating. If I remembered rightly, Mrs Chambers' attempted suicide had been prevented only because her husband had forgotten his briefcase and returned home unexpectedly. Even then, cutting her wrists had led to permanent nerve damage and a vow from Mr Chambers that, if he should ever meet Darrel Everwood face-to-face, he could not be held responsible for his actions.

As if echoing these thoughts, a voice called out across the carpark, "Revolting man, isn't he?"

I turned to find Angela Rowell coming towards me. When we'd arrived yesterday, the housekeeper of Purley had received us by storming out the door of the Victorian rectory and shrieking at Big Sam Urnshaw like a banshee. His lorry had trespassed over the agreed boundary of the fair; didn't he know the stipulations of the contract? No vehicle must come within fifty metres of the house. If he didn't get his load shifted right away, Miss Rowell would be on the phone to the Earl of Aumbry, absentee owner of the property. Looking suitably horrified, Big Sam had jumped back into his cab and backed up halfway across the clearing.

Standing beside me, she now jabbed an outraged finger at the billboard.

"As I said to your father when negotiations for this absurd spectacle began, I'm not a tremendous fan of travelling circuses." I let the mistake pass. "But next to this charlatan, I would welcome a hundred carnivals. The sheer nerve of that man!" I turned to her. Miss Rowell's hands were clasped so tightly together that the knuckles stood out, sharp and bloodless. "They ... That's to say, they ..." She shook her head. "They don't like it up at the house, you know."

"You mean the Earl?" I said. "I thought he never came here?"

"Not in years. As far as Lord Denver is concerned, Purley is a mere curiosity in his property empire. I think he enjoys the bragging rights of owning the most haunted house in England, but otherwise, he's pretty much indifferent."

"So you're talking about?"

"The residents." She held my gaze for a moment before letting it slip to the ground. "The personalities who call the house their home. They cannot abide an imposter, Mr Jericho."

"You mean the ghosts?" I said, making a heroic effort to keep a straight face.

"*Personalities*," she corrected. "And jealous ones at that. Mark my words, they shan't tolerate the likes of Mr Everwood within their walls. There have been consequences in the past for those who have sought to exploit this place."

"Really?"

"Oh yes," she said matter-of-factly. "Madness. Suicide. Murder. However it manifests, the residents of Purley always take their pound of flesh."